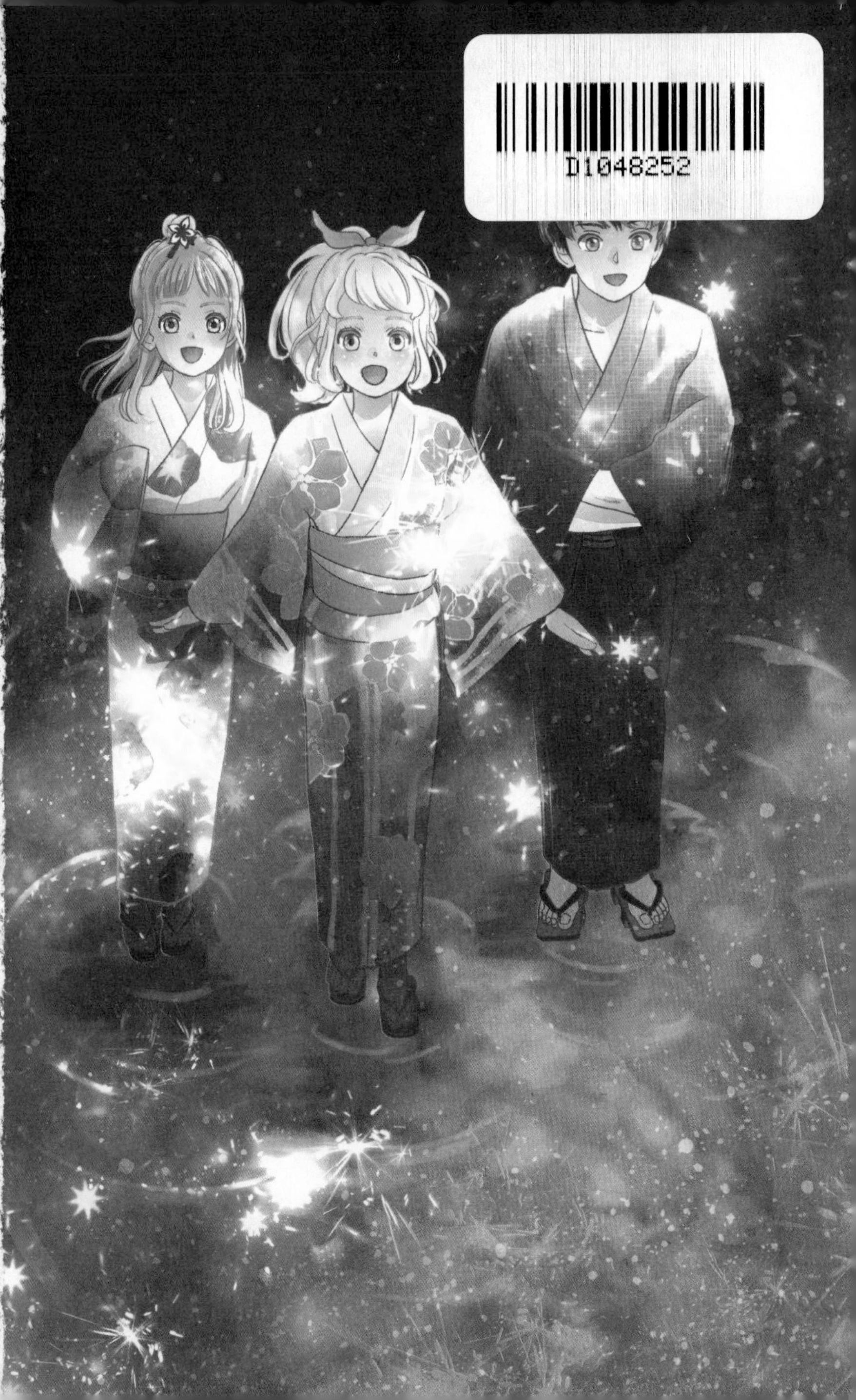

Who is Bibi Blocksberg?

Bibi Blocksberg is a young witch who's known for her practical jokes, her cheerful nature, and —of course— her extraordinary magical abilities! Whether she's brewing magic potions, protecting a dinosaur egg, or even sailing with pirates, you know you're in for a charming adventure!

This little witch and her flying broomstick Apple Pie have captivated the hearts of millions in her German radio series, her live-action blockbuster movies, and even her animated television series!

Check out the back of the book for more behind the scenes content, a letter from the creative team and a travel blog from Bibi!

And now — with a Wizz–Wizz! from Germany's favorite little witch — we bring you to Bibi's first manga adventure!

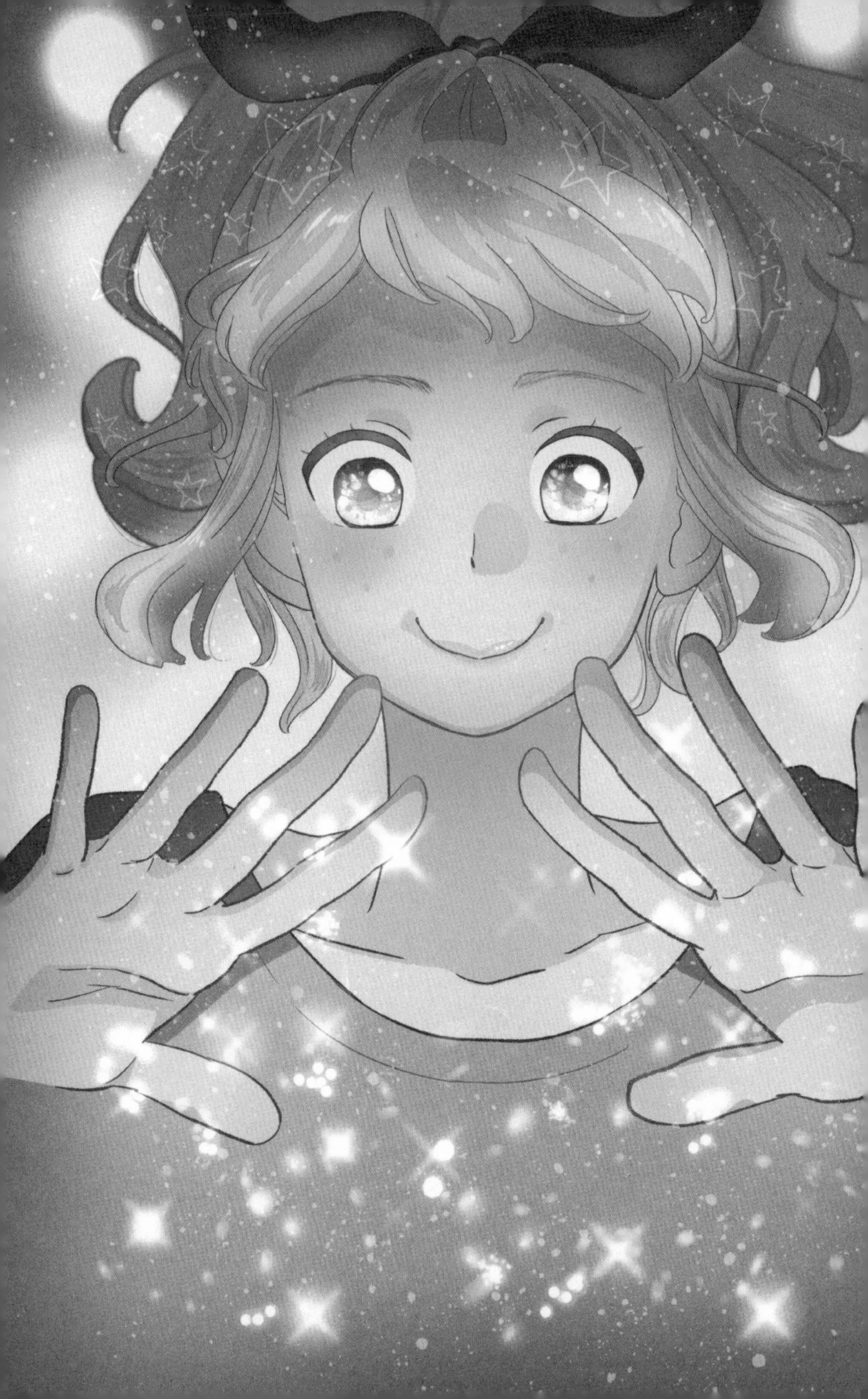

Bibi & Miyu

1

Art: Hirara Natsume
Text: Olivia Vieweg

TOKYOPOP®

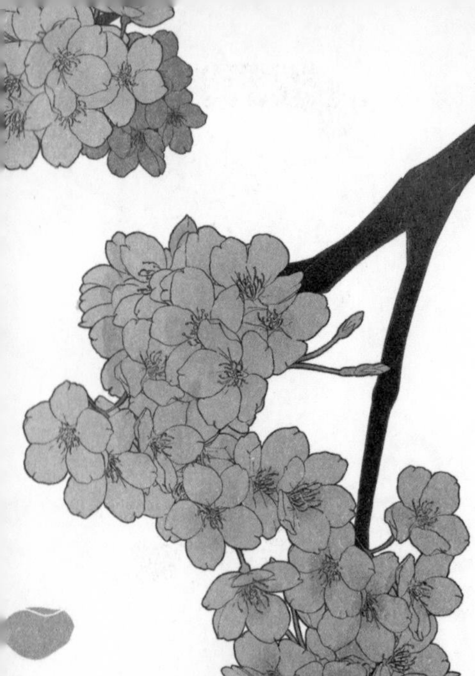

Welcome to Bibi's World!

Are you ready for the start of this brand-new series?! Here are a few characters you'll meet along the way!

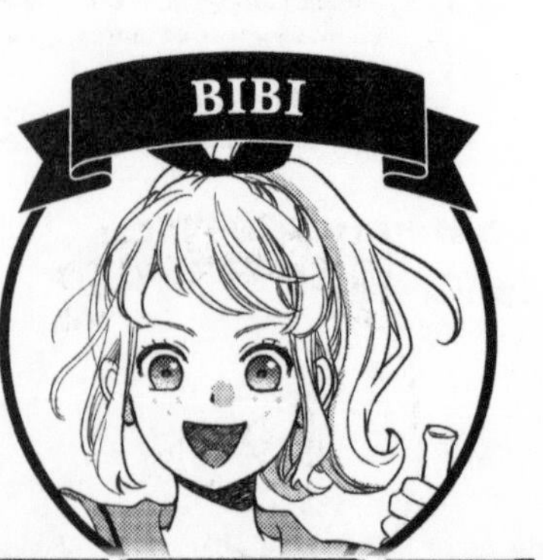
BIBI

Bibi Blocksberg is the most popular young witch in Newtown! Bibi sometimes gets into difficult situations because of her daring magic spells, but she always finds a way to make things better in the end.

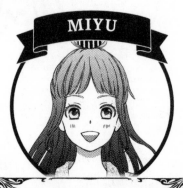

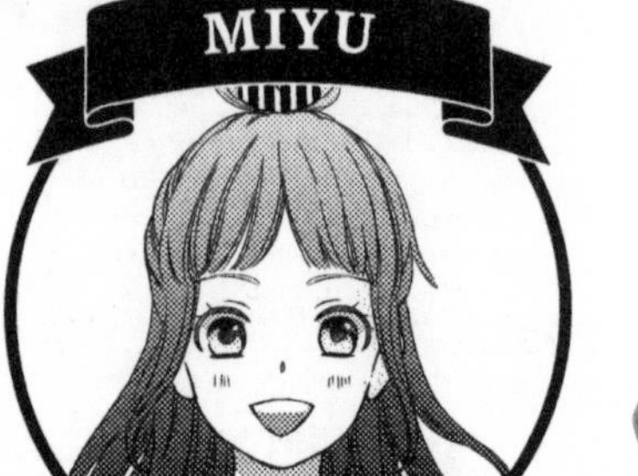
MIYU

You're going to meet the mysterious Miyu for the first time in this story, so we don't want to give too much away. But Miyu is always excited for an adventure!

TAKI

Taki is Miyu's childhood friend. He's always happy to listen to her.

WASABI

Who is Wasabi, really? Bibi still has to find out!

BERNARD

Bibi's father can't do magic, which secretly irritates him. He often gets annoyed by Bibi and Barbara's many spells. Even so, he's very proud of his two "favorite witches."

BARBARA

It isn't always easy for Bibi's mom to balance family and everyday life as a witch.

MONI & MARITA

These two are Bibi's best friends in Newtown. They go on many adventures together.

JOHNATHAN

Johnathan's friends call him Johnny. He's super smart and a true friend to Bibi.

Table of Contents

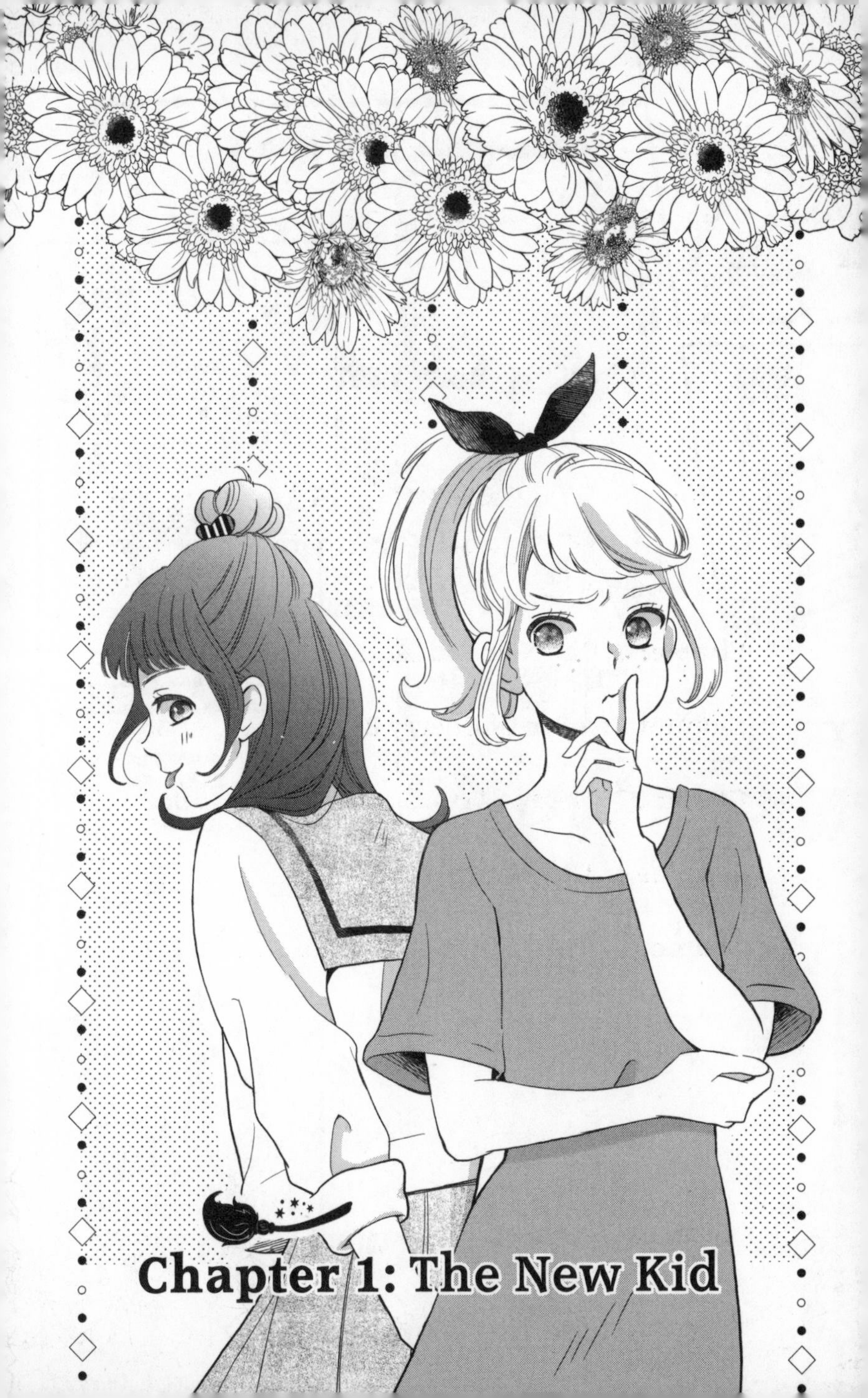

Chapter 1: The New Kid

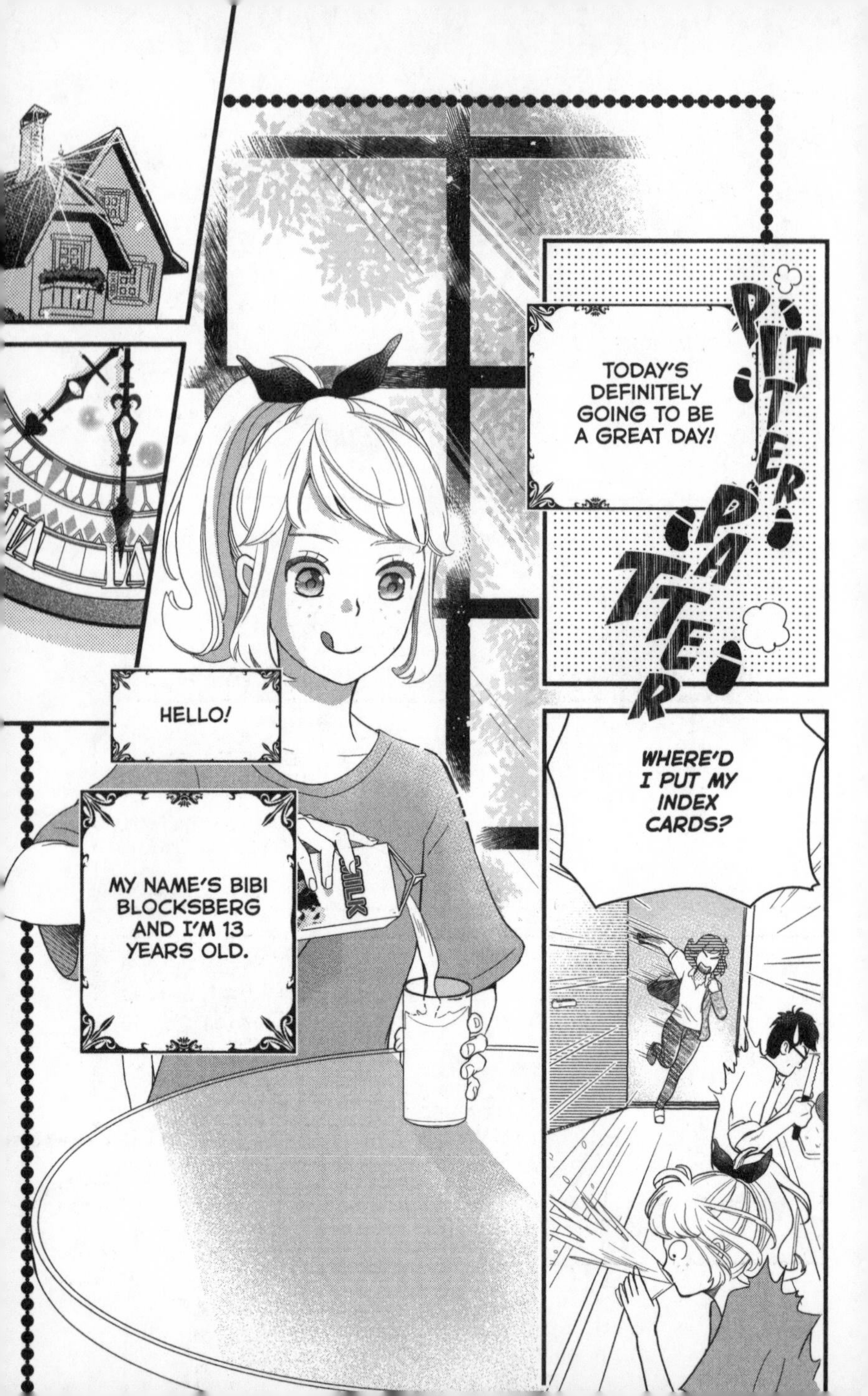
TODAY'S DEFINITELY GOING TO BE A GREAT DAY!
PITTER PATTER
WHERE'D I PUT MY INDEX CARDS?
HELLO!
MY NAME'S BIBI BLOCKSBERG AND I'M 13 YEARS OLD.
MILK

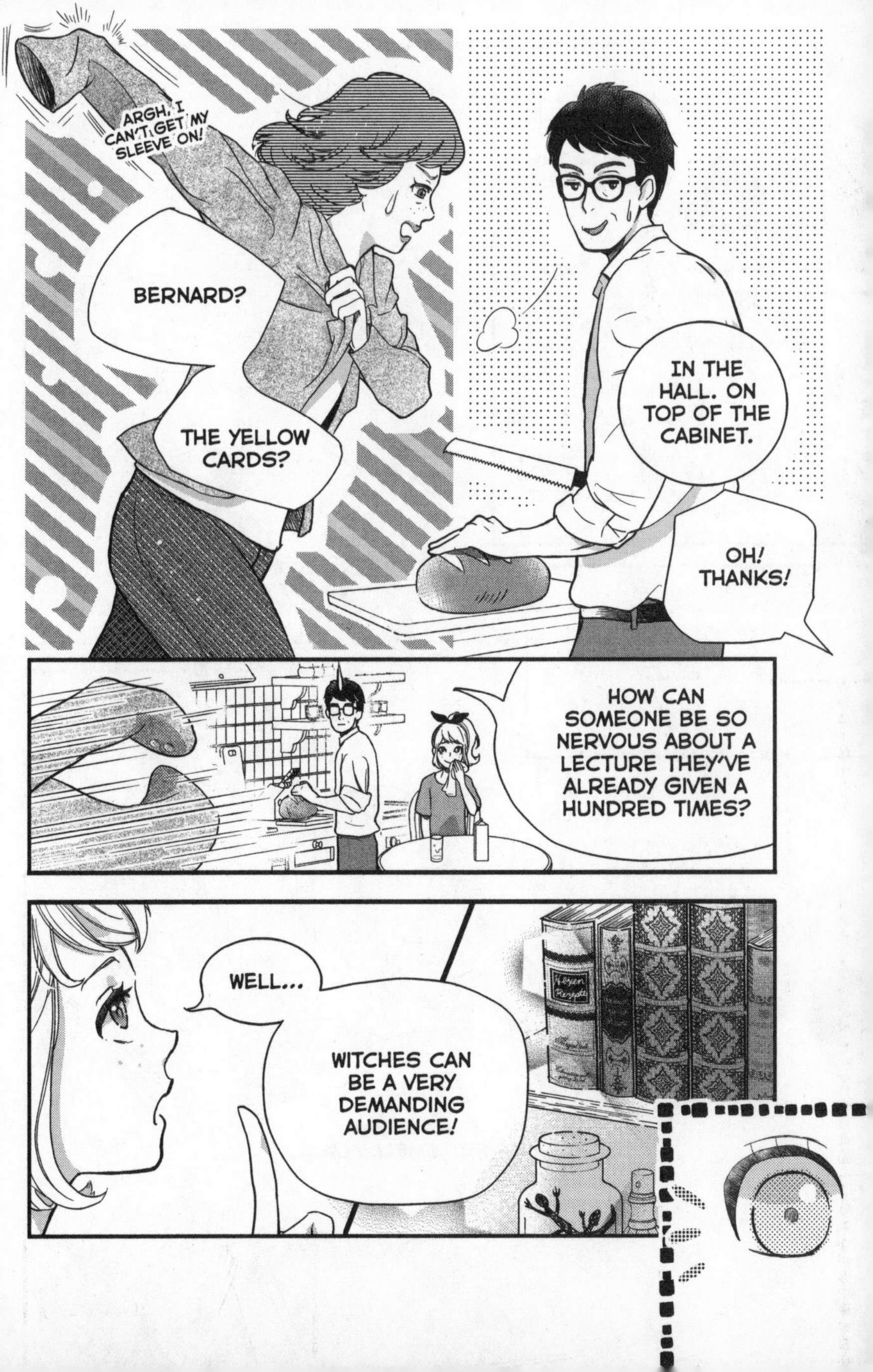
ARGH, I CAN'T GET MY SLEEVE ON!
BERNARD?
THE YELLOW CARDS?
IN THE HALL. ON TOP OF THE CABINET.
OH! THANKS!
HOW CAN SOMEONE BE SO NERVOUS ABOUT A LECTURE THEY'VE ALREADY GIVEN A HUNDRED TIMES?
WELL...
WITCHES CAN BE A VERY DEMANDING AUDIENCE!

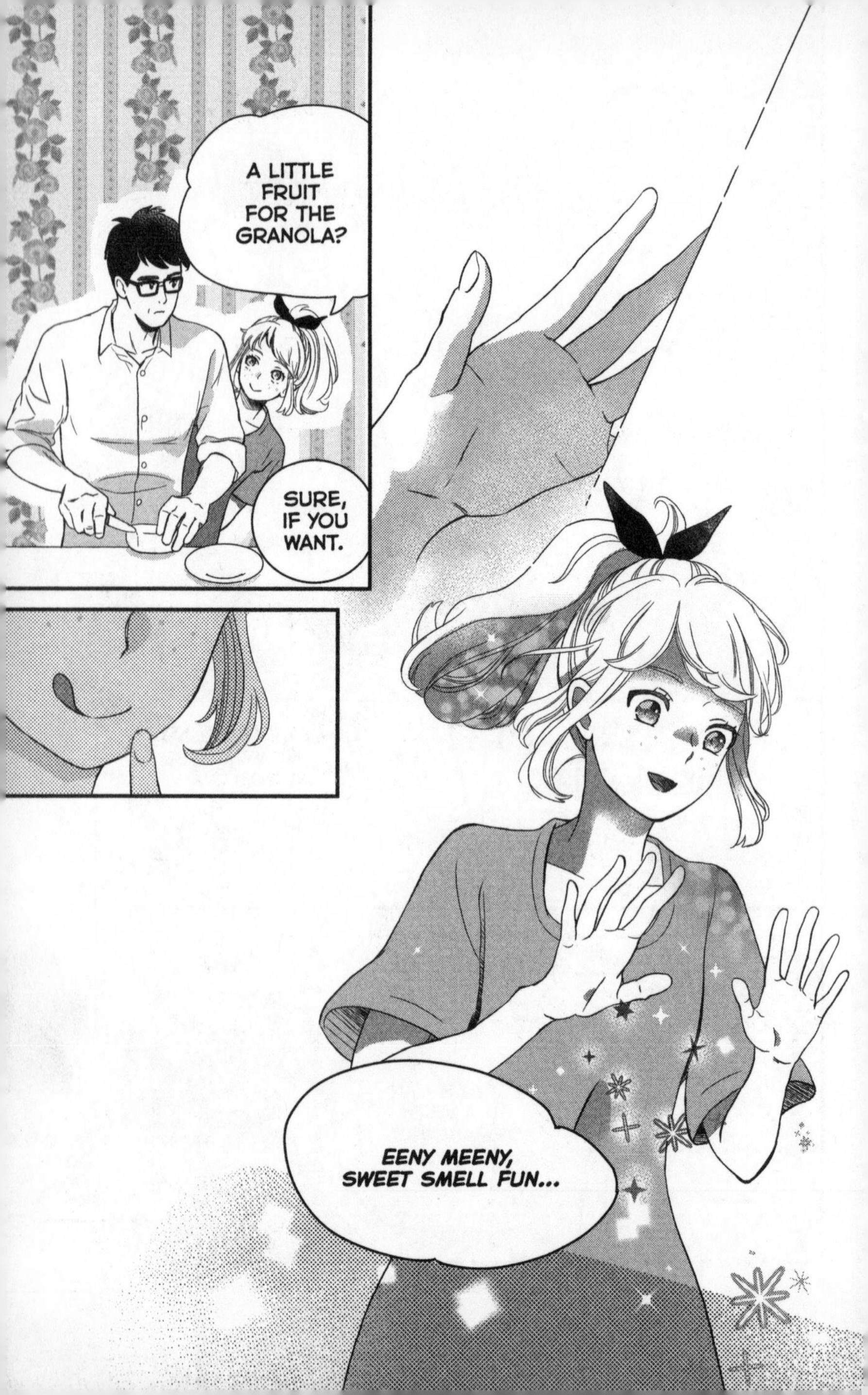
A LITTLE FRUIT FOR THE GRANOLA?
SURE, IF YOU WANT.
EENY MEENY, SWEET SMELL FUN...

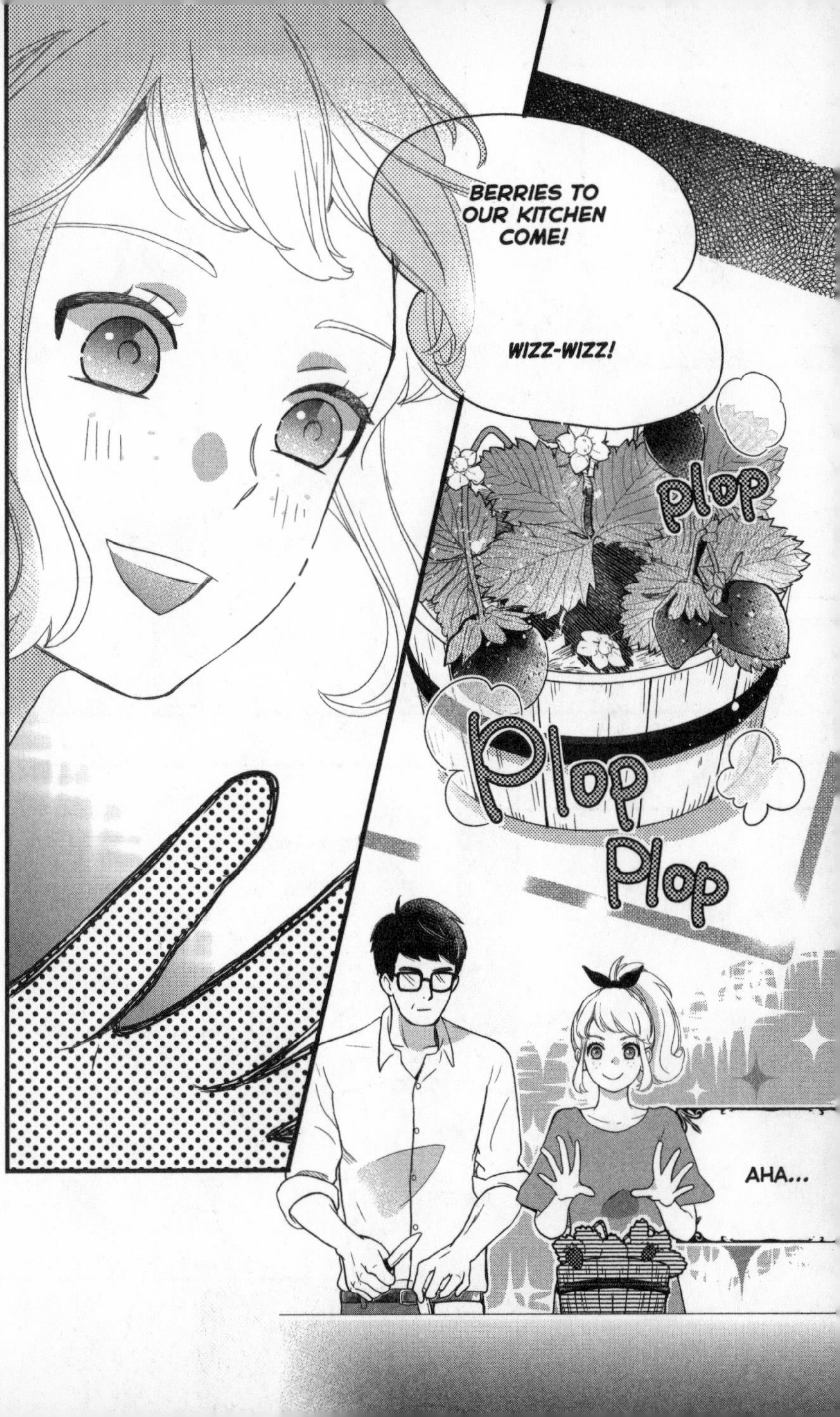
BERRIES TO OUR KITCHEN COME!
WIZZ-WIZZ!
plop
Plop
Plop
AHA...

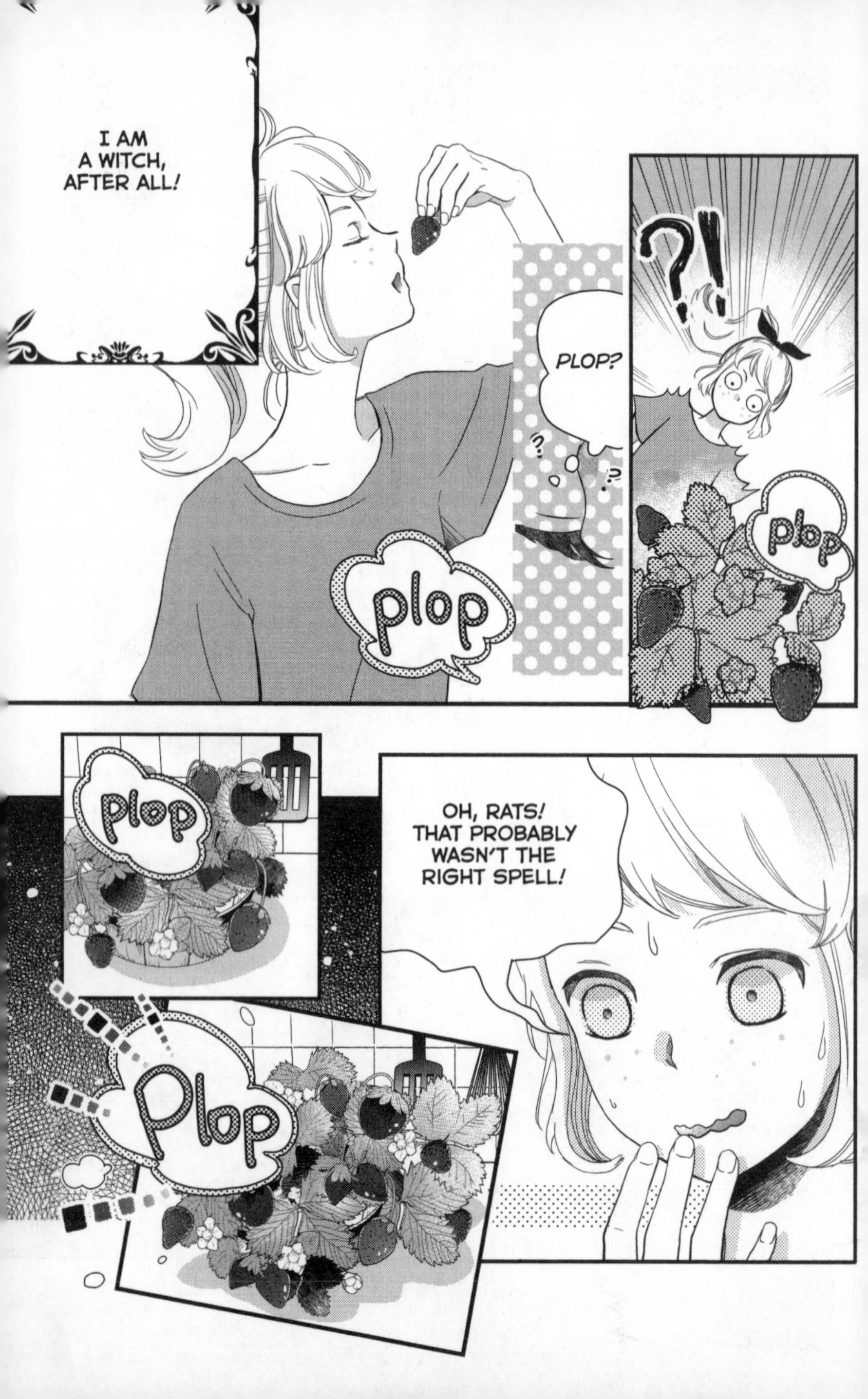
I AM A WITCH, AFTER ALL!
plop
PLOP?
?!
plop
plop
Plop
OH, RATS! THAT PROBABLY WASN'T THE RIGHT SPELL!

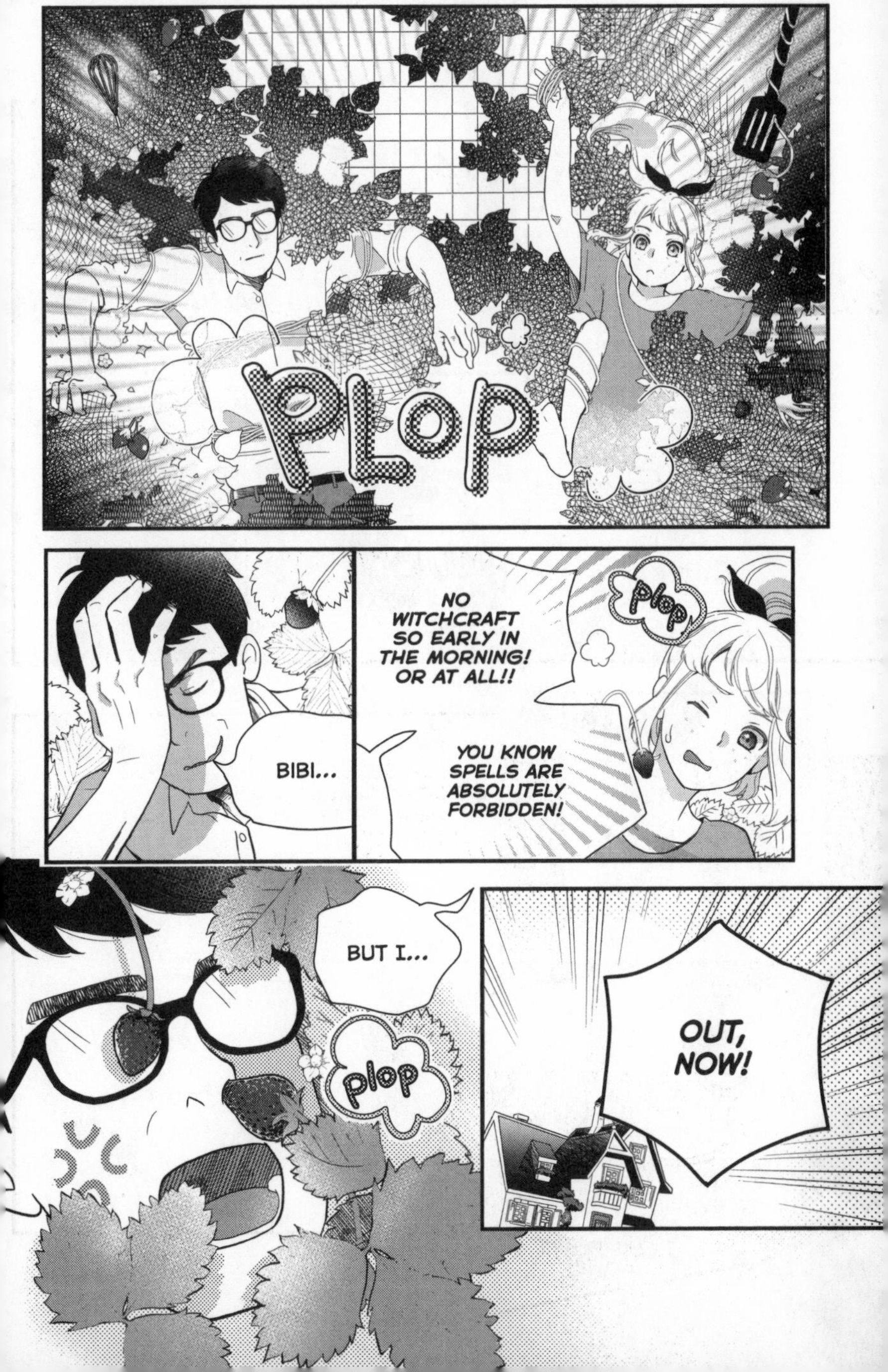
PLOP
BIBI...
NO WITCHCRAFT SO EARLY IN THE MORNING! OR AT ALL!!
plop
YOU KNOW SPELLS ARE ABSOLUTELY FORBIDDEN!
BUT I...
plop
OUT, NOW!

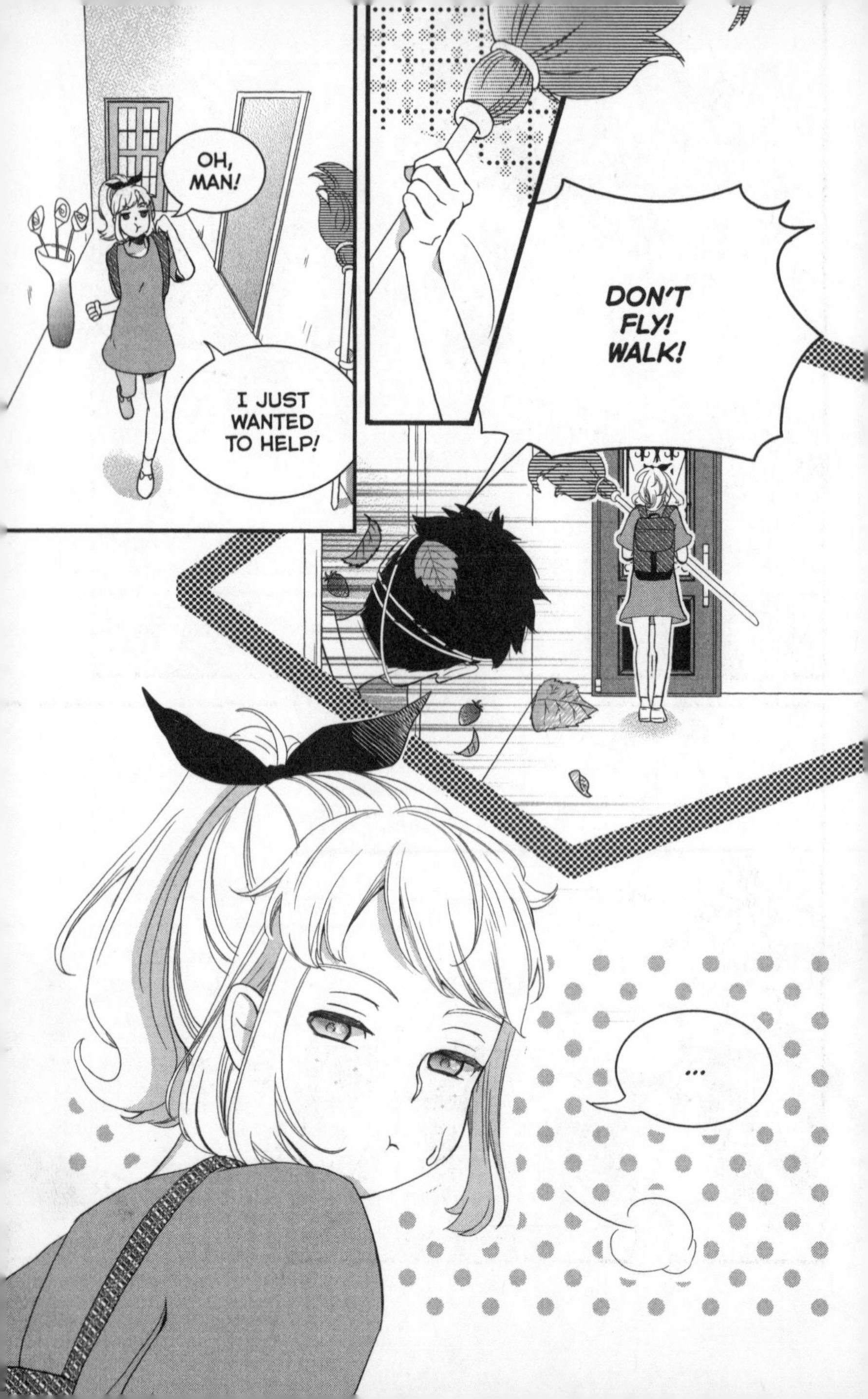
DON'T FLY! WALK!
OH, MAN!
I JUST WANTED TO HELP!
...

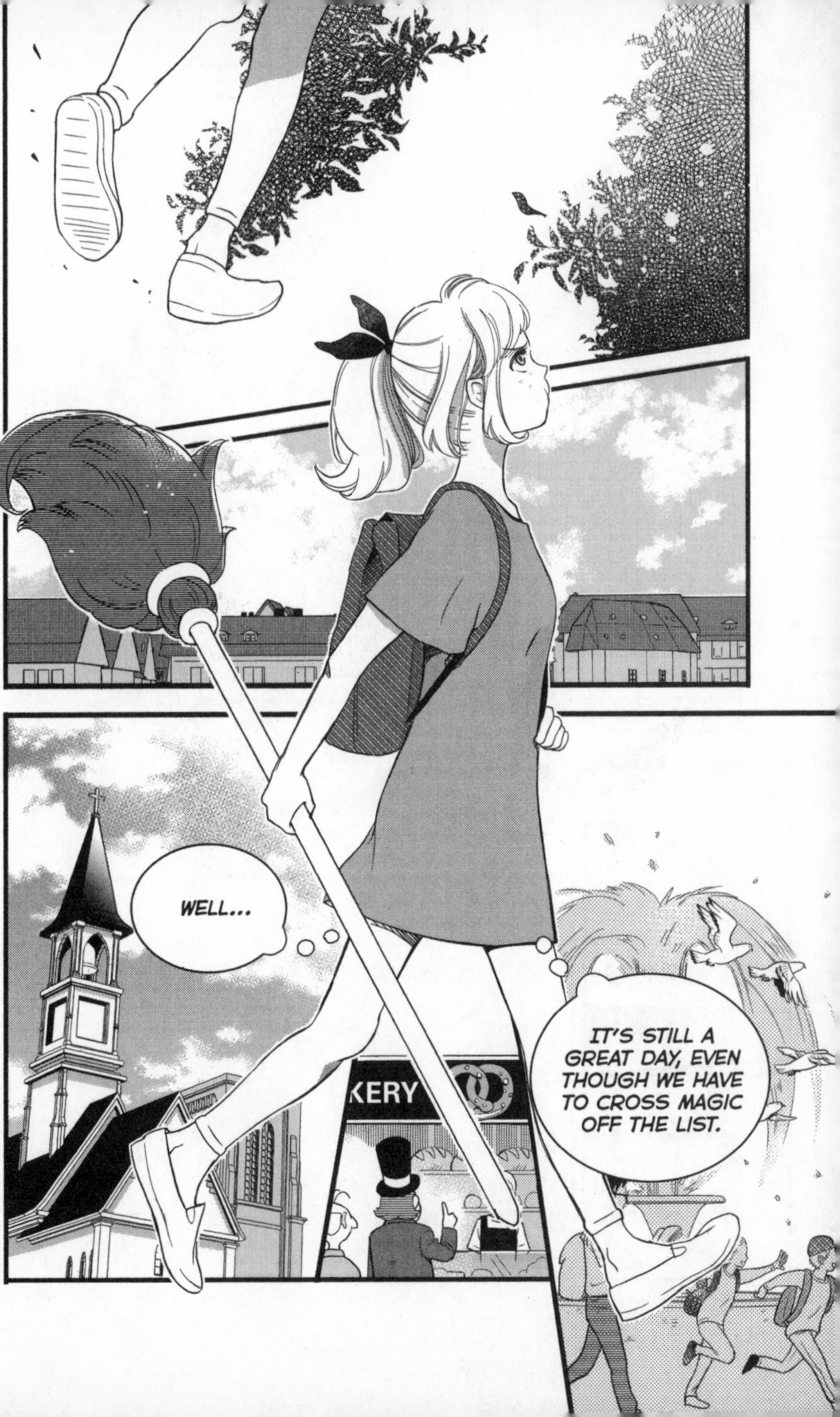
WELL...
IT'S STILL A GREAT DAY, EVEN THOUGH WE HAVE TO CROSS MAGIC OFF THE LIST.
KERY

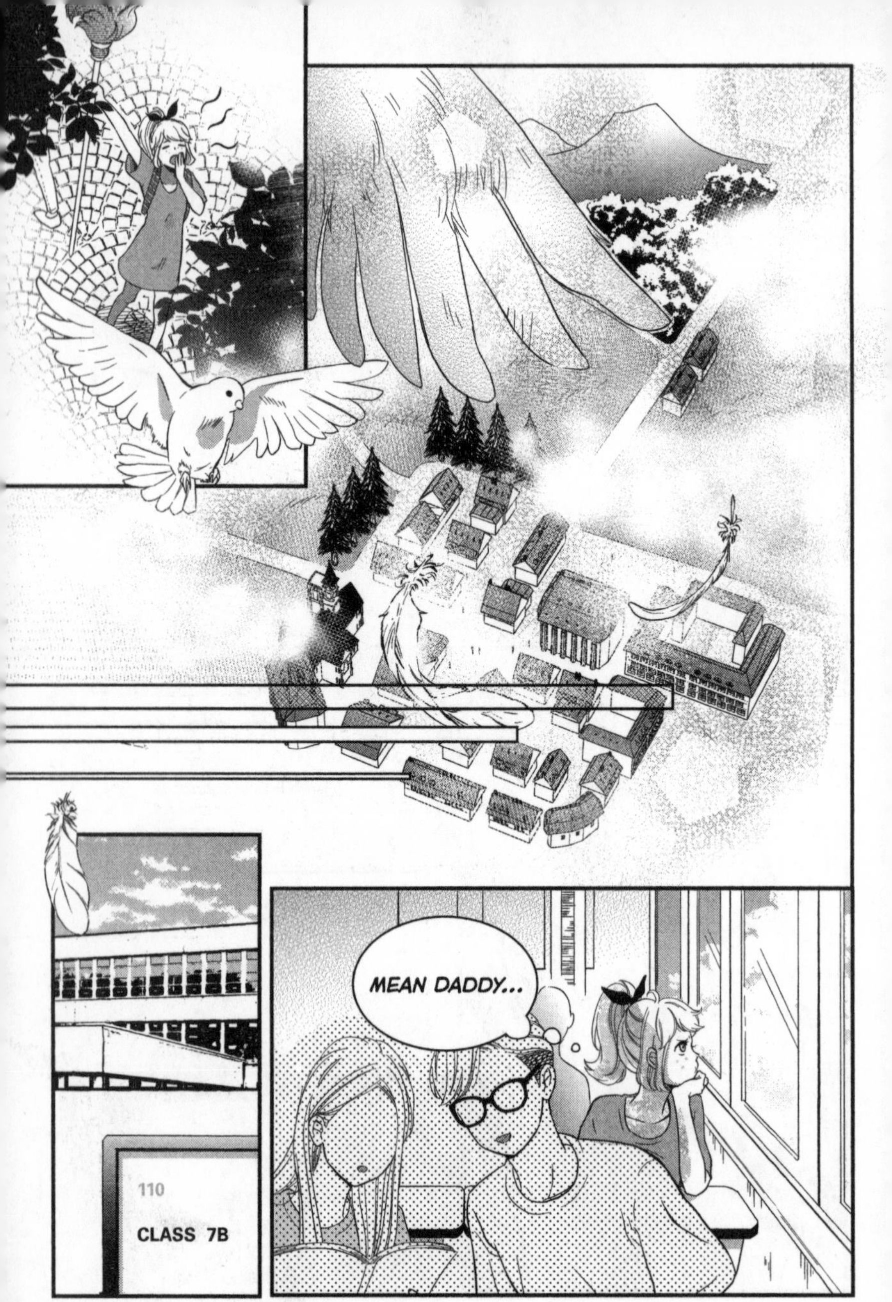
MEAN DADDY...
110
CLASS 7B

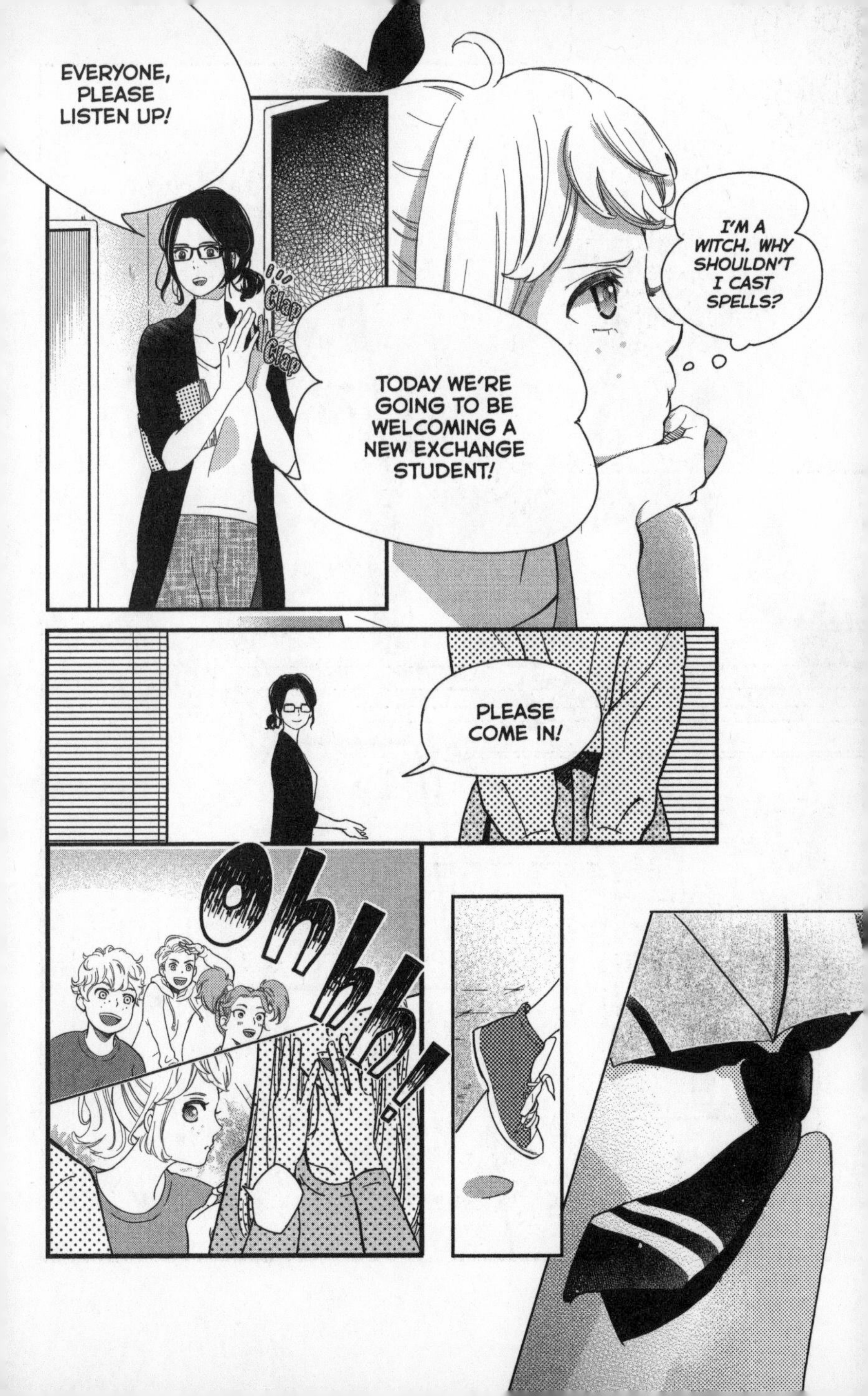
I'M A WITCH. WHY SHOULDN'T I CAST SPELLS?
EVERYONE, PLEASE LISTEN UP!
Clap Clap
TODAY WE'RE GOING TO BE WELCOMING A NEW EXCHANGE STUDENT!
PLEASE COME IN!
Ohhh!!

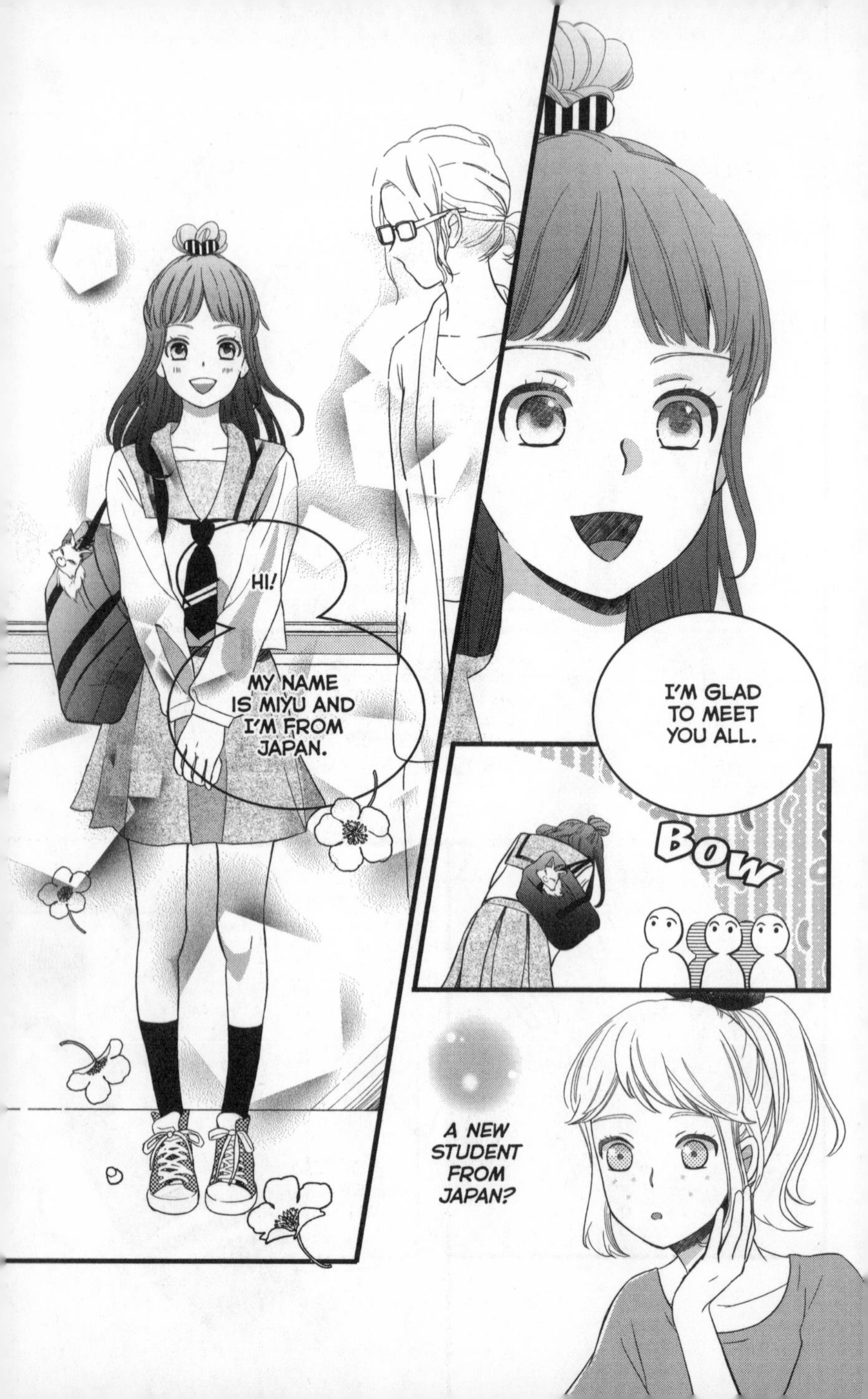
HI!
MY NAME IS MIYU AND I'M FROM JAPAN.
I'M GLAD TO MEET YOU ALL.
BOW
A NEW STUDENT FROM JAPAN?

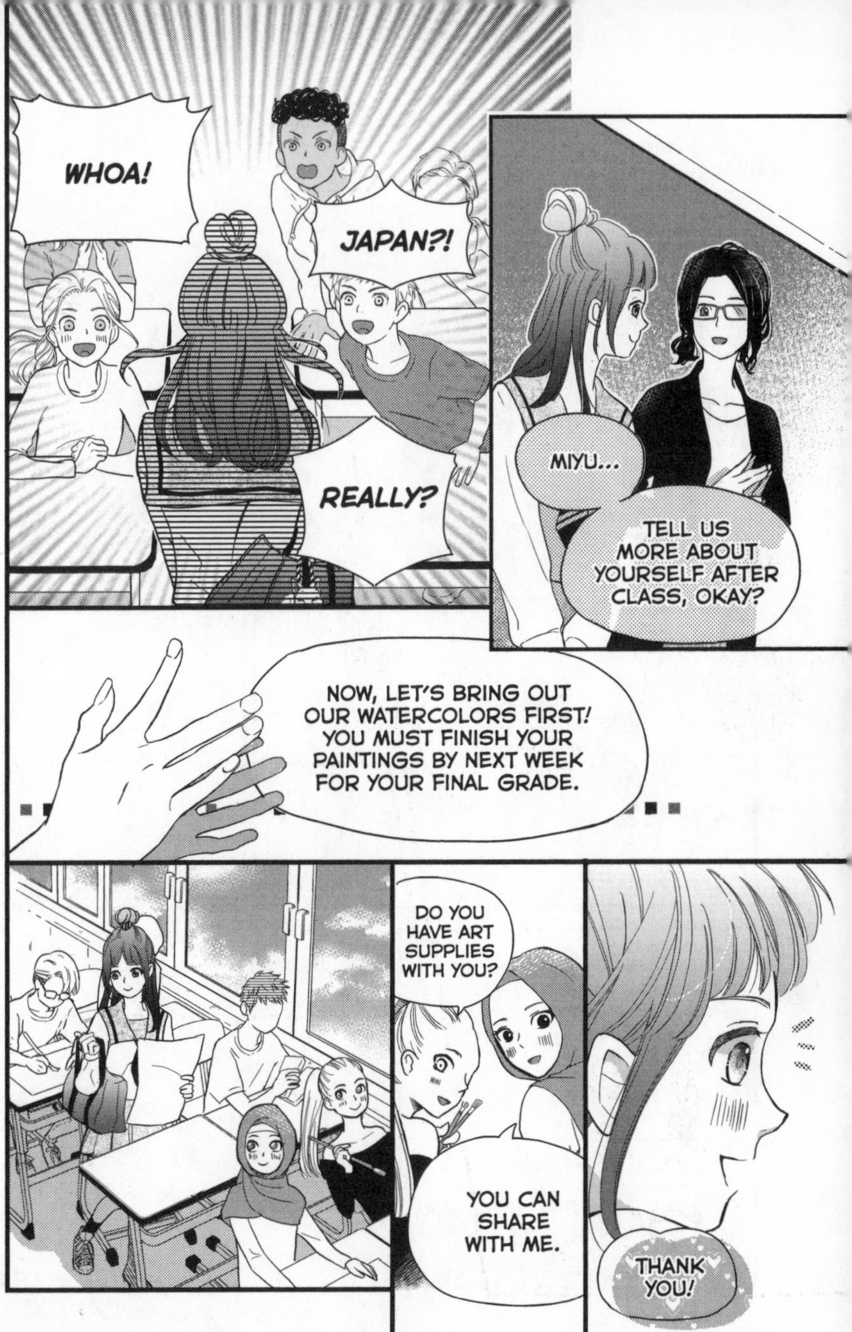
WHOA!
JAPAN?!
REALLY?
MIYU...
TELL US MORE ABOUT YOURSELF AFTER CLASS, OKAY?
NOW, LET'S BRING OUT OUR WATERCOLORS FIRST! YOU MUST FINISH YOUR PAINTINGS BY NEXT WEEK FOR YOUR FINAL GRADE.
DO YOU HAVE ART SUPPLIES WITH YOU?
YOU CAN SHARE WITH ME.
THANK YOU!

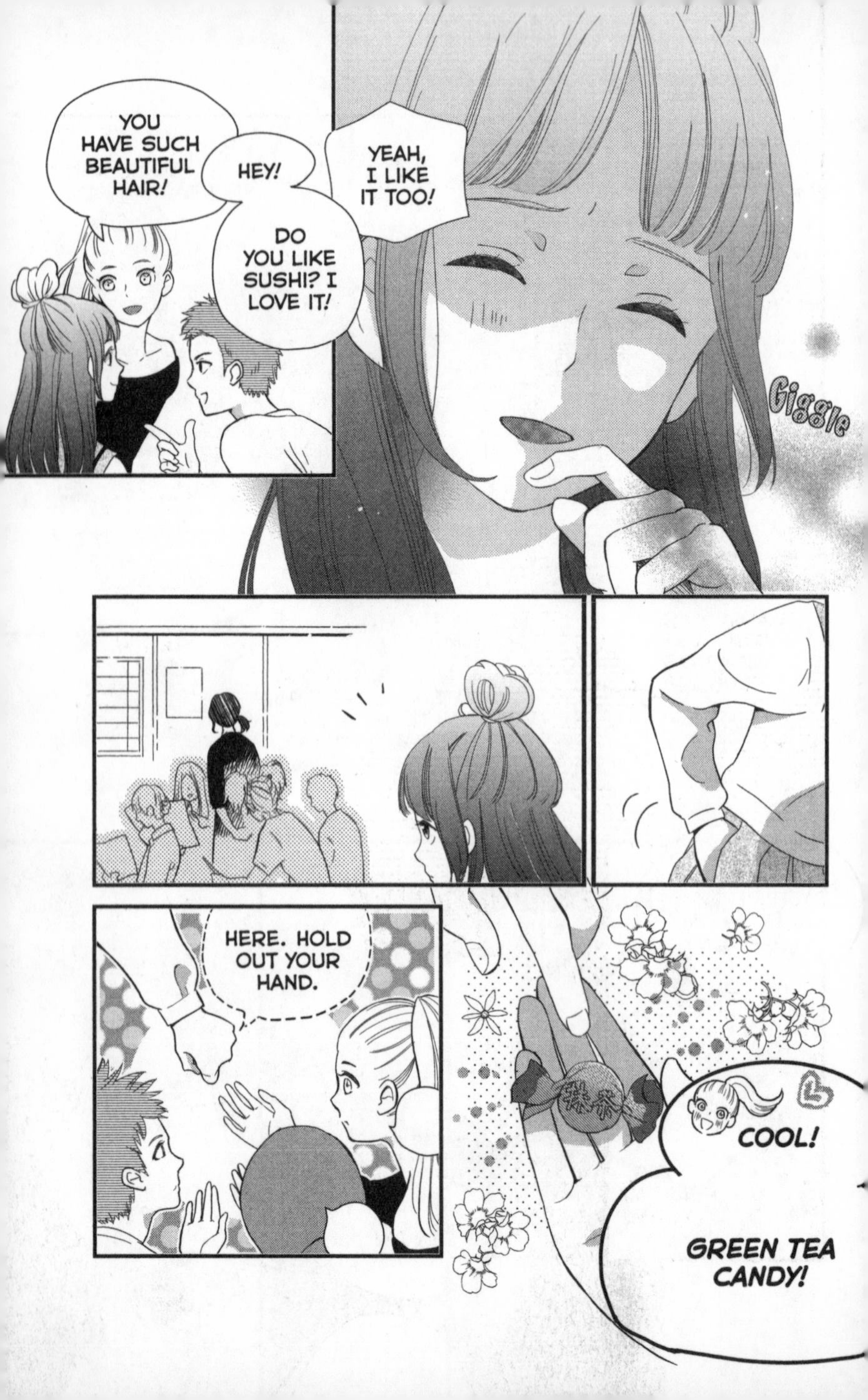
YOU HAVE SUCH BEAUTIFUL HAIR!
HEY!
DO YOU LIKE SUSHI? I LOVE IT!
YEAH, I LIKE IT TOO!
Giggle
HERE. HOLD OUT YOUR HAND.
COOL!
GREEN TEA CANDY!

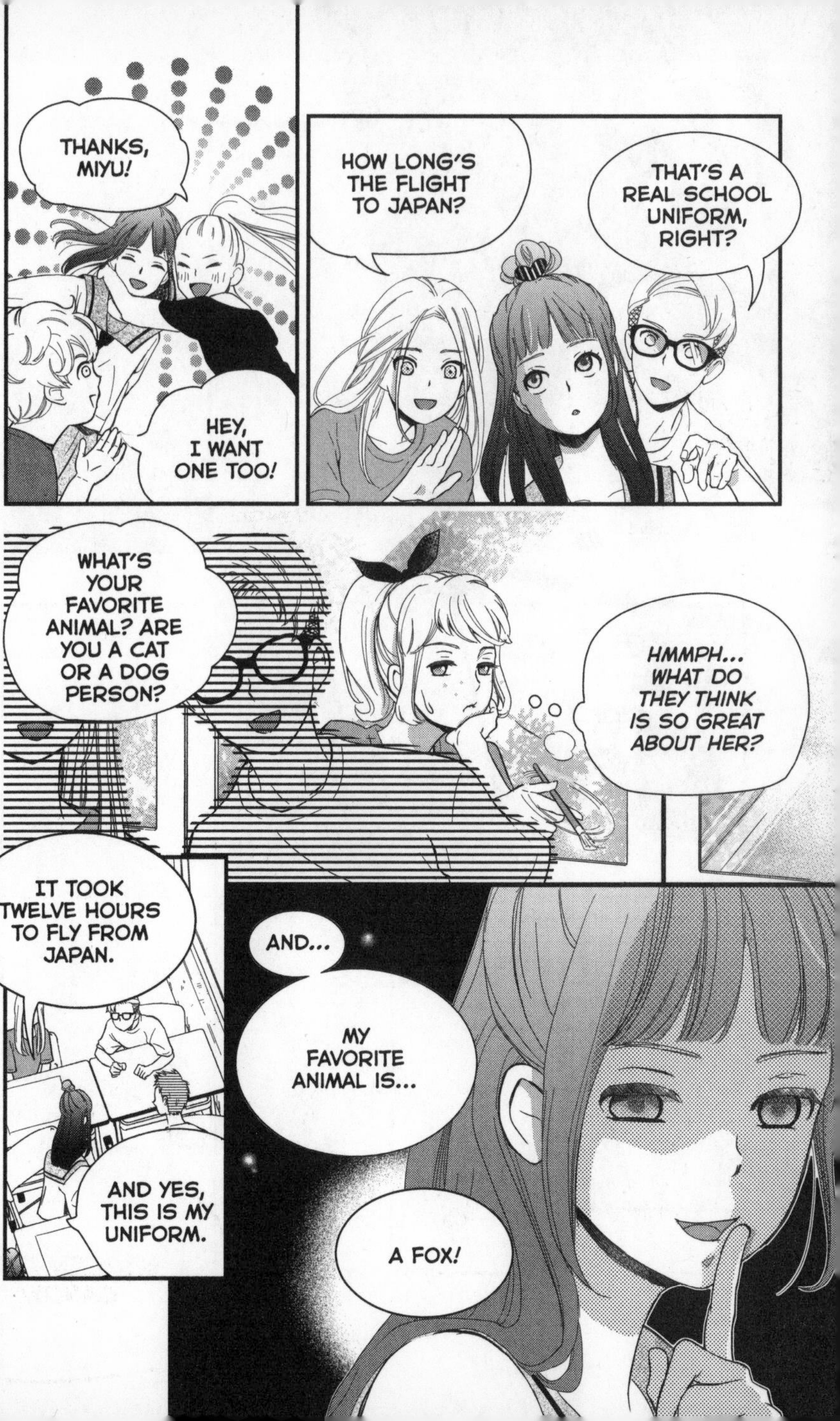
THANKS, MIYU!
HEY, I WANT ONE TOO!
HOW LONG'S THE FLIGHT TO JAPAN?
THAT'S A REAL SCHOOL UNIFORM, RIGHT?
WHAT'S YOUR FAVORITE ANIMAL? ARE YOU A CAT OR A DOG PERSON?
HMMPH... WHAT DO THEY THINK IS SO GREAT ABOUT HER?
IT TOOK TWELVE HOURS TO FLY FROM JAPAN.
AND YES, THIS IS MY UNIFORM.
AND...
MY FAVORITE ANIMAL IS...
A FOX!

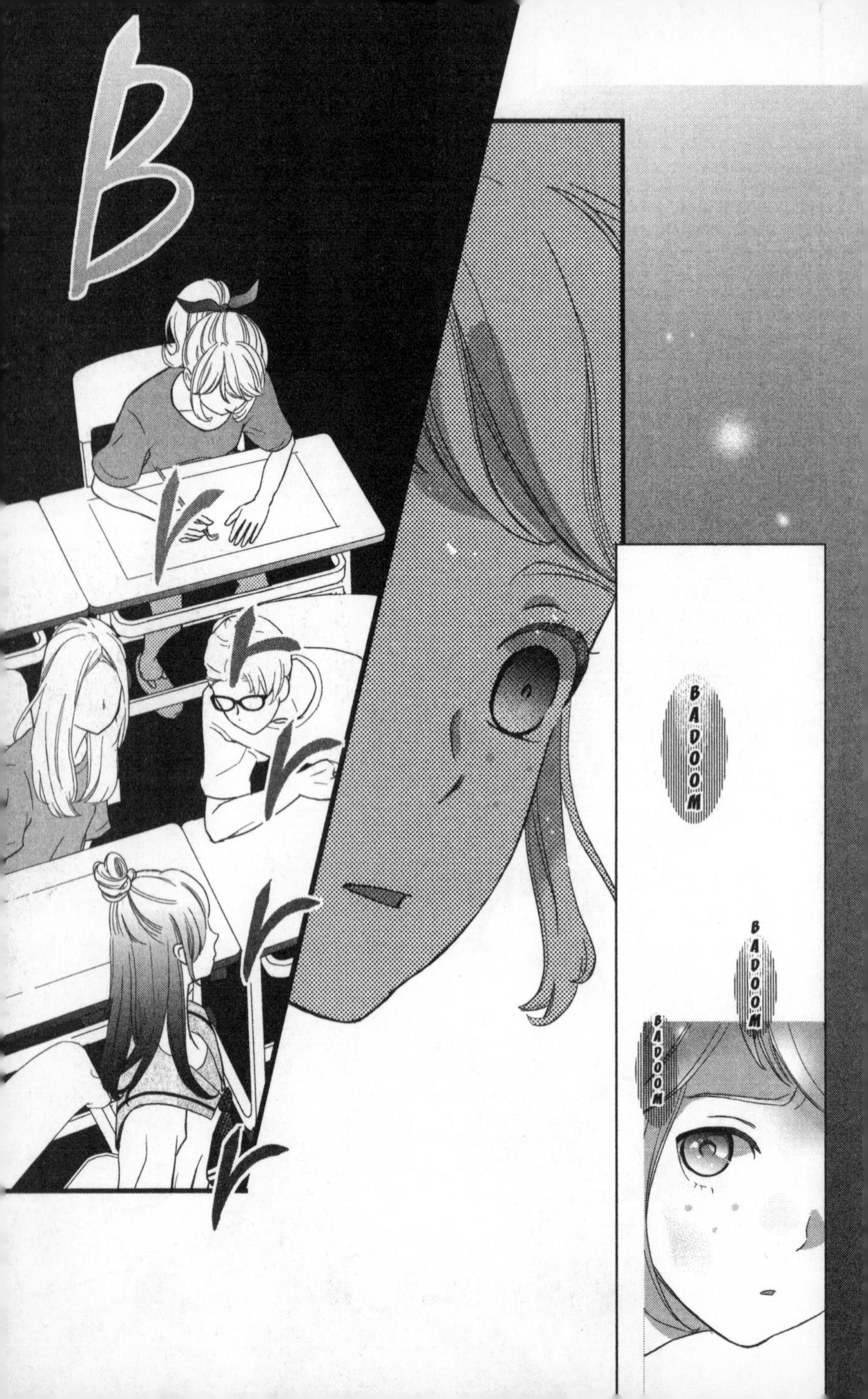
BADOOM
BADOOM
BADOOM
B

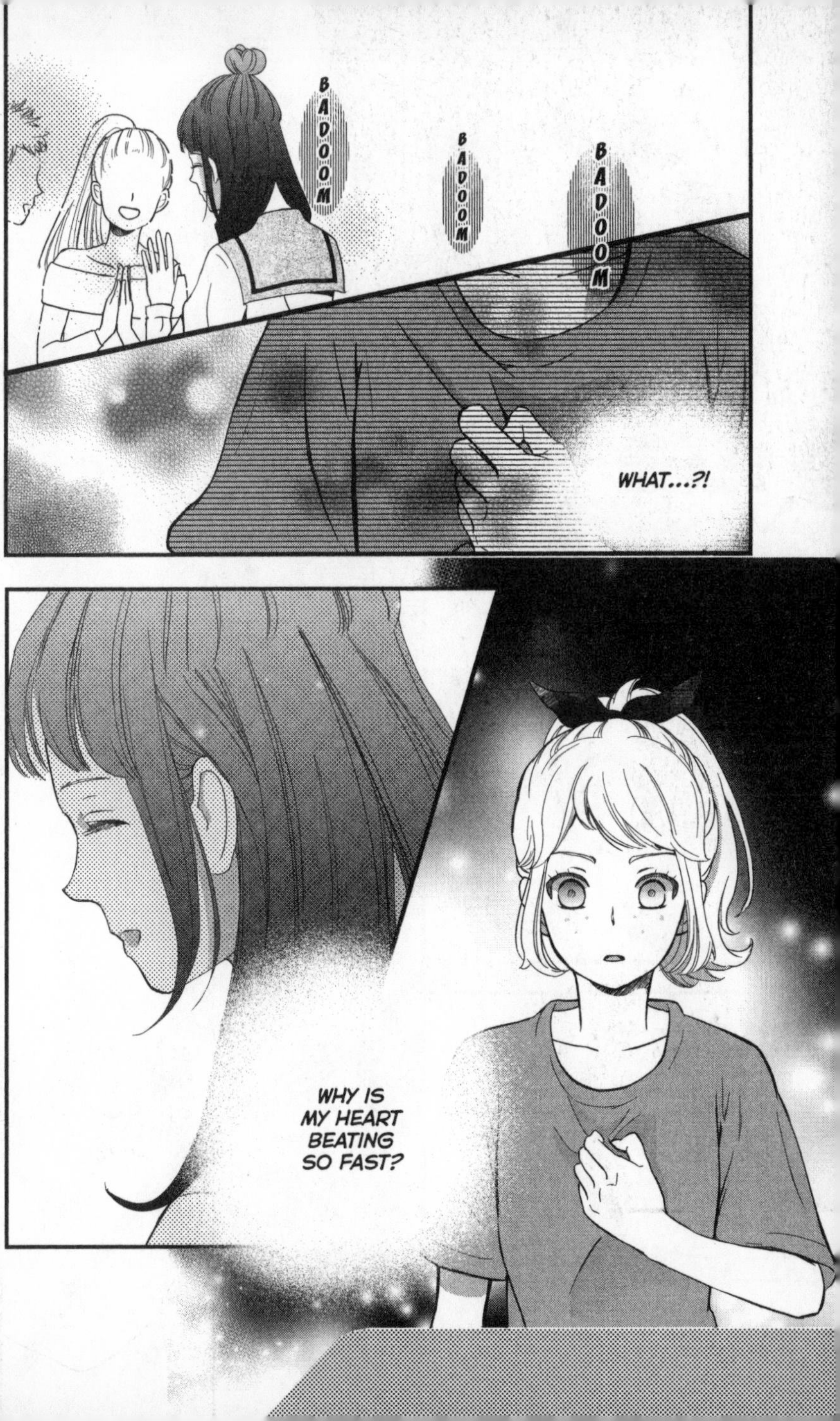
BADOOM
BADOOM
BADOOM
WHAT...?!
WHY IS MY HEART BEATING SO FAST?

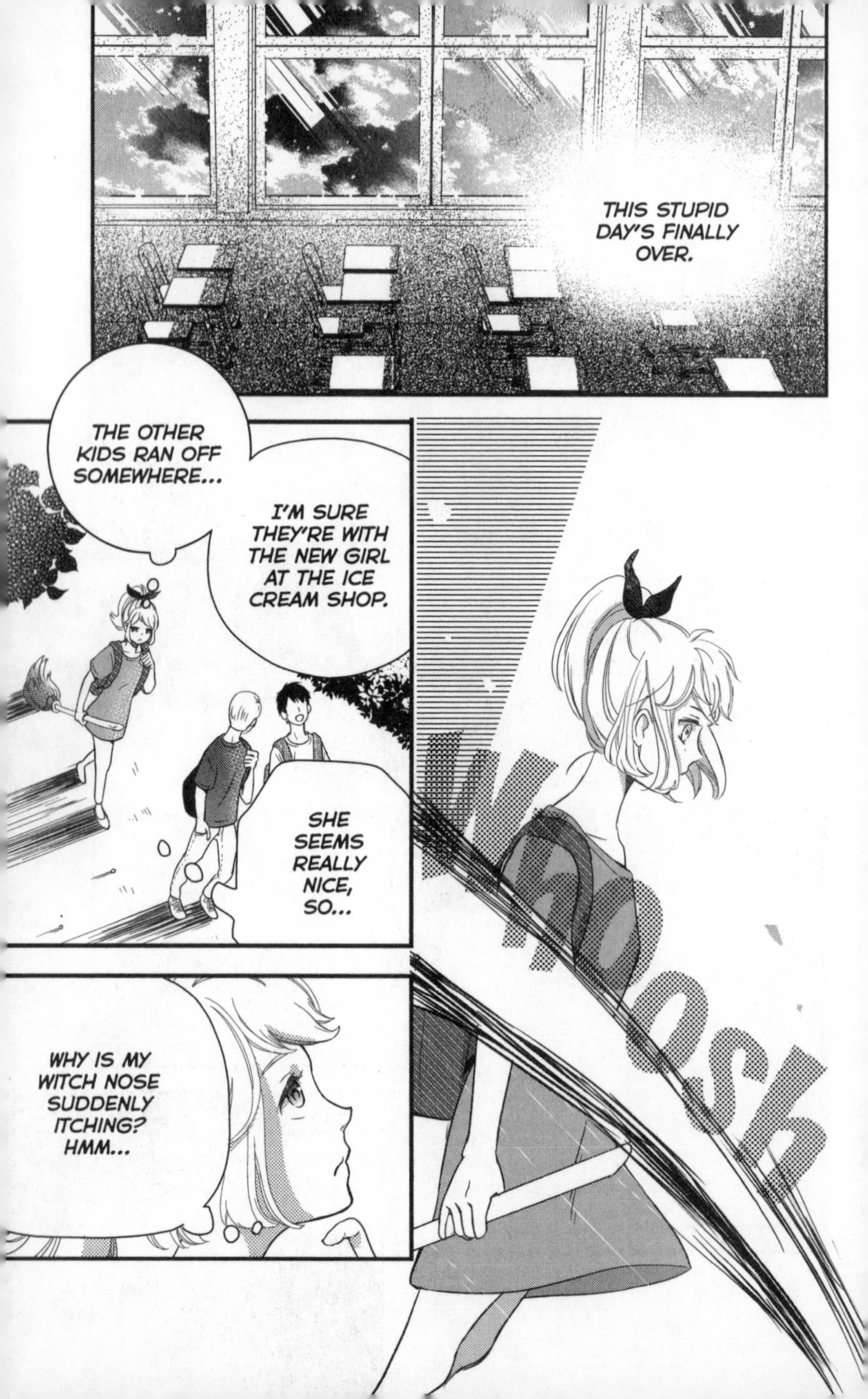
THIS STUPID DAY'S FINALLY OVER.
WHOOSH
THE OTHER KIDS RAN OFF SOMEWHERE...
I'M SURE THEY'RE WITH THE NEW GIRL AT THE ICE CREAM SHOP.
SHE SEEMS REALLY NICE, SO...
WHY IS MY WITCH NOSE SUDDENLY ITCHING? HMM...

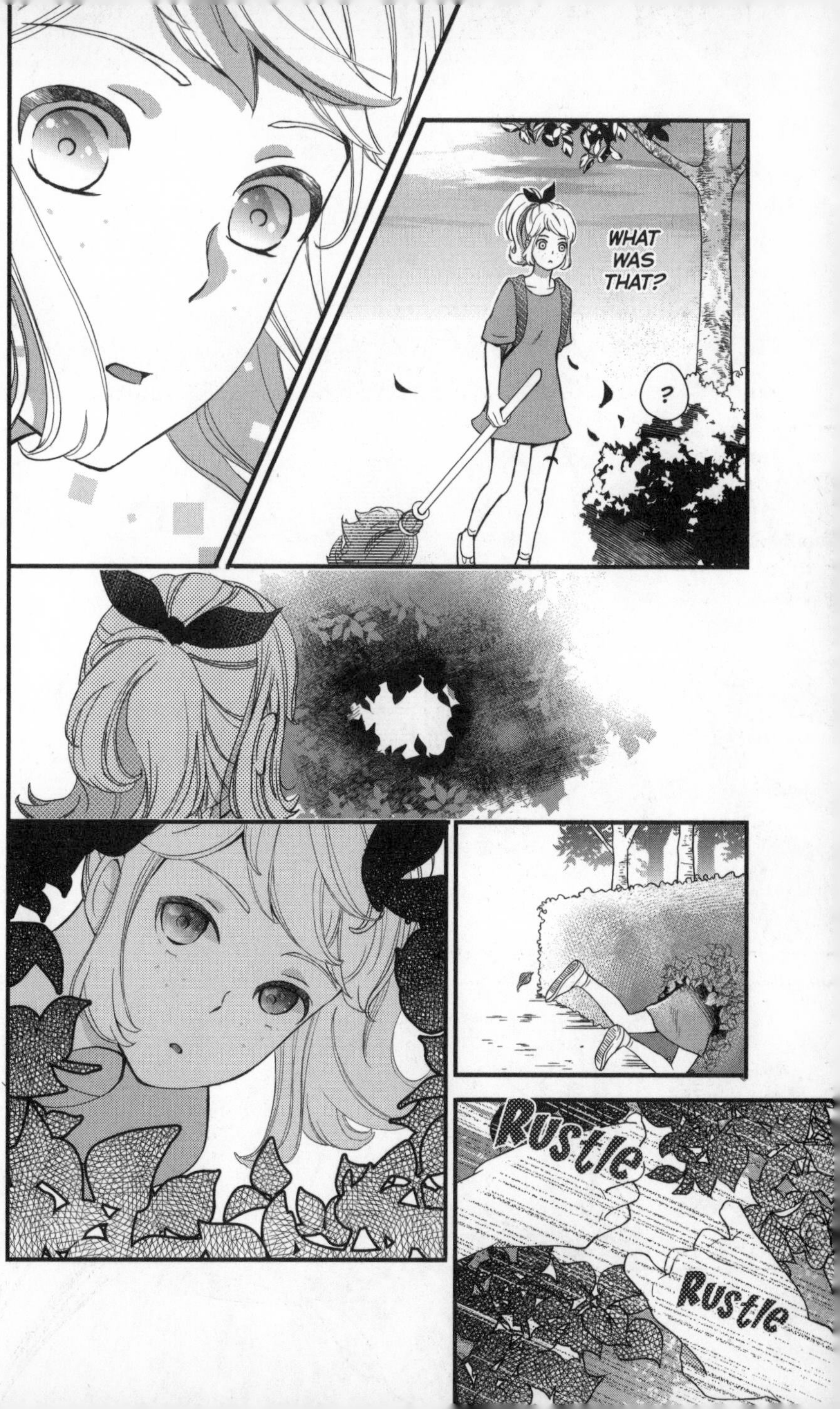
WHAT WAS THAT?
?
Rustle
Rustle

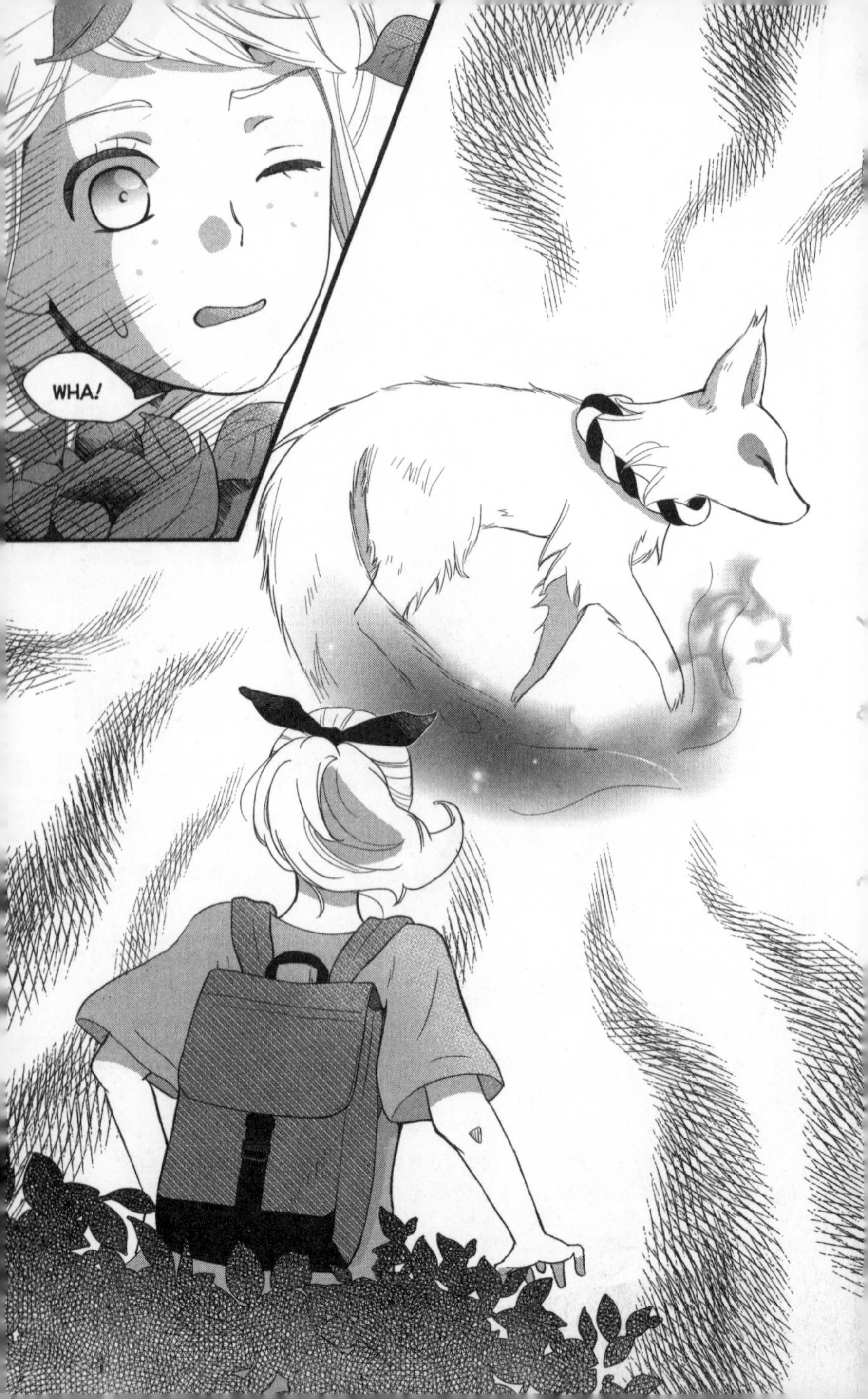
WHA!

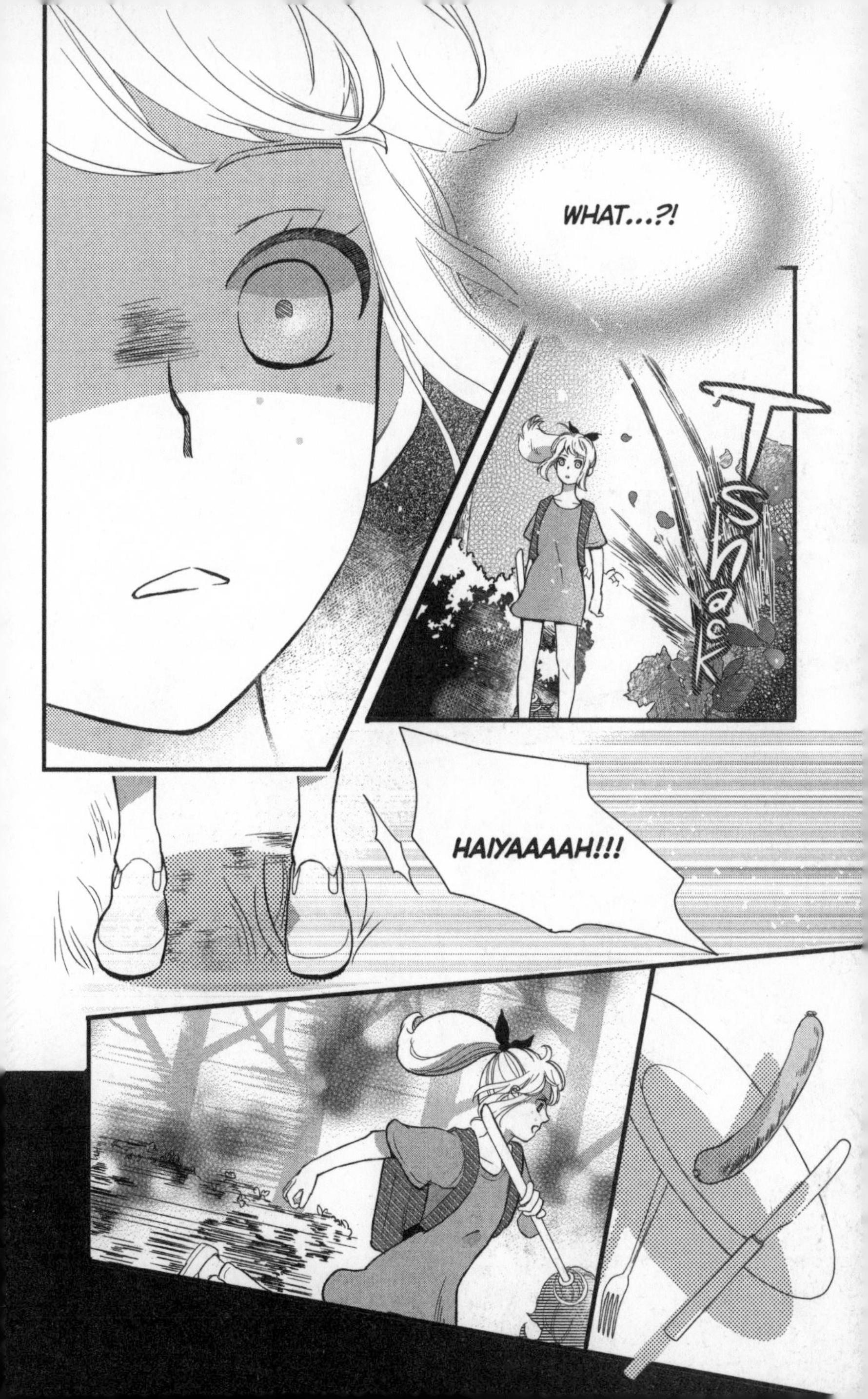
WHAT...?!
T shack
HAIYAAAAH!!!

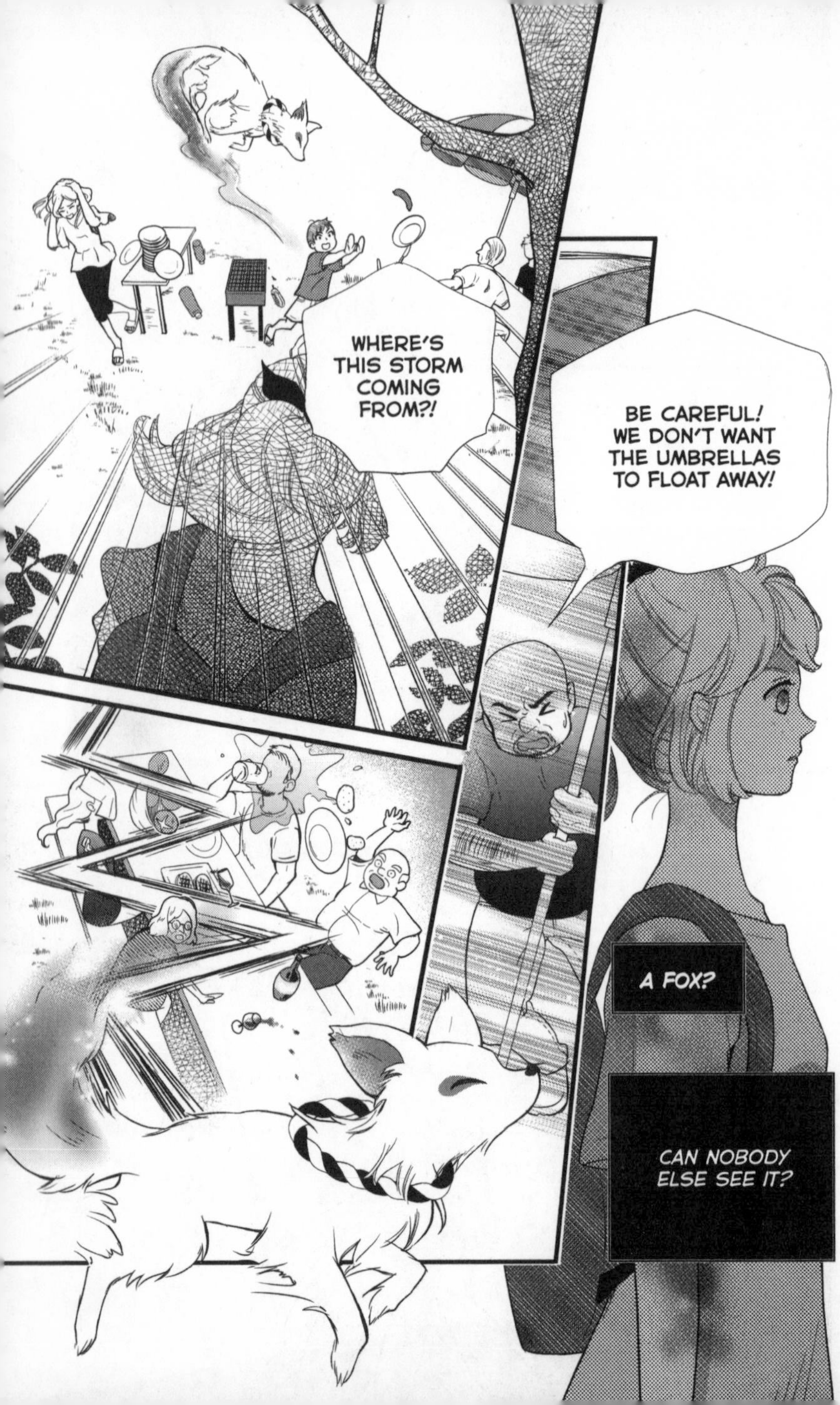
BE CAREFUL! WE DON'T WANT THE UMBRELLAS TO FLOAT AWAY!
WHERE'S THIS STORM COMING FROM?!
A FOX?
CAN NOBODY ELSE SEE IT?

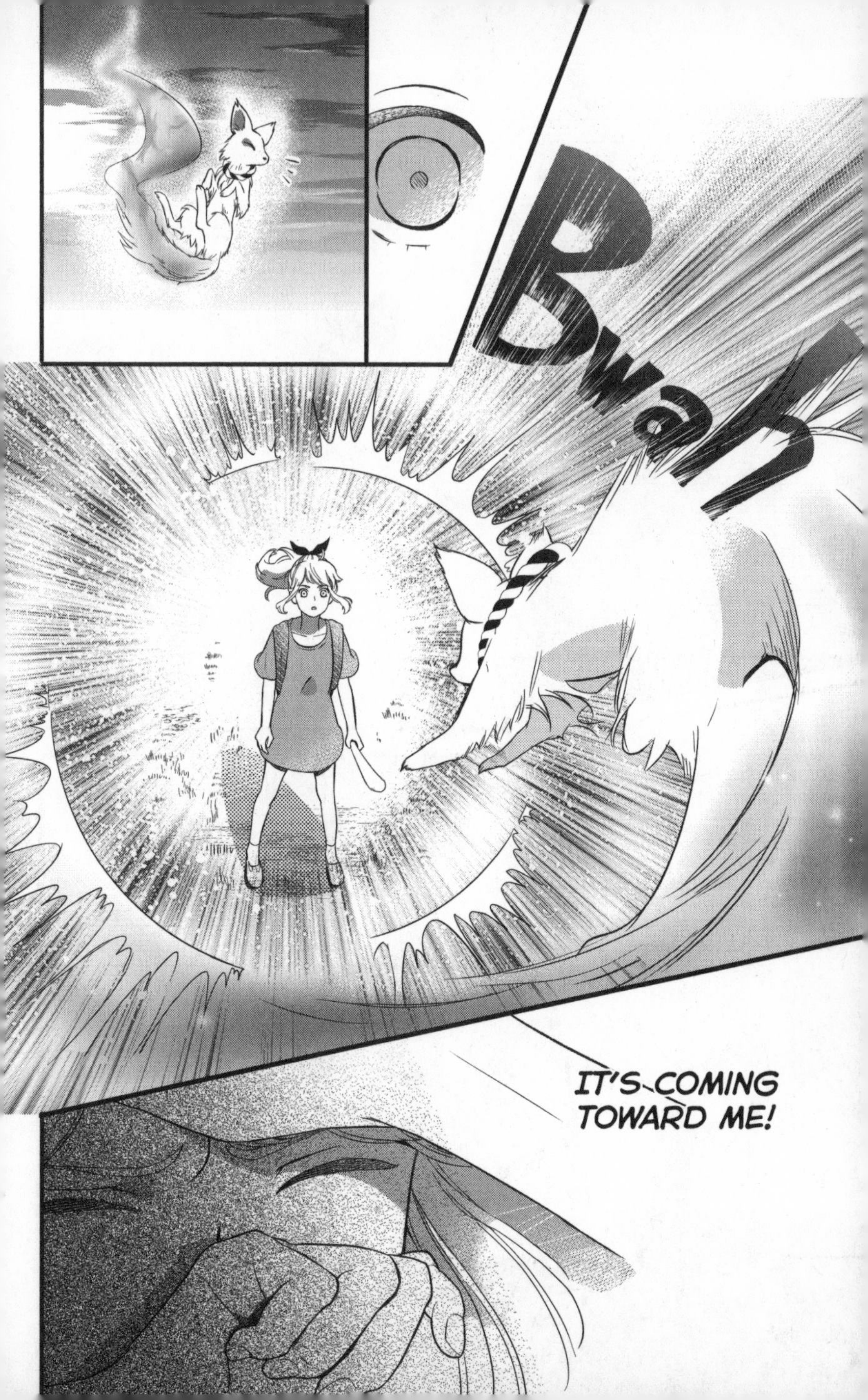
Bwah!
IT'S COMING TOWARD ME!

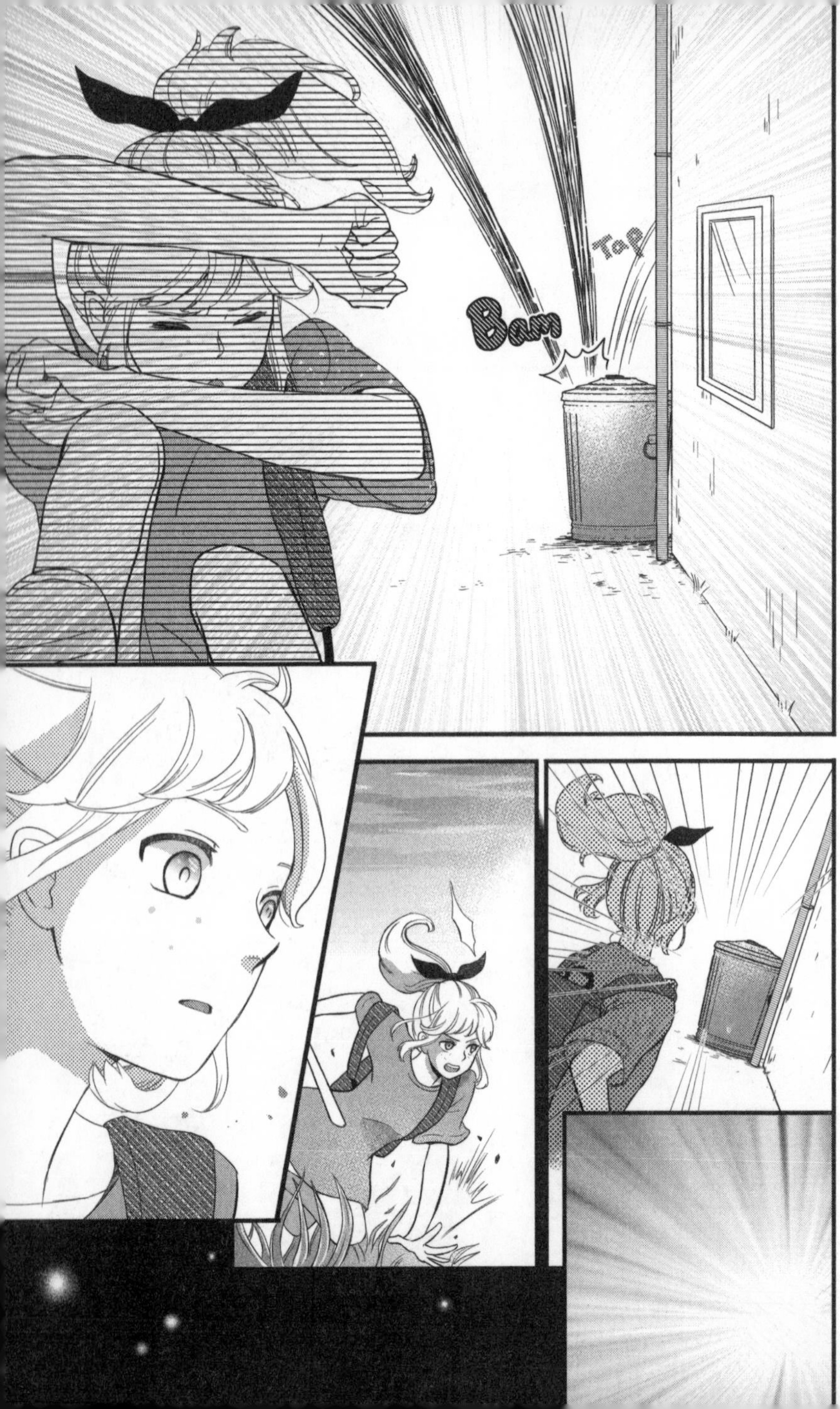
Tap
Bam

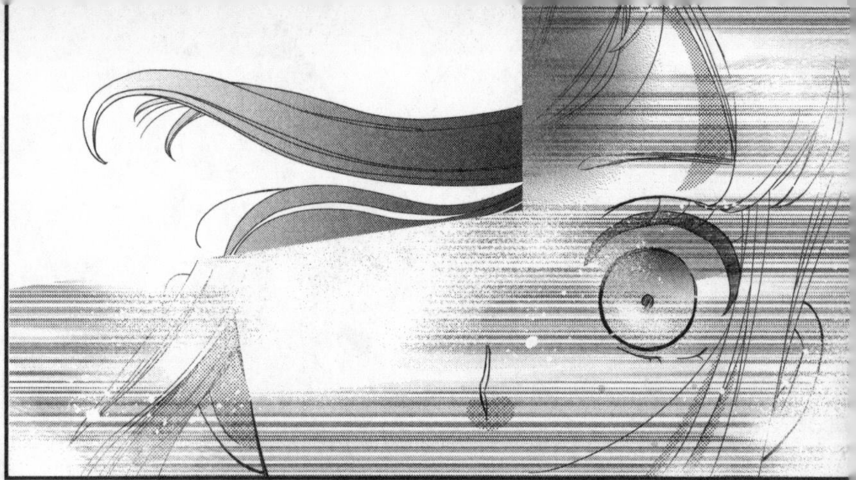
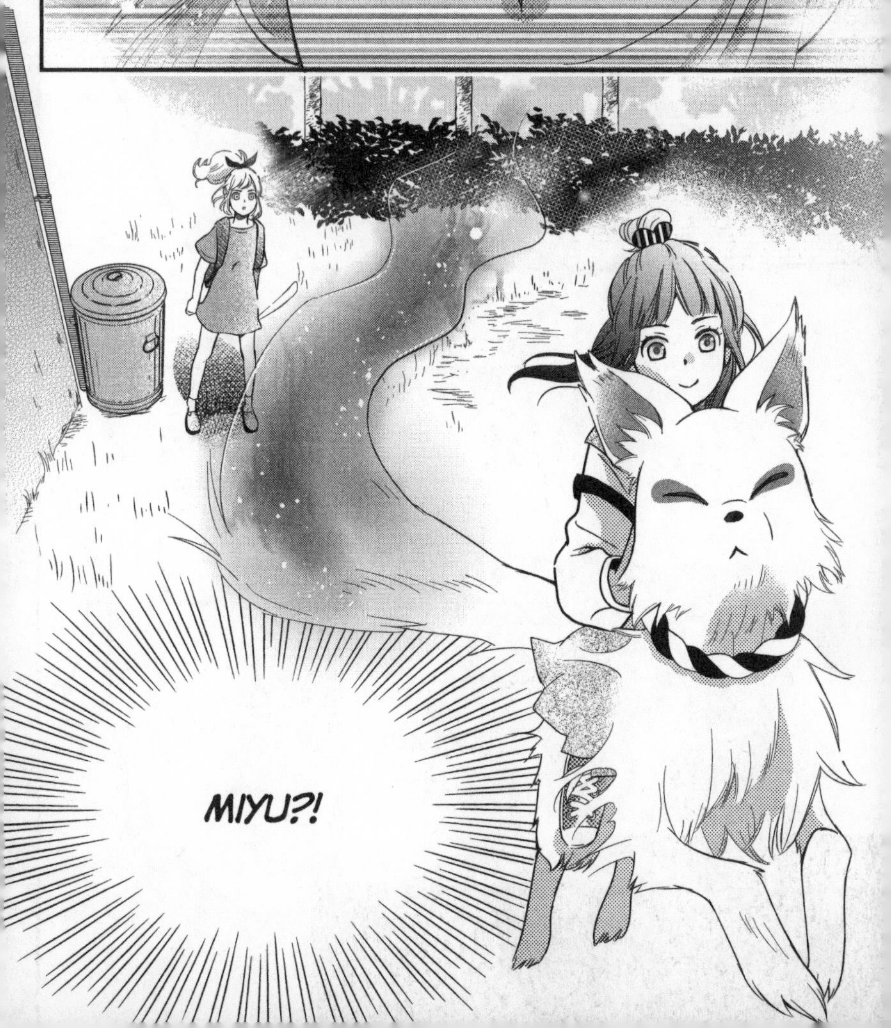
MIYU?!

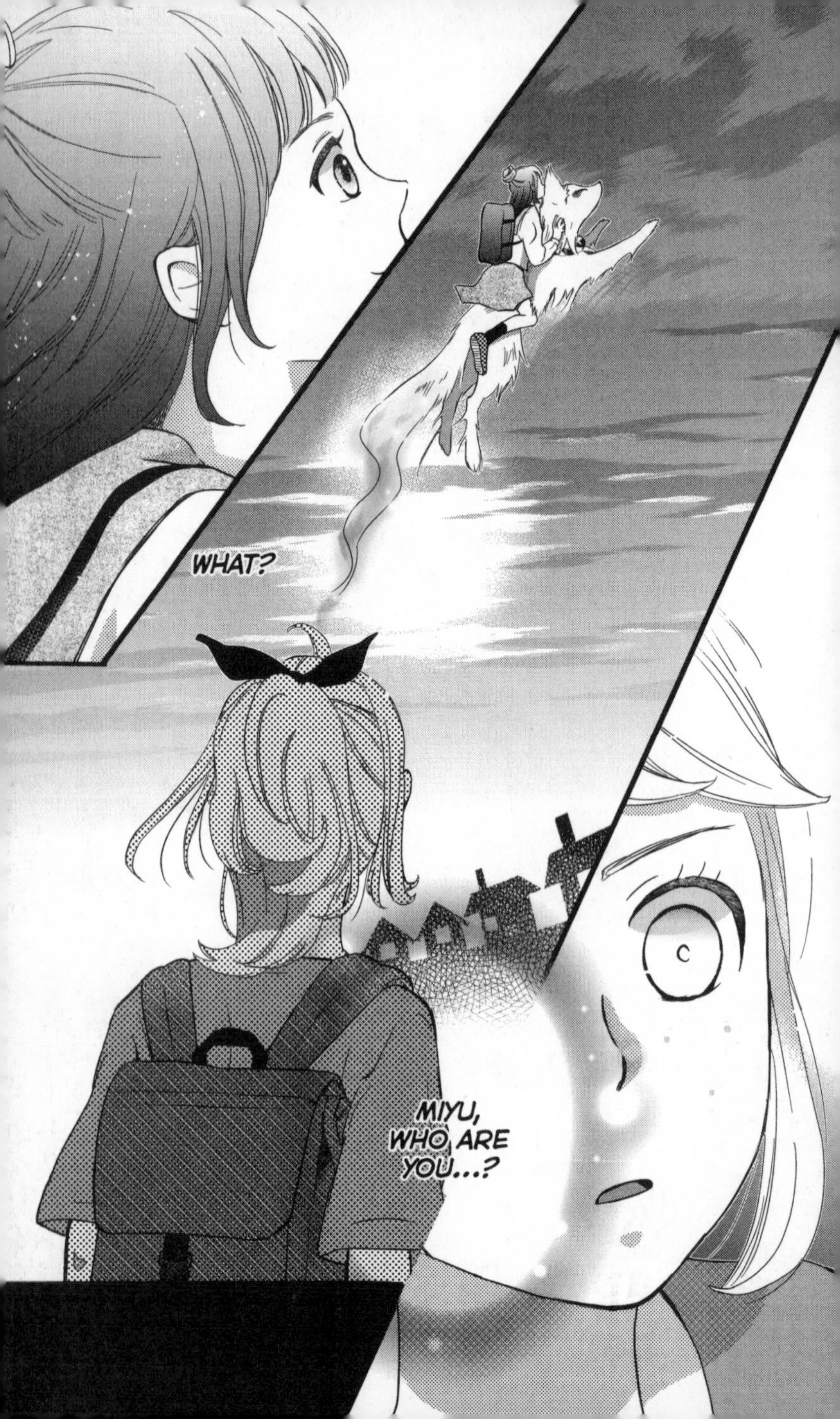
WHAT?
MIYU, WHO ARE YOU...?

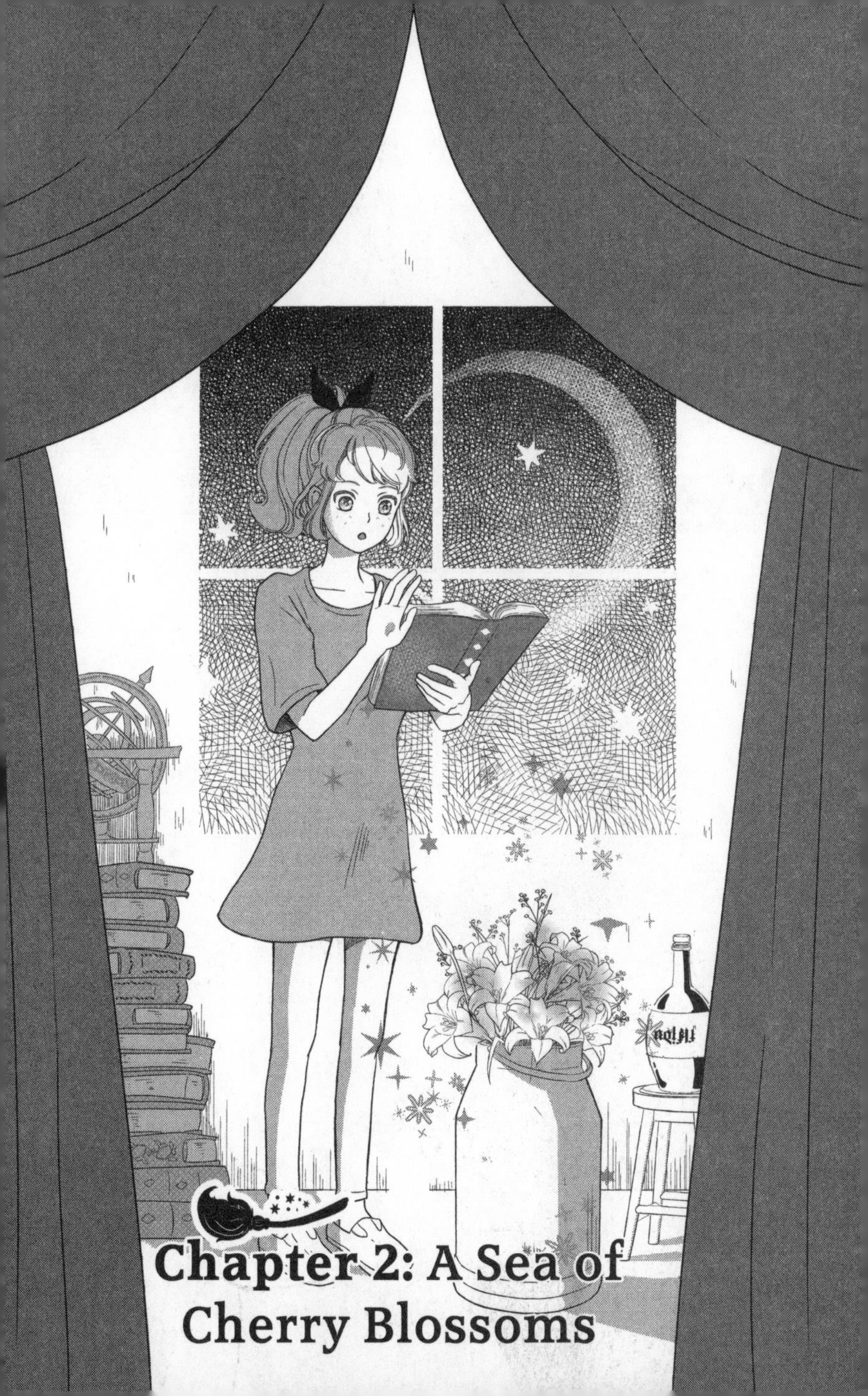

Chapter 2: A Sea of Cherry Blossoms

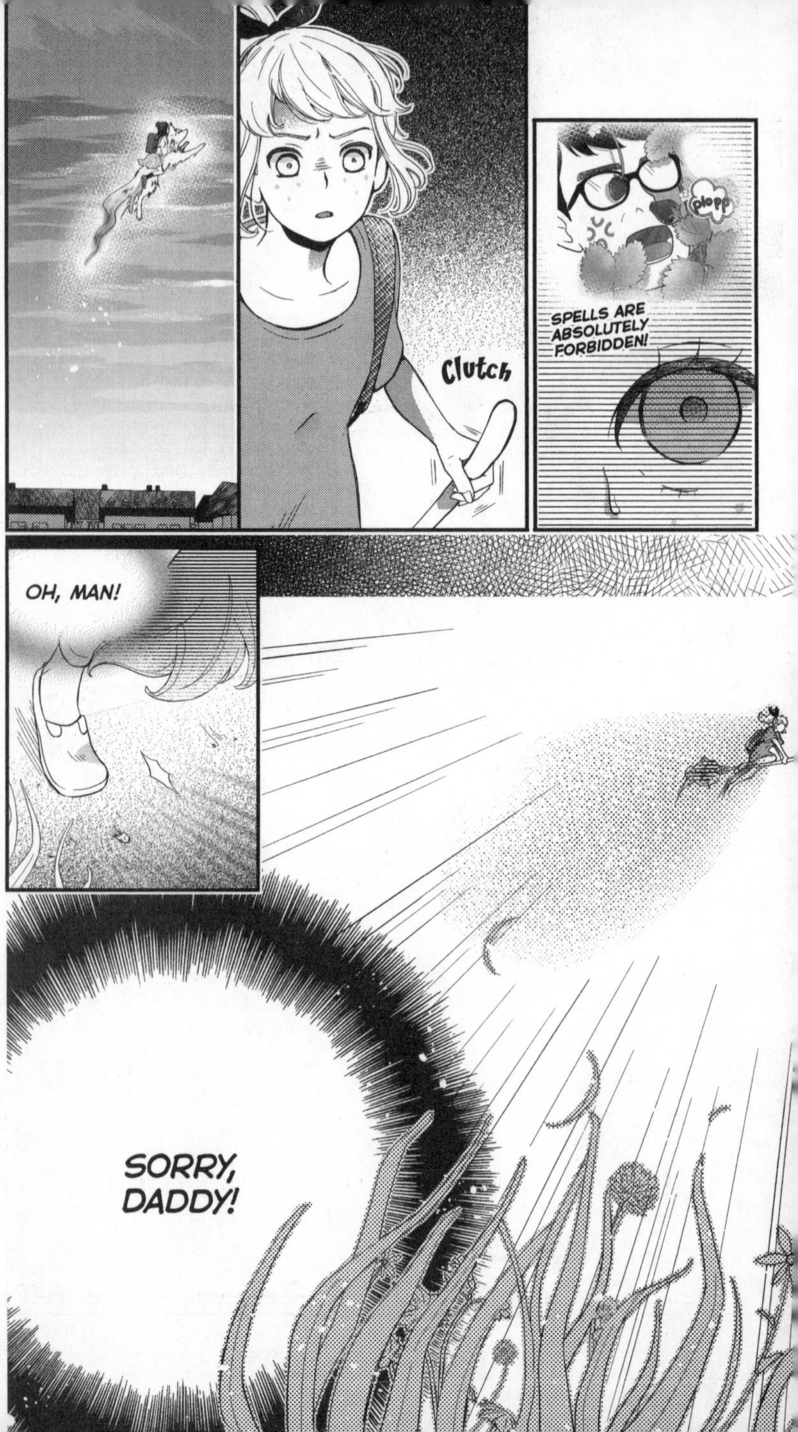
plopp
SPELLS ARE ABSOLUTELY FORBIDDEN!
Clutch
OH, MAN!
SORRY, DADDY!

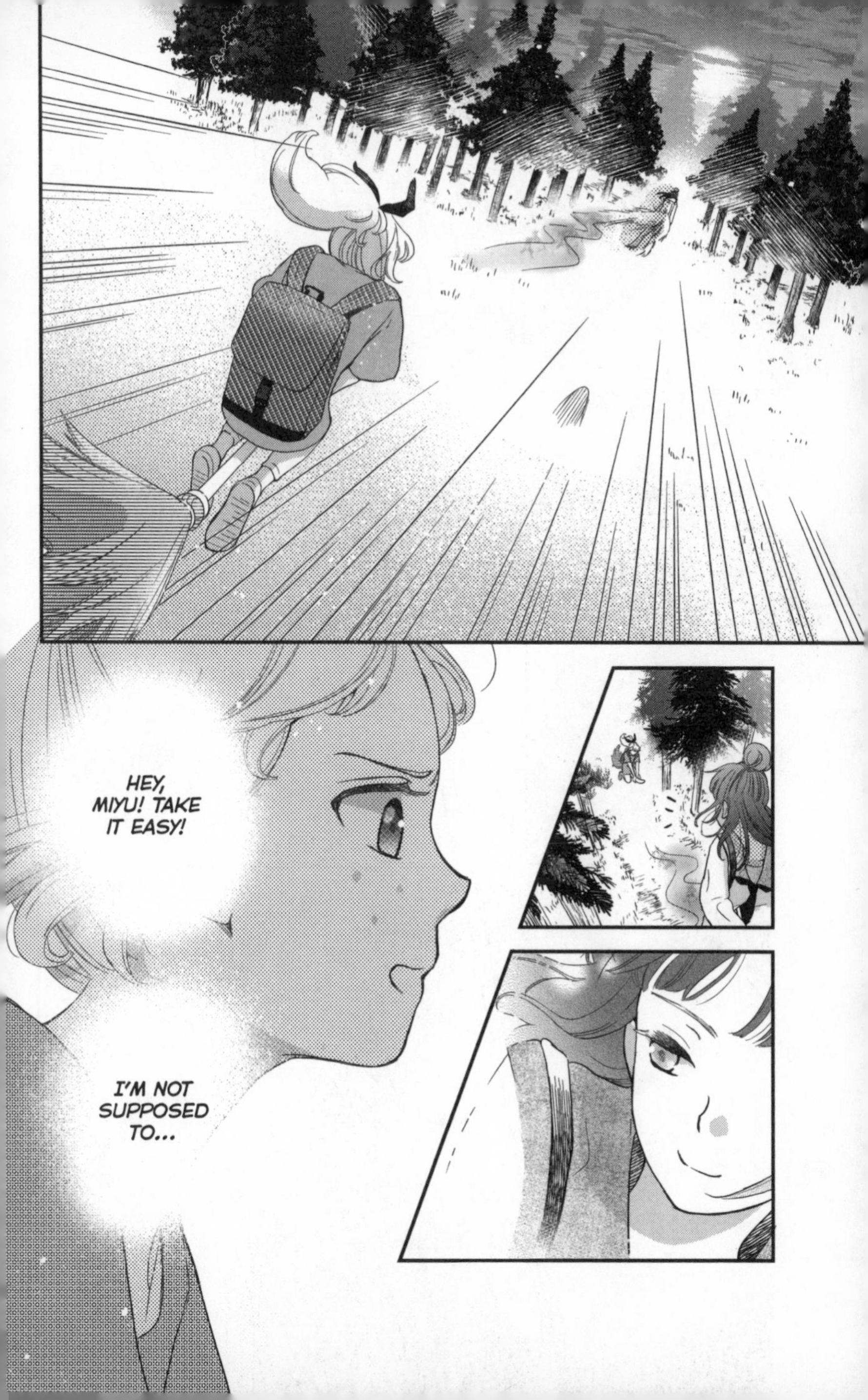
HEY, MIYU! TAKE IT EASY!
I'M NOT SUPPOSED TO...

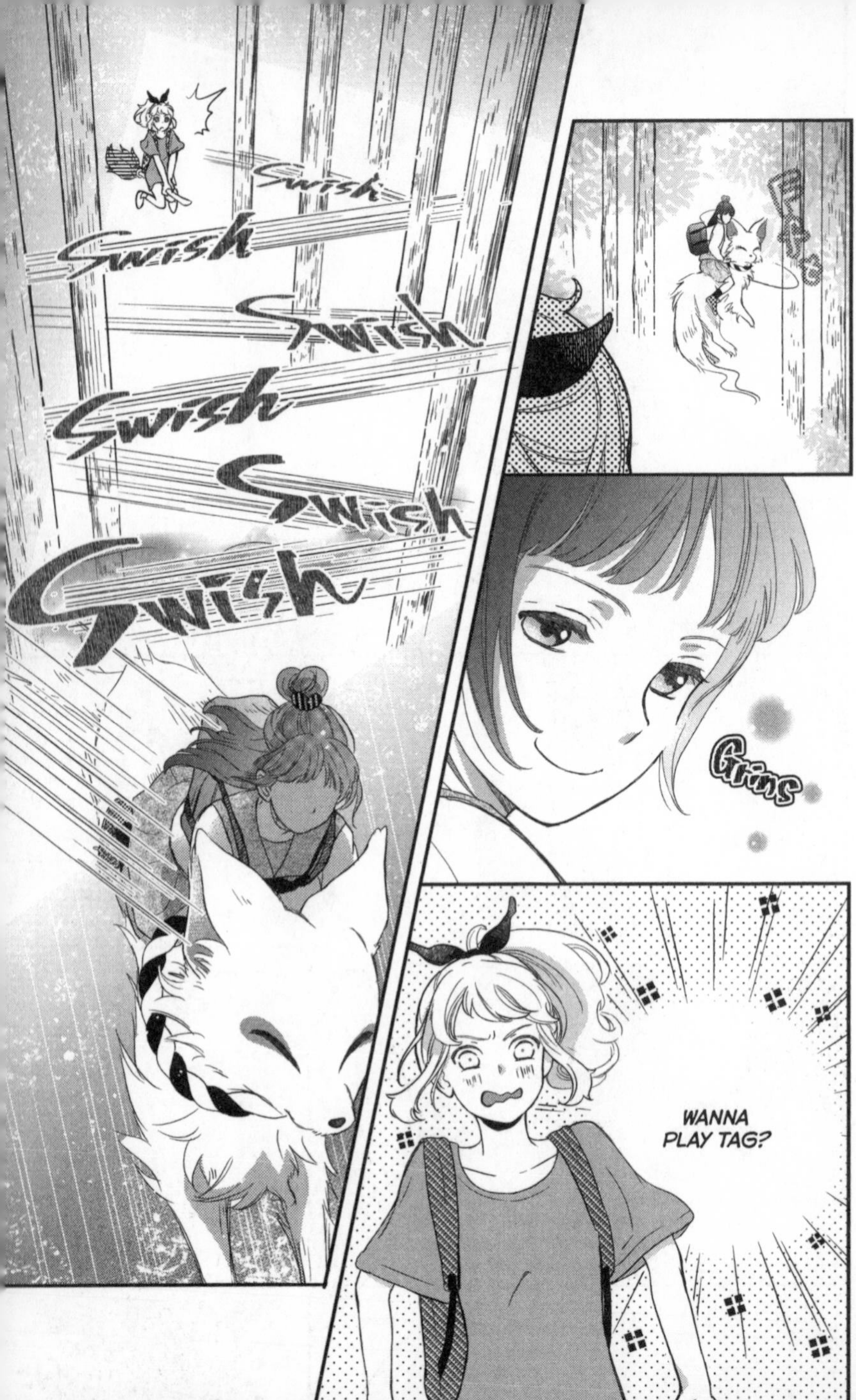
Grins
WANNA PLAY TAG?
Swish
Swish
Swish
Swish
Swish
Swish

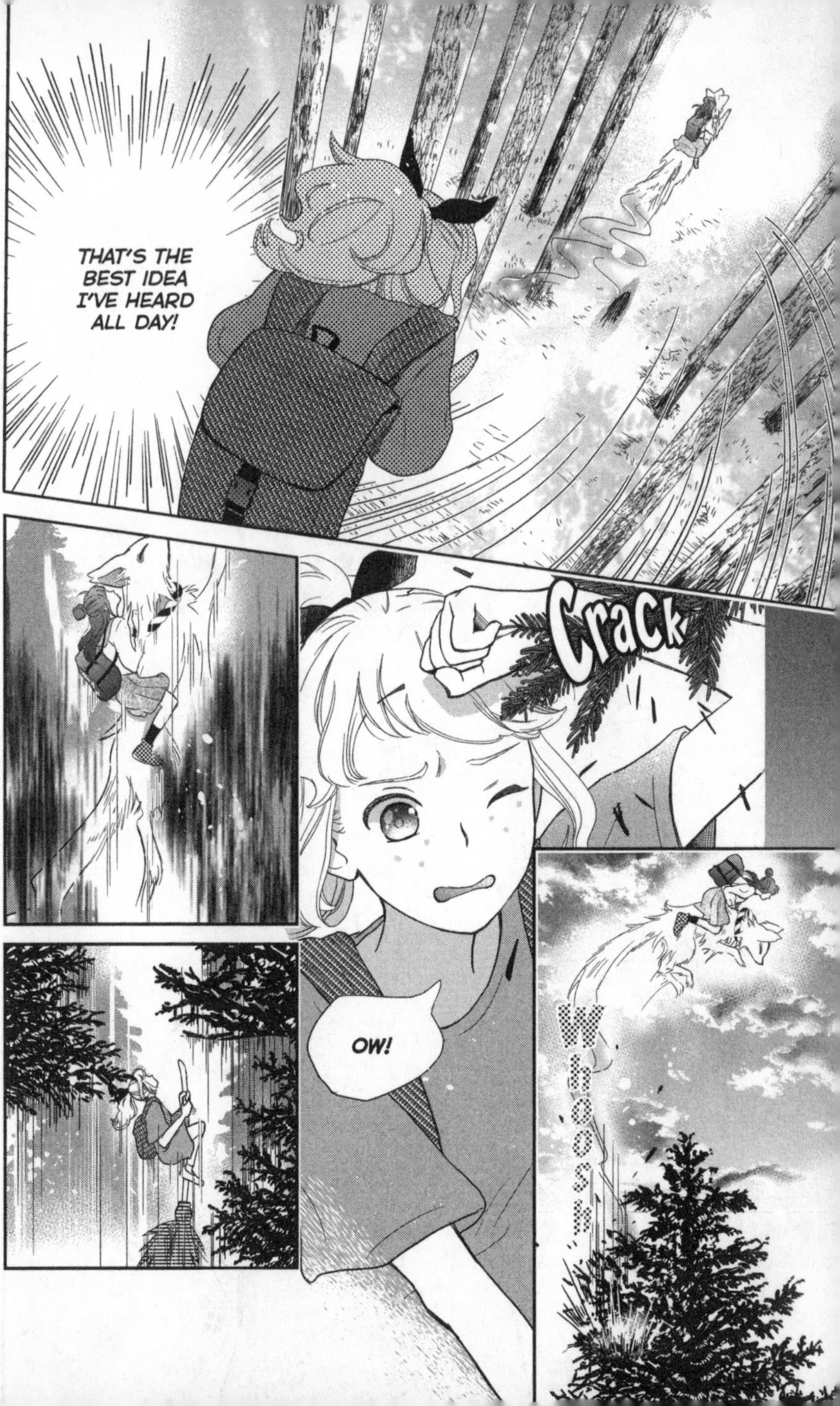
THAT'S THE BEST IDEA I'VE HEARD ALL DAY!
Crack
OW!
Whoosh

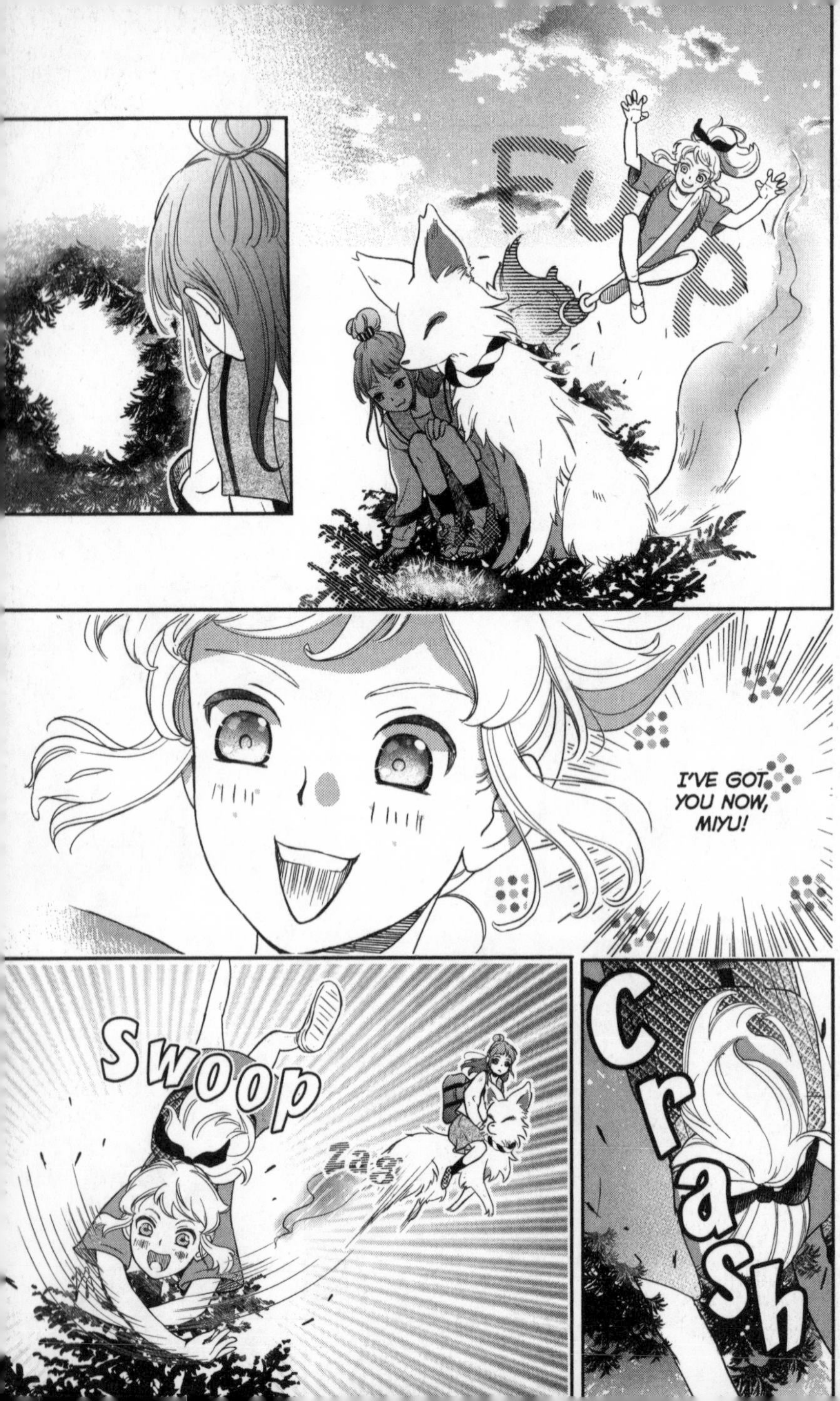
FUP
I'VE GOT YOU NOW, MIYU!
Crash
Swoop
Zag

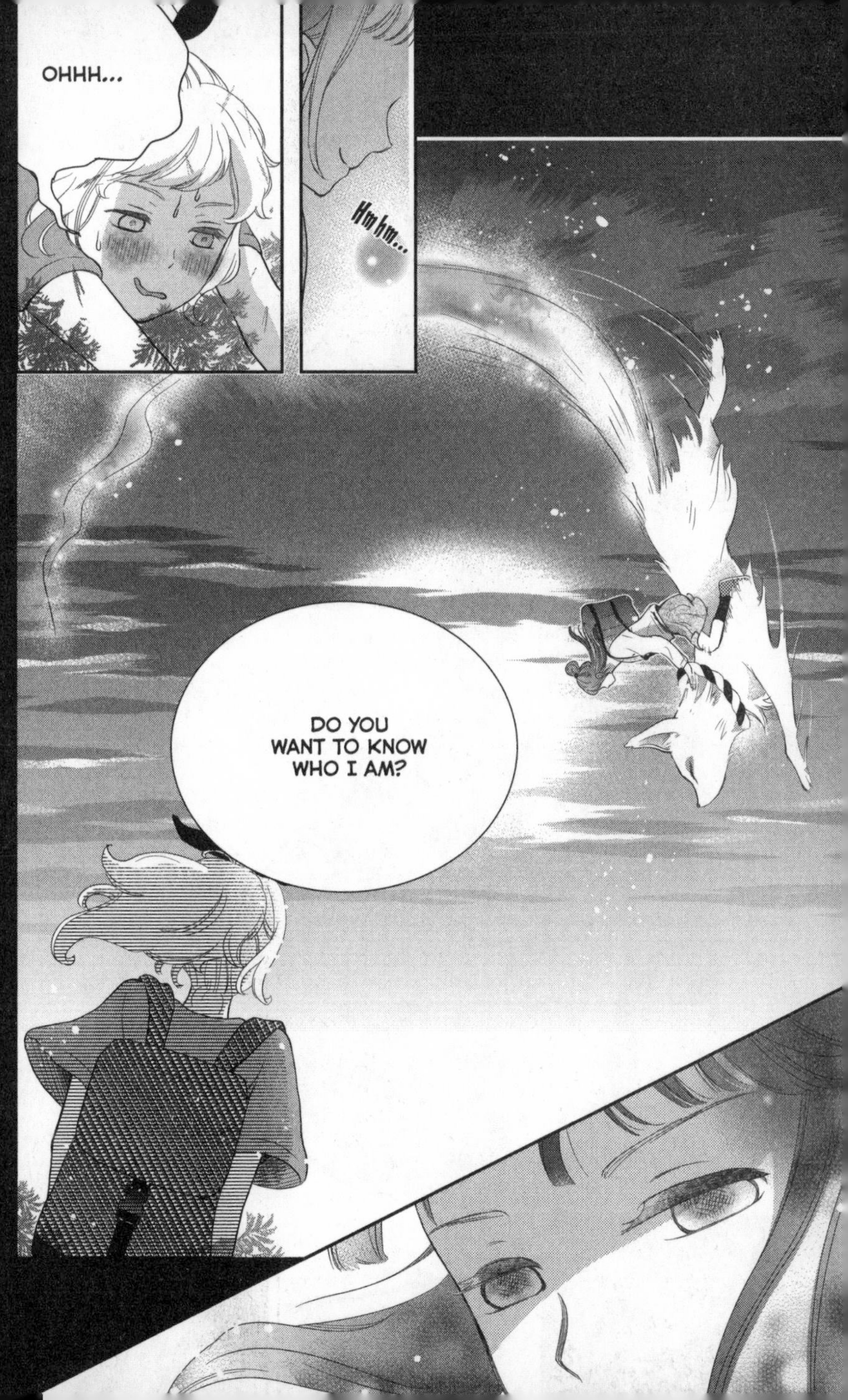
Hm hm...
OHHH...
DO YOU WANT TO KNOW WHO I AM?

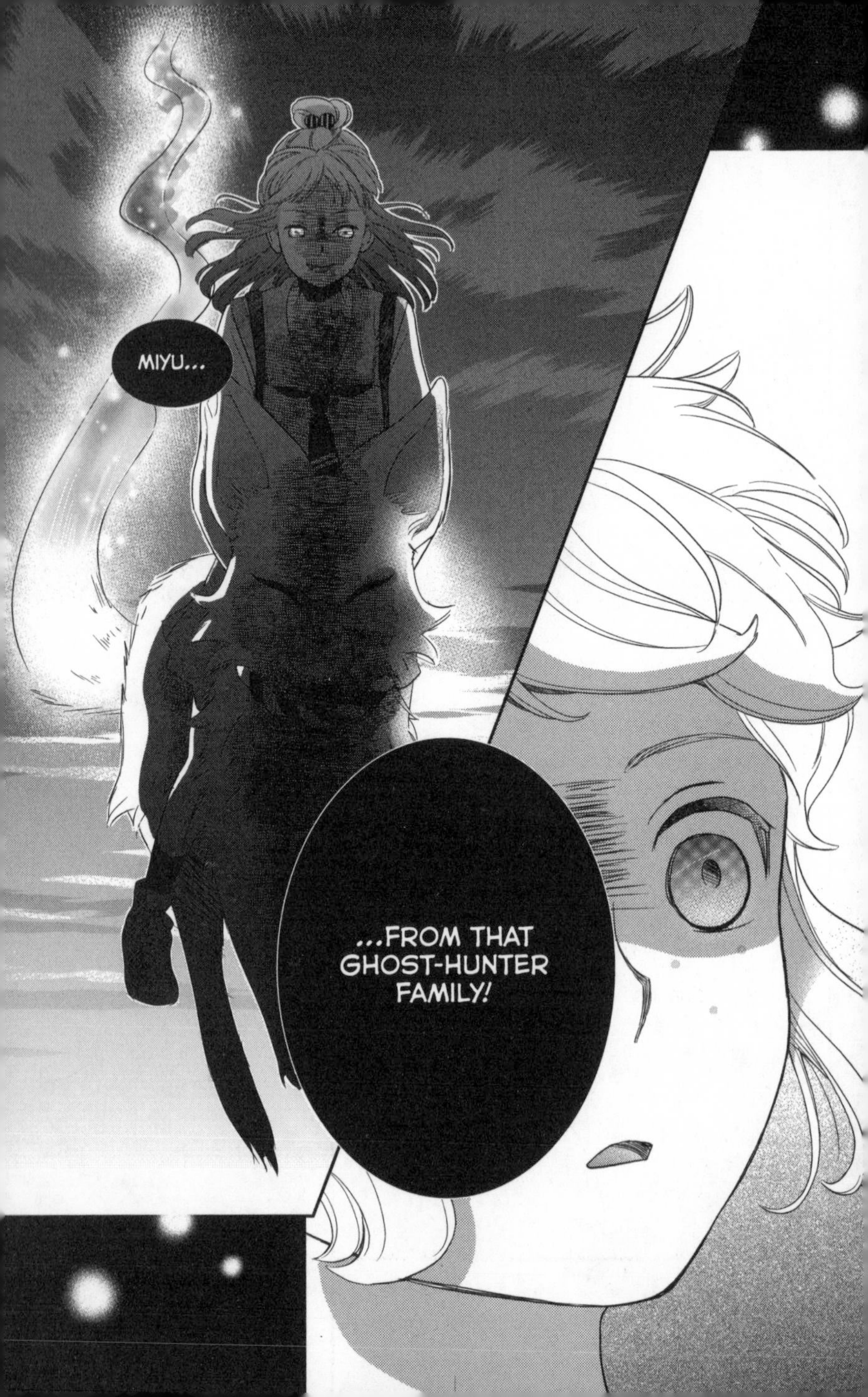
MIYU...
...FROM THAT GHOST-HUNTER FAMILY!

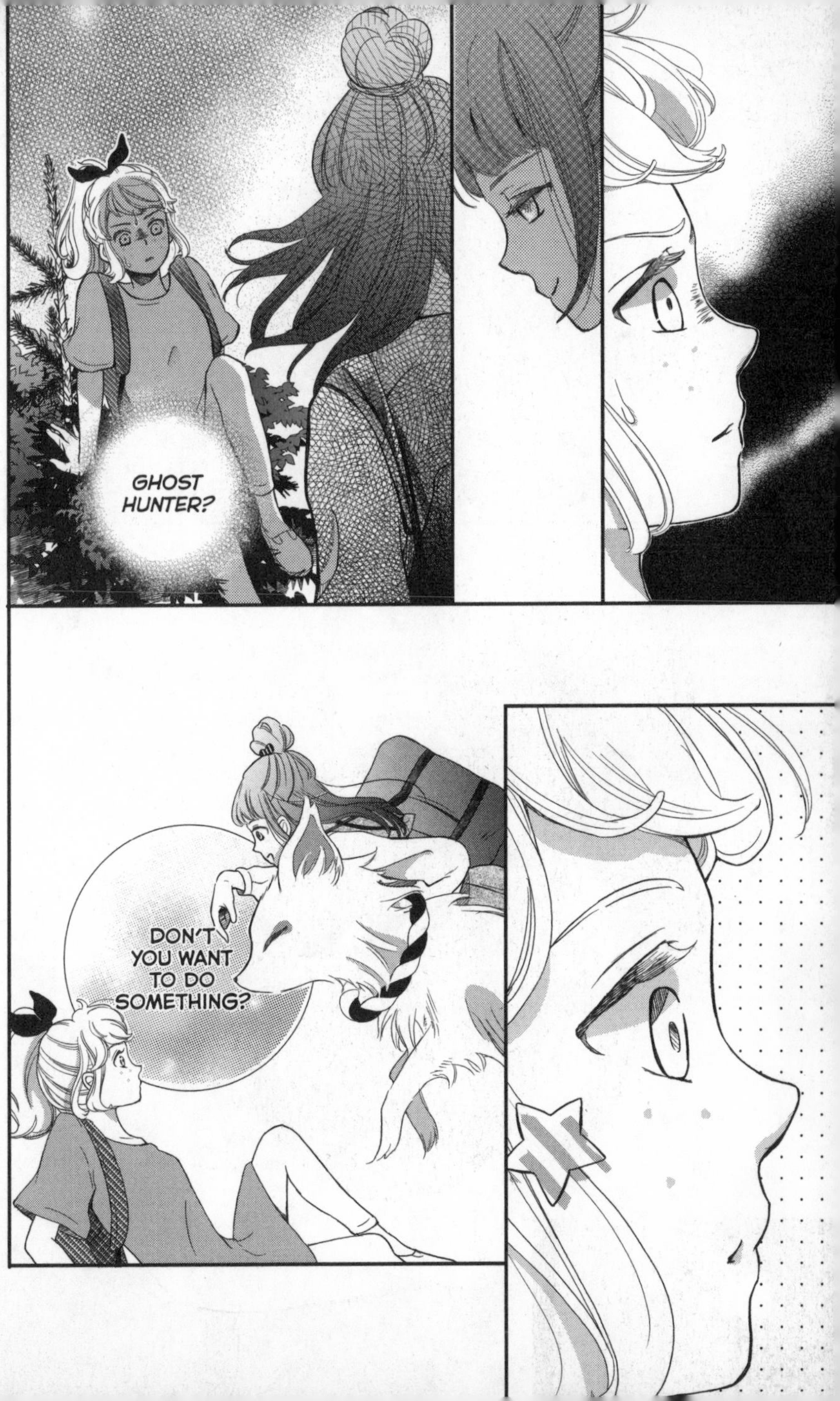
GHOST HUNTER?
DON'T YOU WANT TO DO SOMETHING?

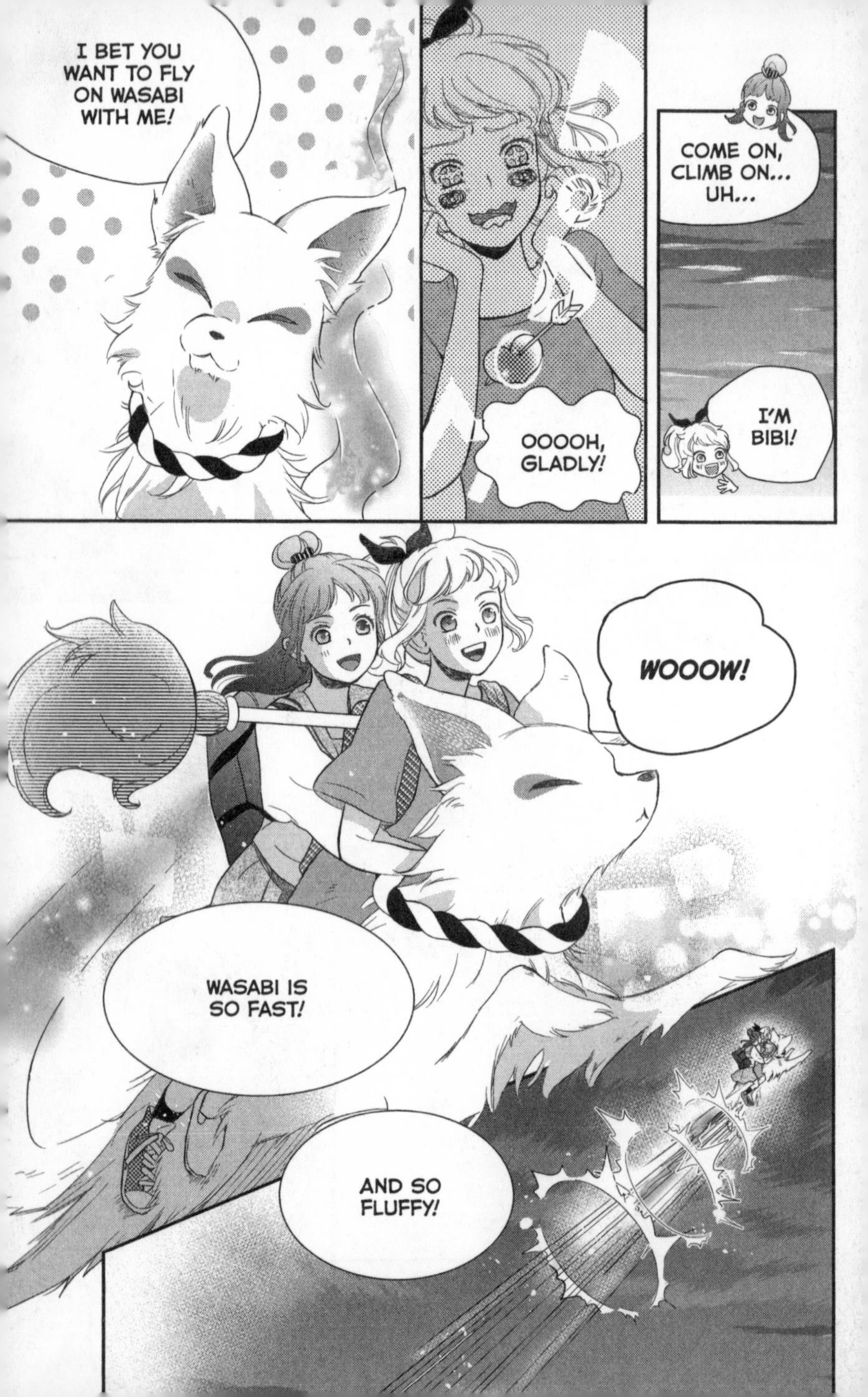
I BET YOU WANT TO FLY ON WASABI WITH ME!
OOOOH, GLADLY!
COME ON, CLIMB ON... UH...
I'M BIBI!
WOOOW!
WASABI IS SO FAST!
AND SO FLUFFY!

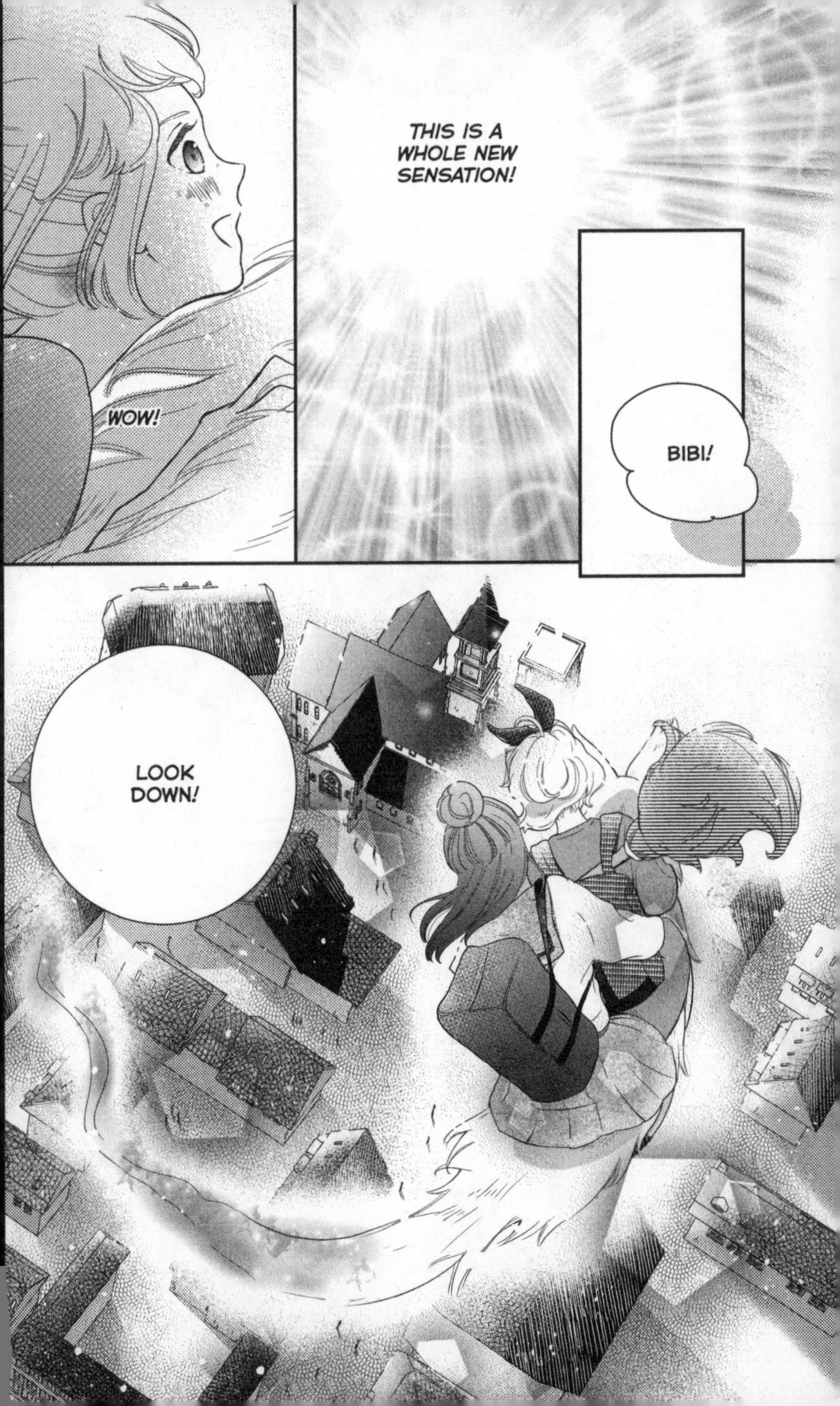
WOW!
THIS IS A WHOLE NEW SENSATION!
BIBI!
LOOK DOWN!

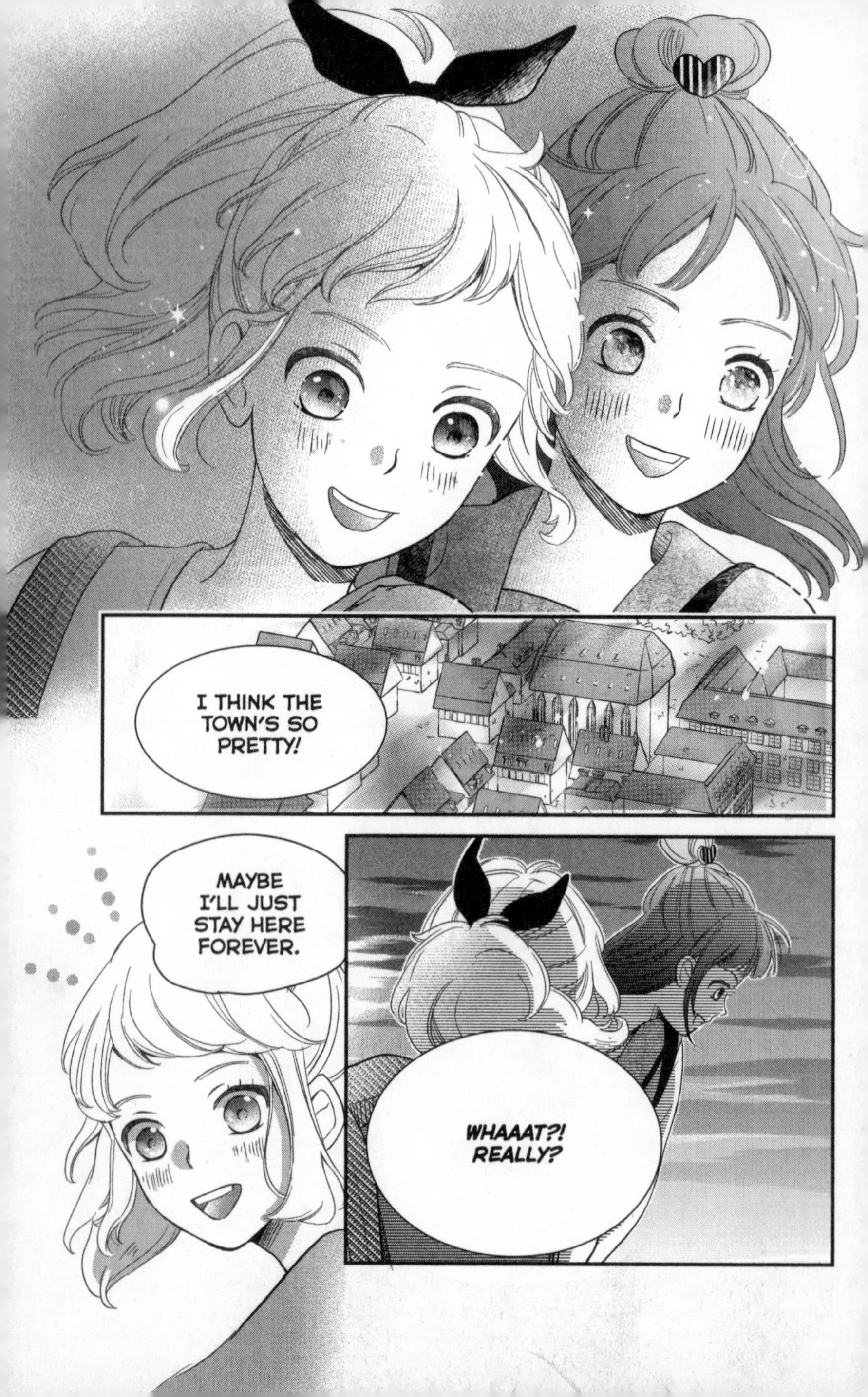
I THINK THE TOWN'S SO PRETTY!
MAYBE I'LL JUST STAY HERE FOREVER.
WHAAAT?! REALLY?

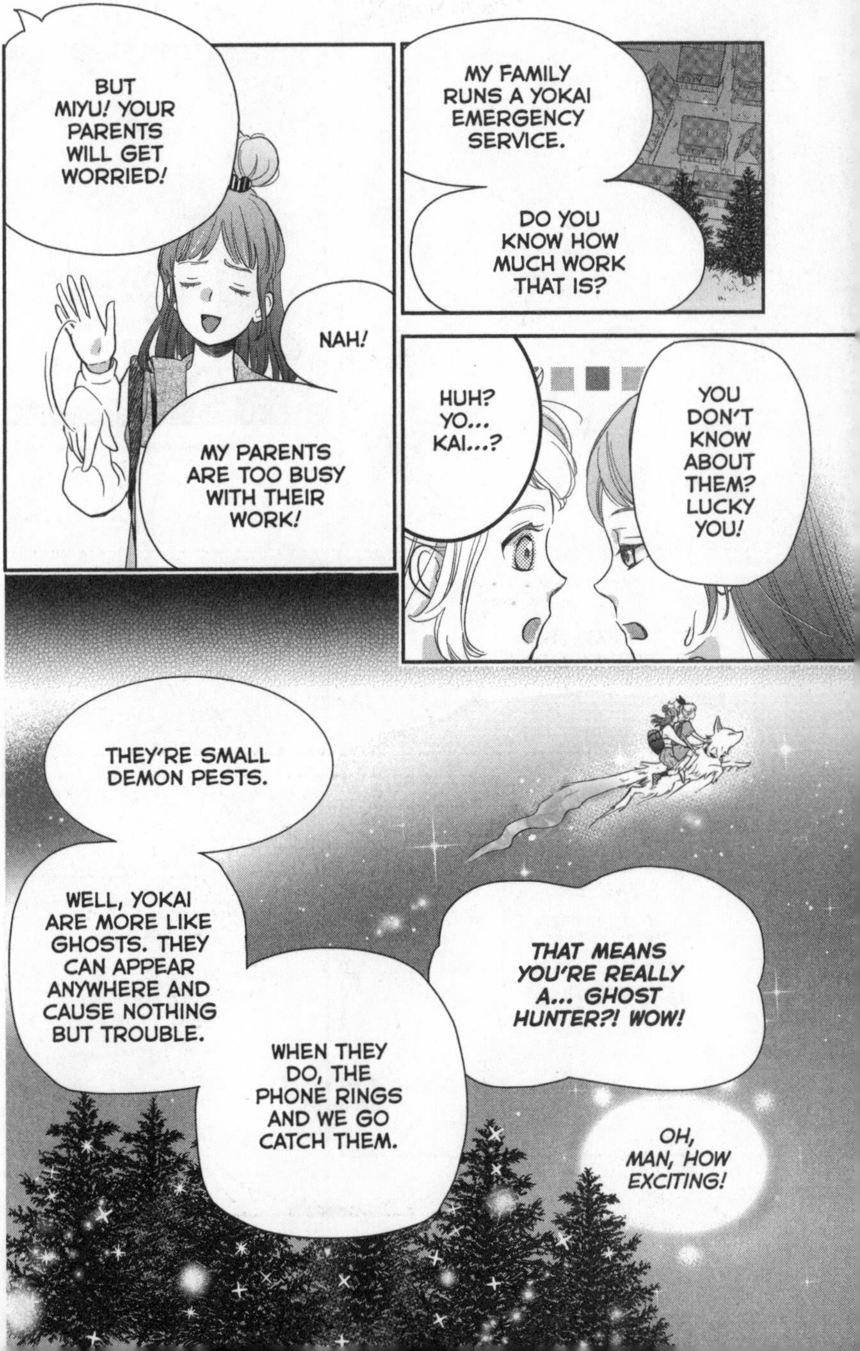
BUT MIYU! YOUR PARENTS WILL GET WORRIED!
NAH!
MY PARENTS ARE TOO BUSY WITH THEIR WORK!
MY FAMILY RUNS A YOKAI EMERGENCY SERVICE.
DO YOU KNOW HOW MUCH WORK THAT IS?
HUH? YO... KAI...?
YOU DON'T KNOW ABOUT THEM? LUCKY YOU!
THEY'RE SMALL DEMON PESTS.
WELL, YOKAI ARE MORE LIKE GHOSTS. THEY CAN APPEAR ANYWHERE AND CAUSE NOTHING BUT TROUBLE.
WHEN THEY DO, THE PHONE RINGS AND WE GO CATCH THEM.
THAT MEANS YOU'RE REALLY A... GHOST HUNTER?! WOW!
OH, MAN, HOW EXCITING!

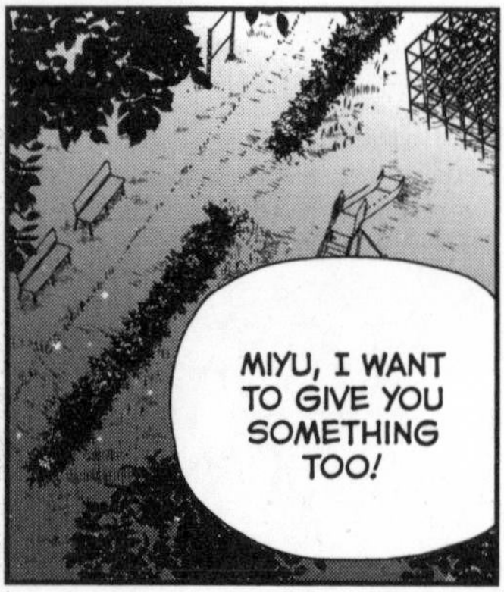
MIYU, I WANT TO GIVE YOU SOMETHING TOO!
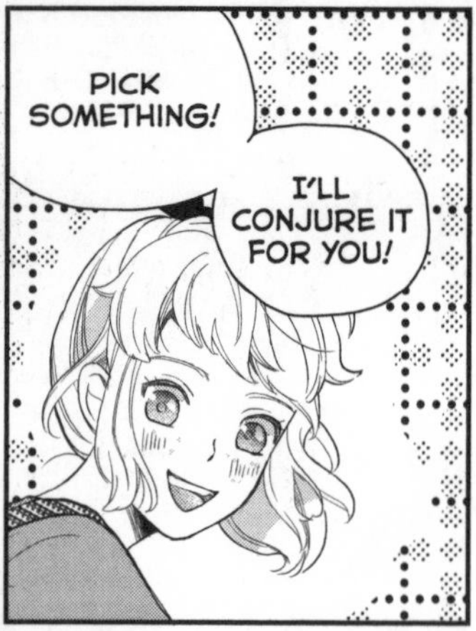
PICK SOMETHING!
I'LL CONJURE IT FOR YOU!
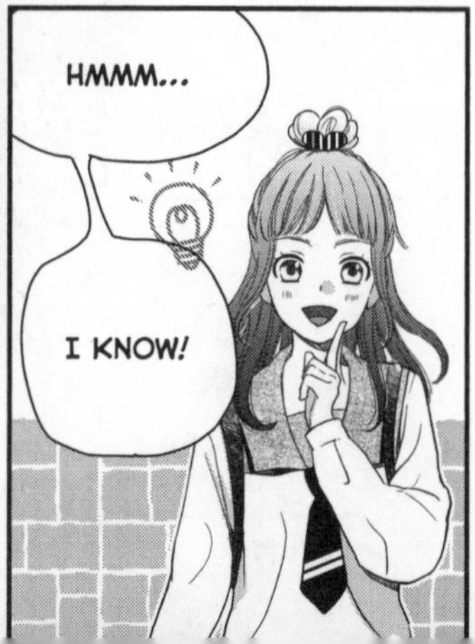
HMMM...
I KNOW!
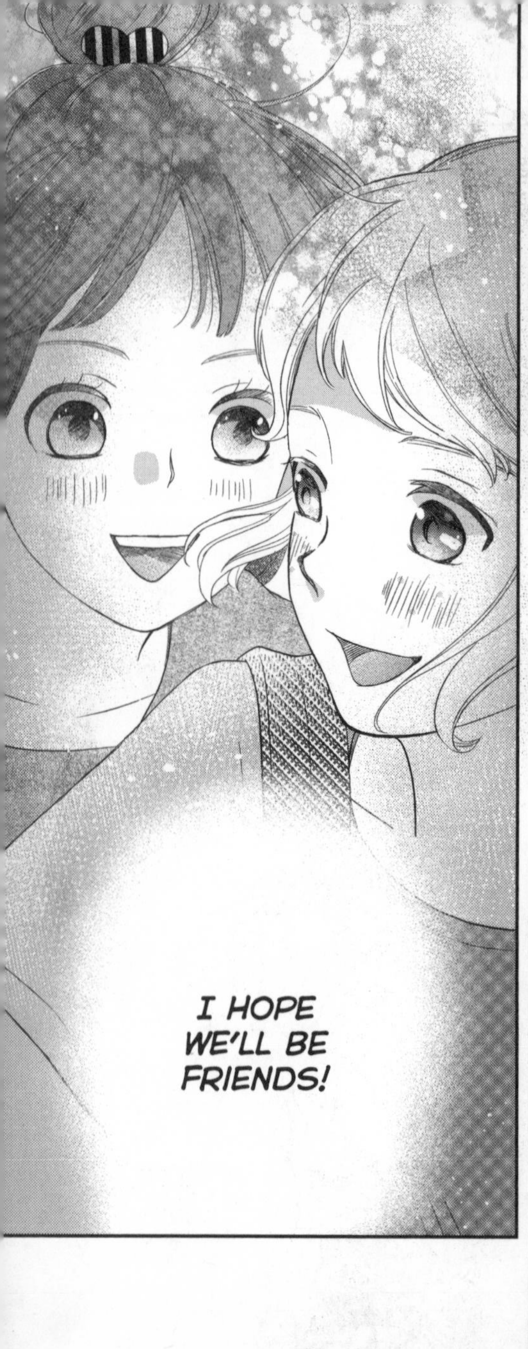
I HOPE WE'LL BE FRIENDS!

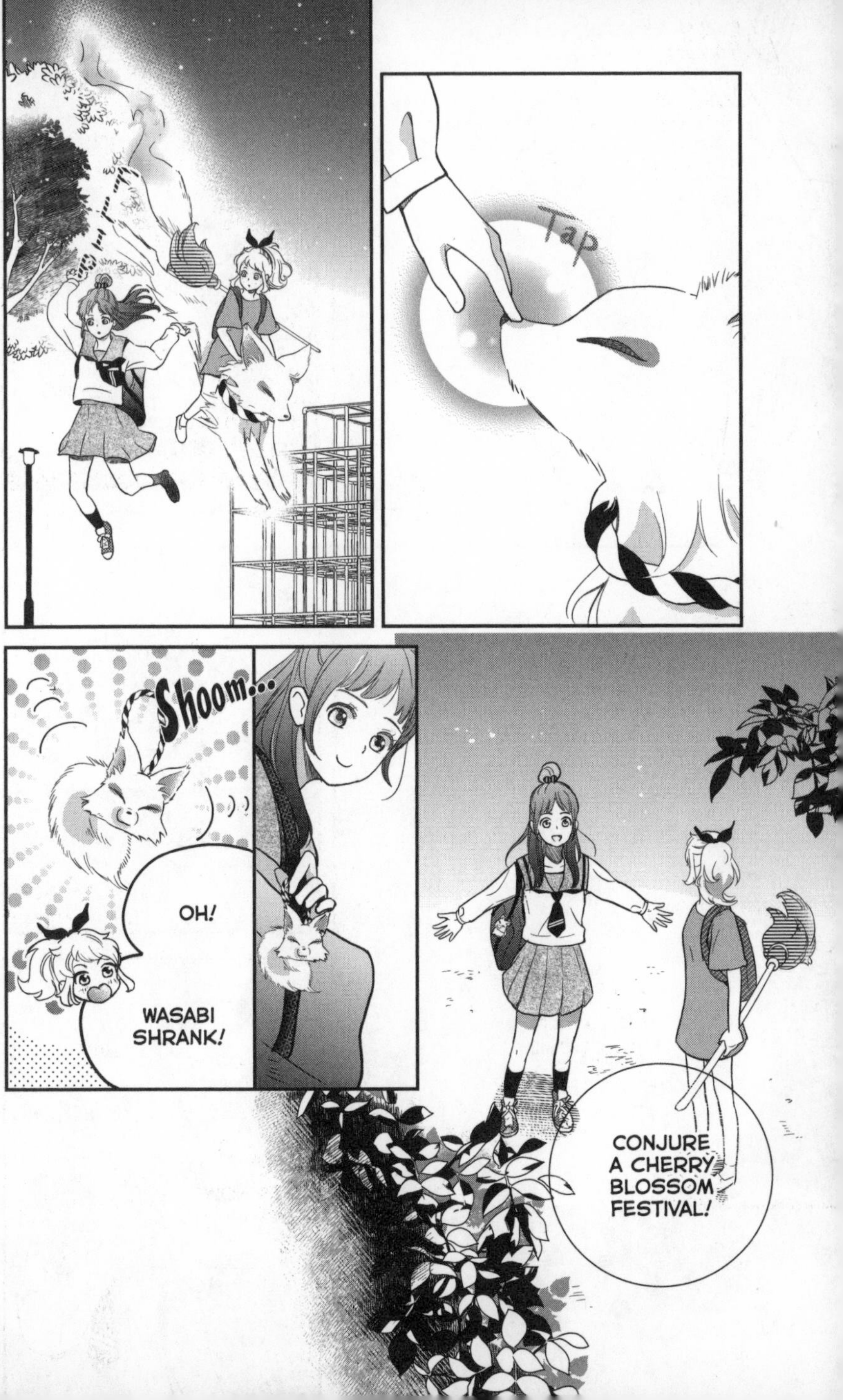
Tap
CONJURE A CHERRY BLOSSOM FESTIVAL!
Shoom...
OH!
WASABI SHRANK!

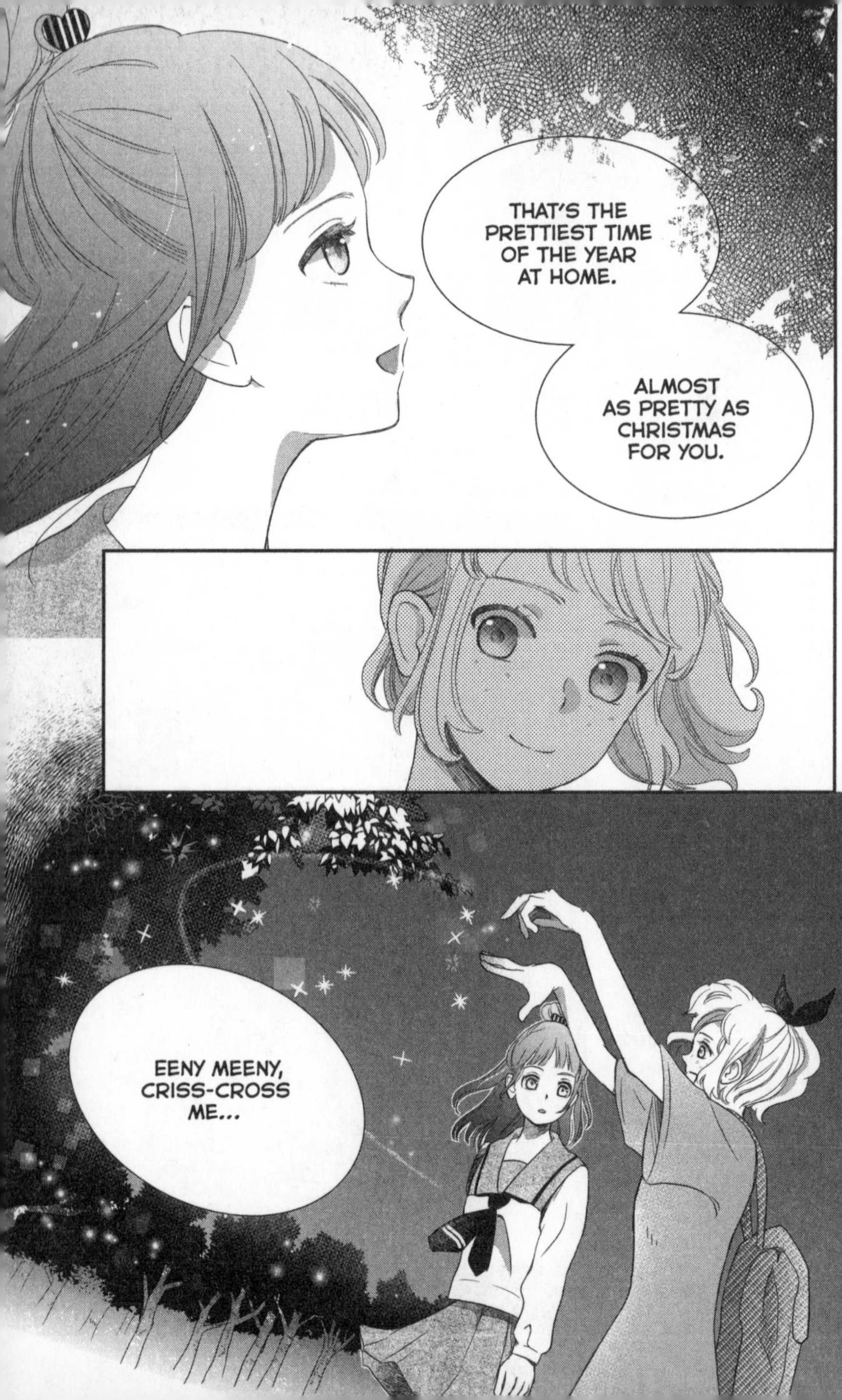
THAT'S THE PRETTIEST TIME OF THE YEAR AT HOME.
ALMOST AS PRETTY AS CHRISTMAS FOR YOU.
EENY MEENY, CRISS-CROSS ME...

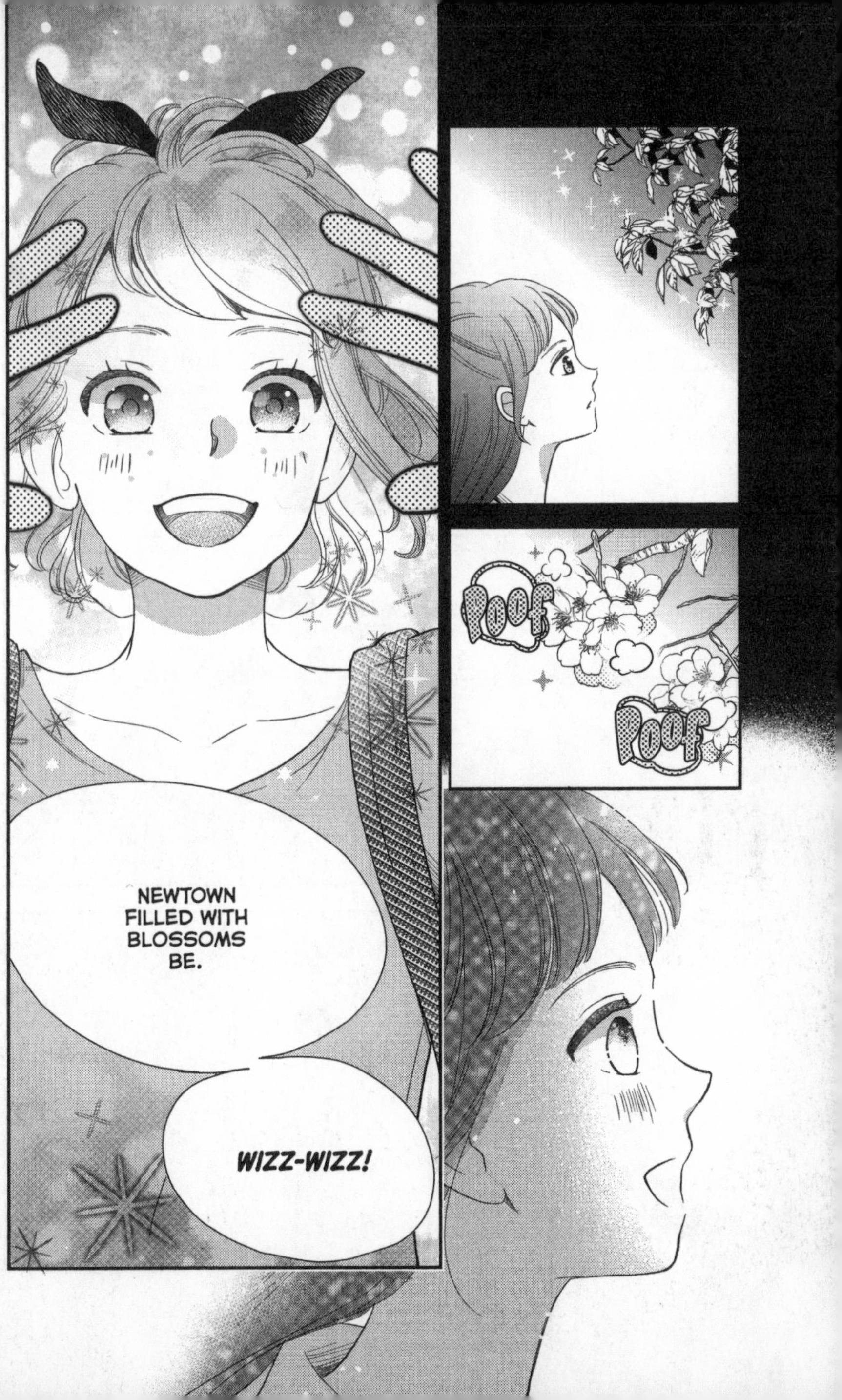
POOF
POOF
NEWTOWN FILLED WITH BLOSSOMS BE.
WIZZ-WIZZ!

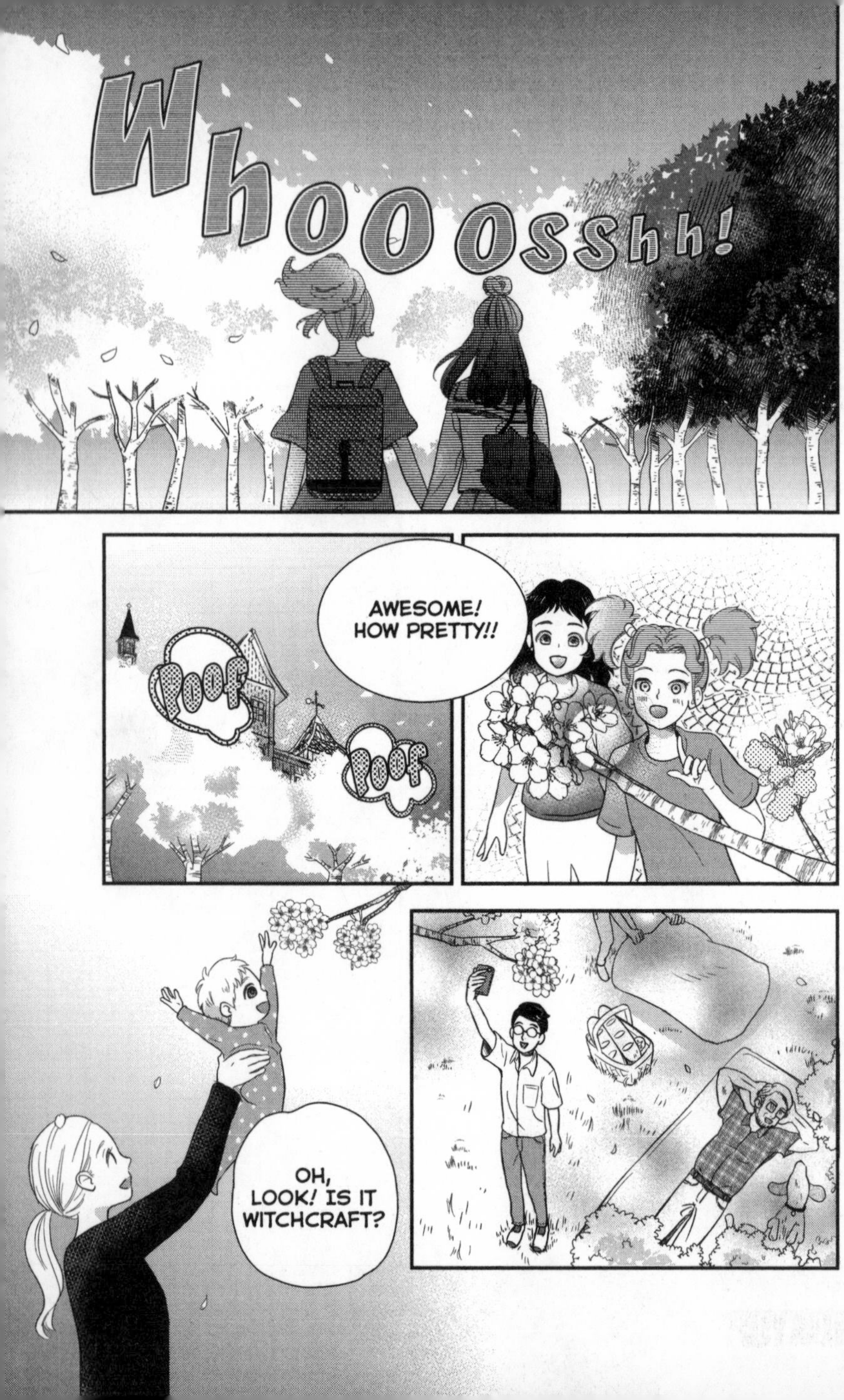
Whooosshh!
AWESOME! HOW PRETTY!!
POOF
POOF
OH, LOOK! IS IT WITCHCRAFT?

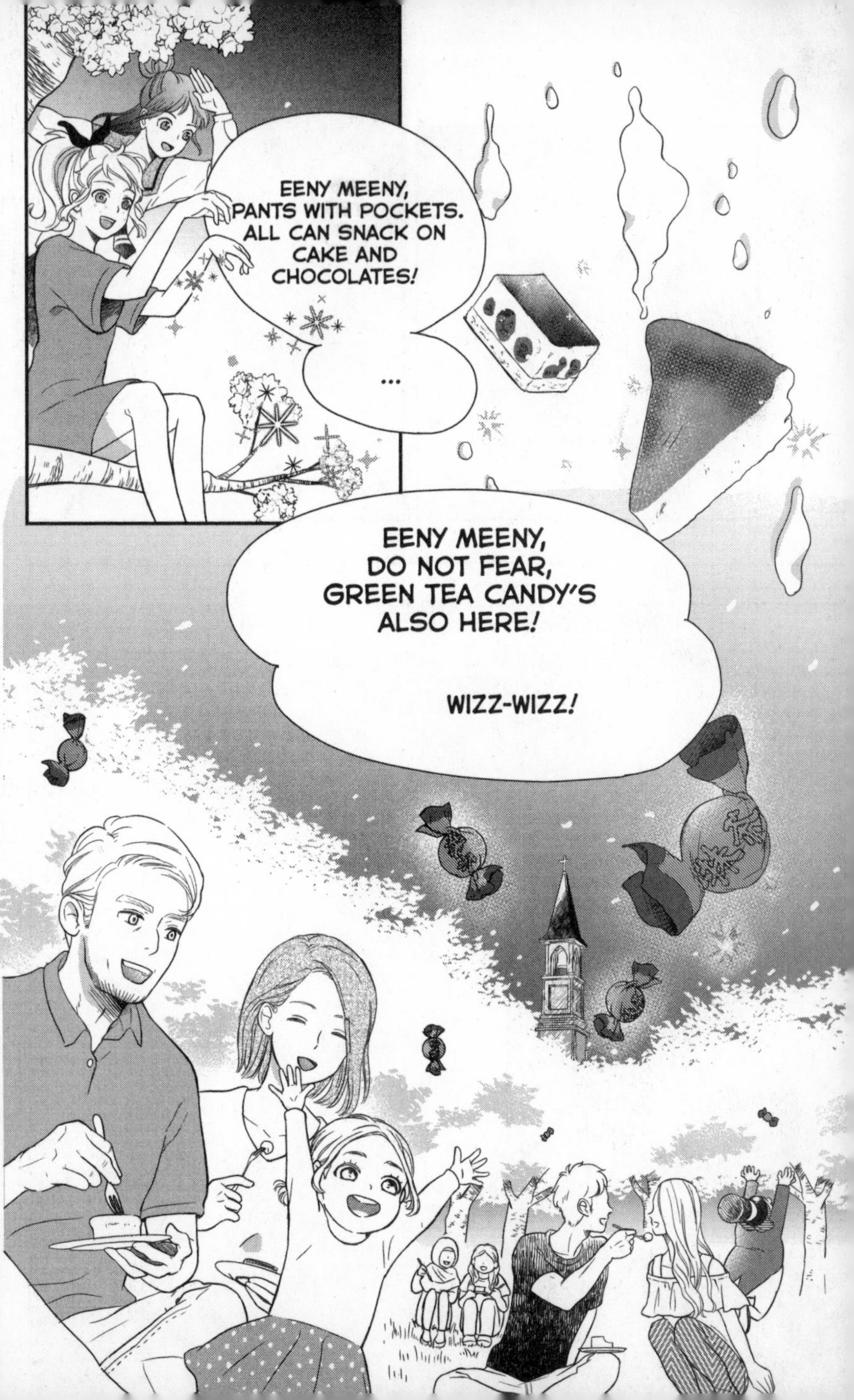
EENY MEENY, PANTS WITH POCKETS. ALL CAN SNACK ON CAKE AND CHOCOLATES!
...
EENY MEENY, DO NOT FEAR, GREEN TEA CANDY'S ALSO HERE!
WIZZ-WIZZ!

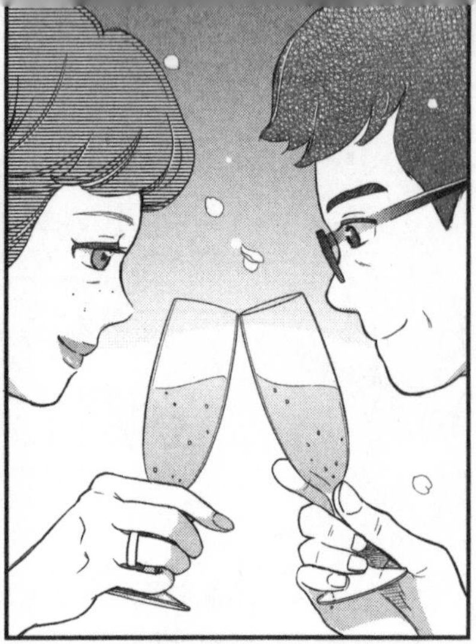
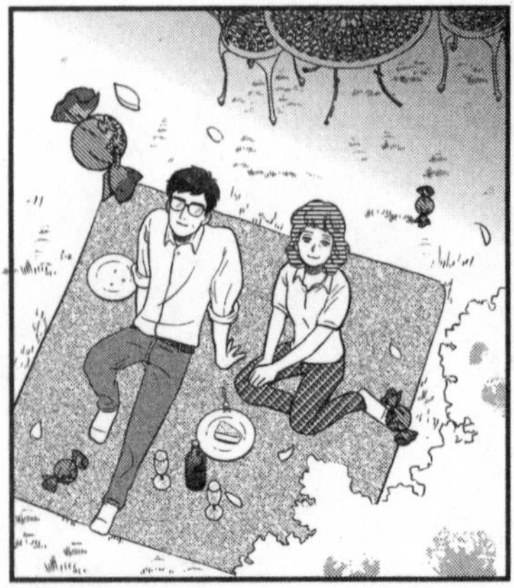
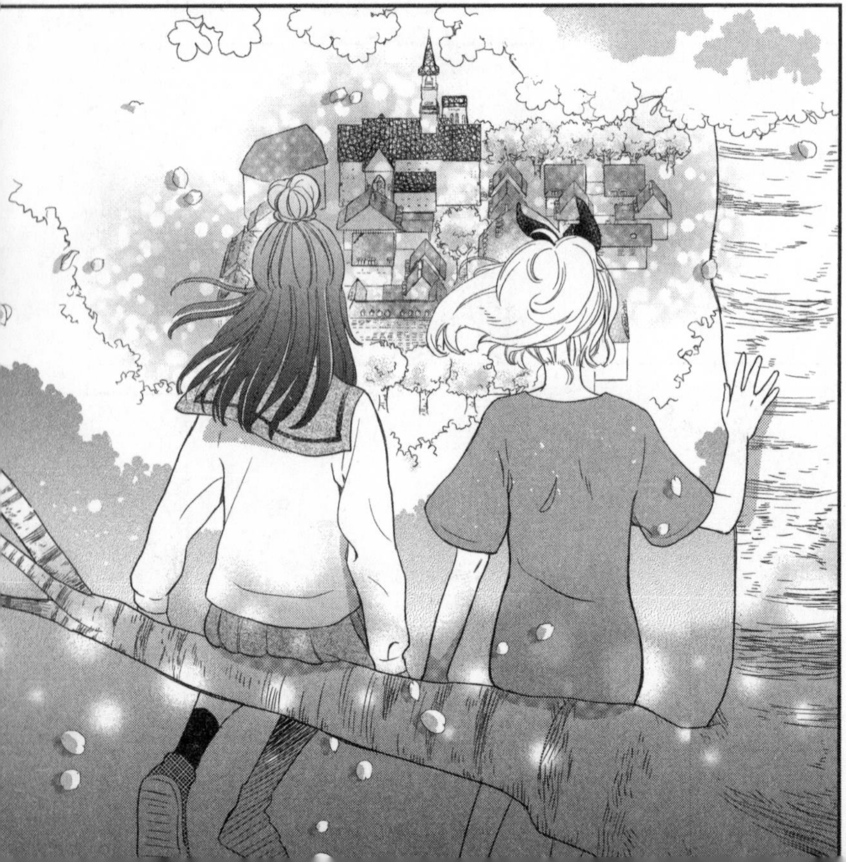

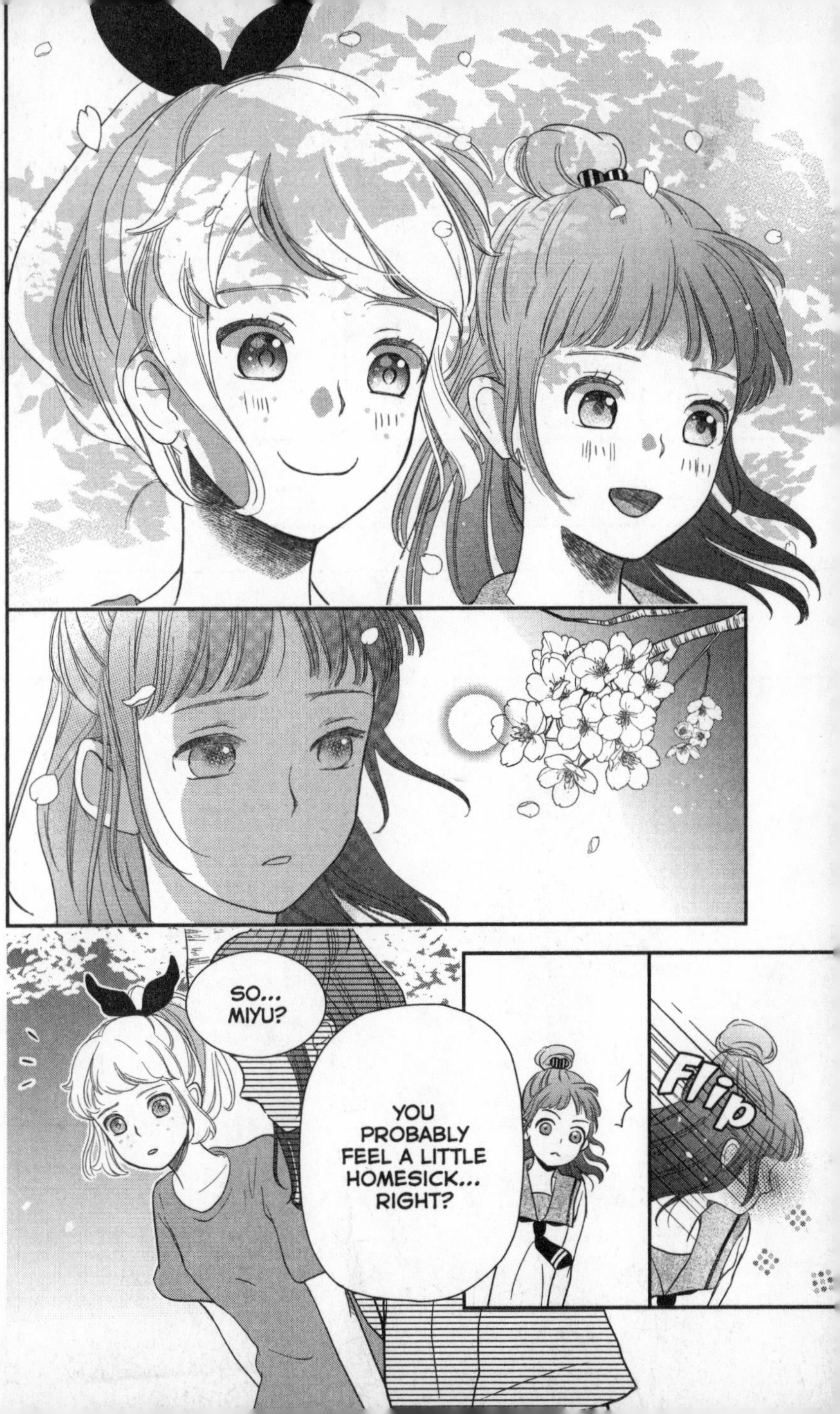
FLIP
SO... MIYU?
YOU PROBABLY FEEL A LITTLE HOMESICK... RIGHT?

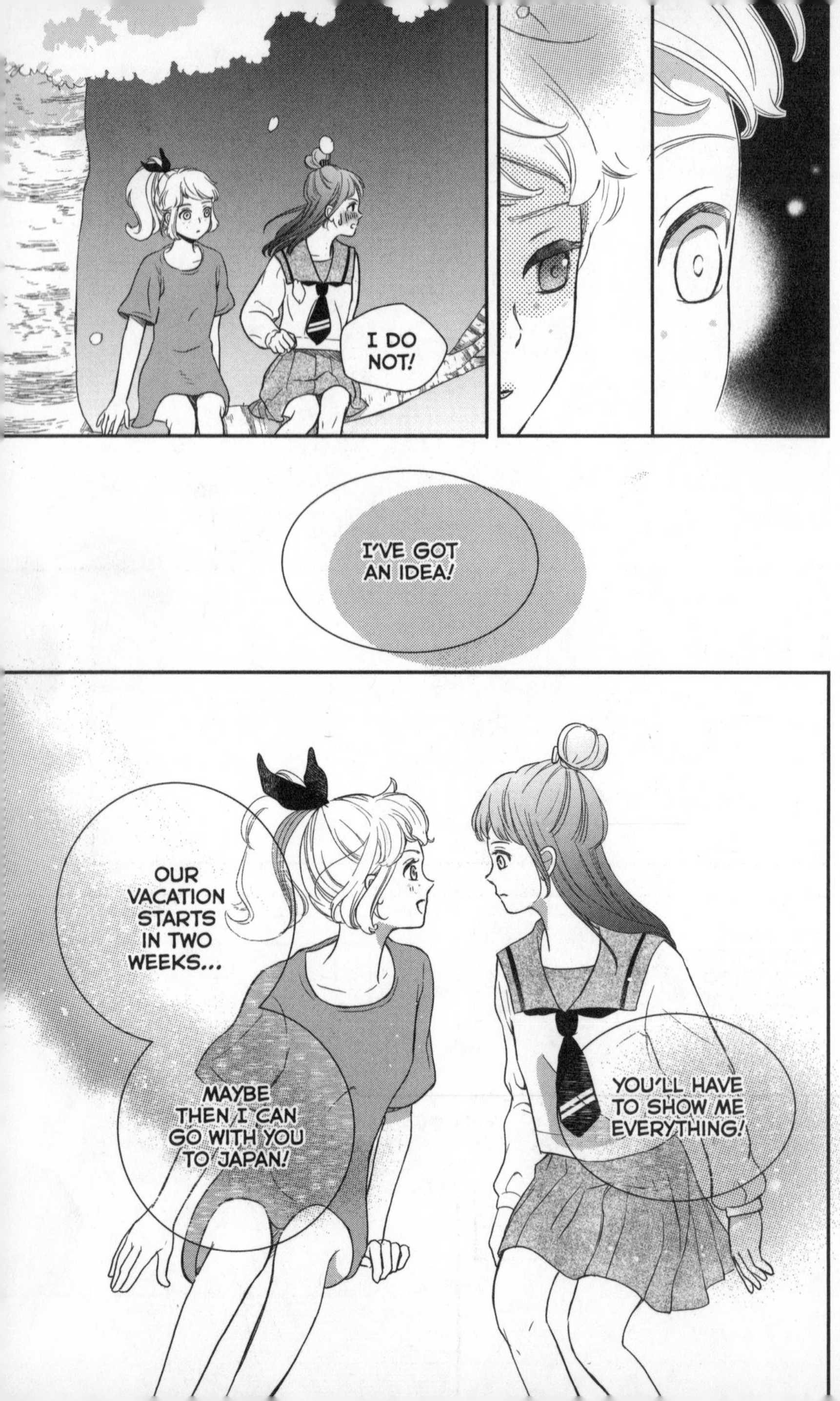
I DO NOT!
I'VE GOT AN IDEA!
OUR VACATION STARTS IN TWO WEEKS...
MAYBE THEN I CAN GO WITH YOU TO JAPAN!
YOU'LL HAVE TO SHOW ME EVERYTHING!

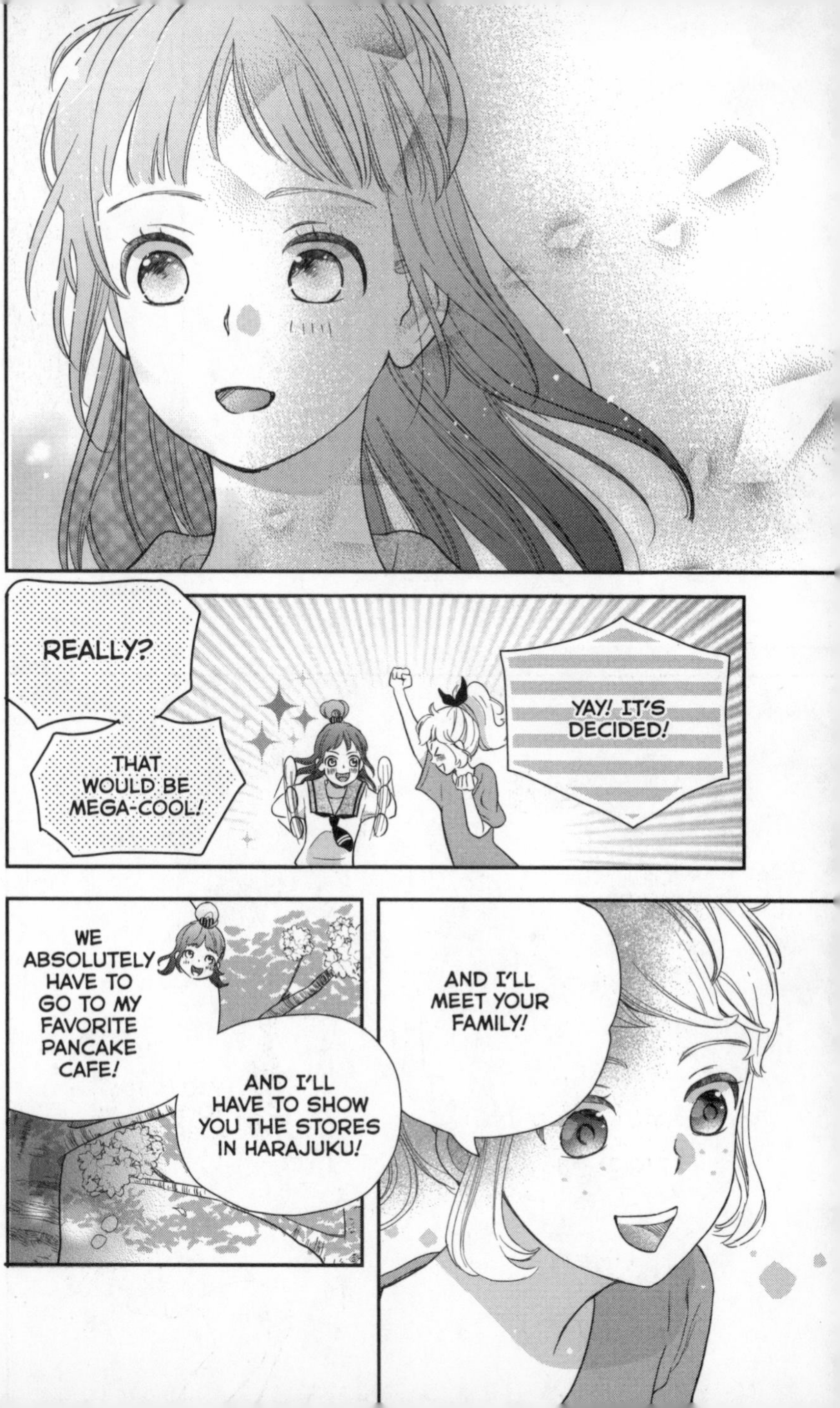
YAY! IT'S DECIDED!
REALLY?
THAT WOULD BE MEGA-COOL!
AND I'LL MEET YOUR FAMILY!
AND I'LL HAVE TO SHOW YOU THE STORES IN HARAJUKU!
WE ABSOLUTELY HAVE TO GO TO MY FAVORITE PANCAKE CAFE!

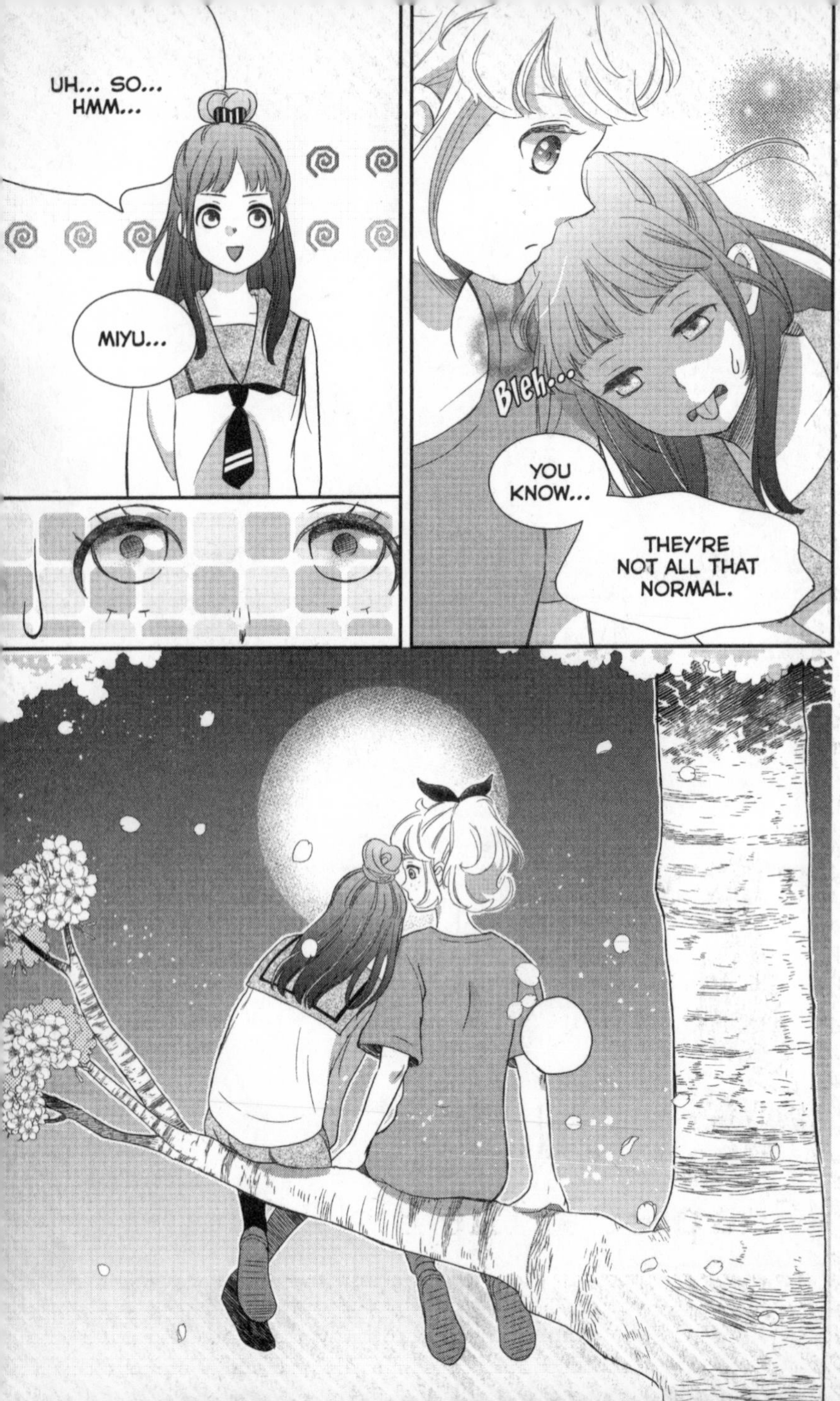
Bleh...
YOU KNOW...
THEY'RE NOT ALL THAT NORMAL.
UH... SO... HMM...
MIYU...

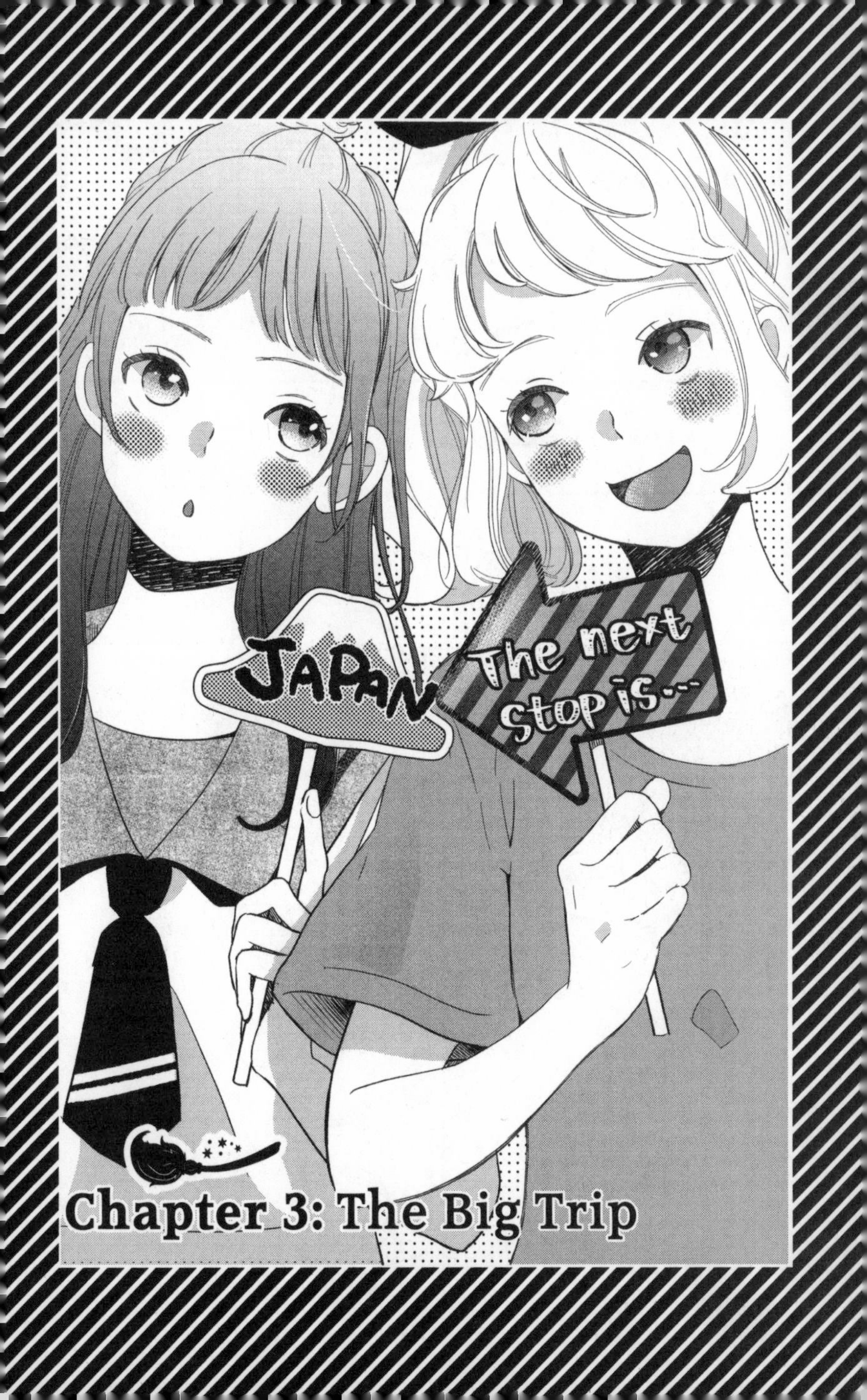
JAPAN
The next stop is...

Chapter 3: The Big Trip

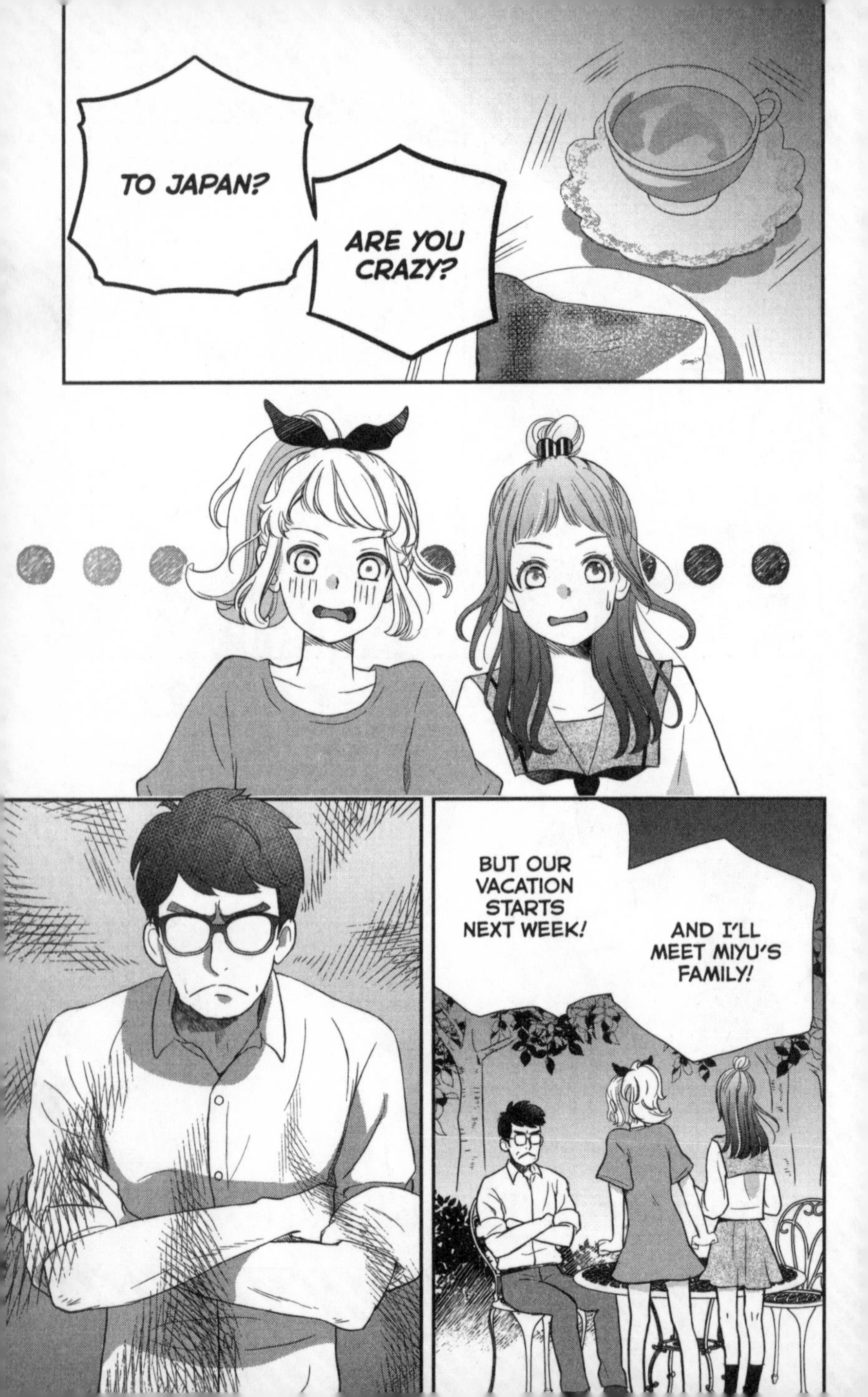
TO JAPAN?
ARE YOU CRAZY?
BUT OUR VACATION STARTS NEXT WEEK!
AND I'LL MEET MIYU'S FAMILY!

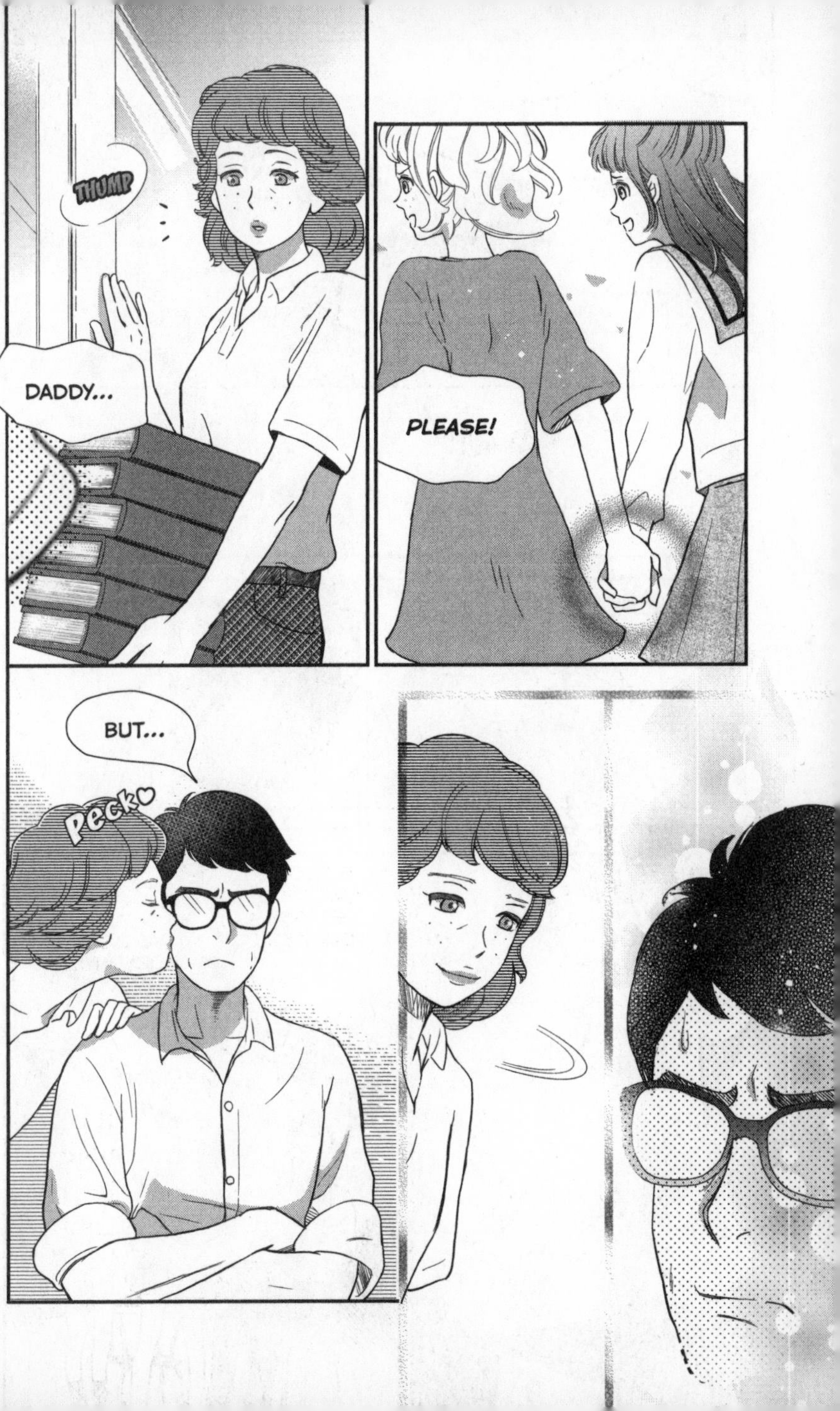
THUMP
DADDY...
PLEASE!
BUT...
Peck♡

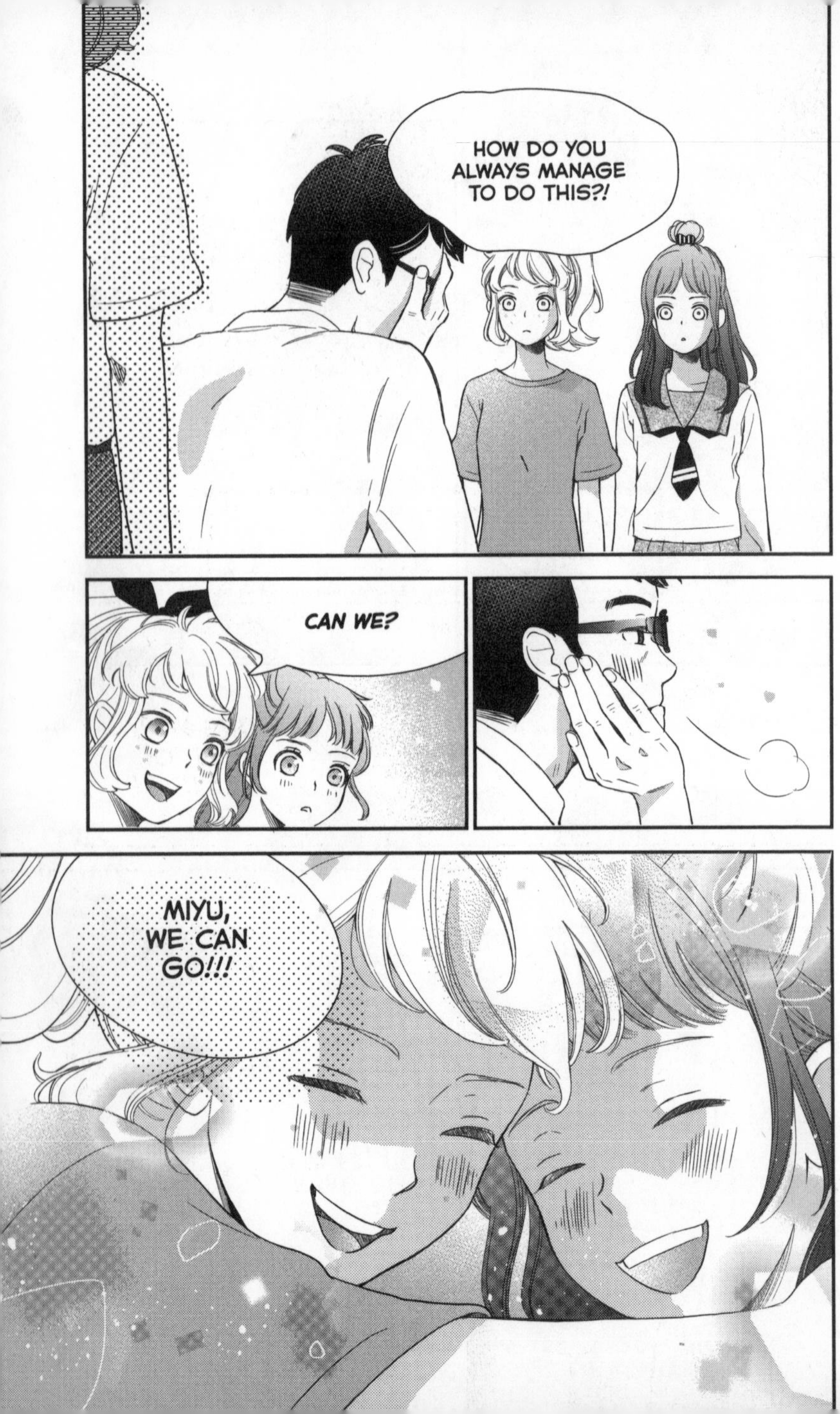
HOW DO YOU ALWAYS MANAGE TO DO THIS?!
CAN WE?
MIYU, WE CAN GO!!!

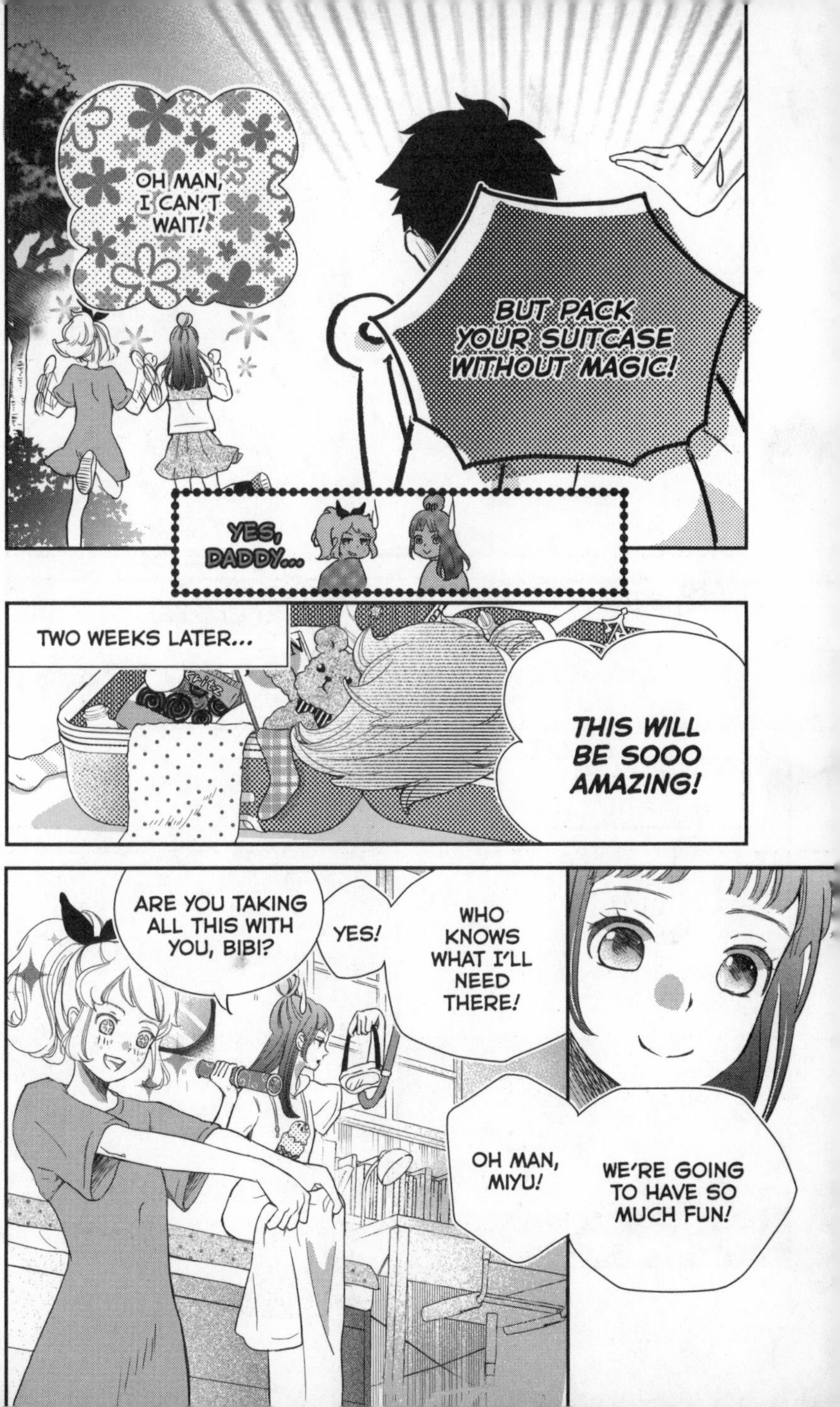
OH MAN, I CAN'T WAIT!
BUT PACK YOUR SUITCASE WITHOUT MAGIC!
YES, DADDY...
TWO WEEKS LATER...
THIS WILL BE SOOO AMAZING!
ARE YOU TAKING ALL THIS WITH YOU, BIBI?
YES!
WHO KNOWS WHAT I'LL NEED THERE!
OH MAN, MIYU!
WE'RE GOING TO HAVE SO MUCH FUN!

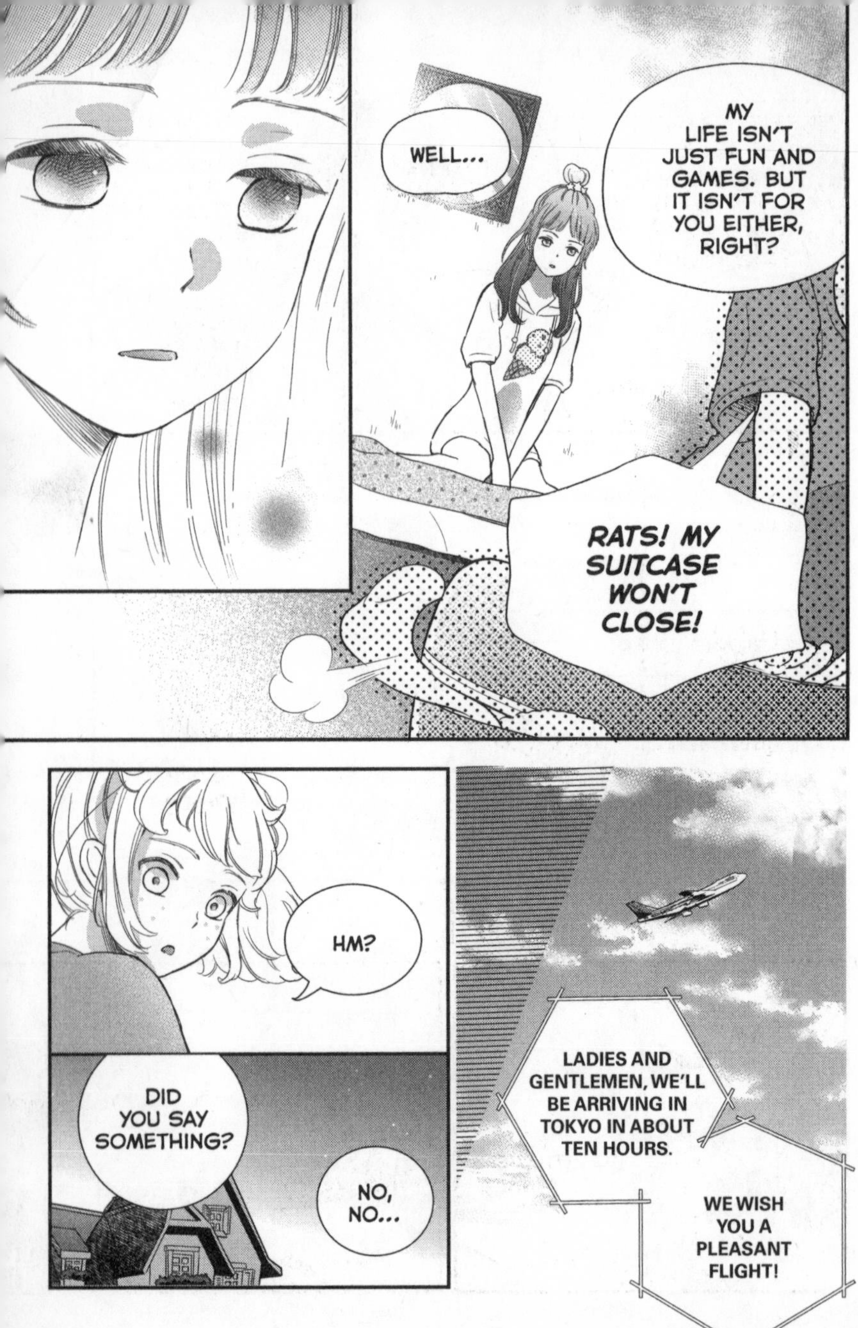
MY LIFE ISN'T JUST FUN AND GAMES. BUT IT ISN'T FOR YOU EITHER, RIGHT?
WELL...
RATS! MY SUITCASE WON'T CLOSE!
LADIES AND GENTLEMEN, WE'LL BE ARRIVING IN TOKYO IN ABOUT TEN HOURS.
WE WISH YOU A PLEASANT FLIGHT!
HM?
DID YOU SAY SOMETHING?
NO, NO...

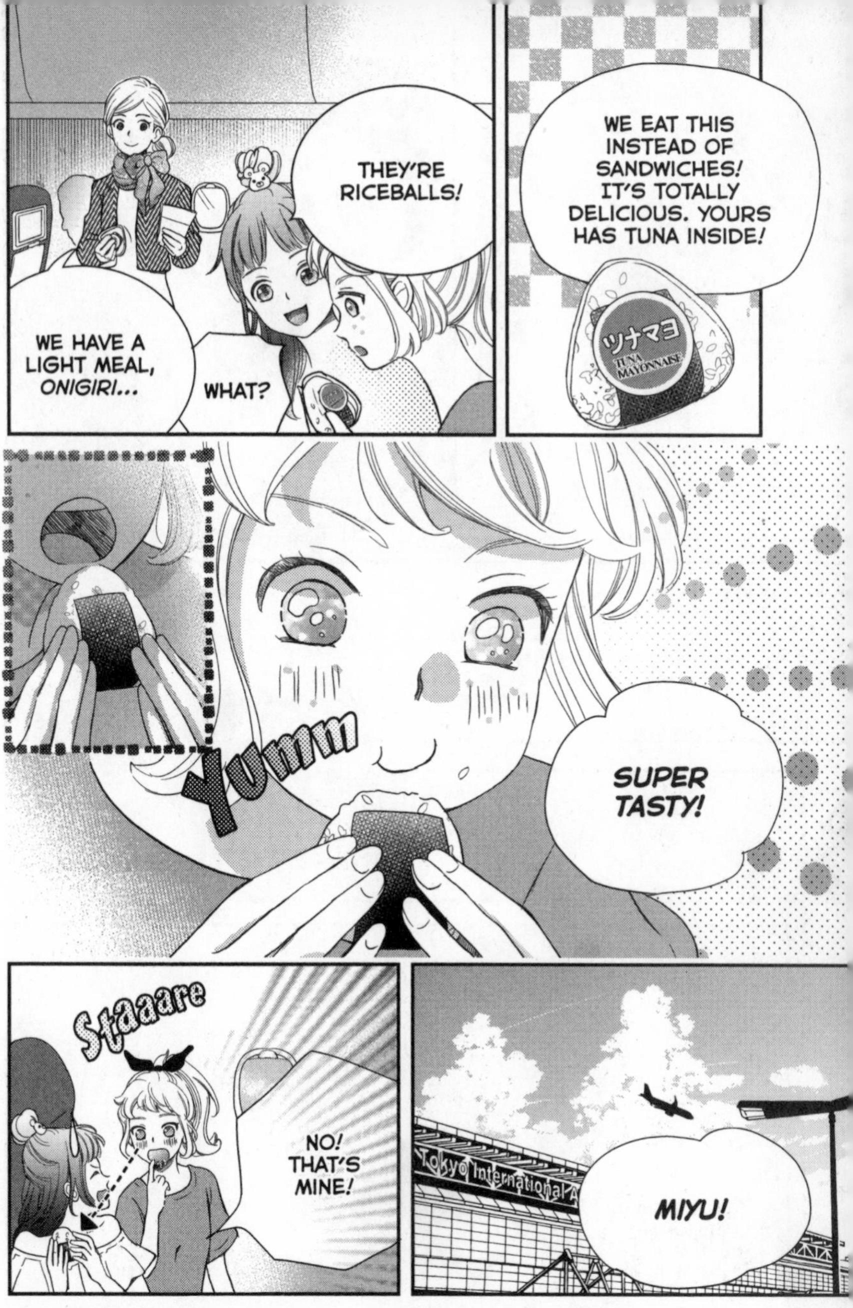
WE HAVE A LIGHT MEAL, ONIGIRI...
WHAT?
THEY'RE RICEBALLS!
WE EAT THIS INSTEAD OF SANDWICHES! IT'S TOTALLY DELICIOUS. YOURS HAS TUNA INSIDE!
ツナマヨ
TUNA MAYONNAISE
Yumm
SUPER TASTY!
Staaare
NO! THAT'S MINE!
Tokyo International A
MIYU!

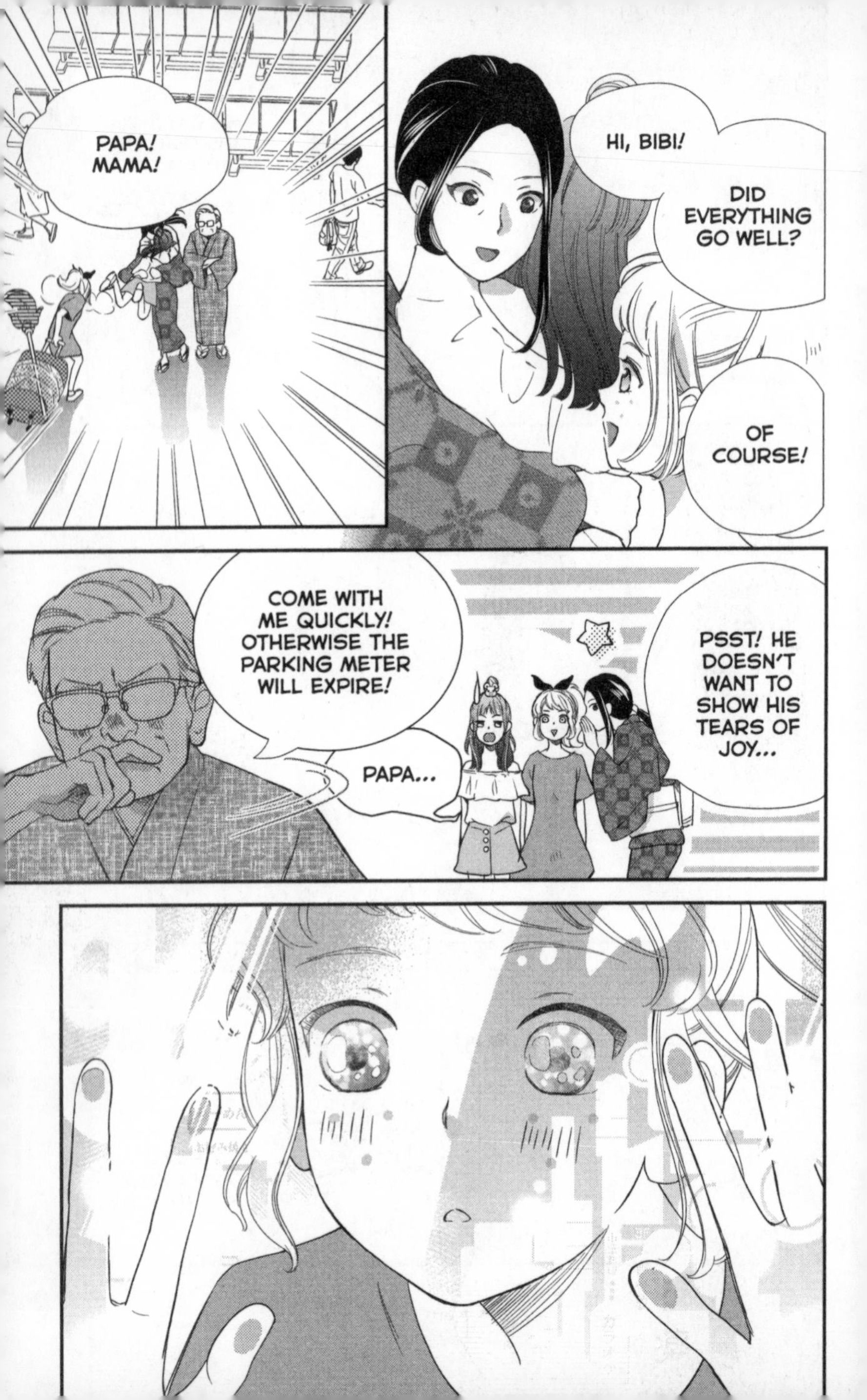
PAPA! MAMA!
HI, BIBI!
DID EVERYTHING GO WELL?
OF COURSE!
COME WITH ME QUICKLY! OTHERWISE THE PARKING METER WILL EXPIRE!
PAPA...
PSST! HE DOESN'T WANT TO SHOW HIS TEARS OF JOY...

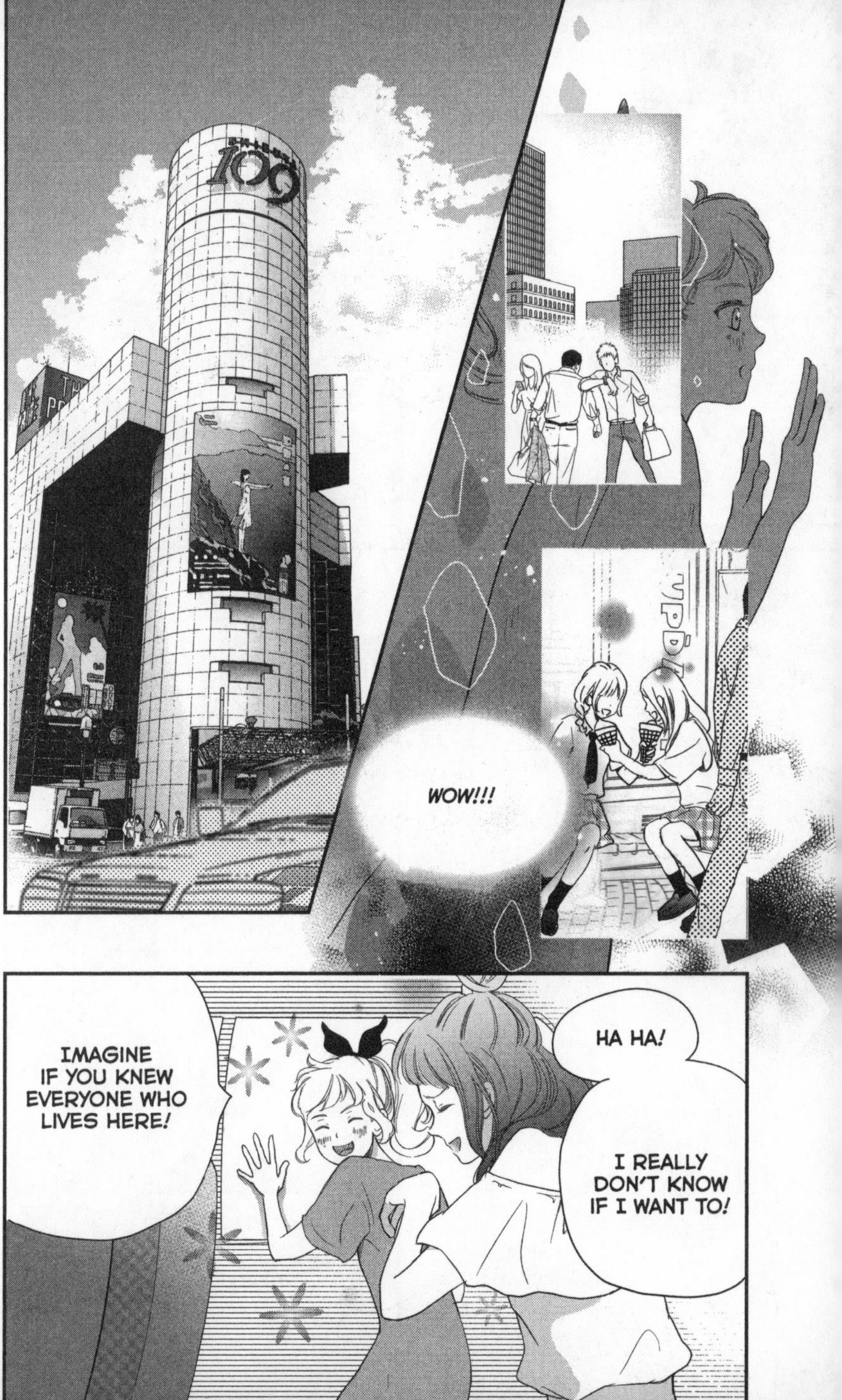
WOW!!!
IMAGINE IF YOU KNEW EVERYONE WHO LIVES HERE!
HA HA!
I REALLY DON'T KNOW IF I WANT TO!

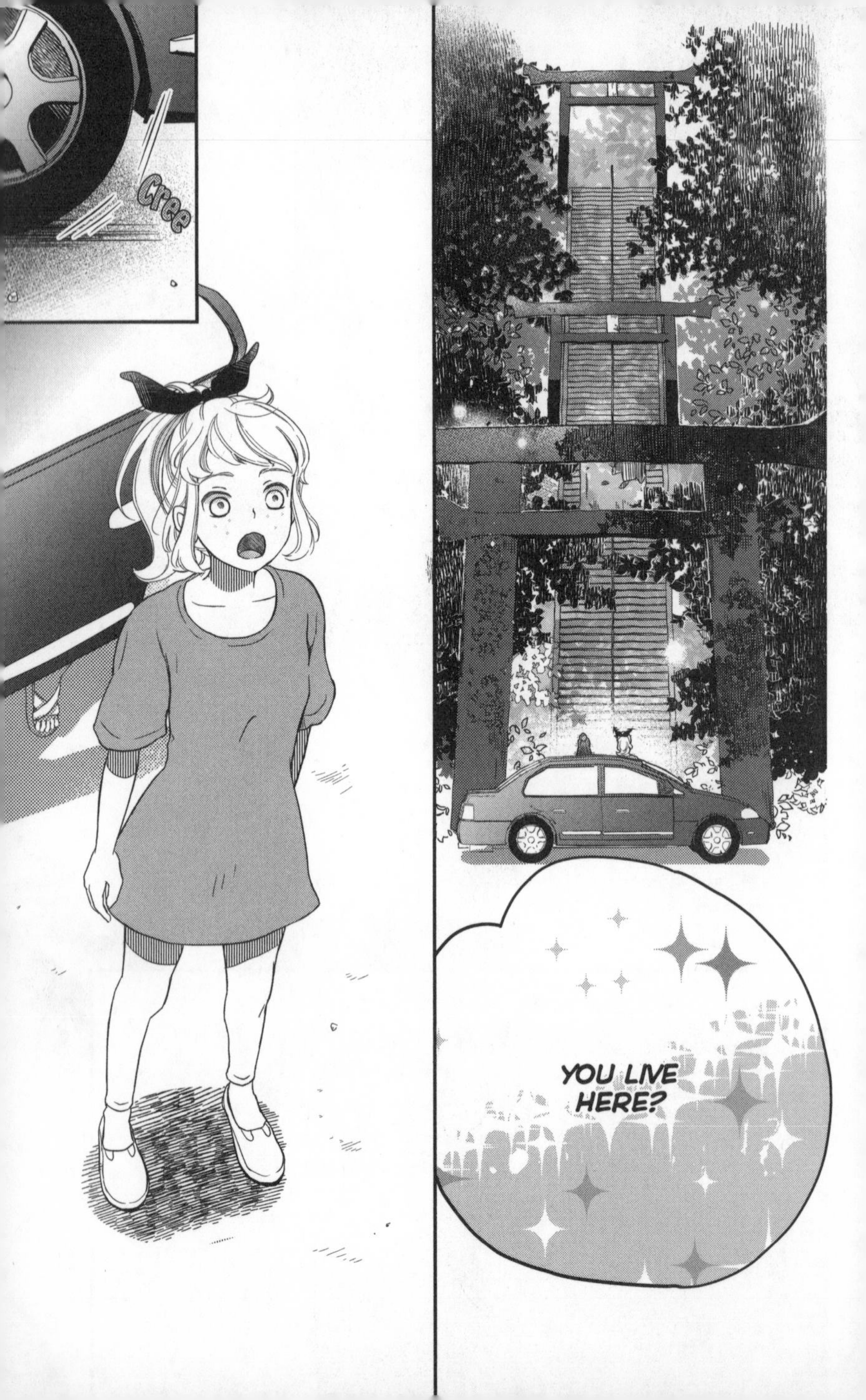
Cree
YOU LIVE HERE?

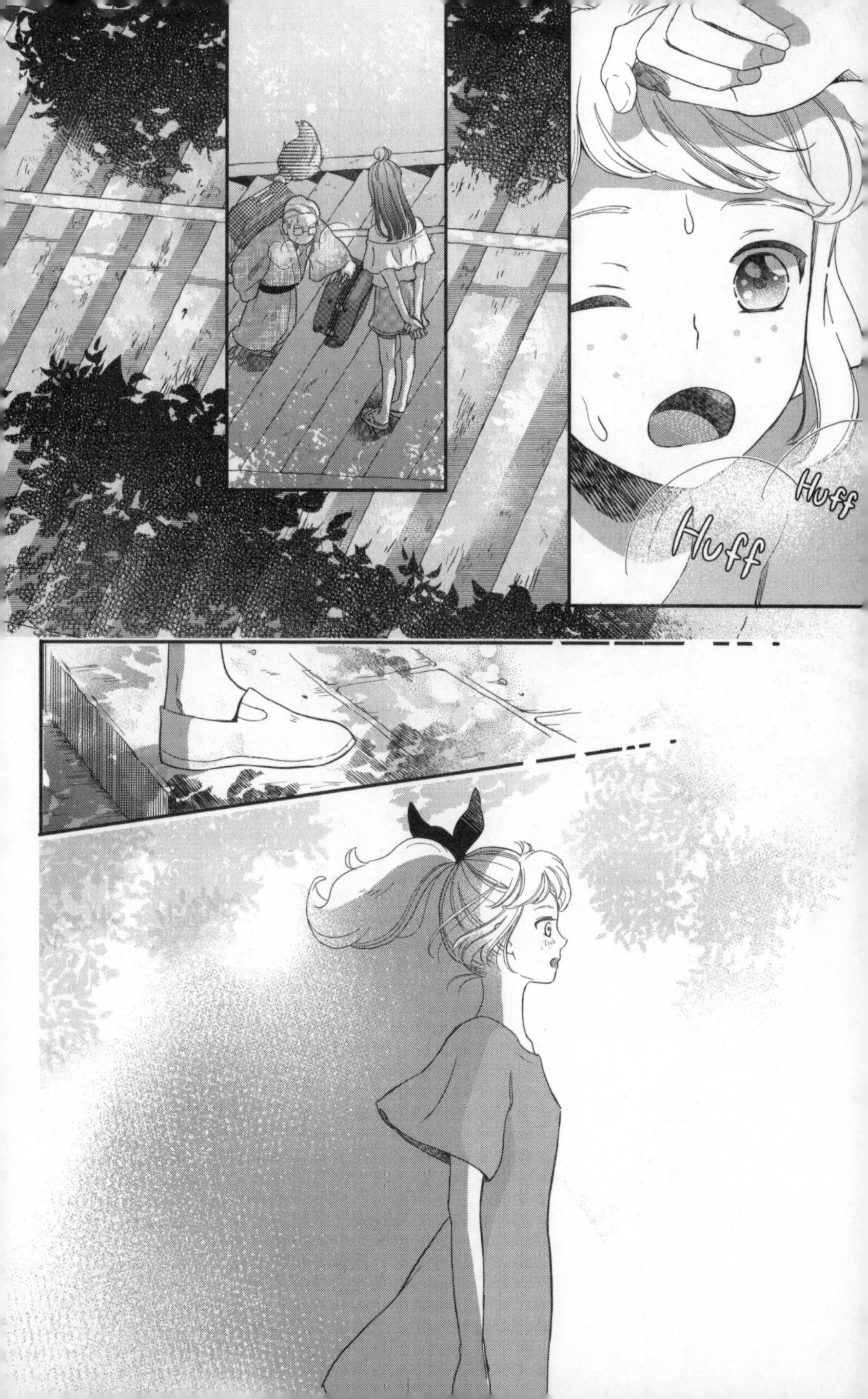
Huff
Huff

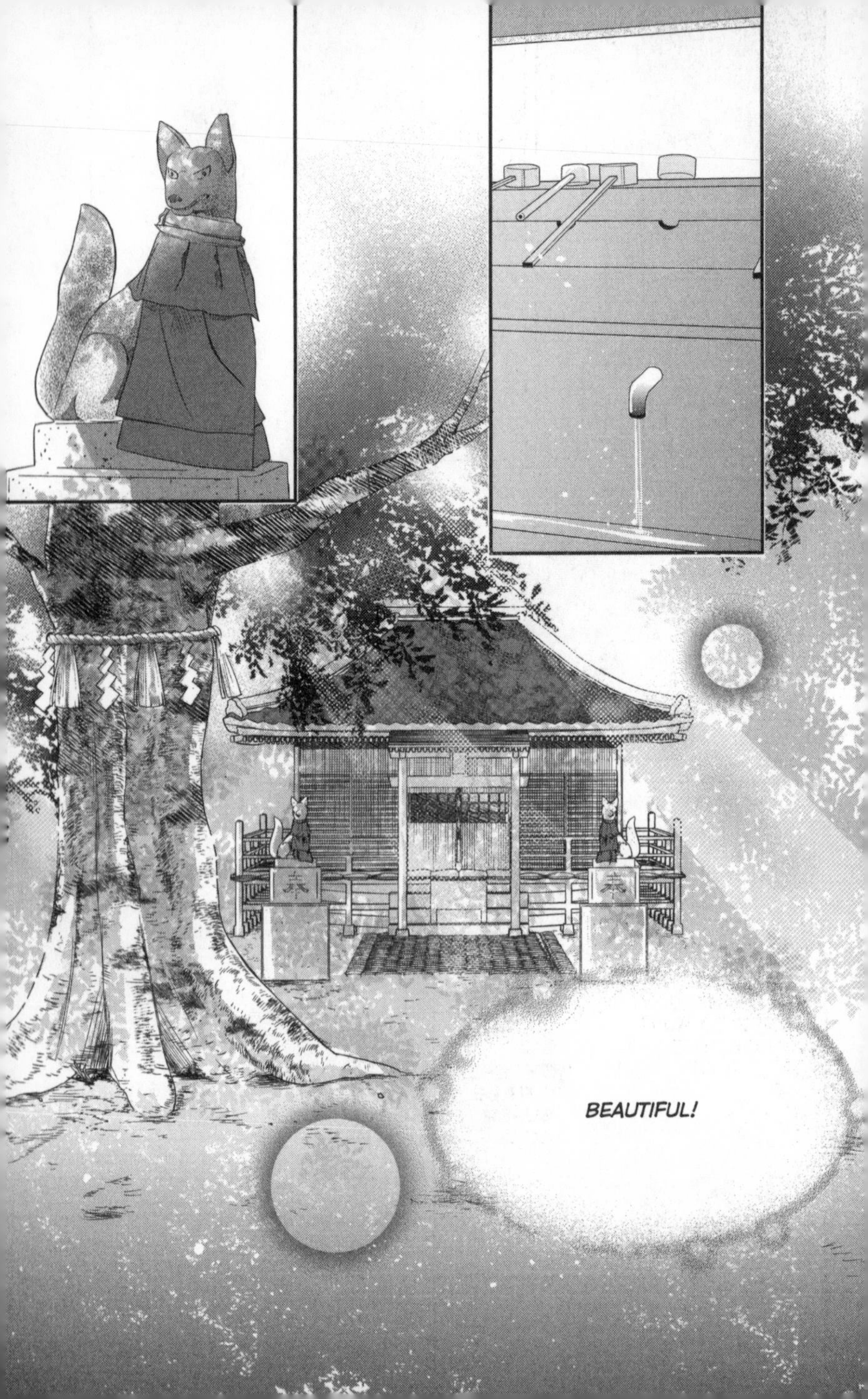
BEAUTIFUL!

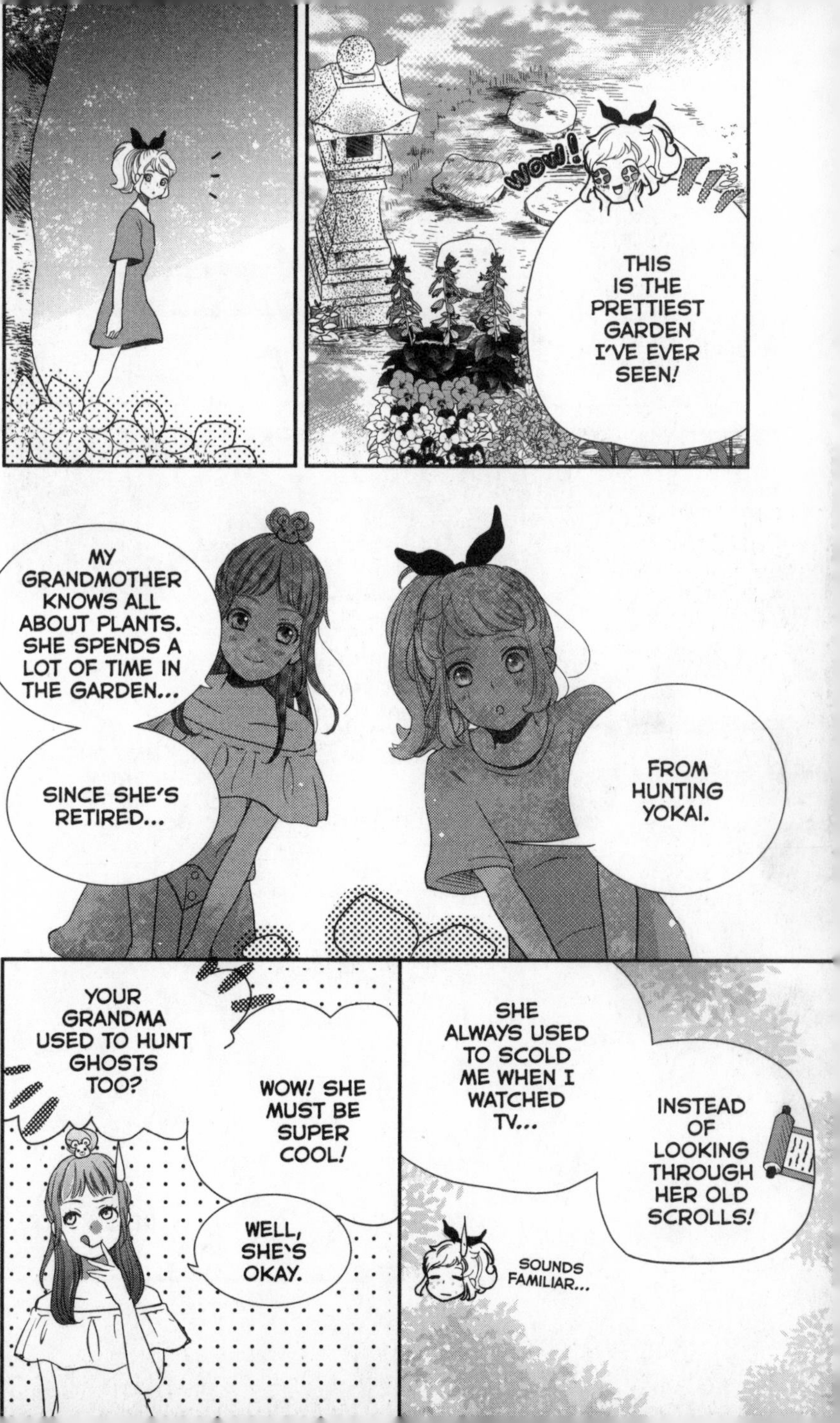
WOW!
THIS IS THE PRETTIEST GARDEN I'VE EVER SEEN!
MY GRANDMOTHER KNOWS ALL ABOUT PLANTS. SHE SPENDS A LOT OF TIME IN THE GARDEN...
SINCE SHE'S RETIRED...
FROM HUNTING YOKAI.
YOUR GRANDMA USED TO HUNT GHOSTS TOO?
WOW! SHE MUST BE SUPER COOL!
WELL, SHE'S OKAY.
SHE ALWAYS USED TO SCOLD ME WHEN I WATCHED TV...
INSTEAD OF LOOKING THROUGH HER OLD SCROLLS!
SOUNDS FAMILIAR...

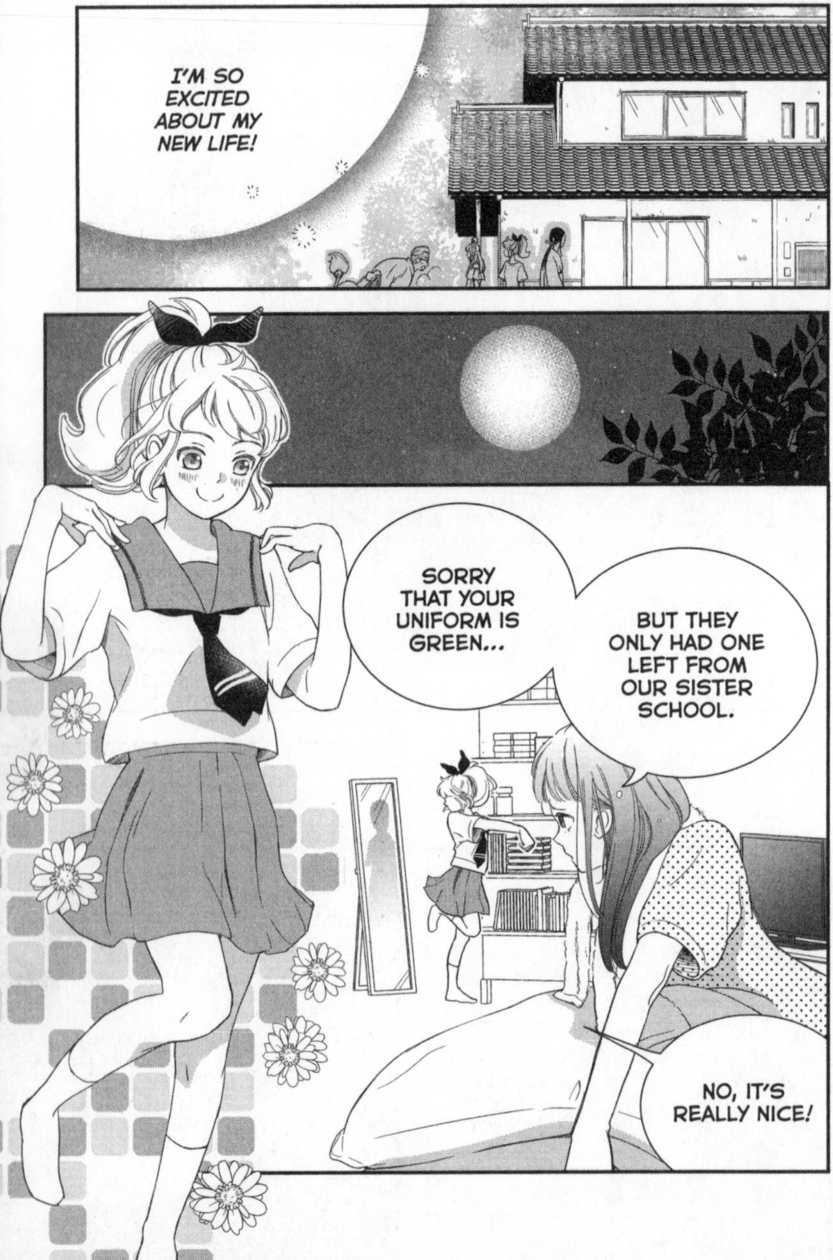
I'M SO EXCITED ABOUT MY NEW LIFE!
SORRY THAT YOUR UNIFORM IS GREEN...
BUT THEY ONLY HAD ONE LEFT FROM OUR SISTER SCHOOL.
NO, IT'S REALLY NICE!

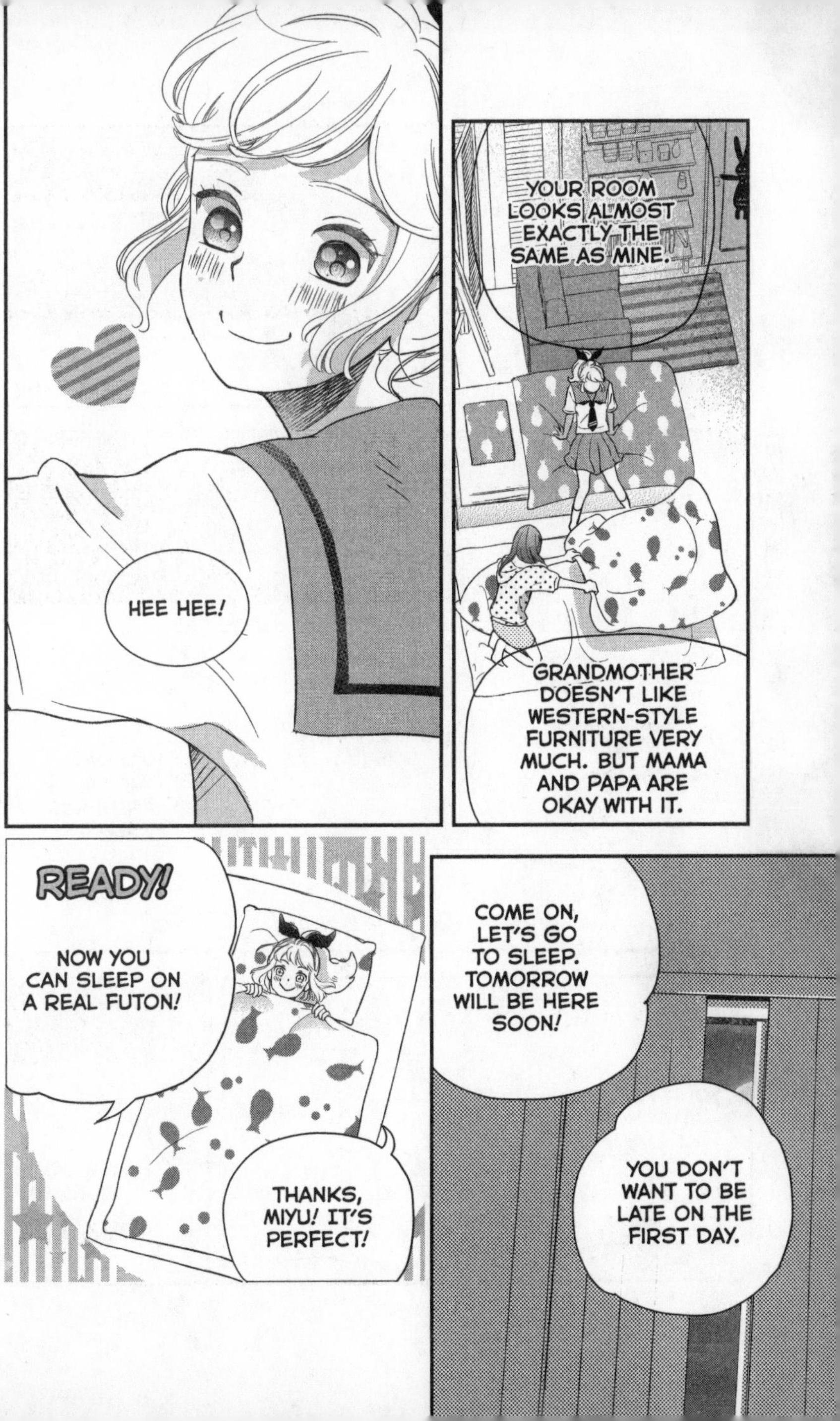
YOUR ROOM LOOKS ALMOST EXACTLY THE SAME AS MINE.
GRANDMOTHER DOESN'T LIKE WESTERN-STYLE FURNITURE VERY MUCH. BUT MAMA AND PAPA ARE OKAY WITH IT.
HEE HEE!
COME ON, LET'S GO TO SLEEP. TOMORROW WILL BE HERE SOON!
YOU DON'T WANT TO BE LATE ON THE FIRST DAY.
READY!
NOW YOU CAN SLEEP ON A REAL FUTON!
THANKS, MIYU! IT'S PERFECT!

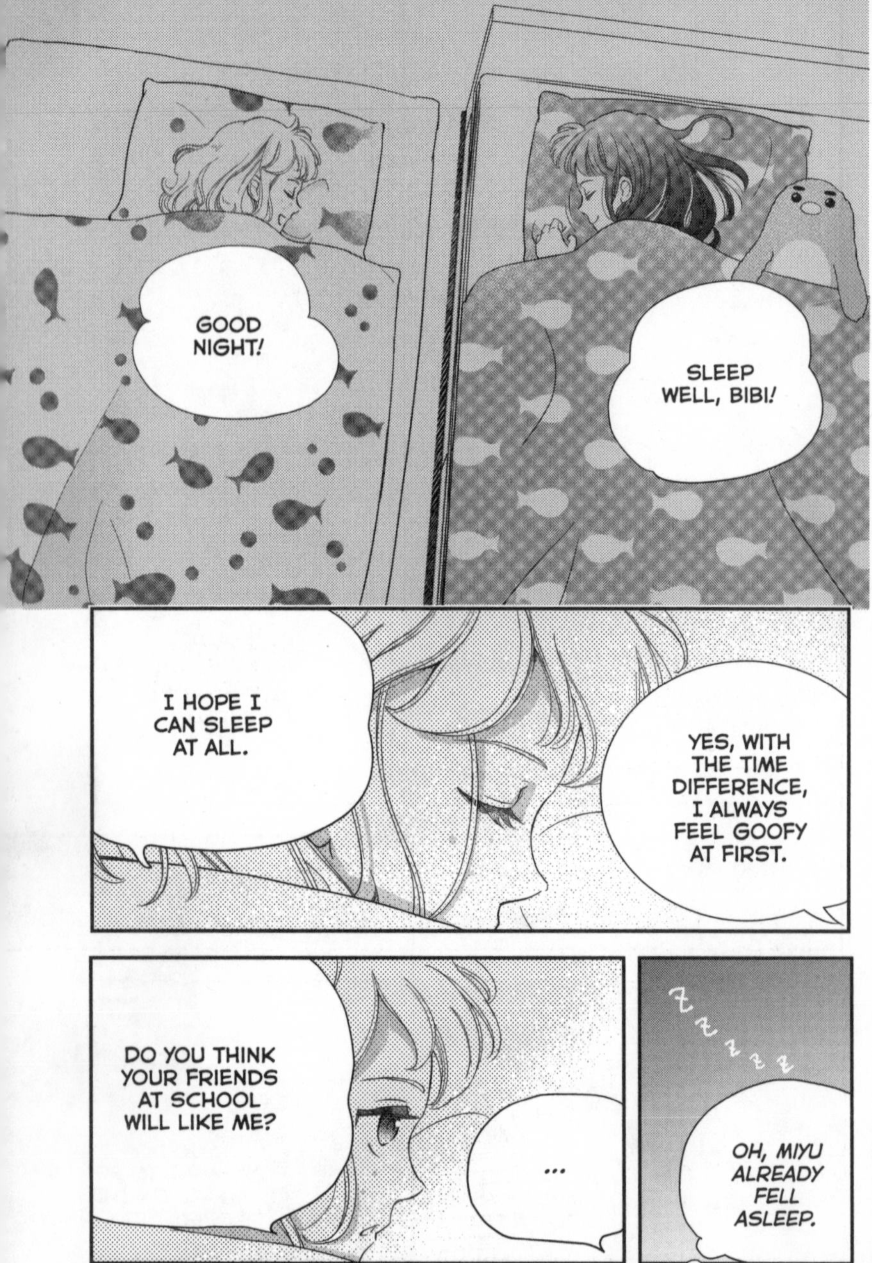
GOOD NIGHT!
SLEEP WELL, BIBI!
I HOPE I CAN SLEEP AT ALL.
YES, WITH THE TIME DIFFERENCE, I ALWAYS FEEL GOOFY AT FIRST.
DO YOU THINK YOUR FRIENDS AT SCHOOL WILL LIKE ME?
...
Z Z Z Z Z
OH, MIYU ALREADY FELL ASLEEP.

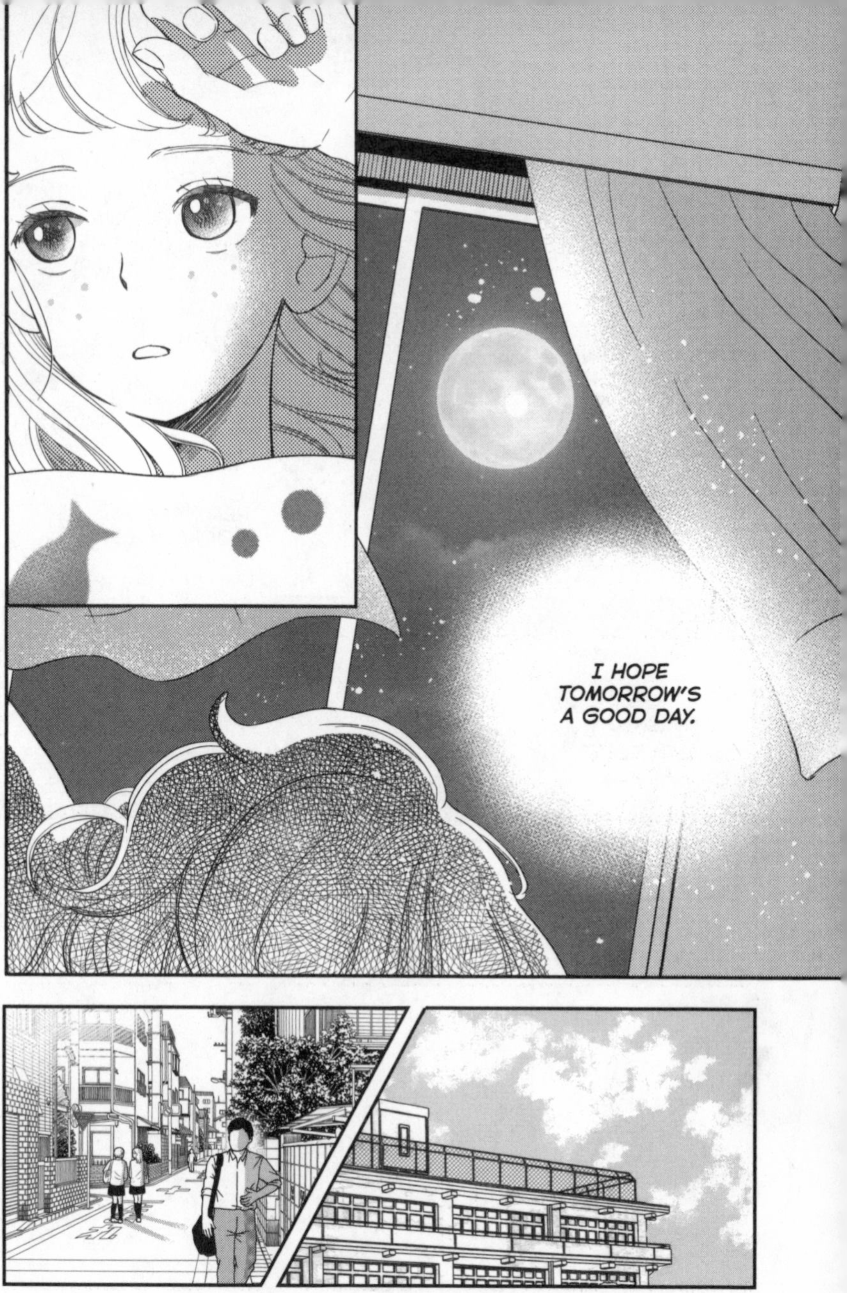
I HOPE TOMORROW'S A GOOD DAY.

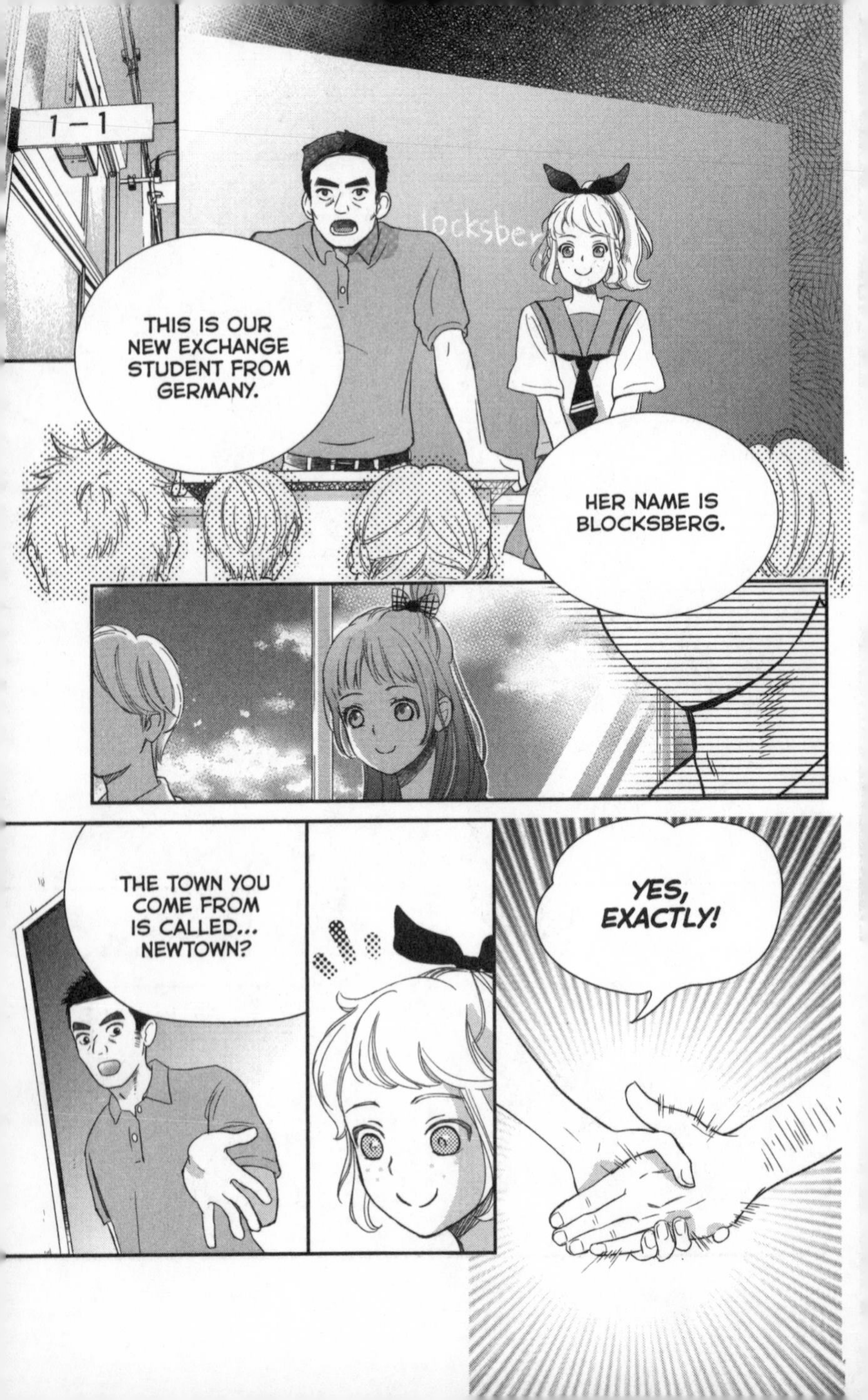
1-1
THIS IS OUR NEW EXCHANGE STUDENT FROM GERMANY.
HER NAME IS BLOCKSBERG.
THE TOWN YOU COME FROM IS CALLED... NEWTOWN?
YES, EXACTLY!

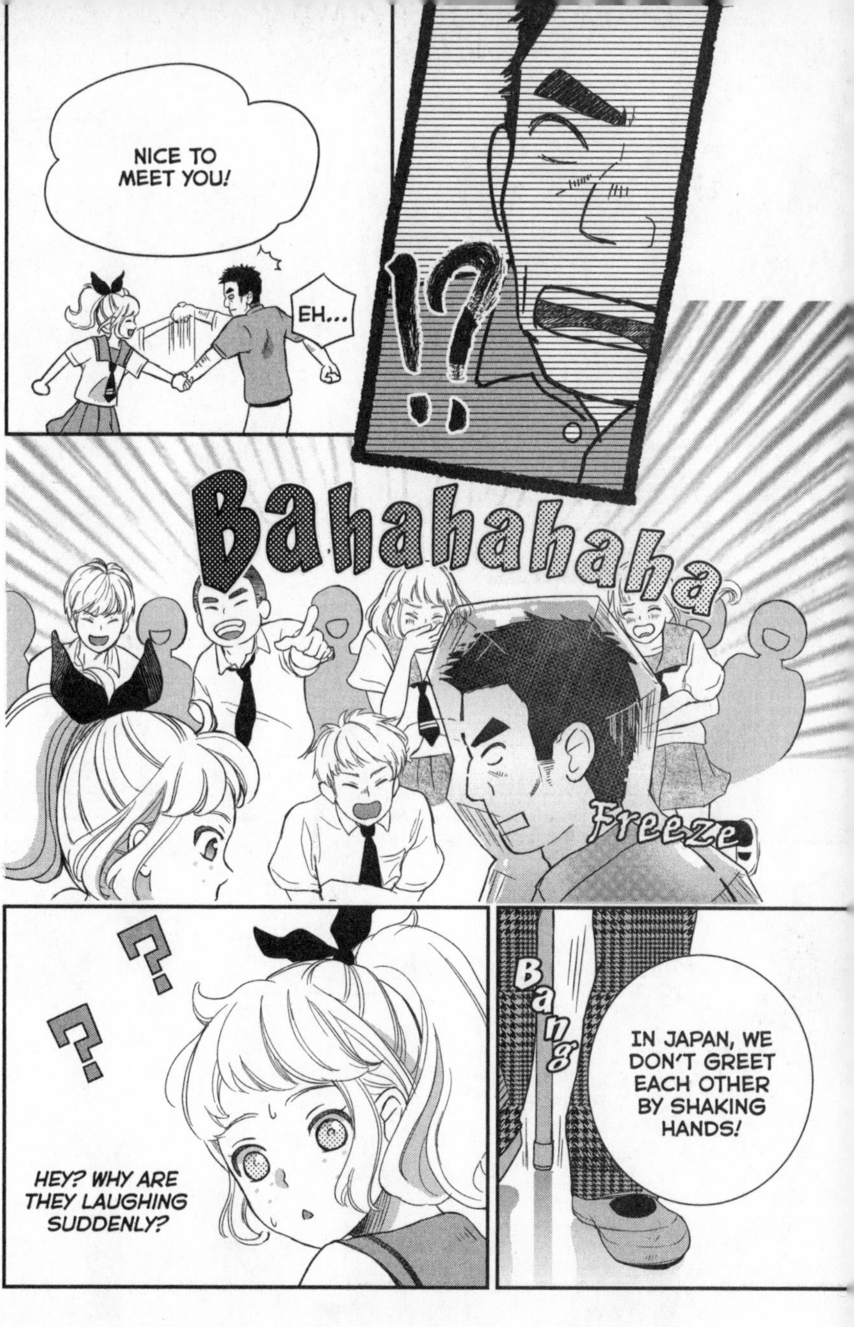
NICE TO MEET YOU!
EH...
!?
Bahahahahaha
Freeze
HEY? WHY ARE THEY LAUGHING SUDDENLY?
Bang
IN JAPAN, WE DON'T GREET EACH OTHER BY SHAKING HANDS!

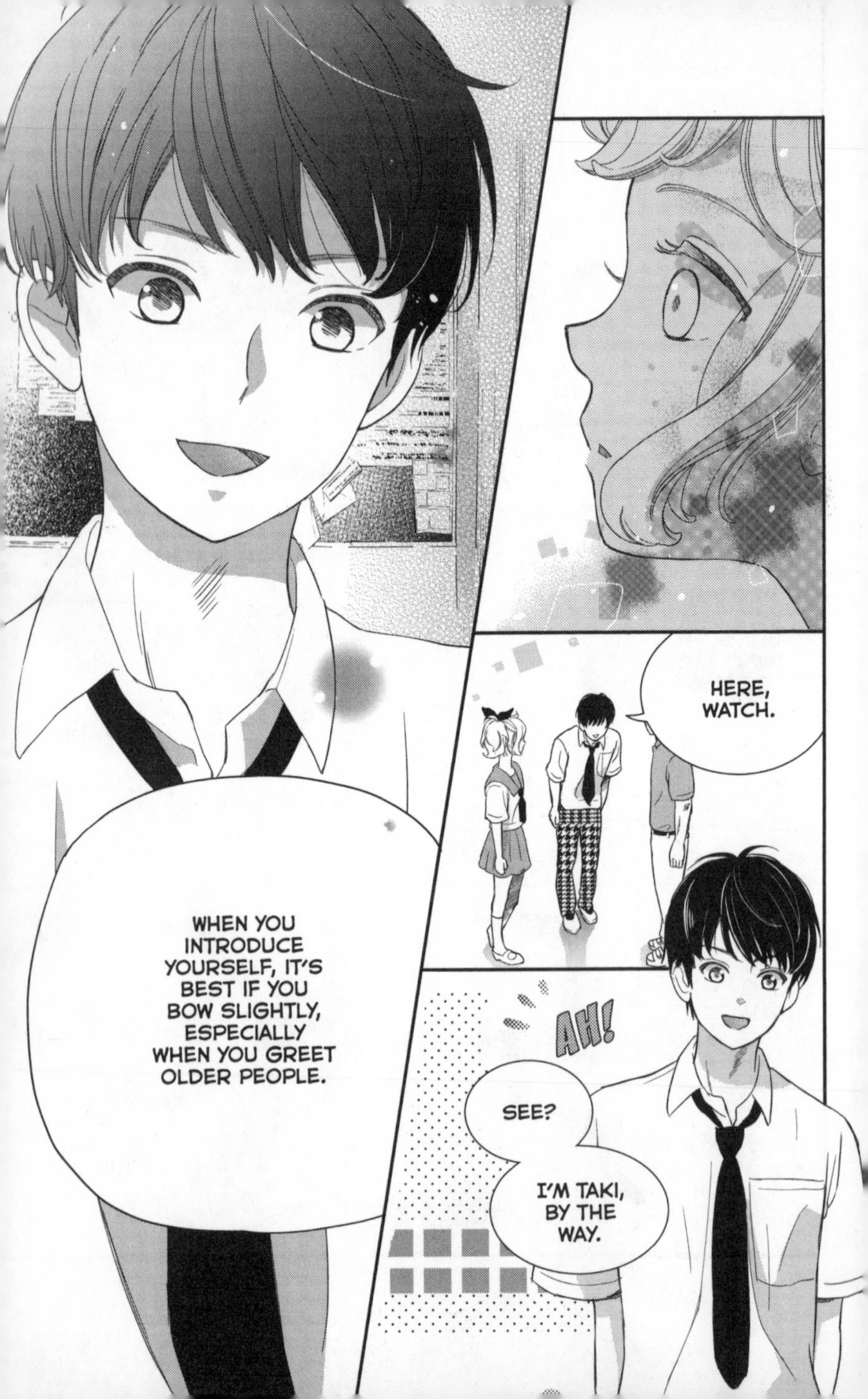
WHEN YOU INTRODUCE YOURSELF, IT'S BEST IF YOU BOW SLIGHTLY, ESPECIALLY WHEN YOU GREET OLDER PEOPLE.
HERE, WATCH.
AH!
SEE?
I'M TAKI, BY THE WAY.

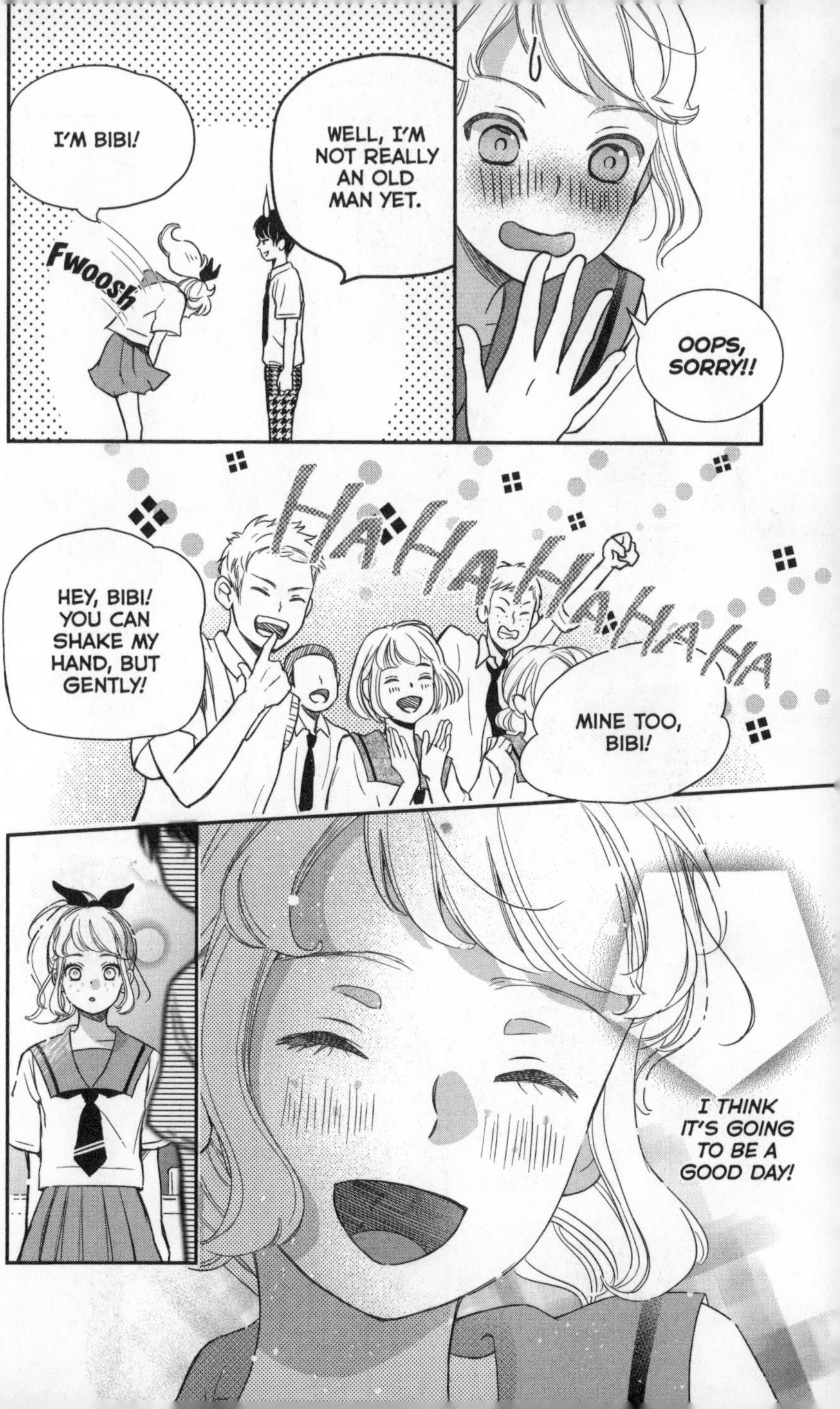
I'M BIBI!
Fwoosh
WELL, I'M NOT REALLY AN OLD MAN YET.
OOPS, SORRY!!
HA HA HA HA HA HA HA
HEY, BIBI! YOU CAN SHAKE MY HAND, BUT GENTLY!
MINE TOO, BIBI!
I THINK IT'S GOING TO BE A GOOD DAY!

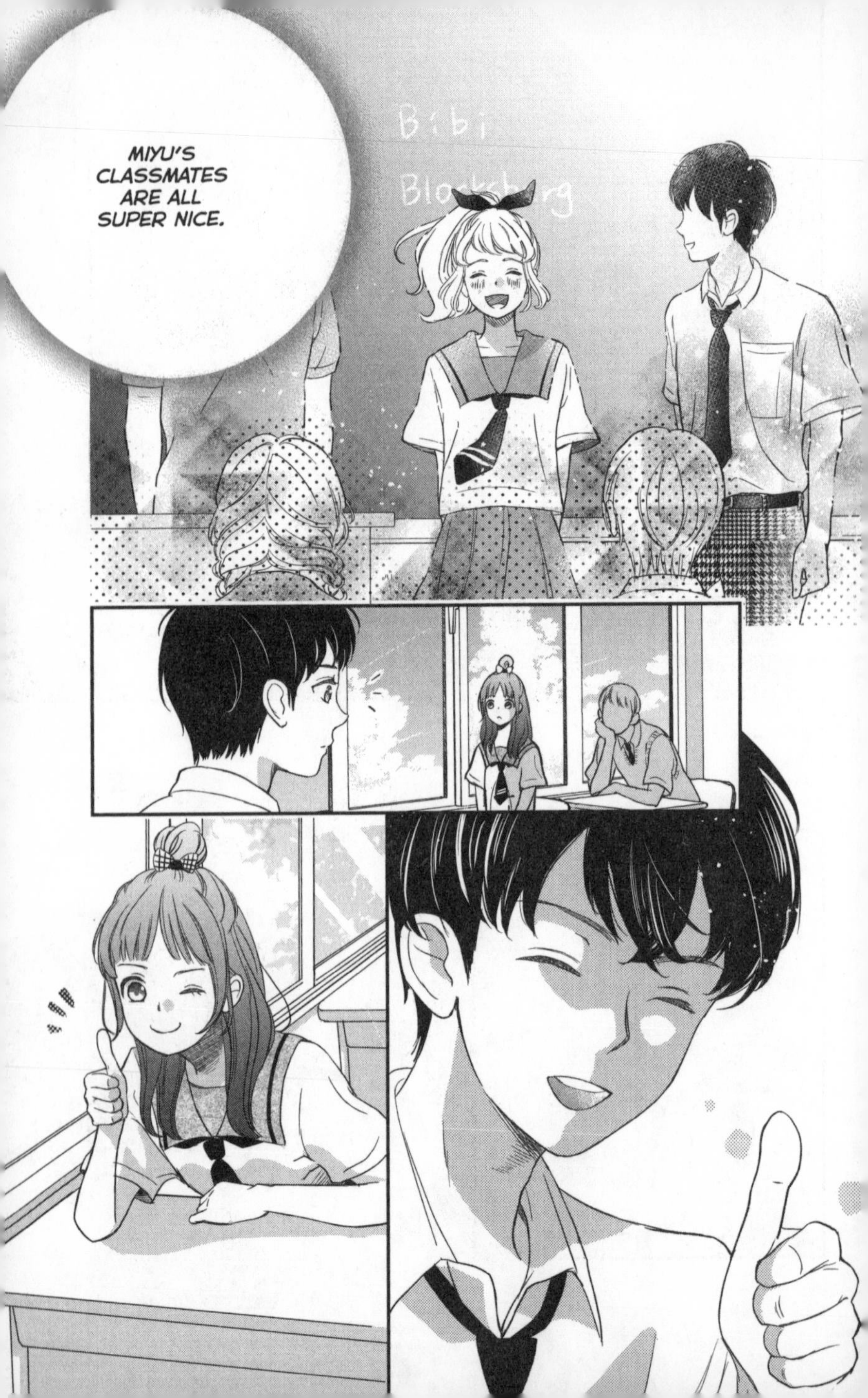
MIYU'S CLASSMATES ARE ALL SUPER NICE.
Bibi Blocksberg

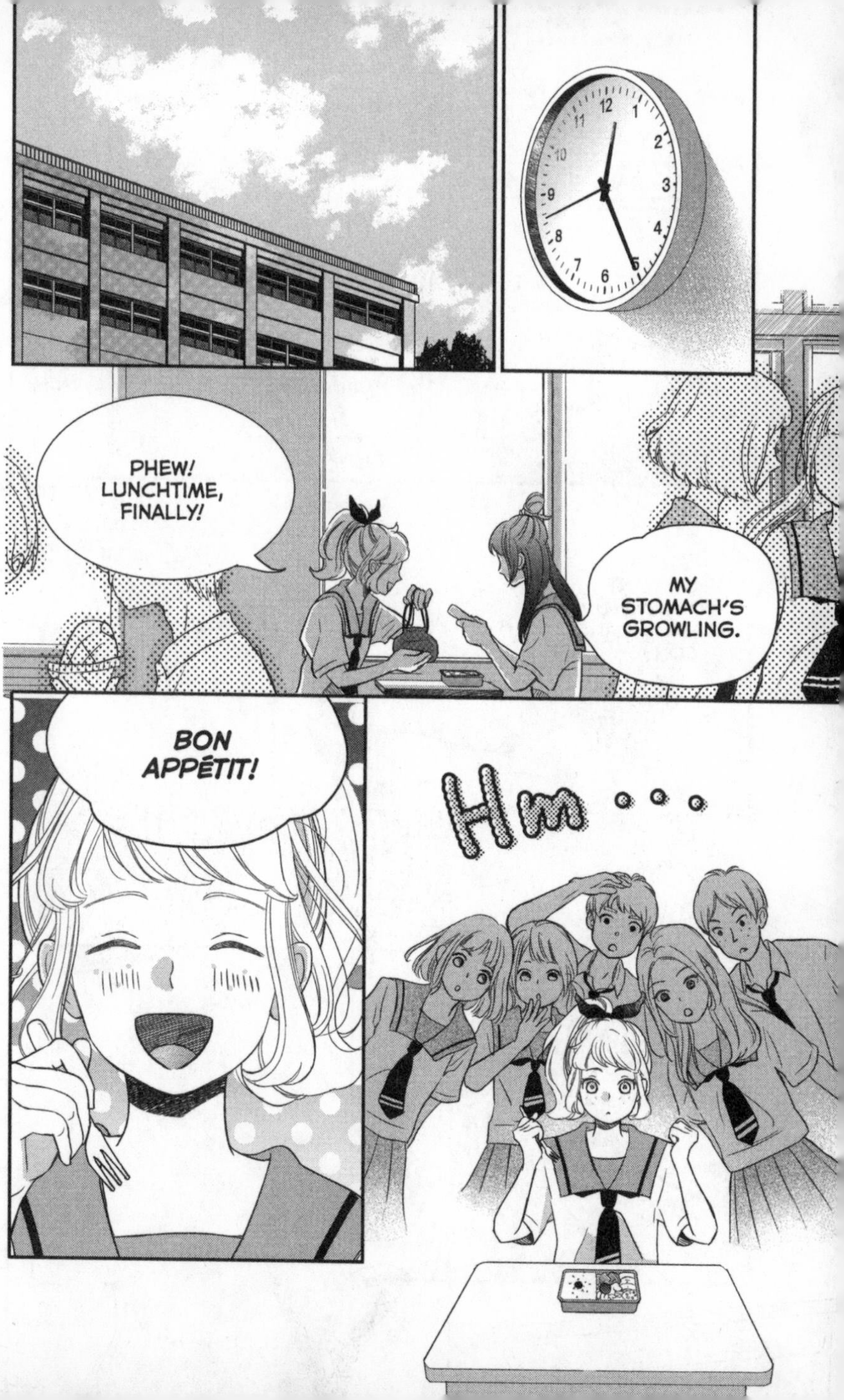
PHEW! LUNCHTIME, FINALLY!
MY STOMACH'S GROWLING.
BON APPÉTIT!
Hm...

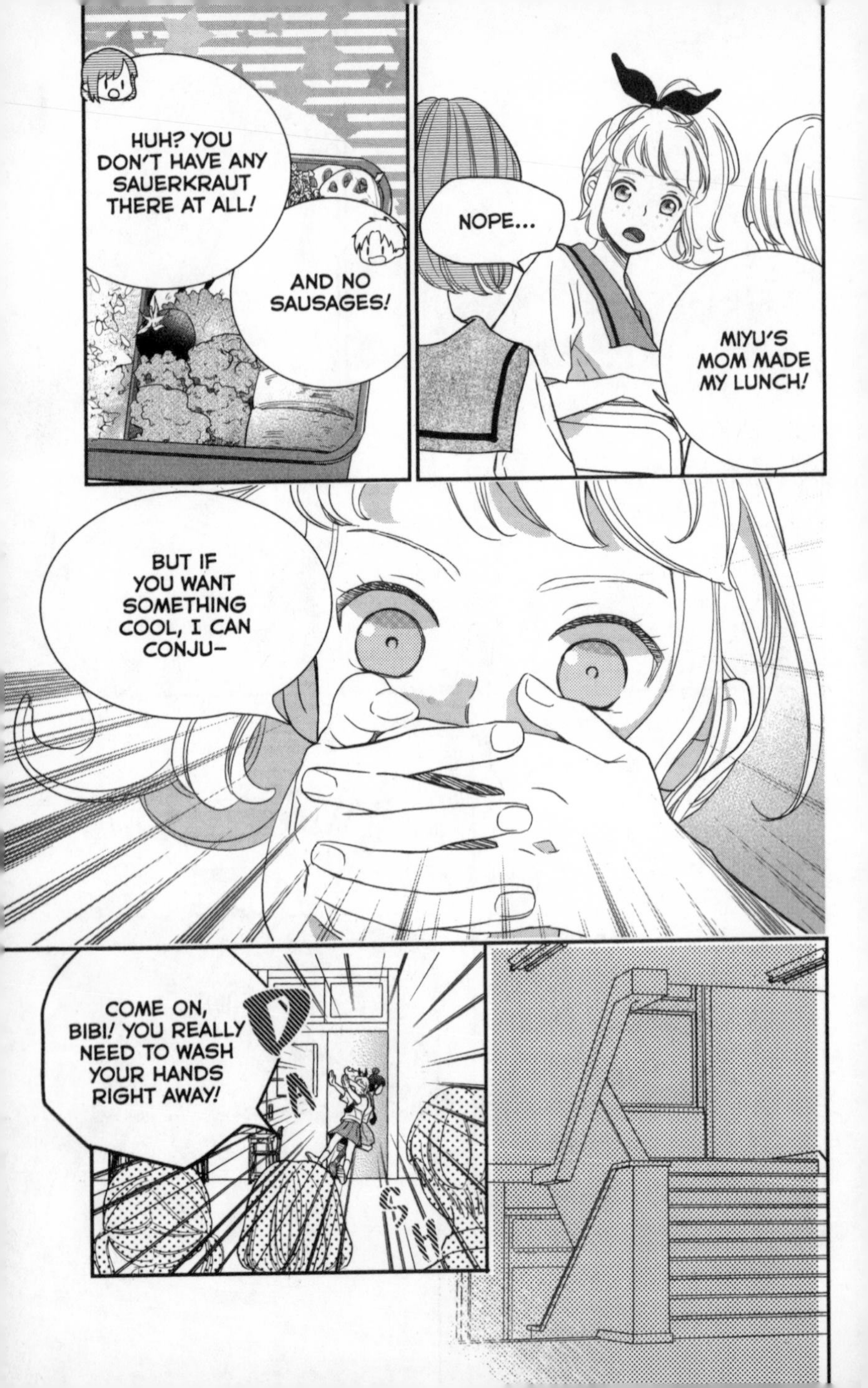
HUH? YOU DON'T HAVE ANY SAUERKRAUT THERE AT ALL!
AND NO SAUSAGES!
NOPE...
MIYU'S MOM MADE MY LUNCH!
BUT IF YOU WANT SOMETHING COOL, I CAN CONJU–
COME ON, BIBI! YOU REALLY NEED TO WASH YOUR HANDS RIGHT AWAY!

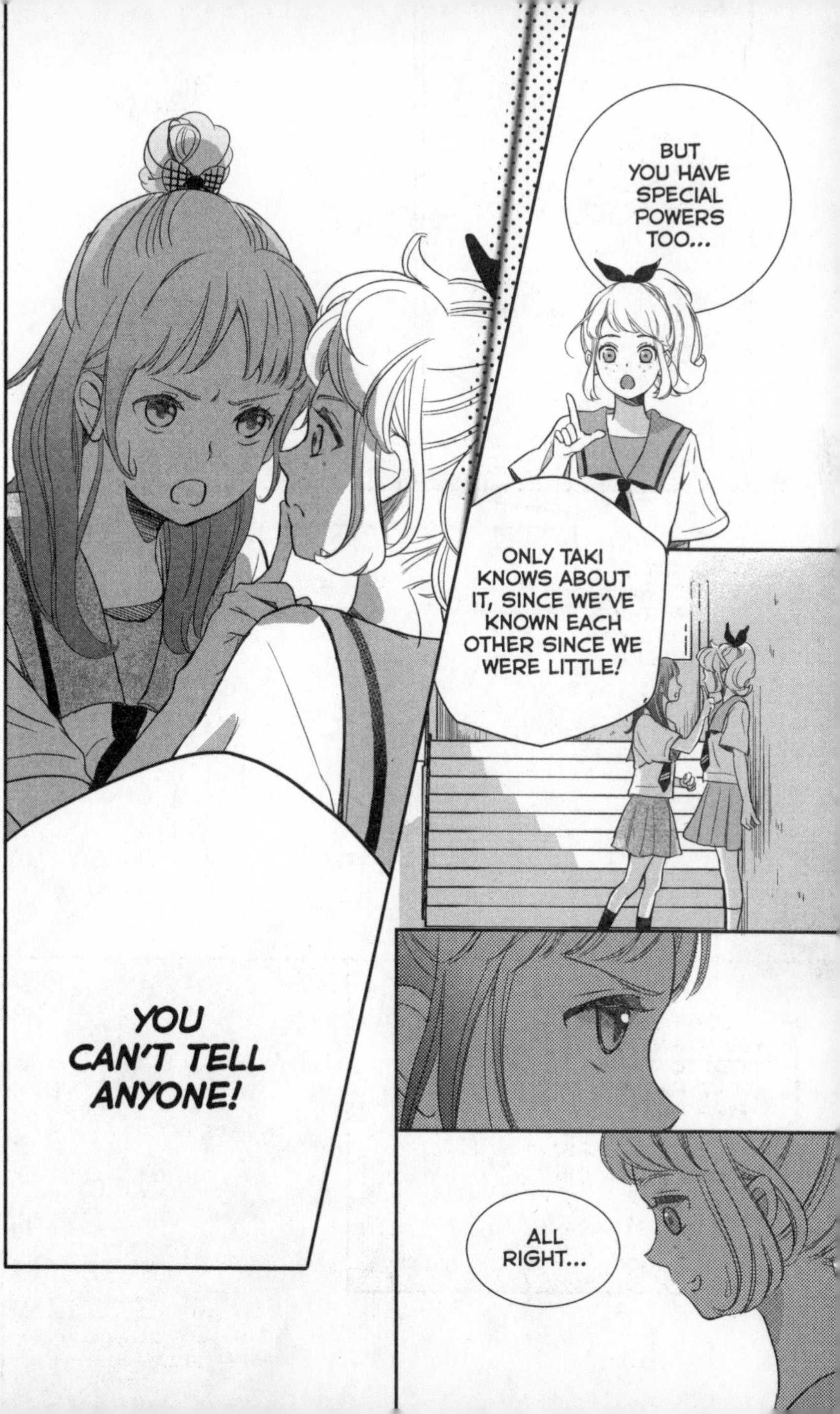
BUT YOU HAVE SPECIAL POWERS TOO...
ONLY TAKI KNOWS ABOUT IT, SINCE WE'VE KNOWN EACH OTHER SINCE WE WERE LITTLE!
ALL RIGHT...
YOU CAN'T TELL ANYONE!

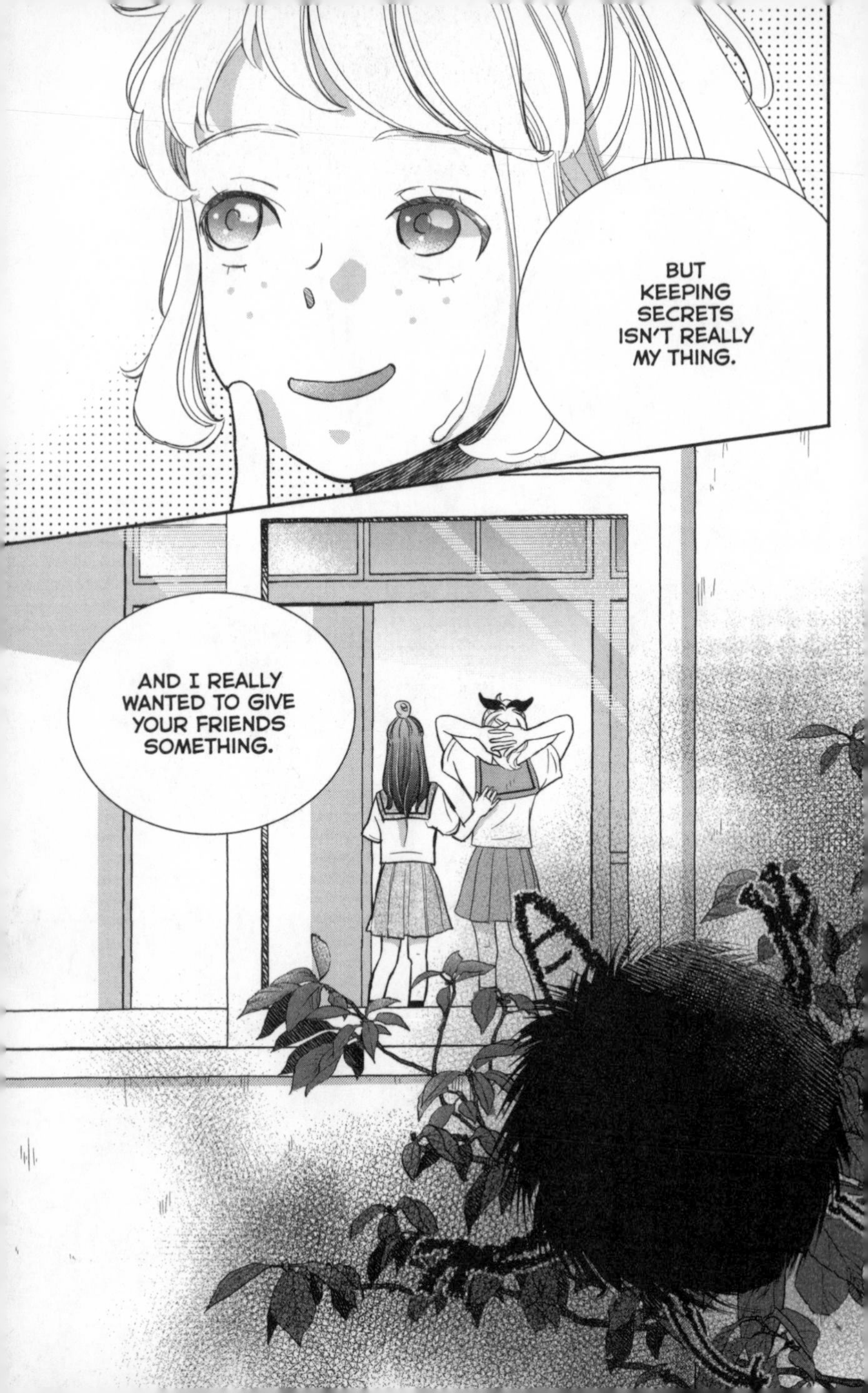
BUT KEEPING SECRETS ISN'T REALLY MY THING.
AND I REALLY WANTED TO GIVE YOUR FRIENDS SOMETHING.

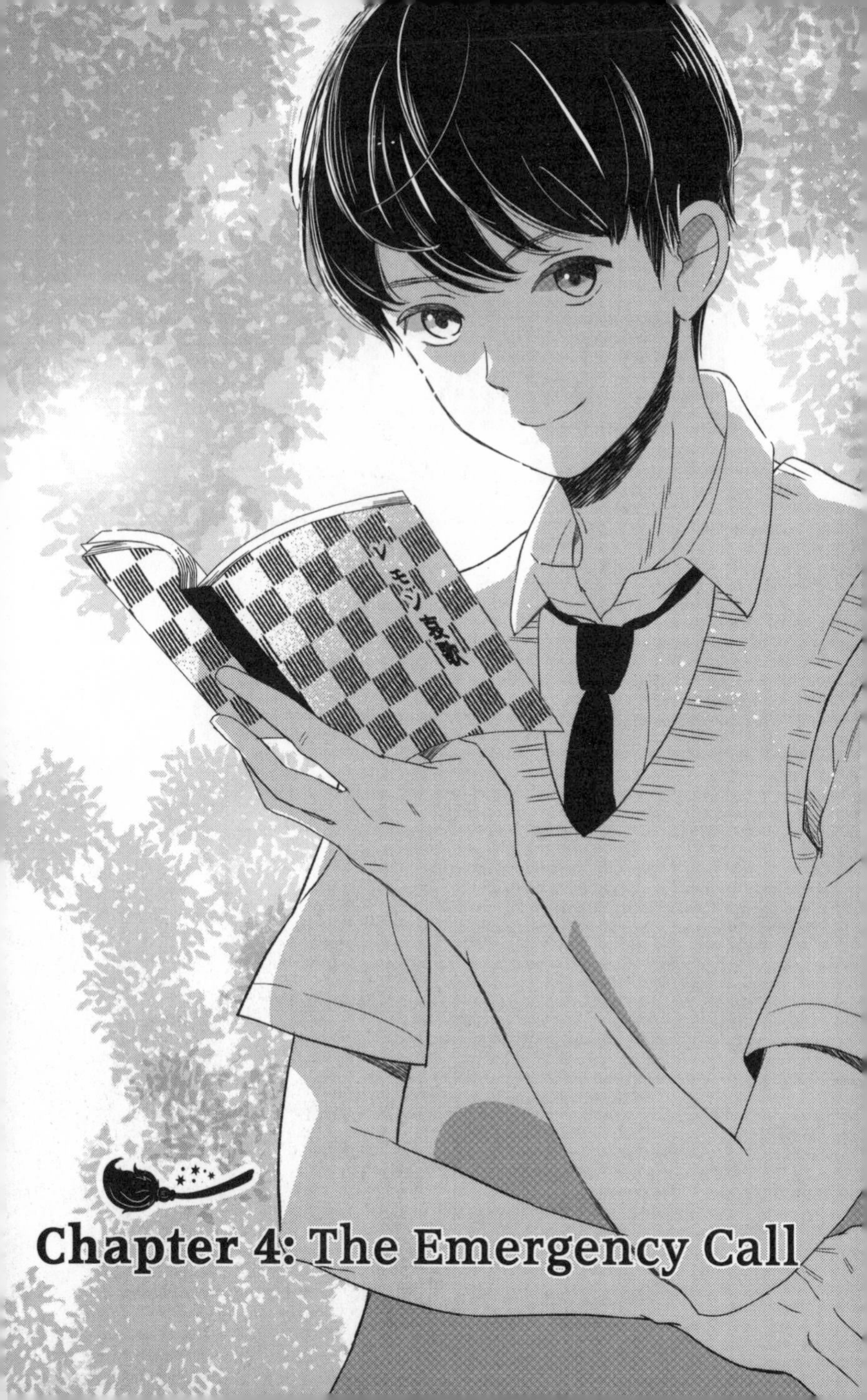

Chapter 4: The Emergency Call

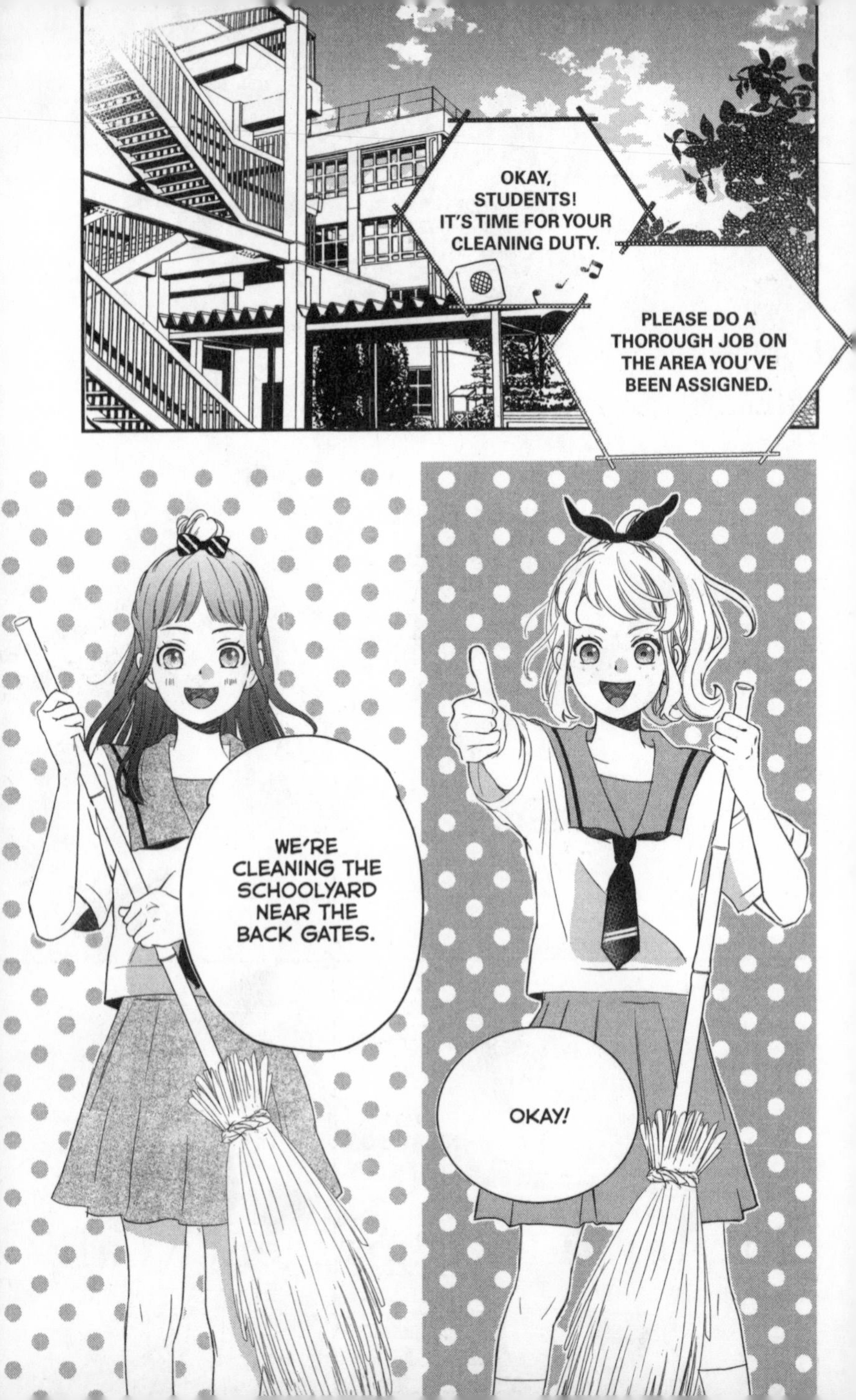
OKAY, STUDENTS! IT'S TIME FOR YOUR CLEANING DUTY.
PLEASE DO A THOROUGH JOB ON THE AREA YOU'VE BEEN ASSIGNED.
WE'RE CLEANING THE SCHOOLYARD NEAR THE BACK GATES.
OKAY!

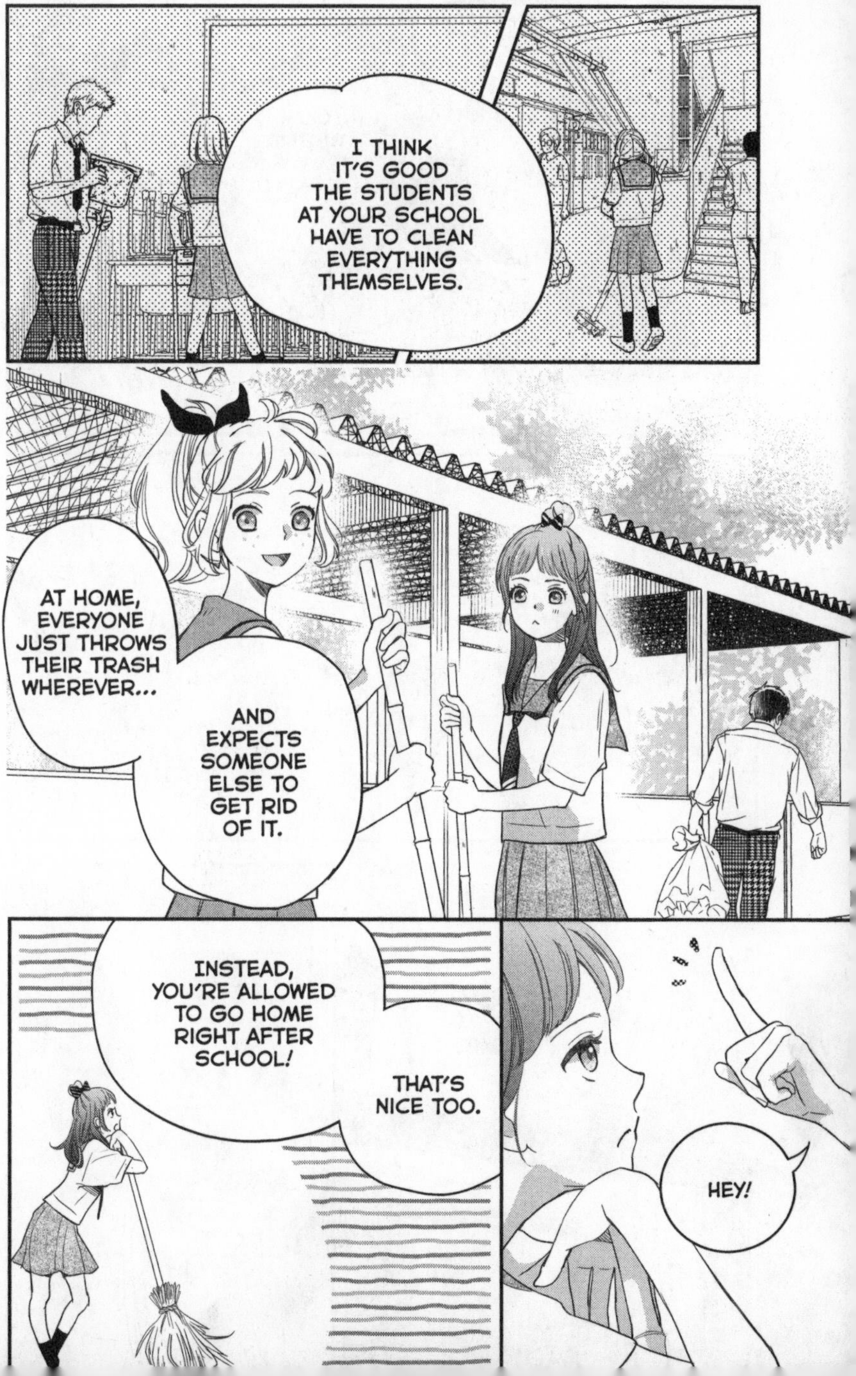
I THINK IT'S GOOD THE STUDENTS AT YOUR SCHOOL HAVE TO CLEAN EVERYTHING THEMSELVES.
AT HOME, EVERYONE JUST THROWS THEIR TRASH WHEREVER...
AND EXPECTS SOMEONE ELSE TO GET RID OF IT.
INSTEAD, YOU'RE ALLOWED TO GO HOME RIGHT AFTER SCHOOL!
THAT'S NICE TOO.
HEY!

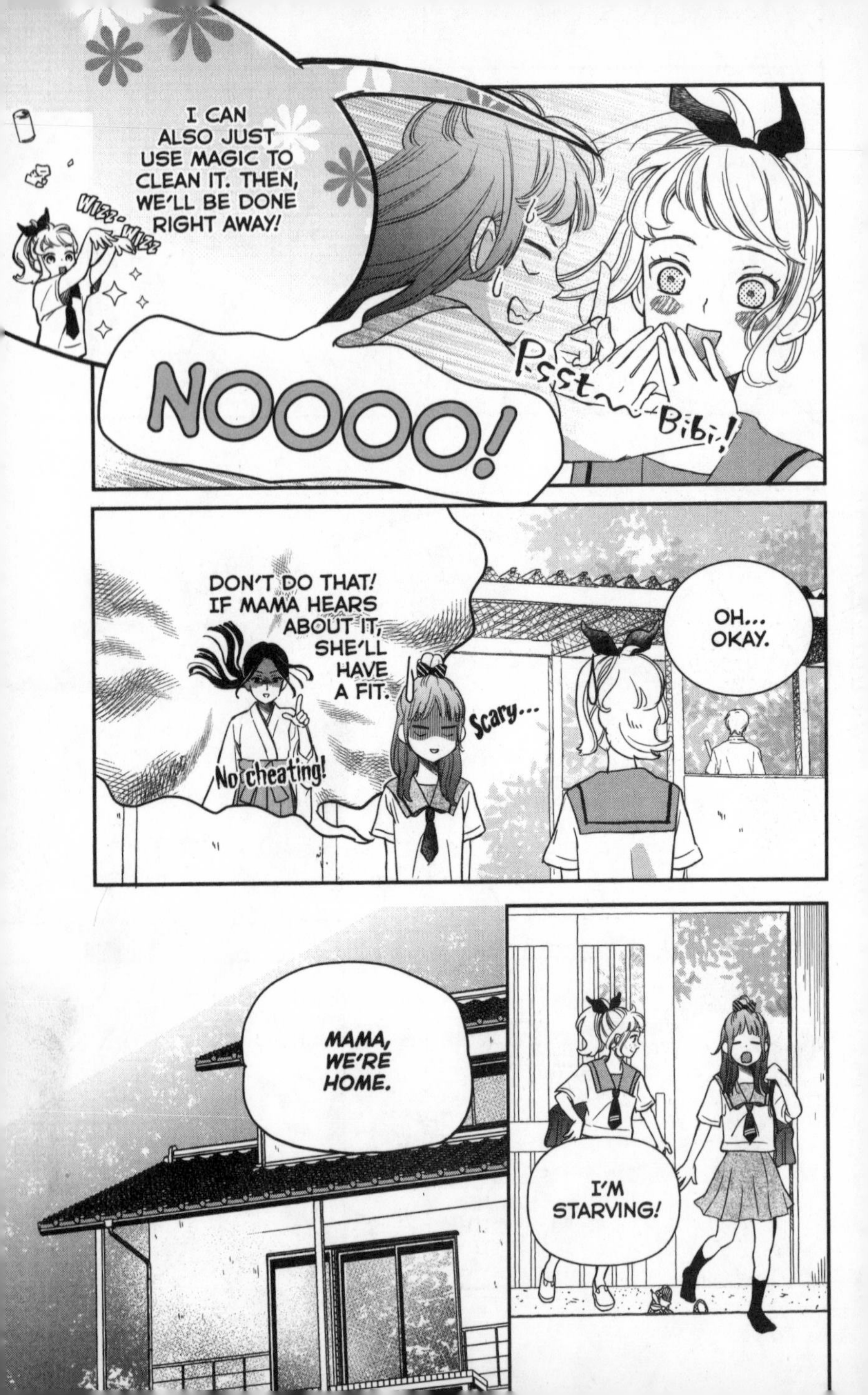
I CAN ALSO JUST USE MAGIC TO CLEAN IT. THEN, WE'LL BE DONE RIGHT AWAY!
WIZZ-WIZZ
NOOOO!
Psst...Bibi!
OH... OKAY.
DON'T DO THAT! IF MAMA HEARS ABOUT IT, SHE'LL HAVE A FIT.
Scary...
No cheating!
MAMA, WE'RE HOME.
I'M STARVING!

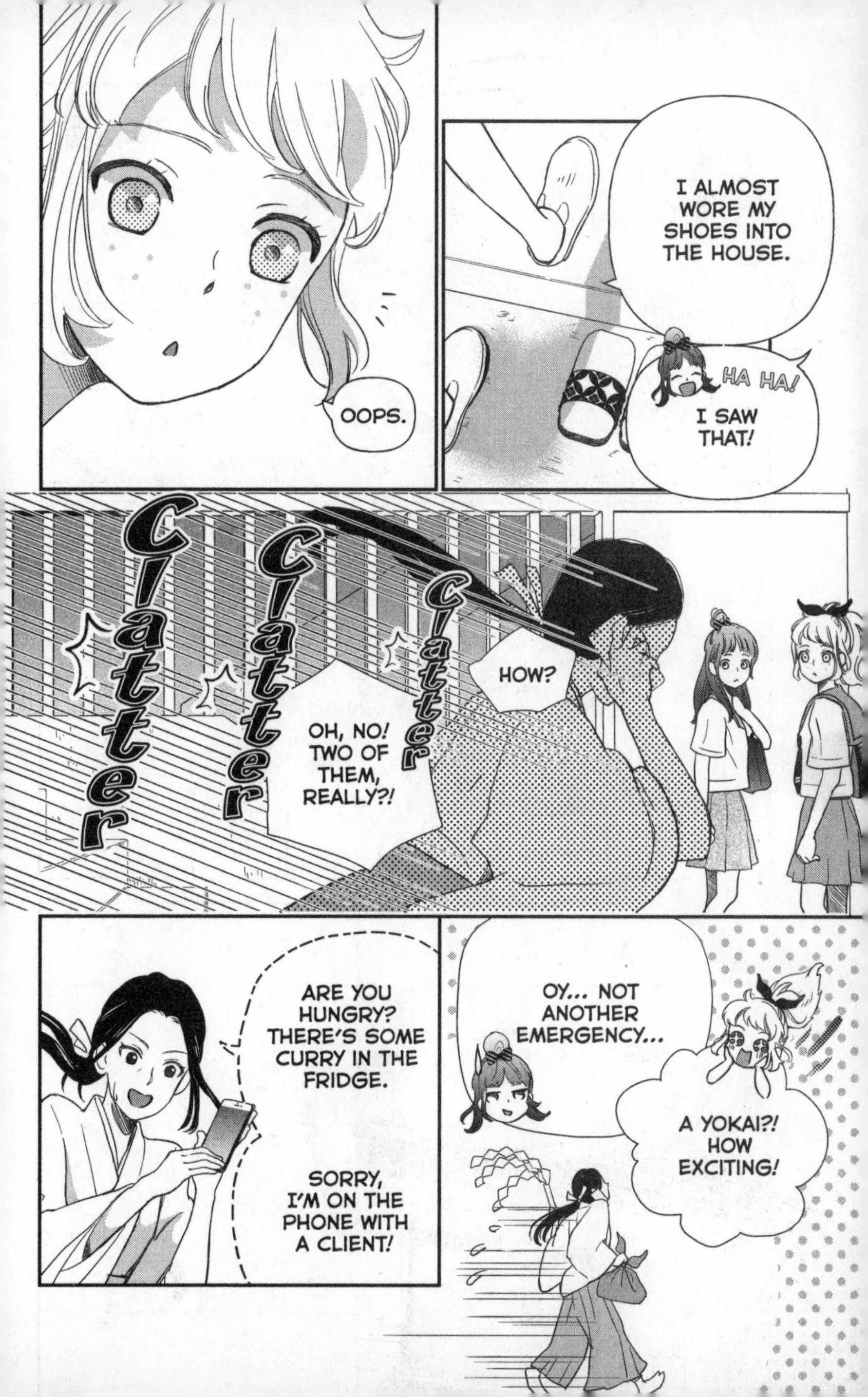
I ALMOST WORE MY SHOES INTO THE HOUSE.
HA HA!
I SAW THAT!
OOPS.
HOW?
Clatter
Clatter
Clatter
OH, NO! TWO OF THEM, REALLY?!
OY... NOT ANOTHER EMERGENCY...
A YOKAI?! HOW EXCITING!
ARE YOU HUNGRY? THERE'S SOME CURRY IN THE FRIDGE.
SORRY, I'M ON THE PHONE WITH A CLIENT!

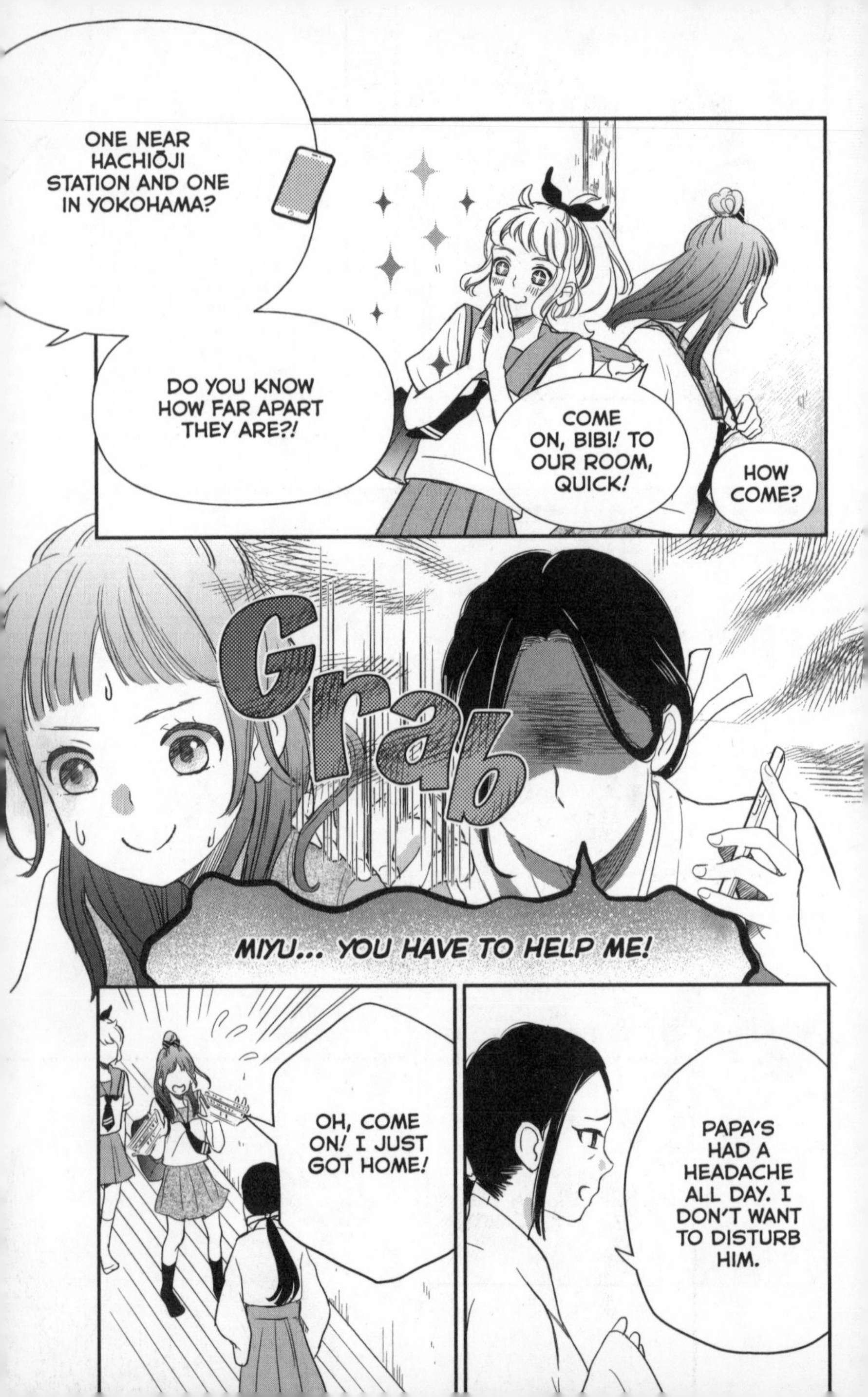
HOW COME?
COME ON, BIBI! TO OUR ROOM, QUICK!
ONE NEAR HACHIŌJI STATION AND ONE IN YOKOHAMA?
DO YOU KNOW HOW FAR APART THEY ARE?!
Grab
MIYU... YOU HAVE TO HELP ME!
PAPA'S HAD A HEADACHE ALL DAY. I DON'T WANT TO DISTURB HIM.
OH, COME ON! I JUST GOT HOME!

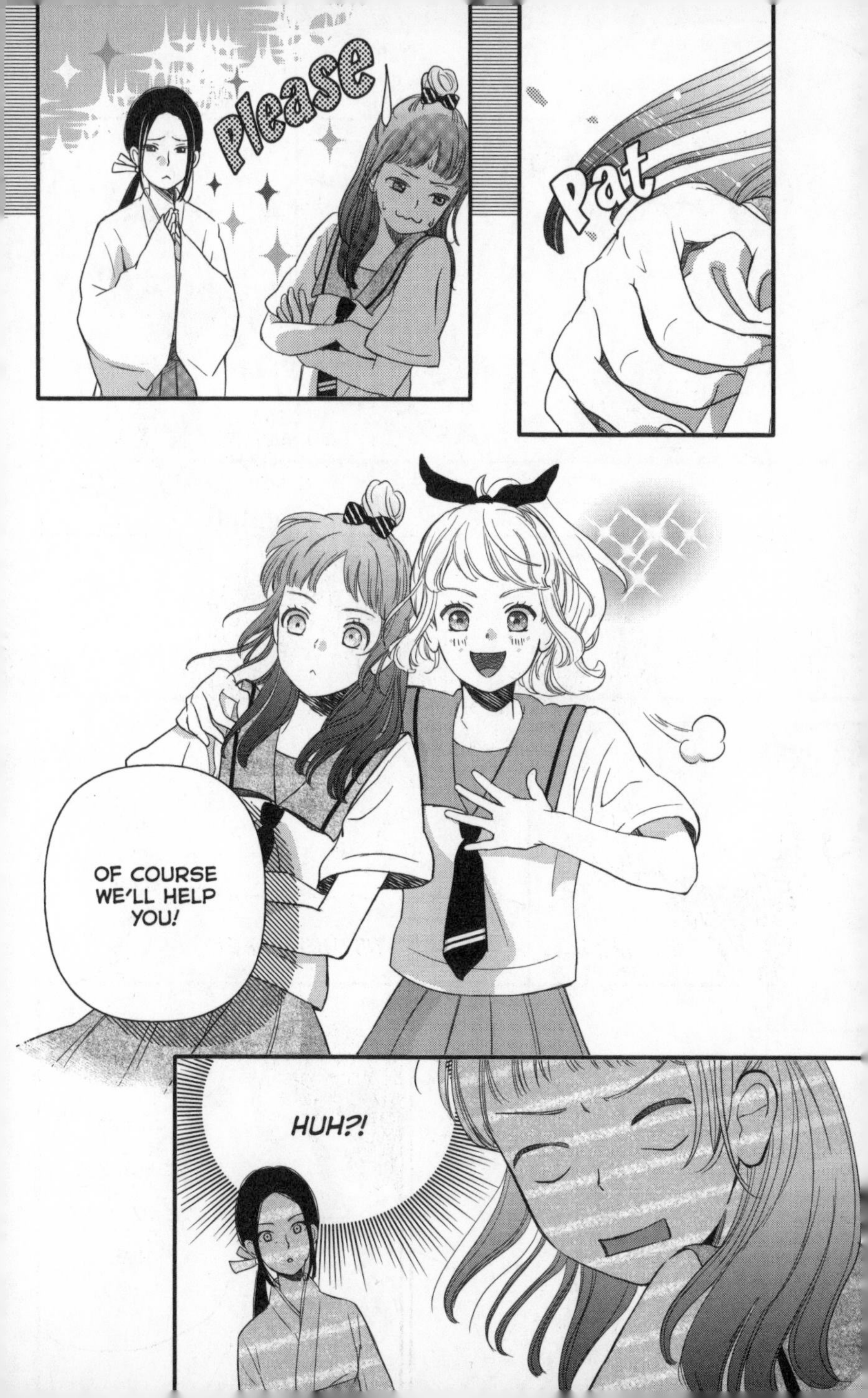
Pat
Please
OF COURSE WE'LL HELP YOU!
HUH?!

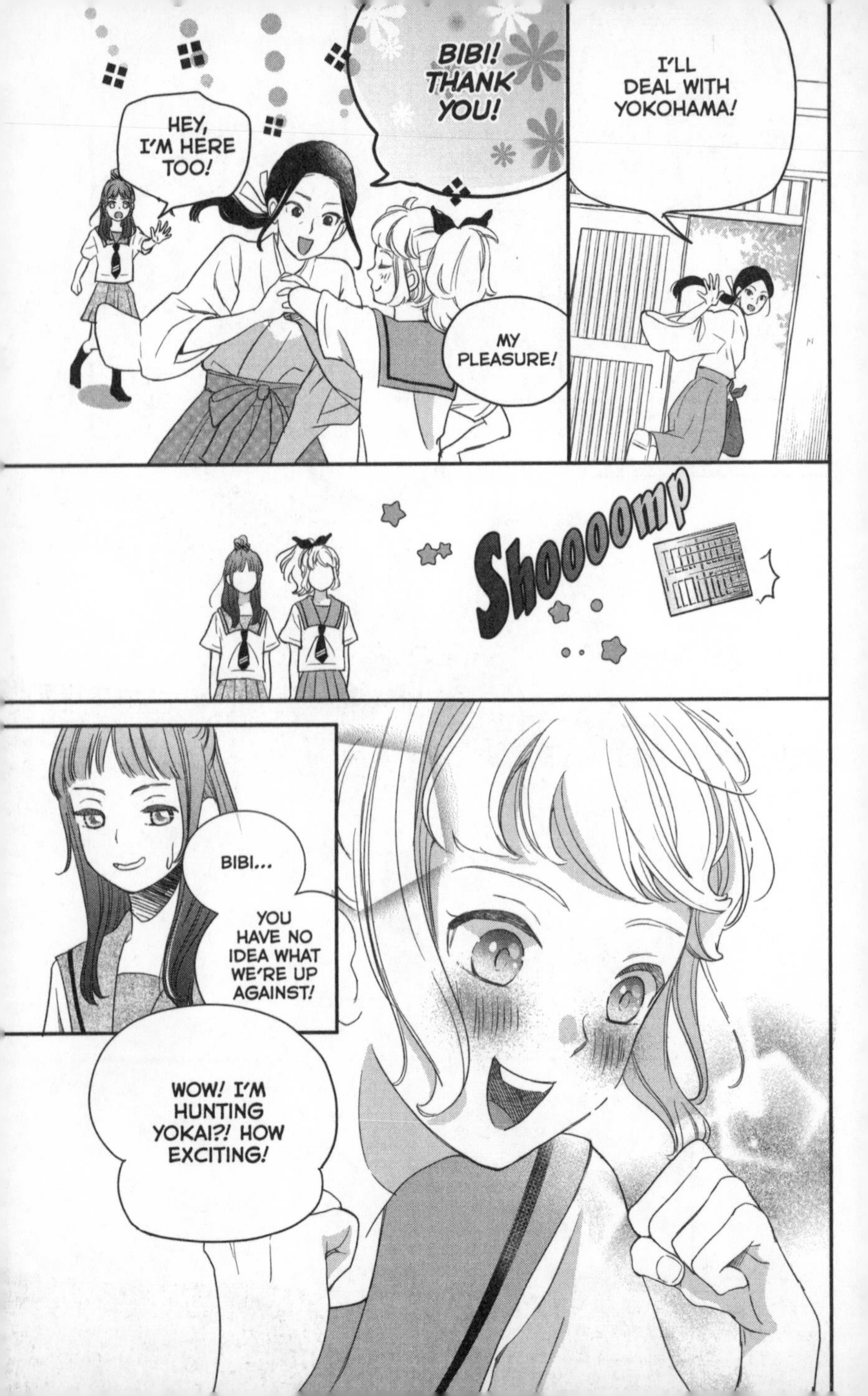
I'LL DEAL WITH YOKOHAMA!
BIBI! THANK YOU!
MY PLEASURE!
HEY, I'M HERE TOO!
Shoooomp
WOW! I'M HUNTING YOKAI?! HOW EXCITING!
BIBI... YOU HAVE NO IDEA WHAT WE'RE UP AGAINST!

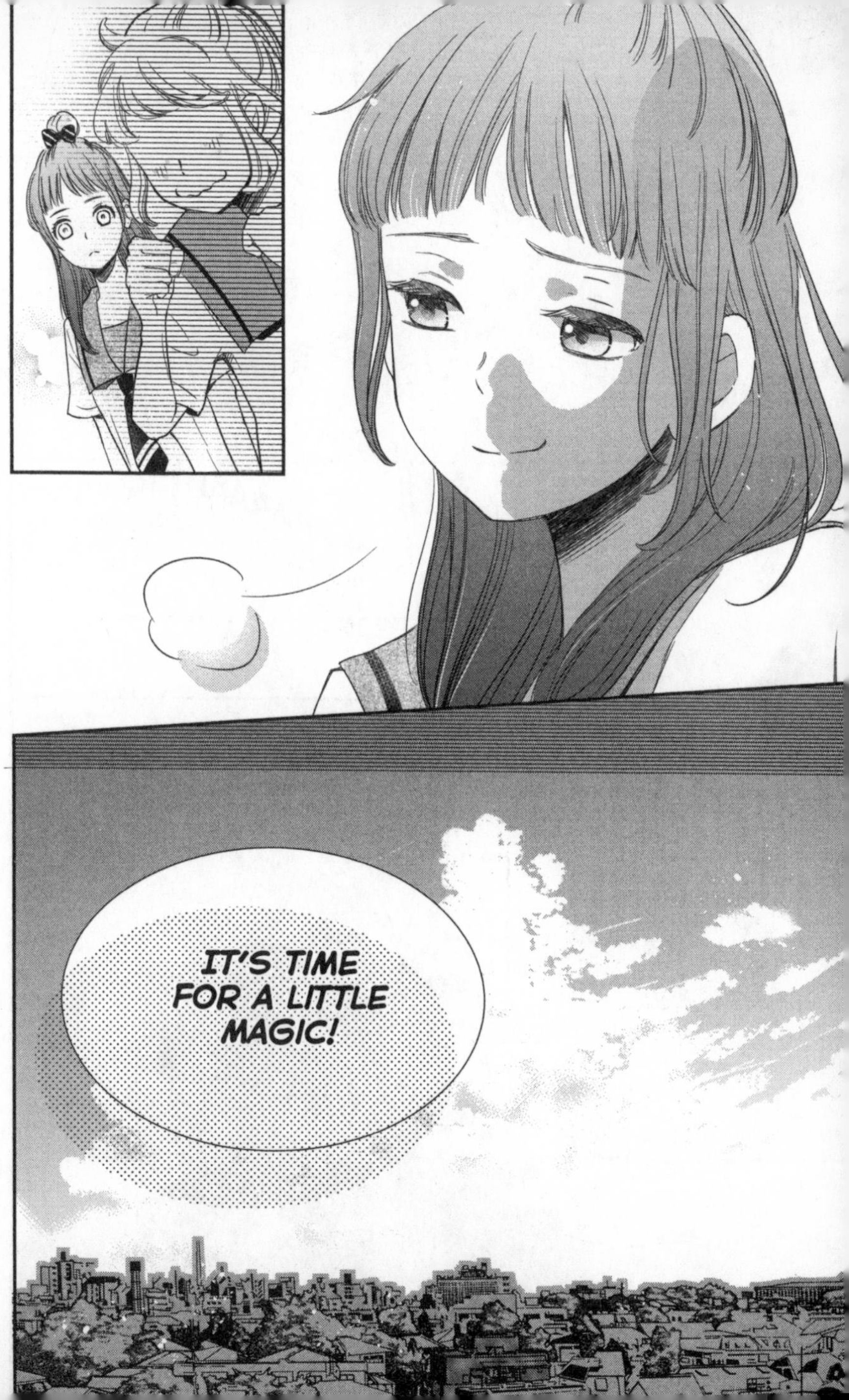
IT'S TIME FOR A LITTLE MAGIC!

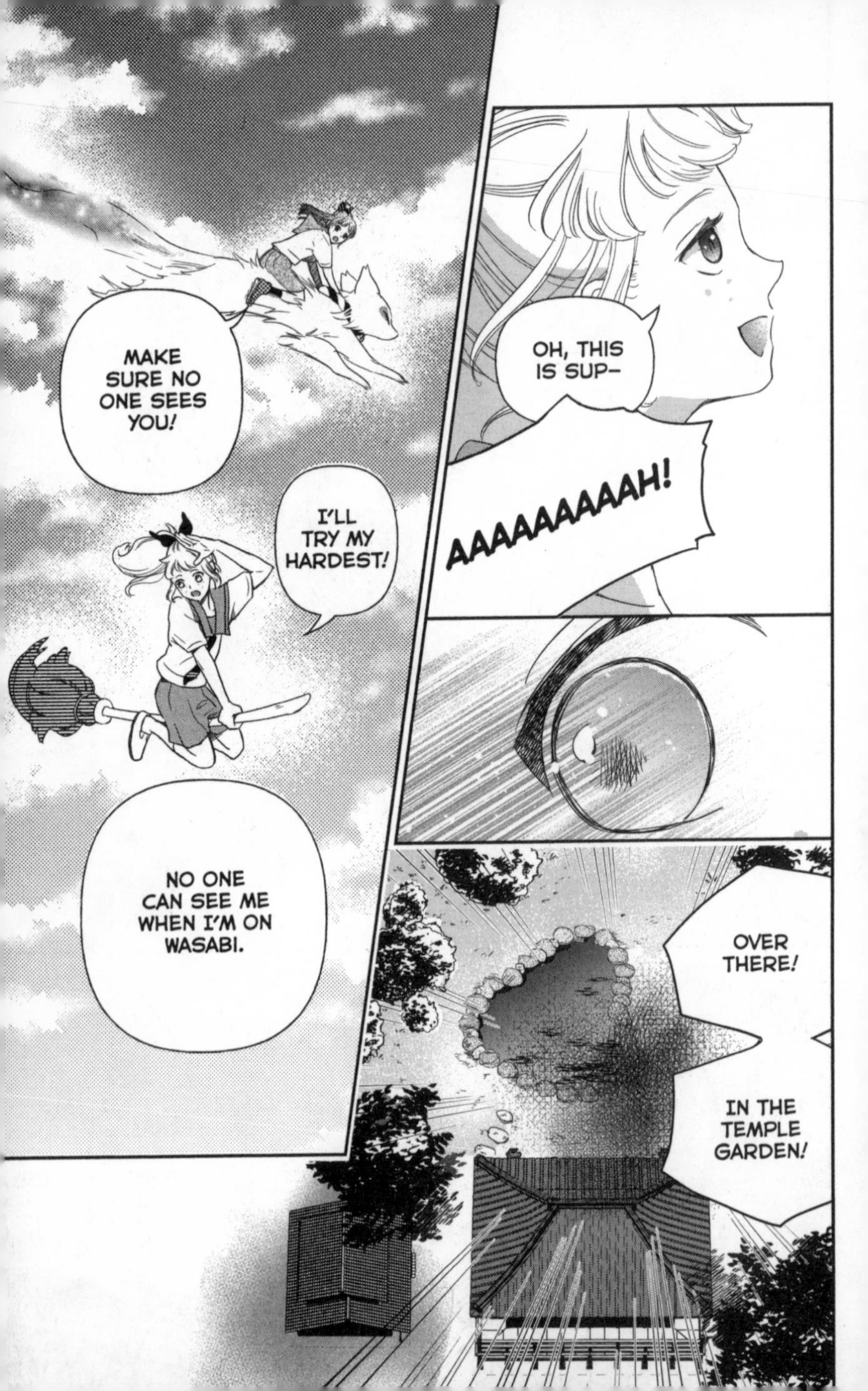
MAKE SURE NO ONE SEES YOU!
I'LL TRY MY HARDEST!
NO ONE CAN SEE ME WHEN I'M ON WASABI.
OH, THIS IS SUP-
AAAAAAAAAH!
OVER THERE!
IN THE TEMPLE GARDEN!

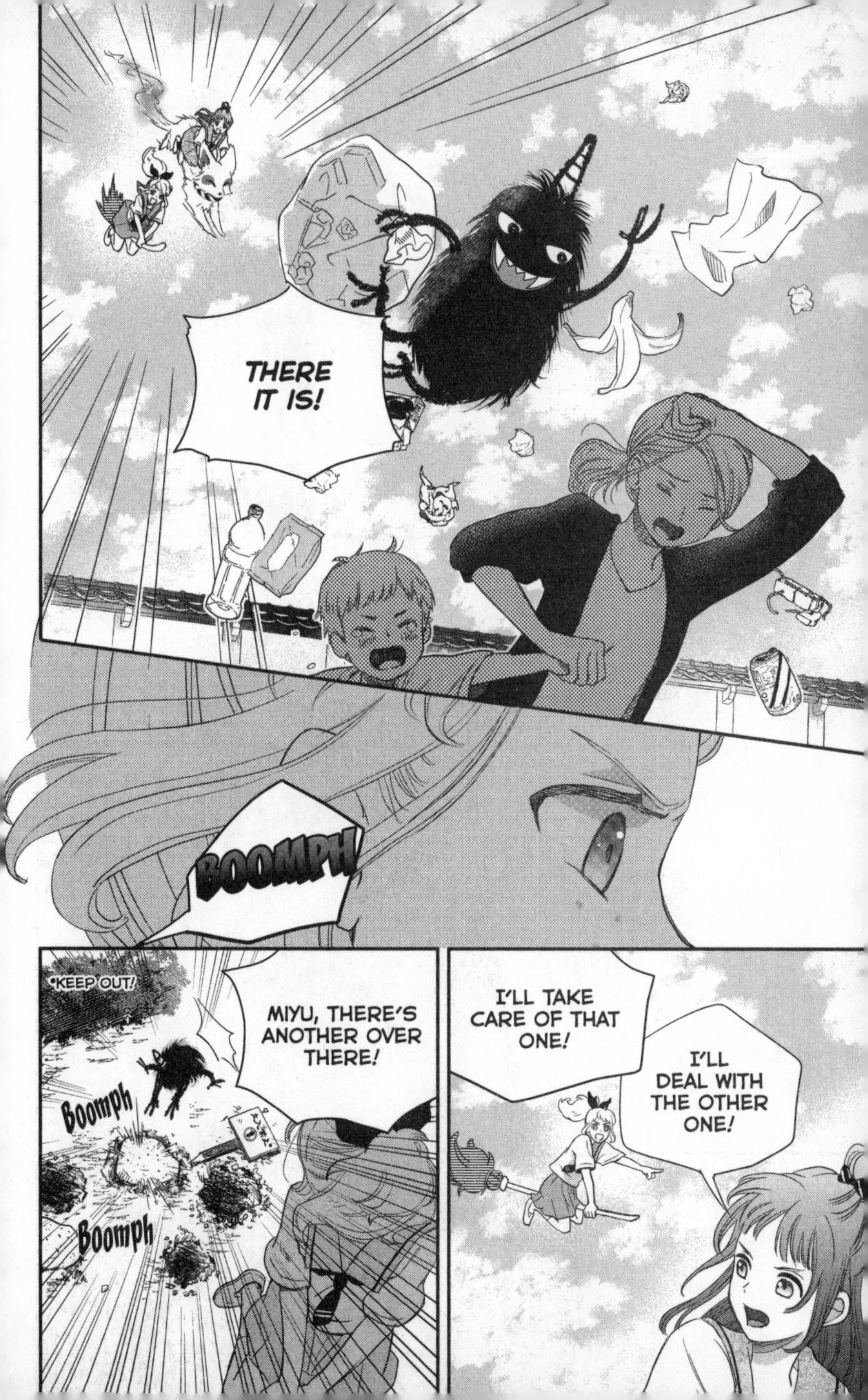
THERE IT IS!
BOOMPH
I'LL TAKE CARE OF THAT ONE!
I'LL DEAL WITH THE OTHER ONE!
MIYU, THERE'S ANOTHER OVER THERE!
*KEEP OUT!
Boomph
Boomph

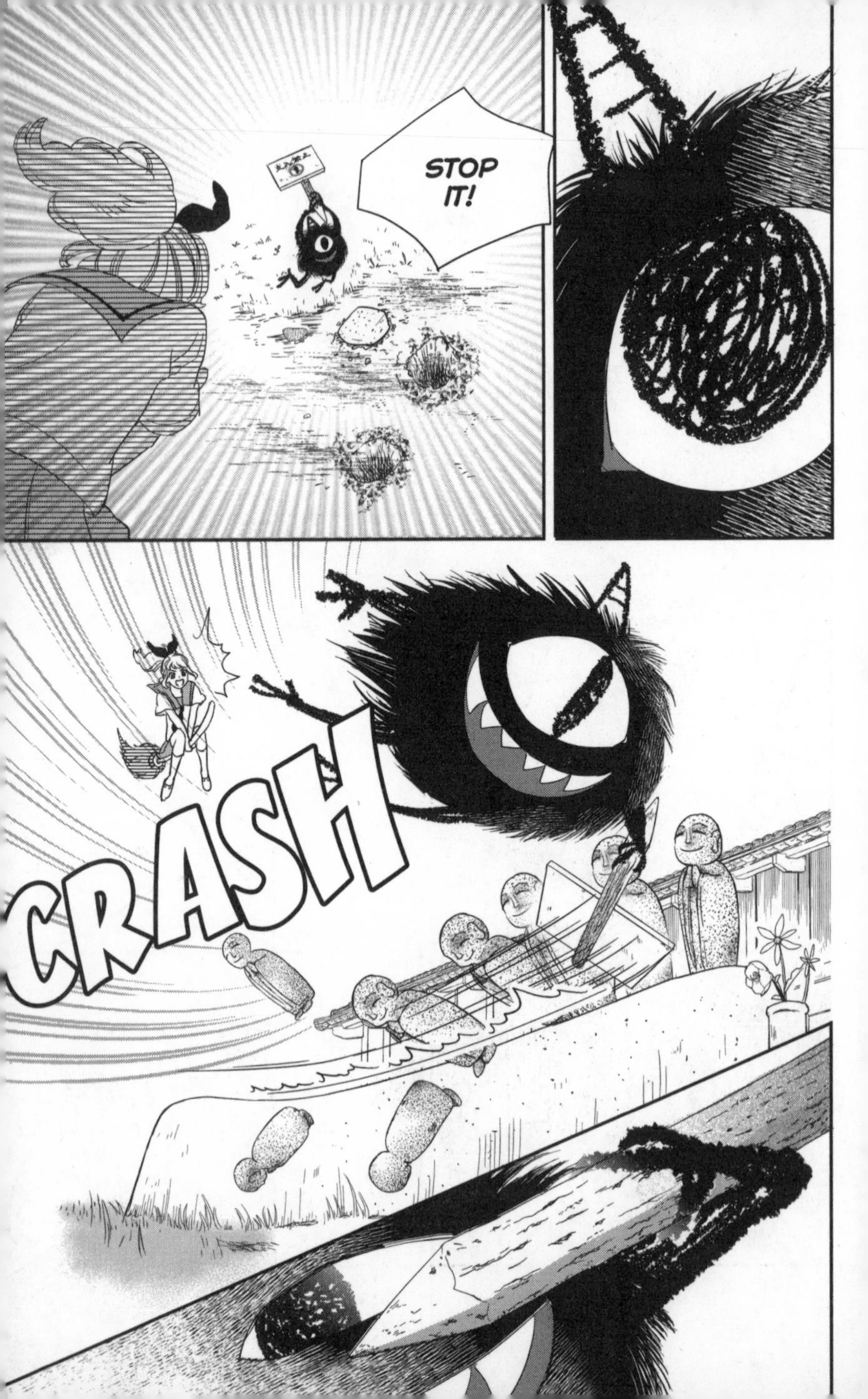
STOP IT!
CRASH

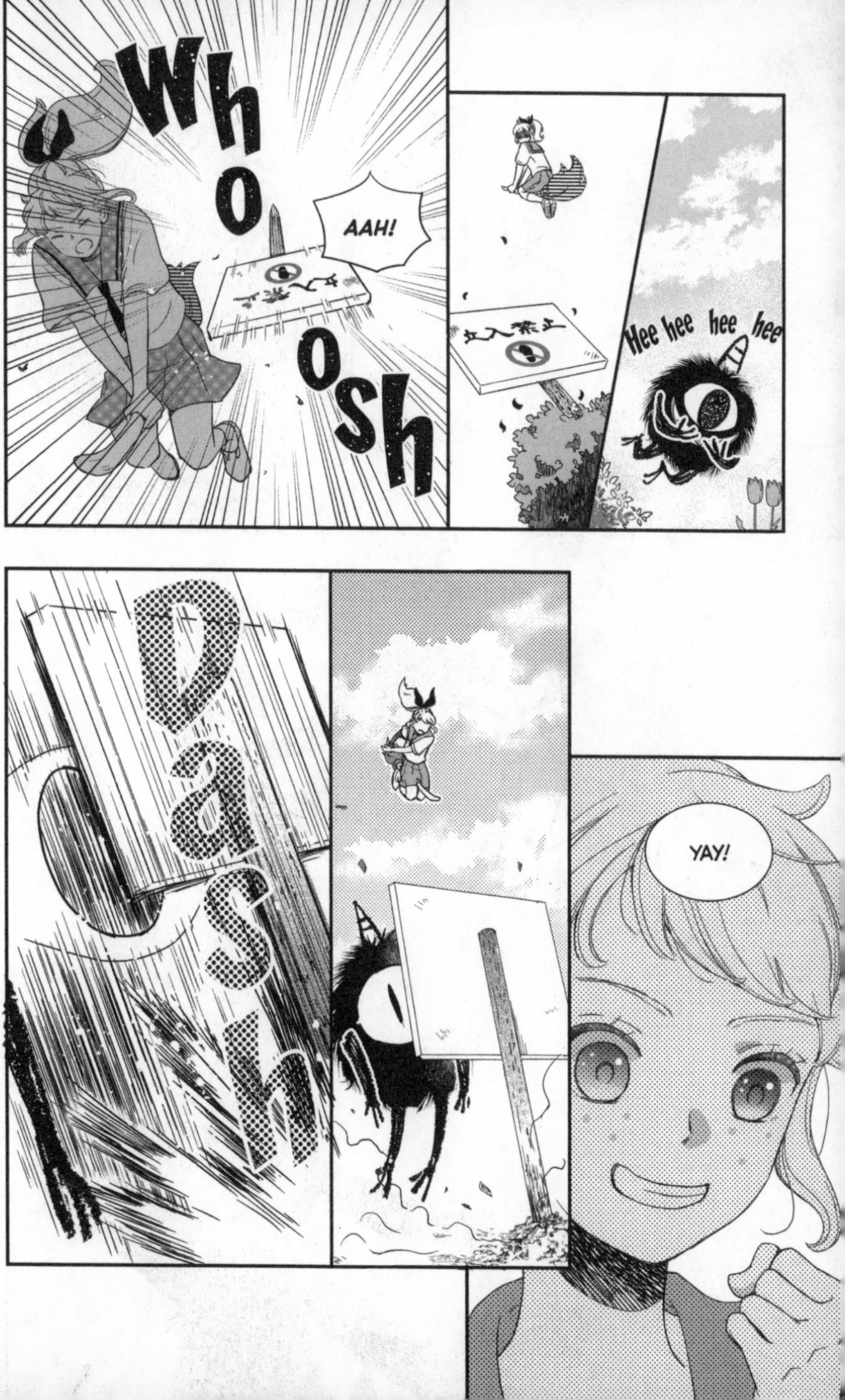

立入禁止
Hee hee hee hee
Whoosh
AAH!
YAY!
Dash

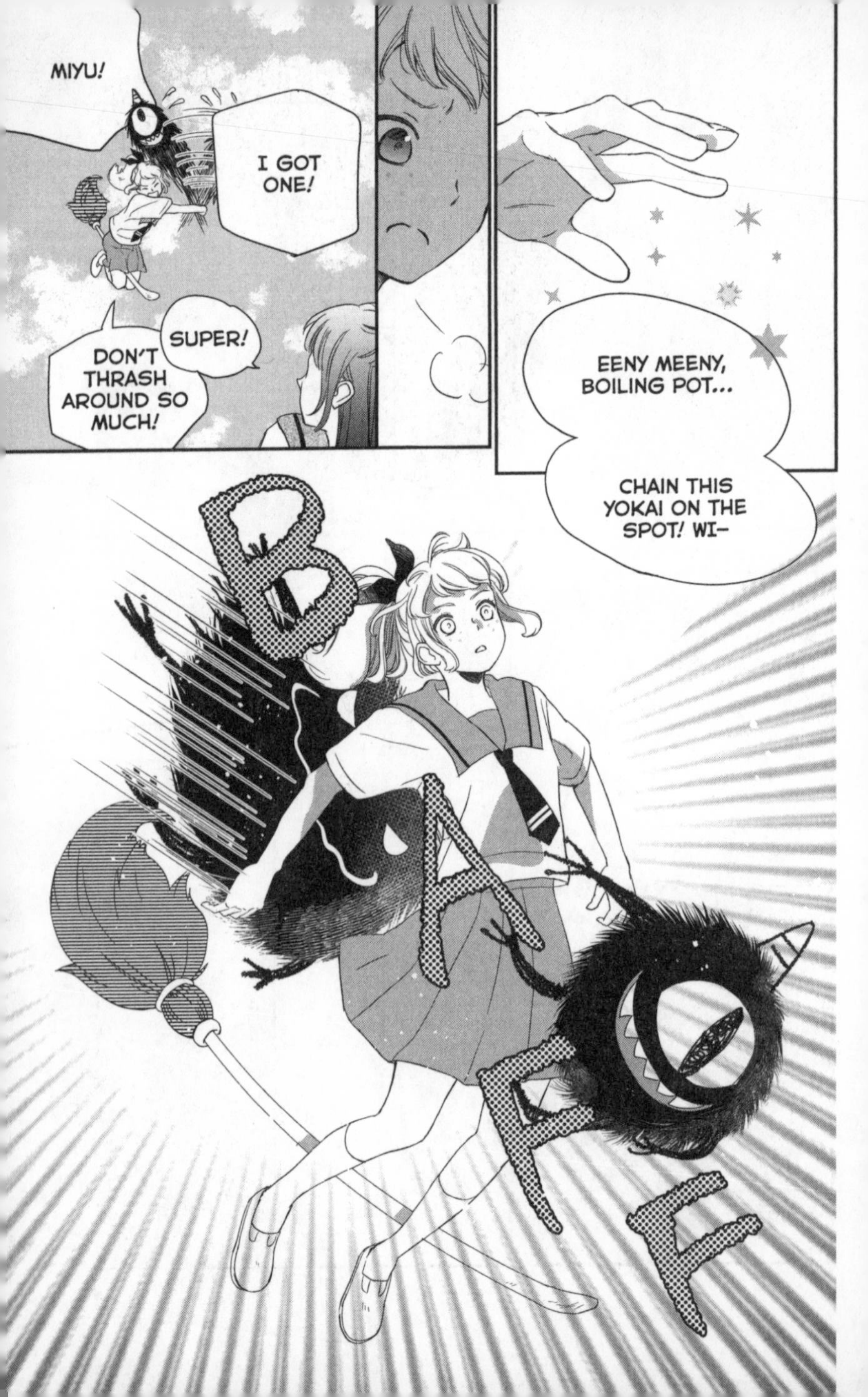
EENY MEENY, BOILING POT...
CHAIN THIS YOKAI ON THE SPOT! WI–
MIYU!
I GOT ONE!
SUPER!
DON'T THRASH AROUND SO MUCH!
BAF

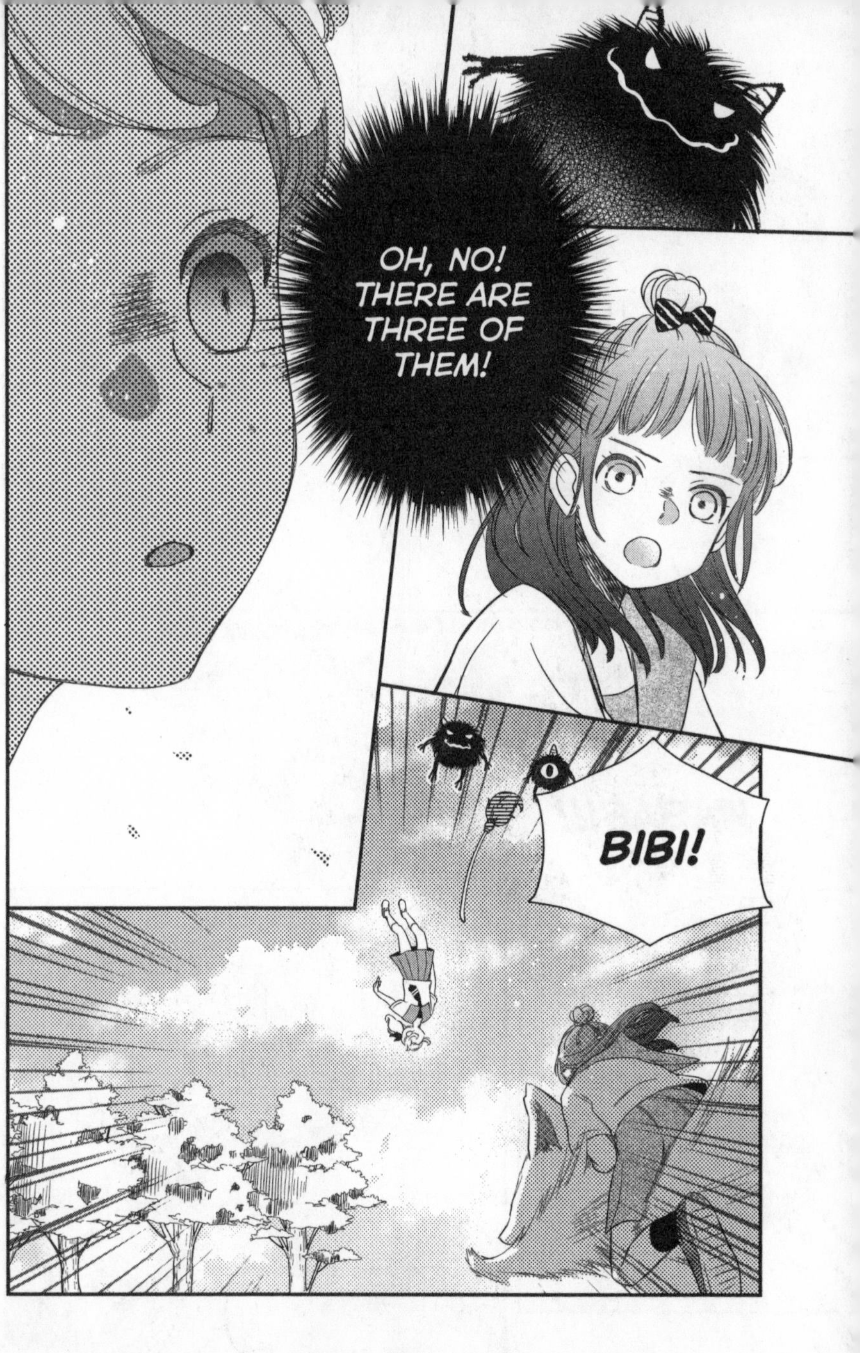
OH, NO! THERE ARE THREE OF THEM!
BIBI!

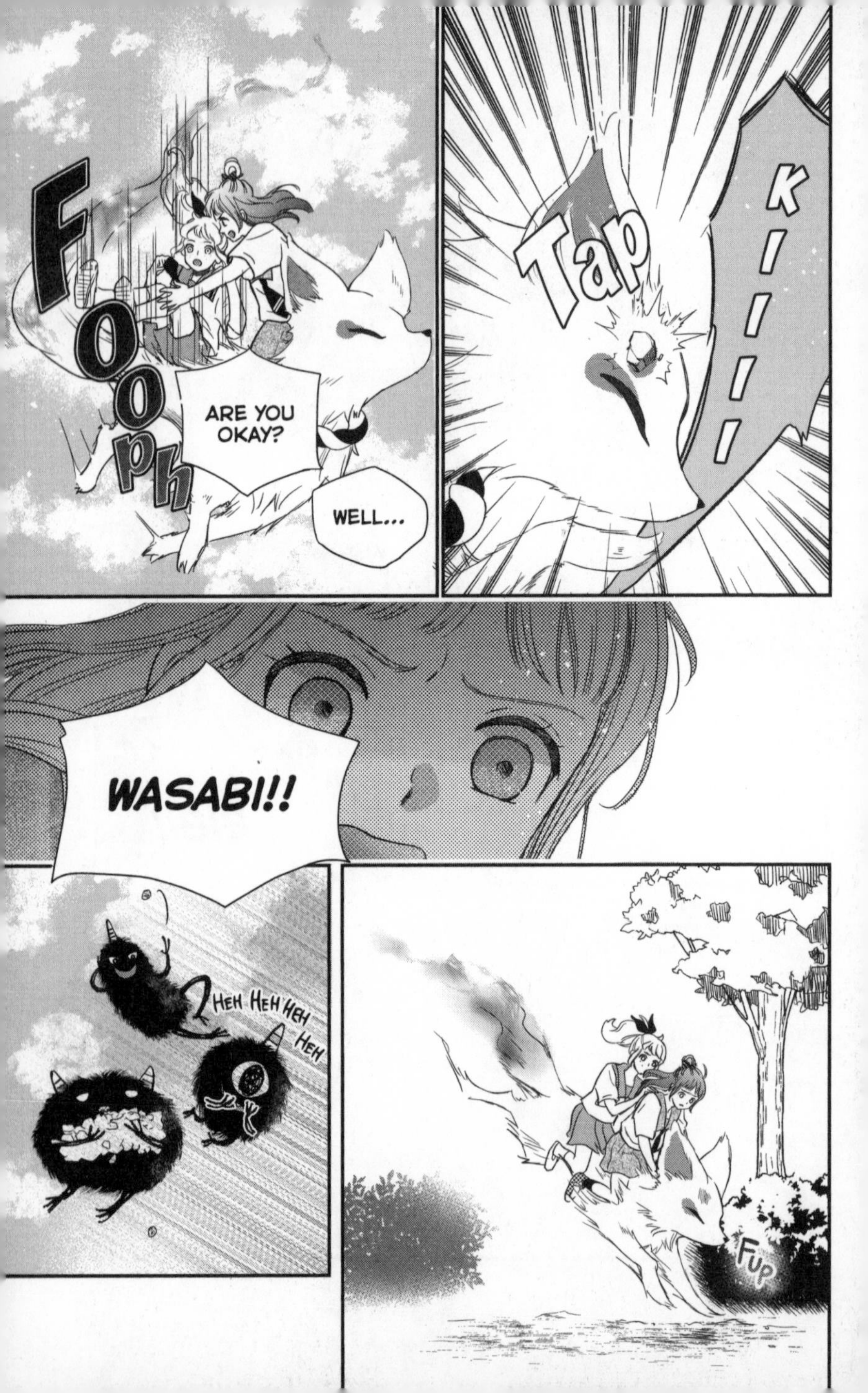

Tap
KIIIIII
Fooph
ARE YOU OKAY?
WELL...
WASABI!!
FUP
HEH HEH HEH HEH HEH

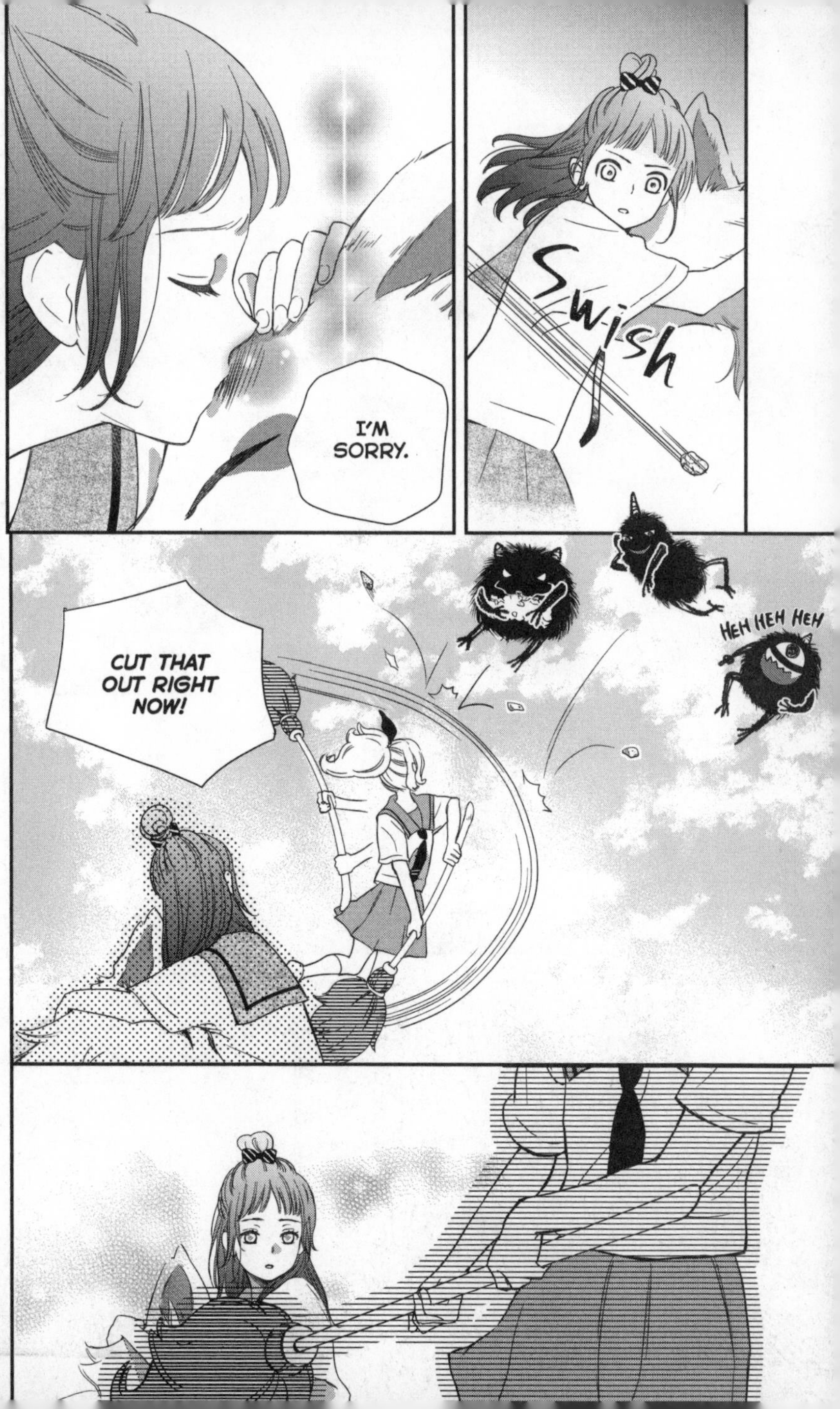
Swish
I'M SORRY.
HEH HEH HEH
CUT THAT OUT RIGHT NOW!

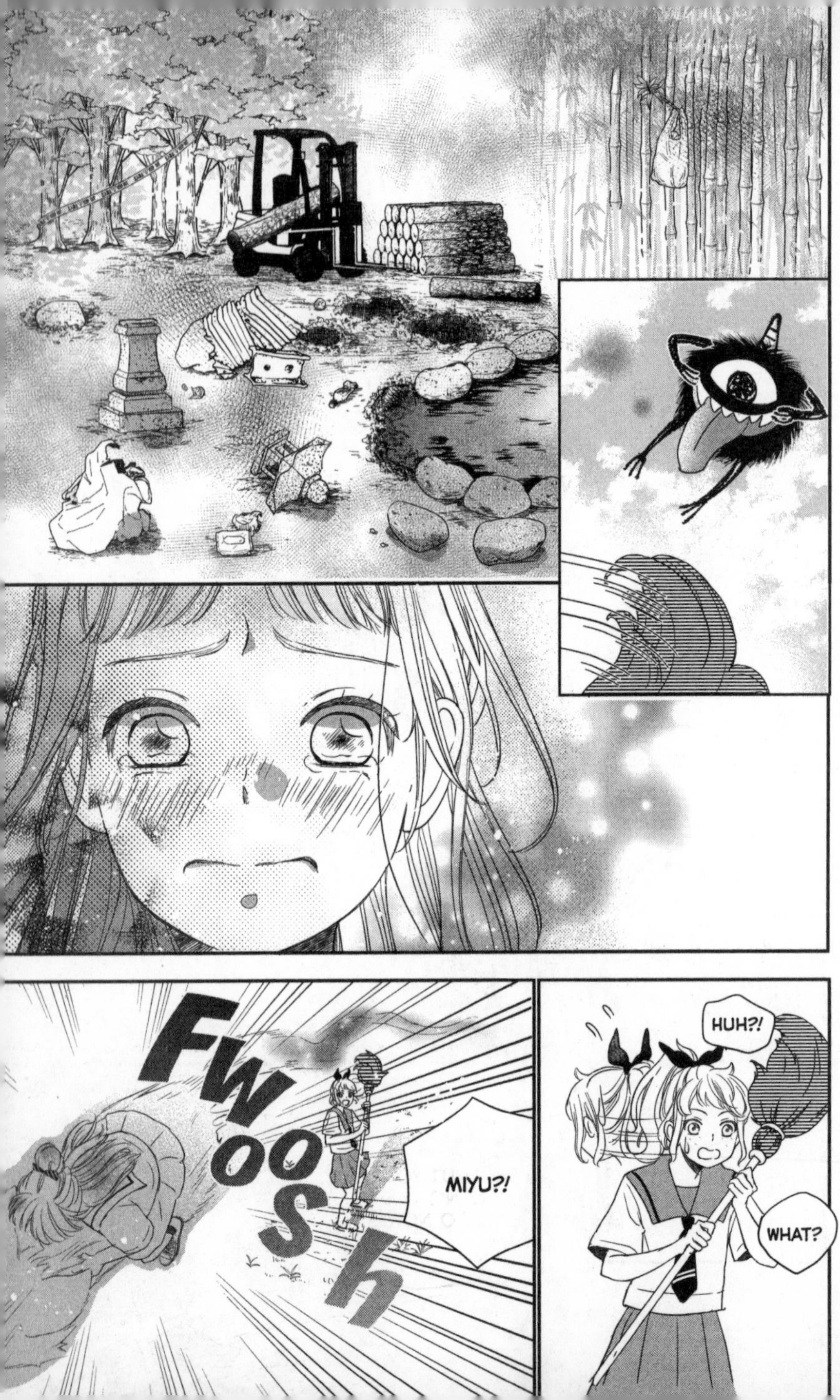
HUH?!
WHAT?
MIYU?!
FWOOSh

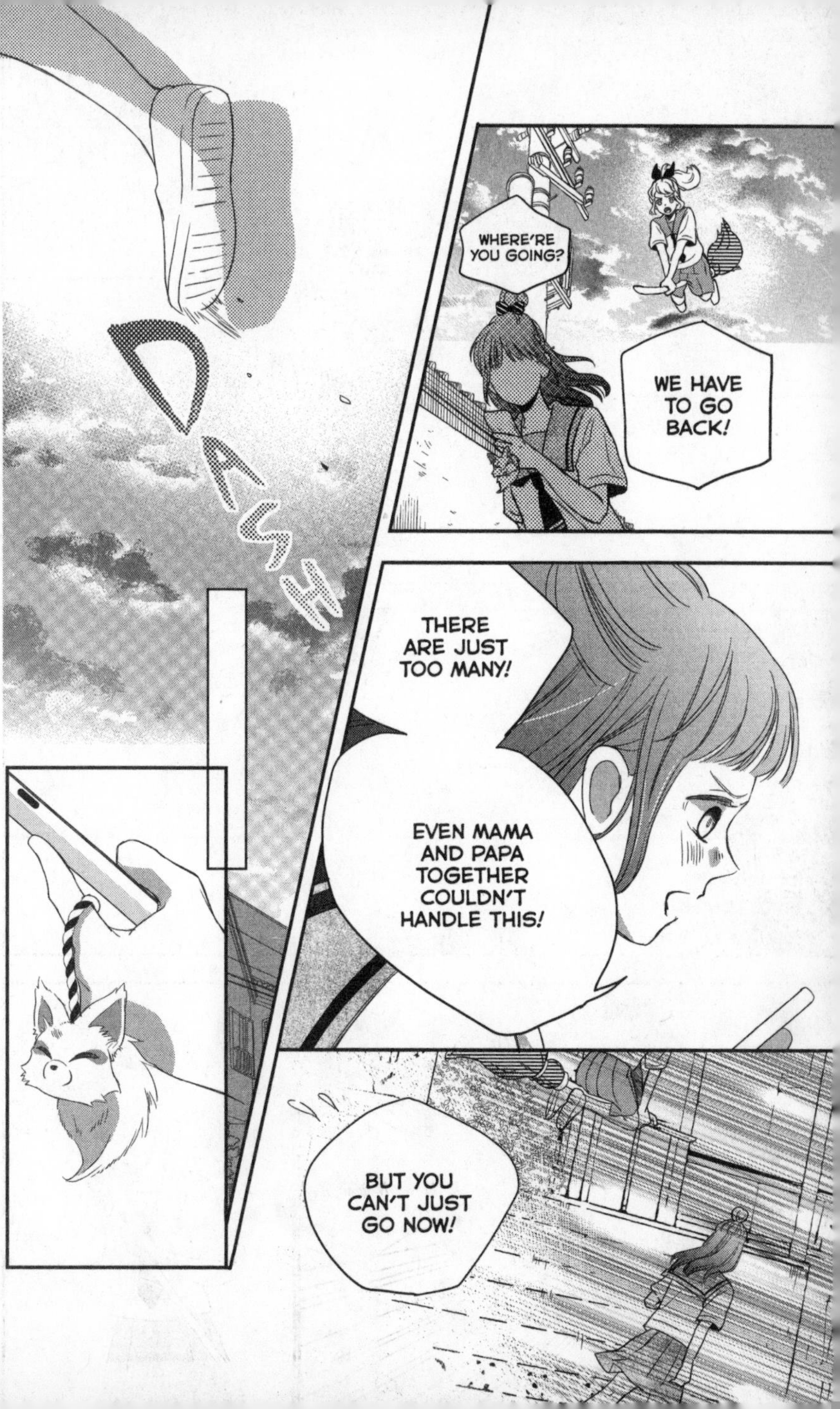
WHERE'RE YOU GOING?
WE HAVE TO GO BACK!
THERE ARE JUST TOO MANY!
EVEN MAMA AND PAPA TOGETHER COULDN'T HANDLE THIS!
BUT YOU CAN'T JUST GO NOW!
DASH

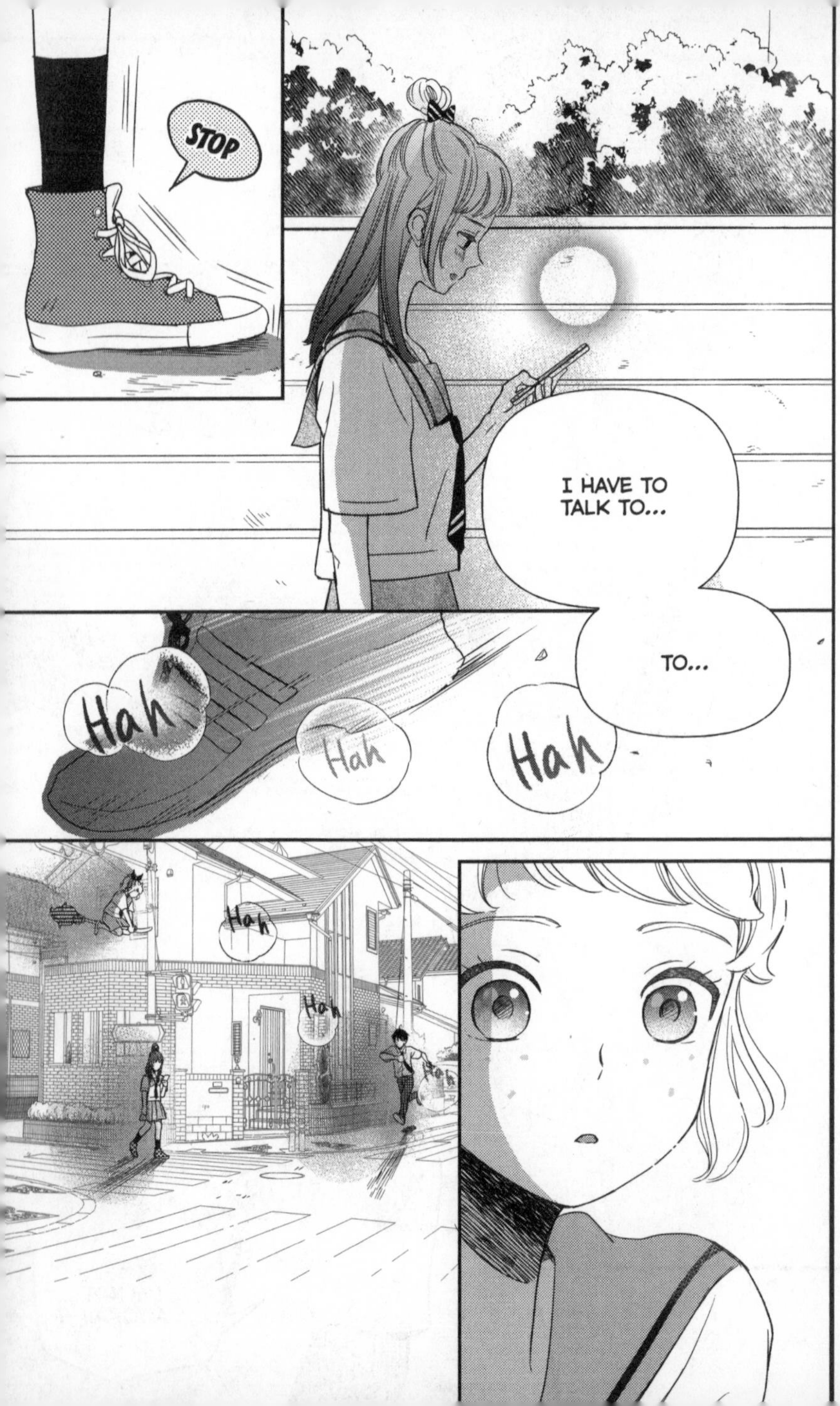
I HAVE TO TALK TO...
STOP
TO...
Hah
Hah
Hah
Hah
Hah

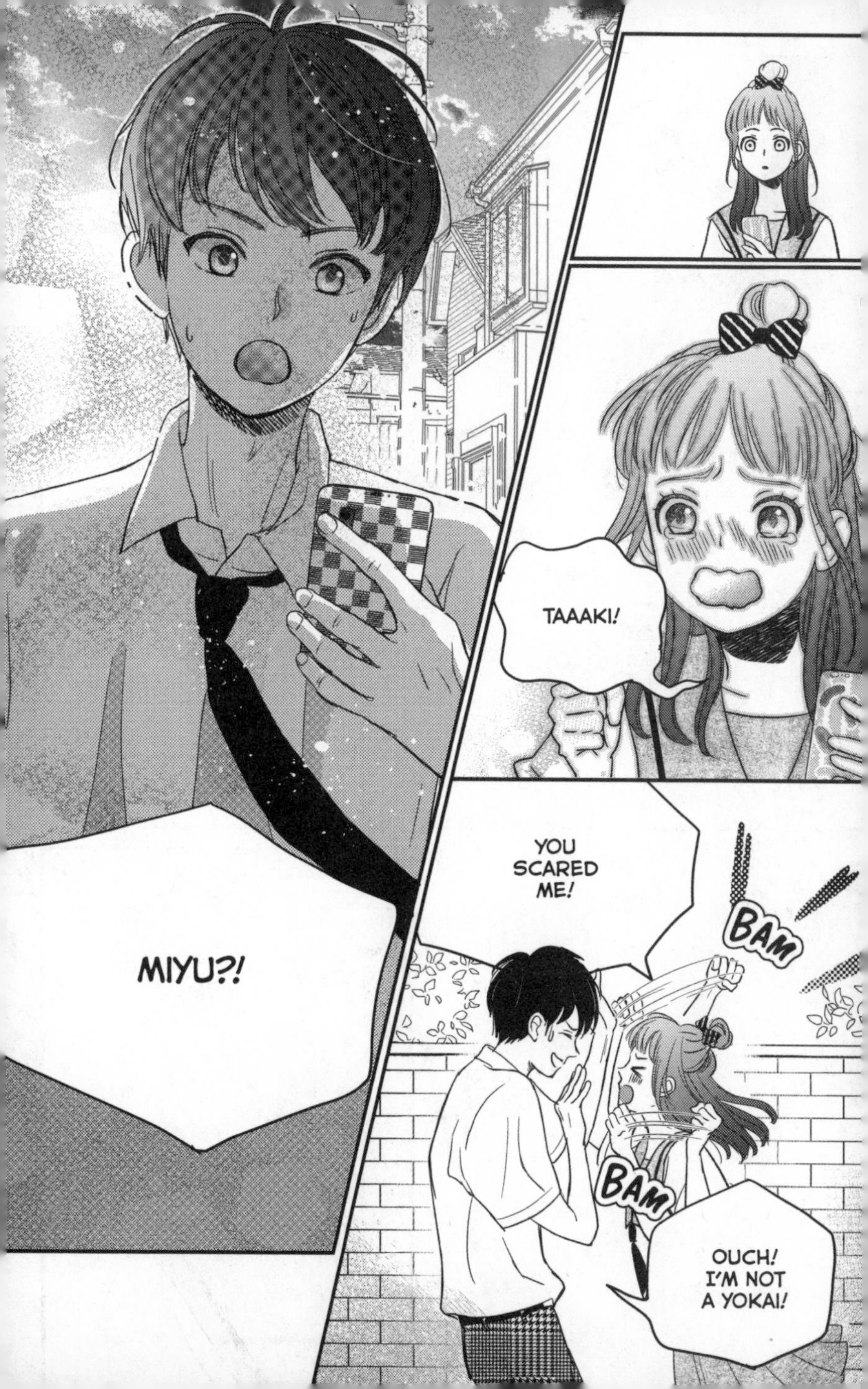
TAAAKI!
YOU SCARED ME!
BAM
BAM
OUCH! I'M NOT A YOKAI!
MIYU?!

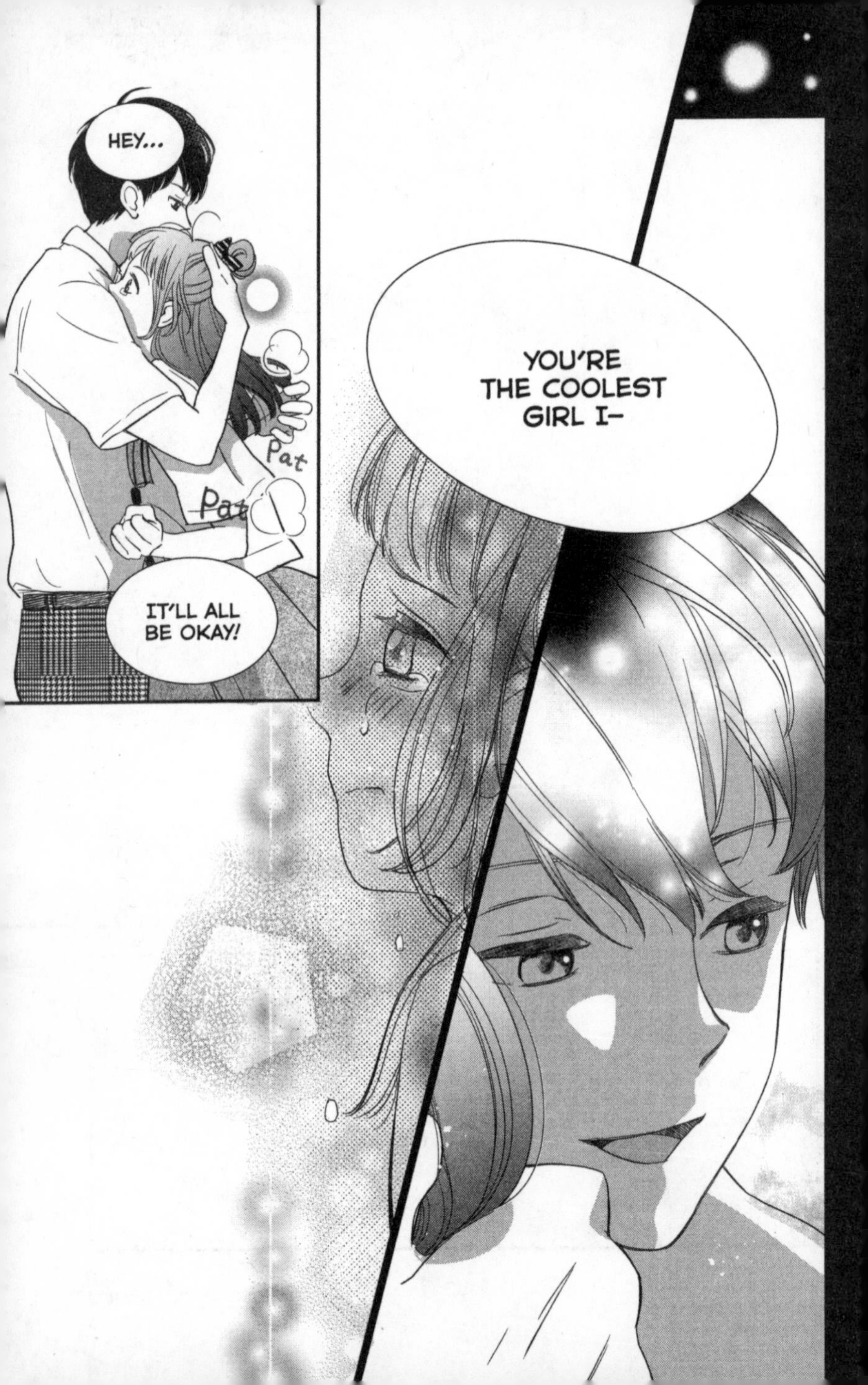
HEY...
Pat
Pat
IT'LL ALL BE OKAY!
YOU'RE THE COOLEST GIRL I-

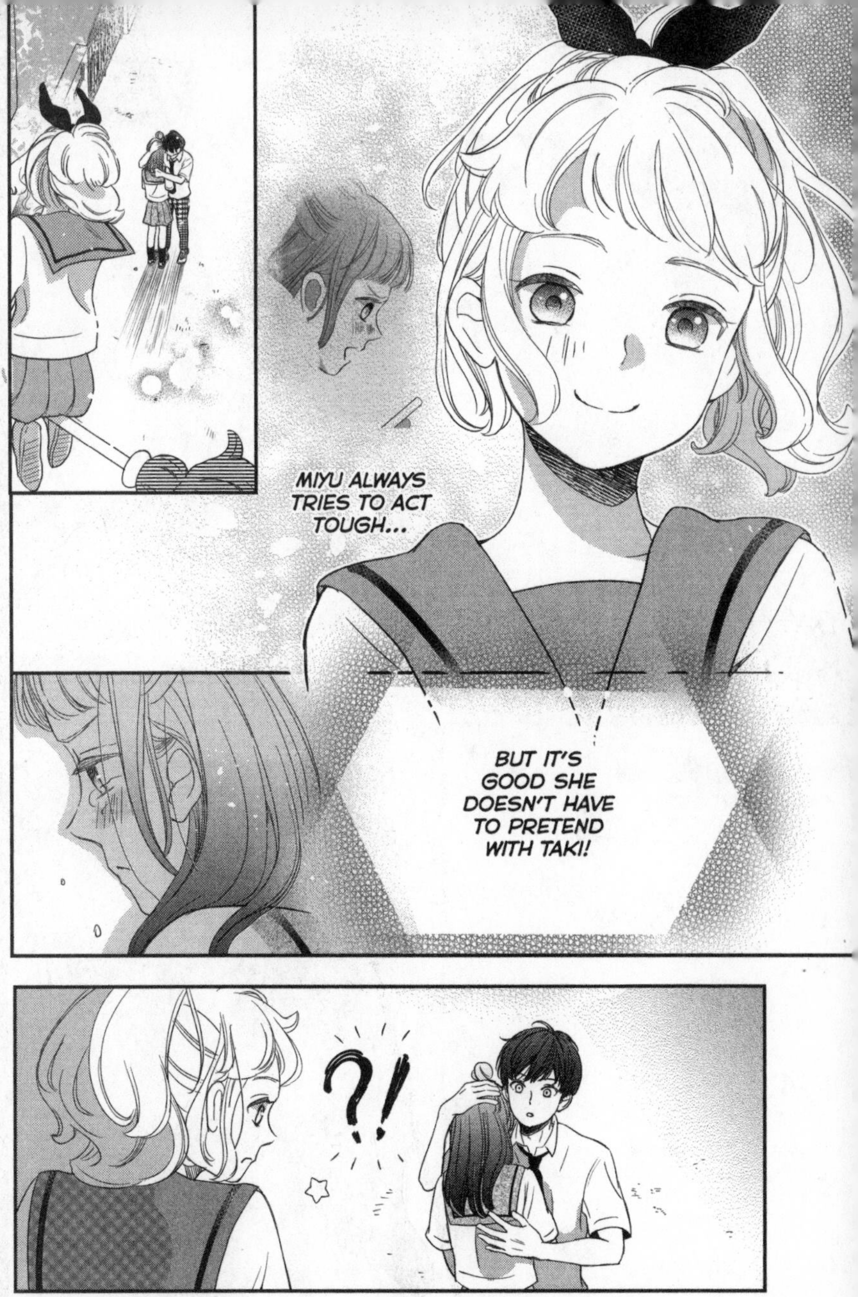
MIYU ALWAYS TRIES TO ACT TOUGH...
BUT IT'S GOOD SHE DOESN'T HAVE TO PRETEND WITH TAKI!
?!

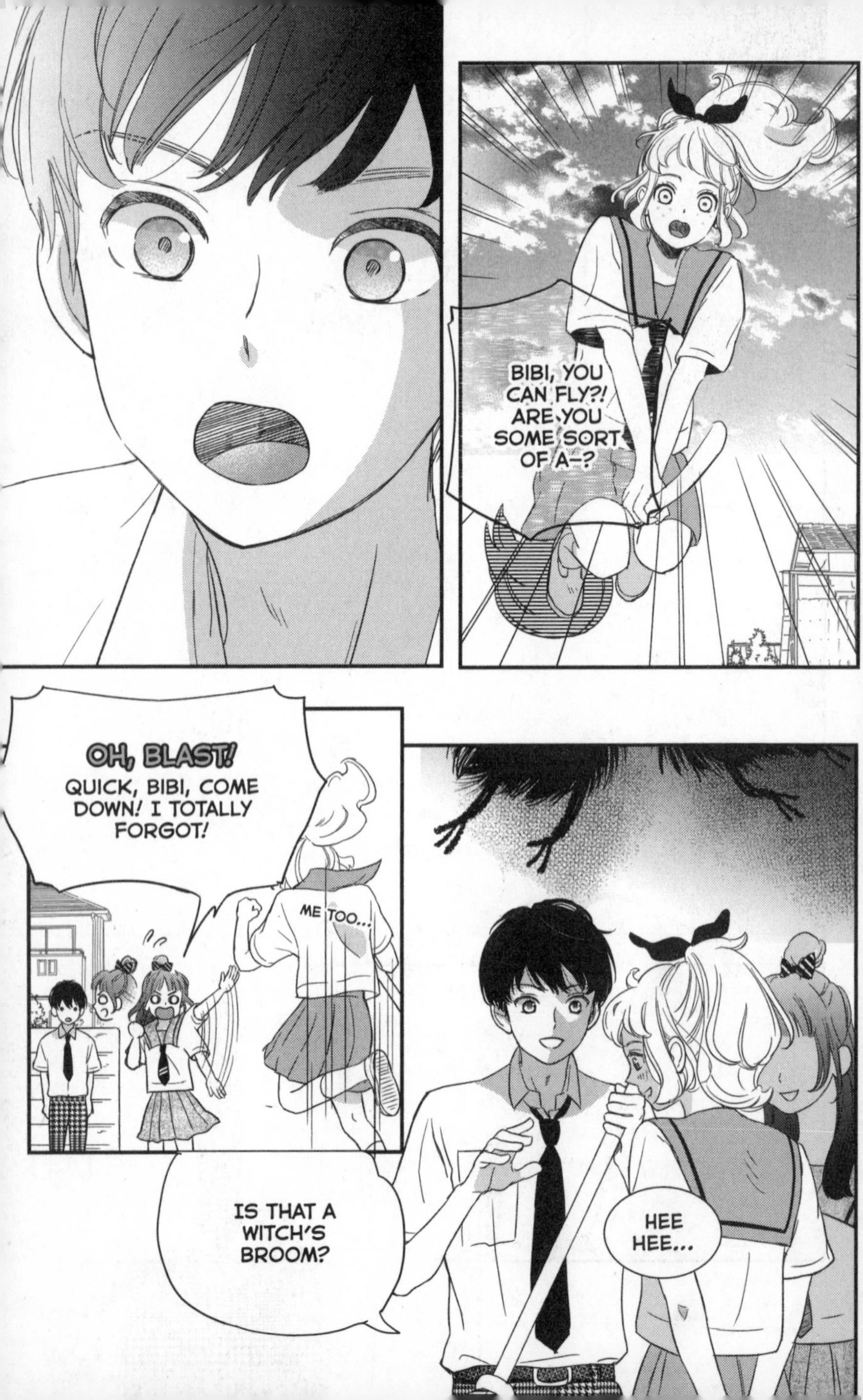
BIBI, YOU CAN FLY?! ARE YOU SOME SORT OF A-?
OH, BLAST!
QUICK, BIBI, COME DOWN! I TOTALLY FORGOT!
ME TOO...
IS THAT A WITCH'S BROOM?
HEE HEE...

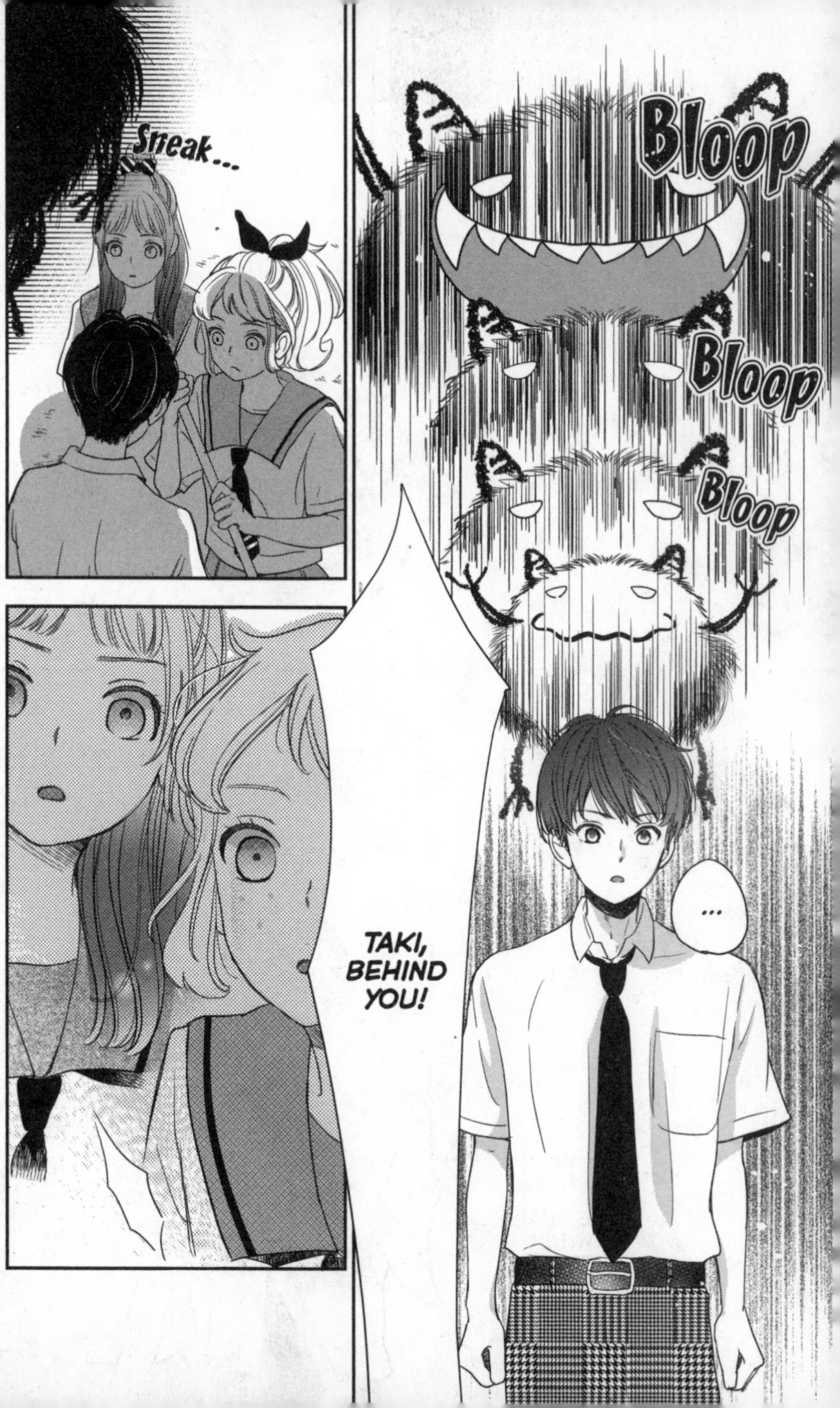
Bloop
Bloop
Bloop
...
TAKI, BEHIND YOU!
Sneak...

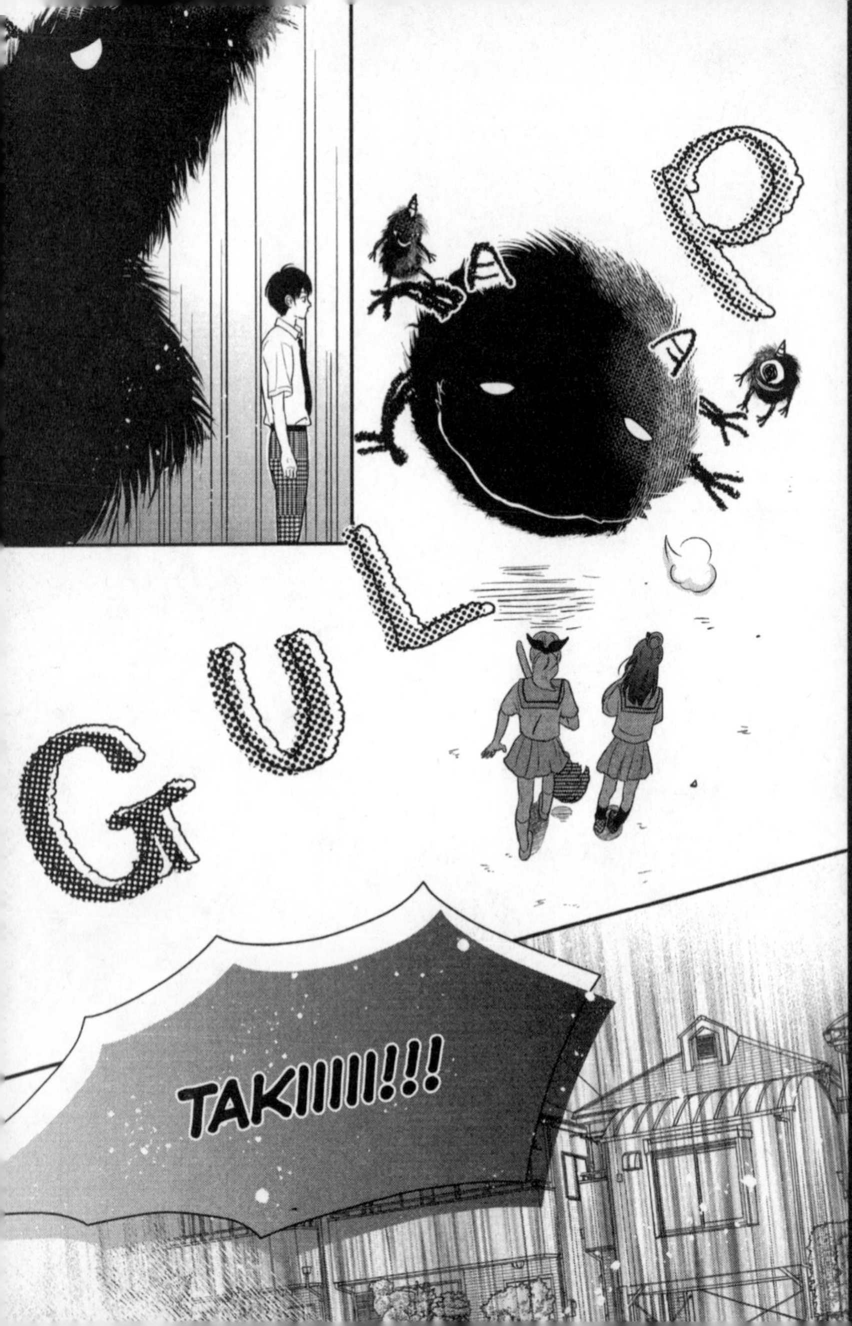
GULP
TAKIIIIII!!!

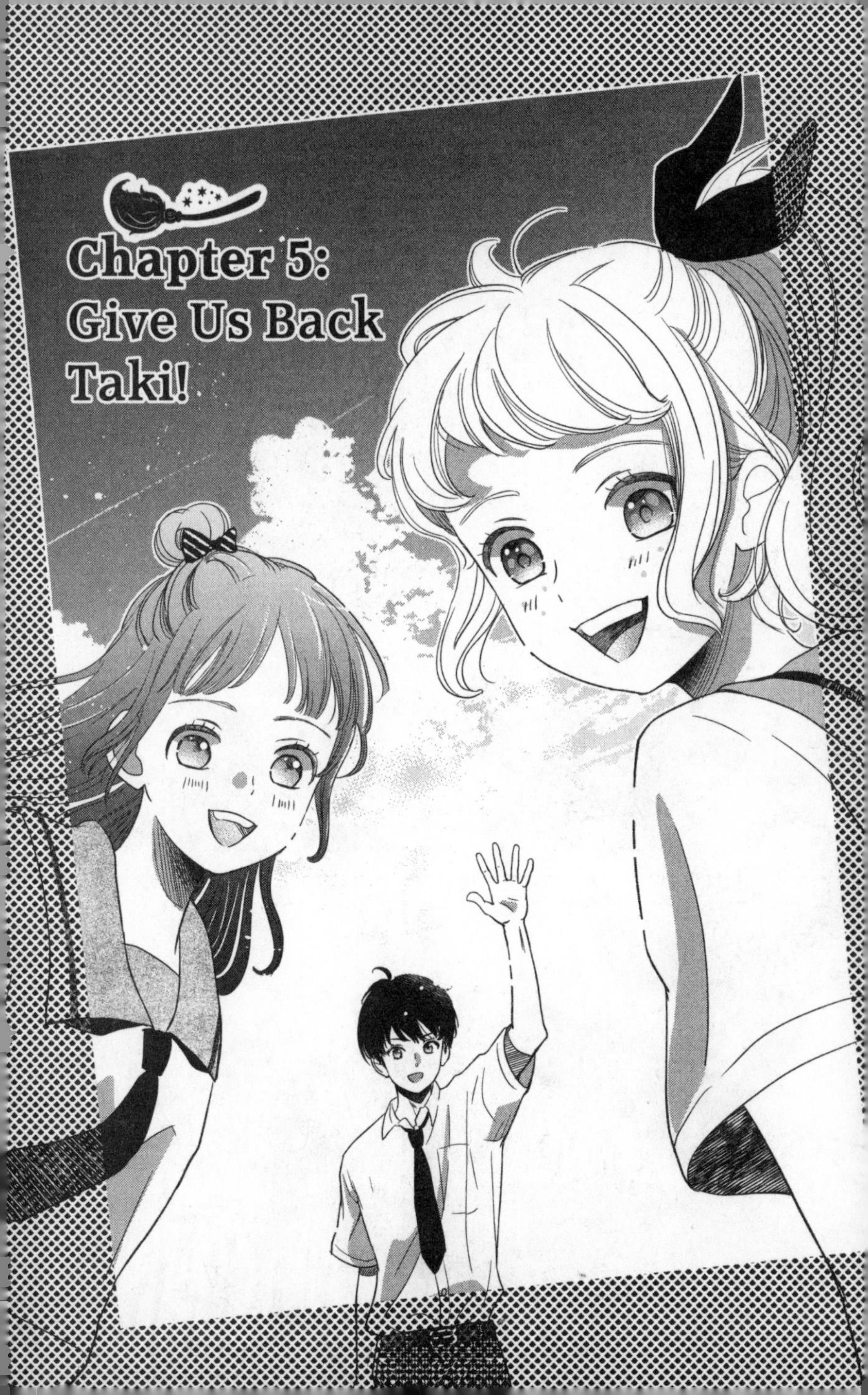
Chapter 5:
Give Us Back
Taki!

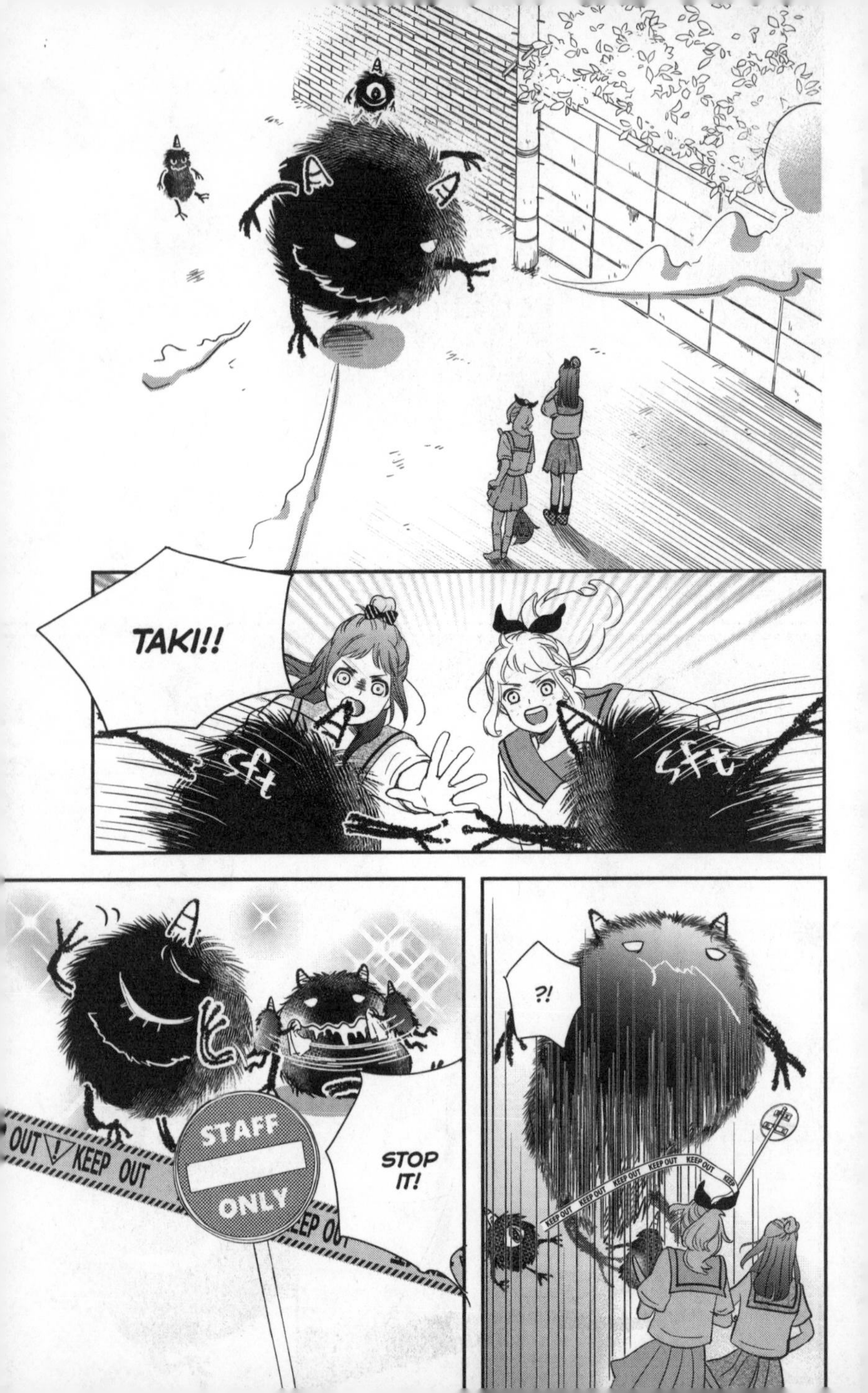
TAKI!!
sft
sft
?!
STOP IT!
STAFF
ONLY
OUT KEEP OUT
KEEP OU

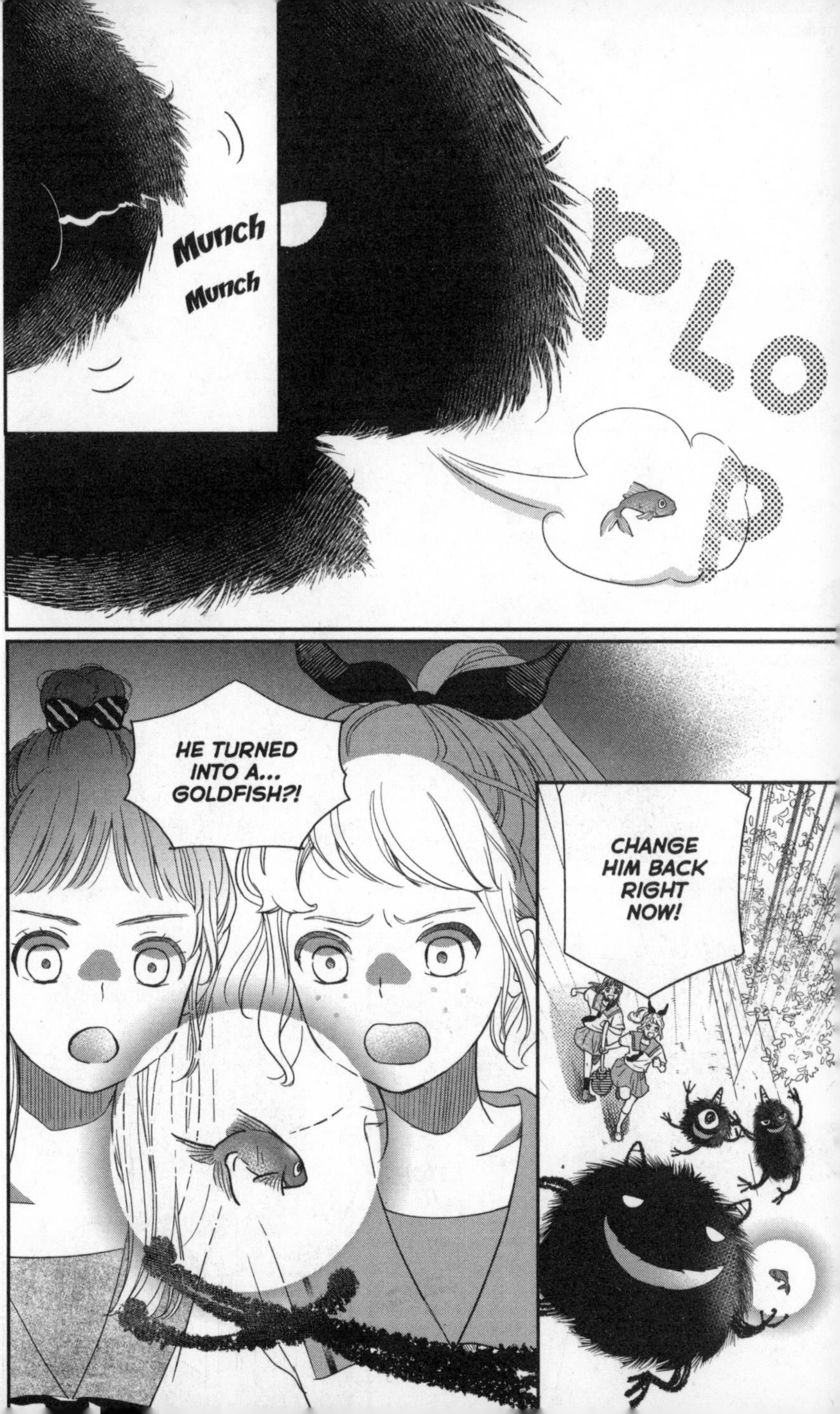
PLOP
Munch
Munch
CHANGE HIM BACK RIGHT NOW!
HE TURNED INTO A... GOLDFISH?!

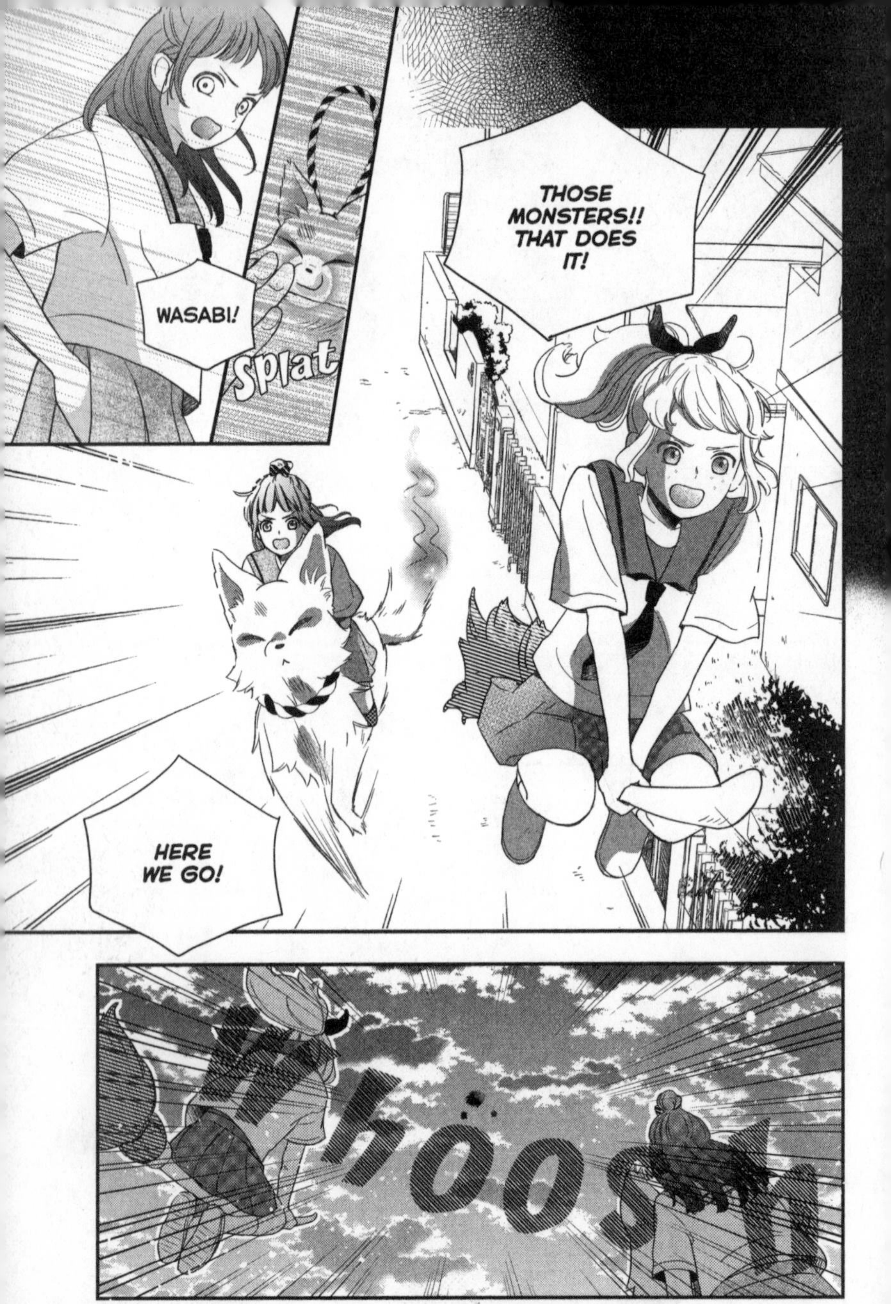
THOSE MONSTERS!! THAT DOES IT!
WASABI!
Splat
HERE WE GO!
WHOOSH

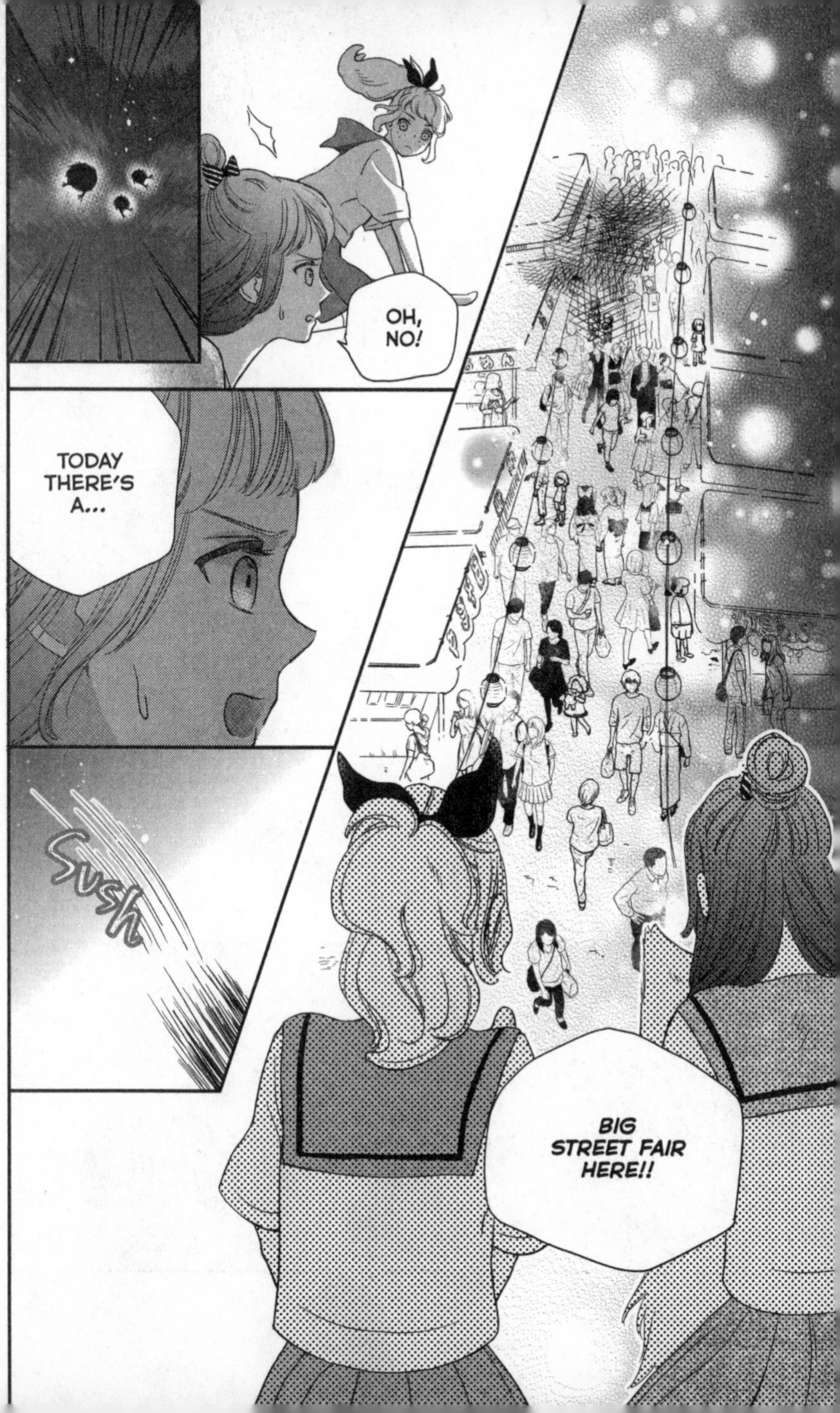
OH, NO!
TODAY THERE'S A...
Sush
BIG STREET FAIR HERE!!

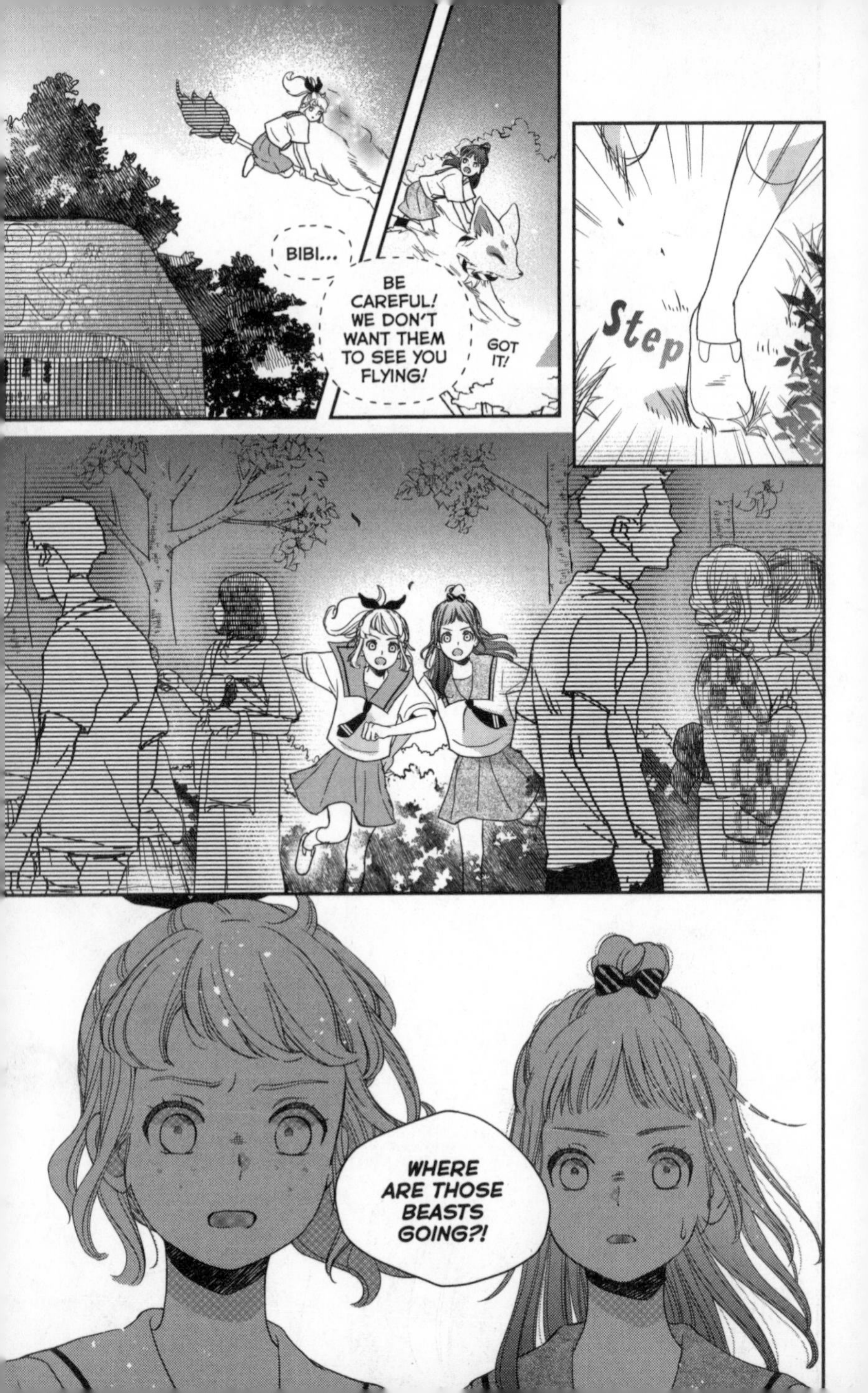
Step
BIBI...
BE CAREFUL! WE DON'T WANT THEM TO SEE YOU FLYING!
GOT IT!
WHERE ARE THOSE BEASTS GOING?!

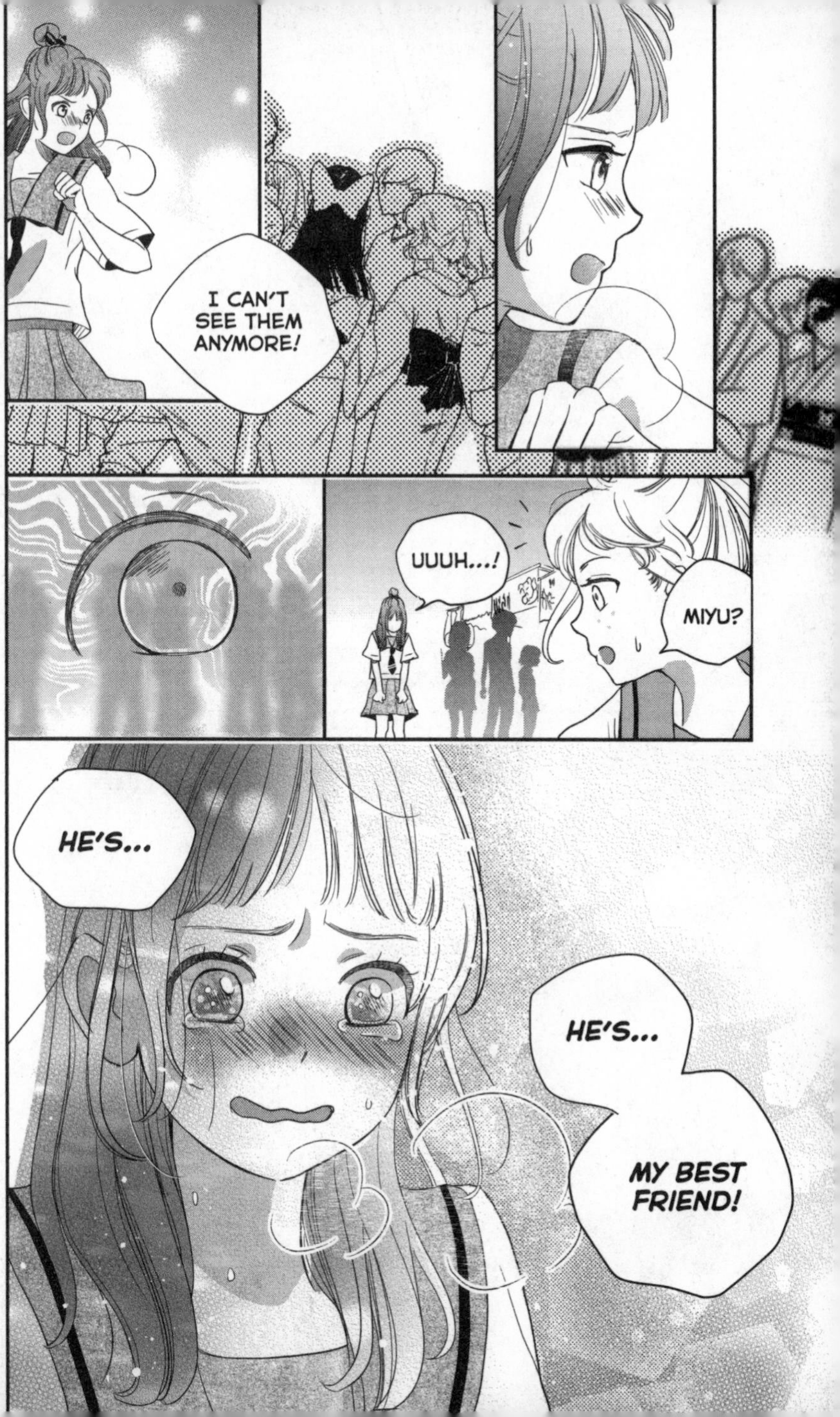
I CAN'T SEE THEM ANYMORE!
MIYU?
UUUH...!
HE'S...
HE'S...
MY BEST FRIEND!

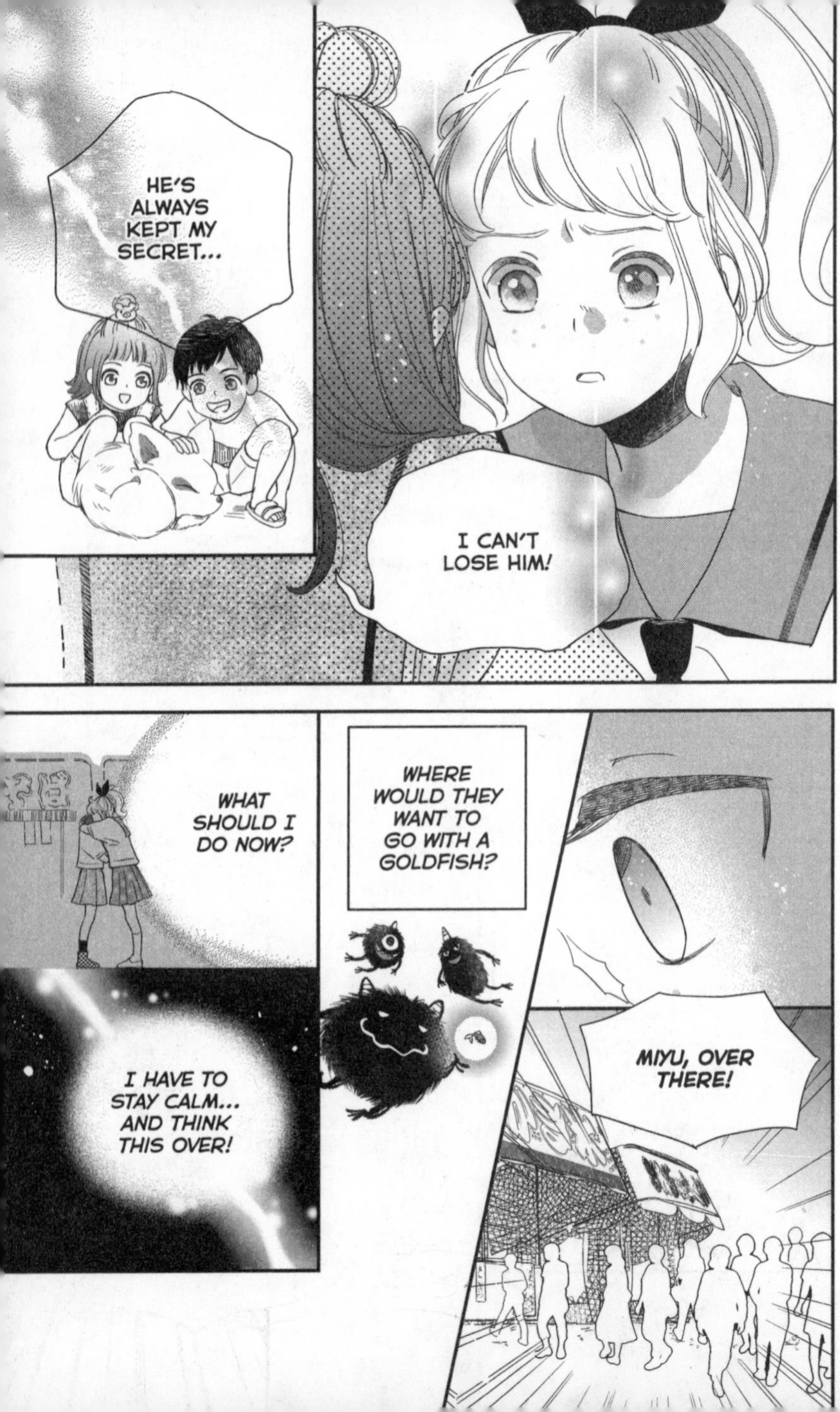
HE'S ALWAYS KEPT MY SECRET...
I CAN'T LOSE HIM!
WHAT SHOULD I DO NOW?
I HAVE TO STAY CALM... AND THINK THIS OVER!
WHERE WOULD THEY WANT TO GO WITH A GOLDFISH?
MIYU, OVER THERE!

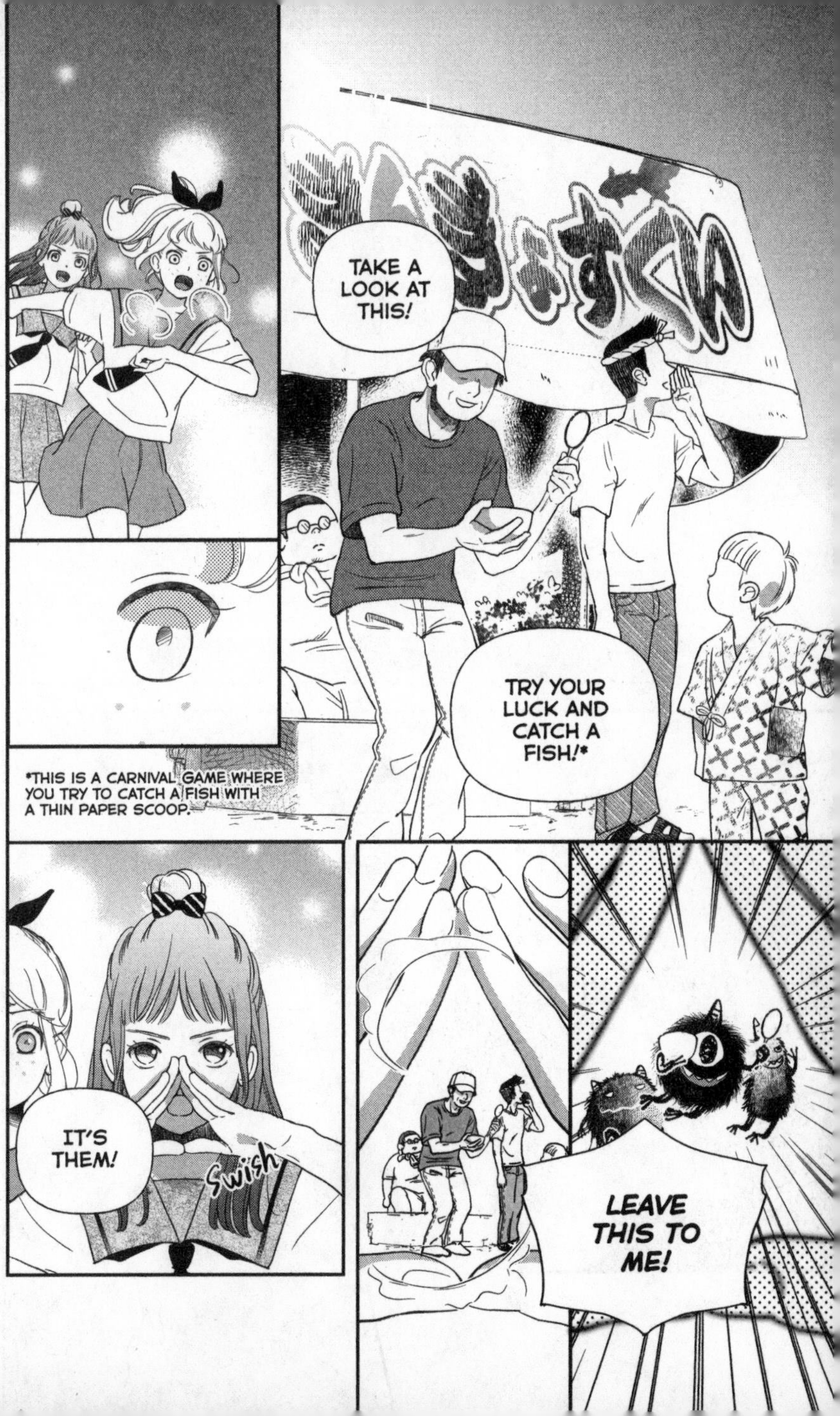
TAKE A LOOK AT THIS!
TRY YOUR LUCK AND CATCH A FISH!*
*THIS IS A CARNIVAL GAME WHERE YOU TRY TO CATCH A FISH WITH A THIN PAPER SCOOP.
LEAVE THIS TO ME!
IT'S THEM!
Swish

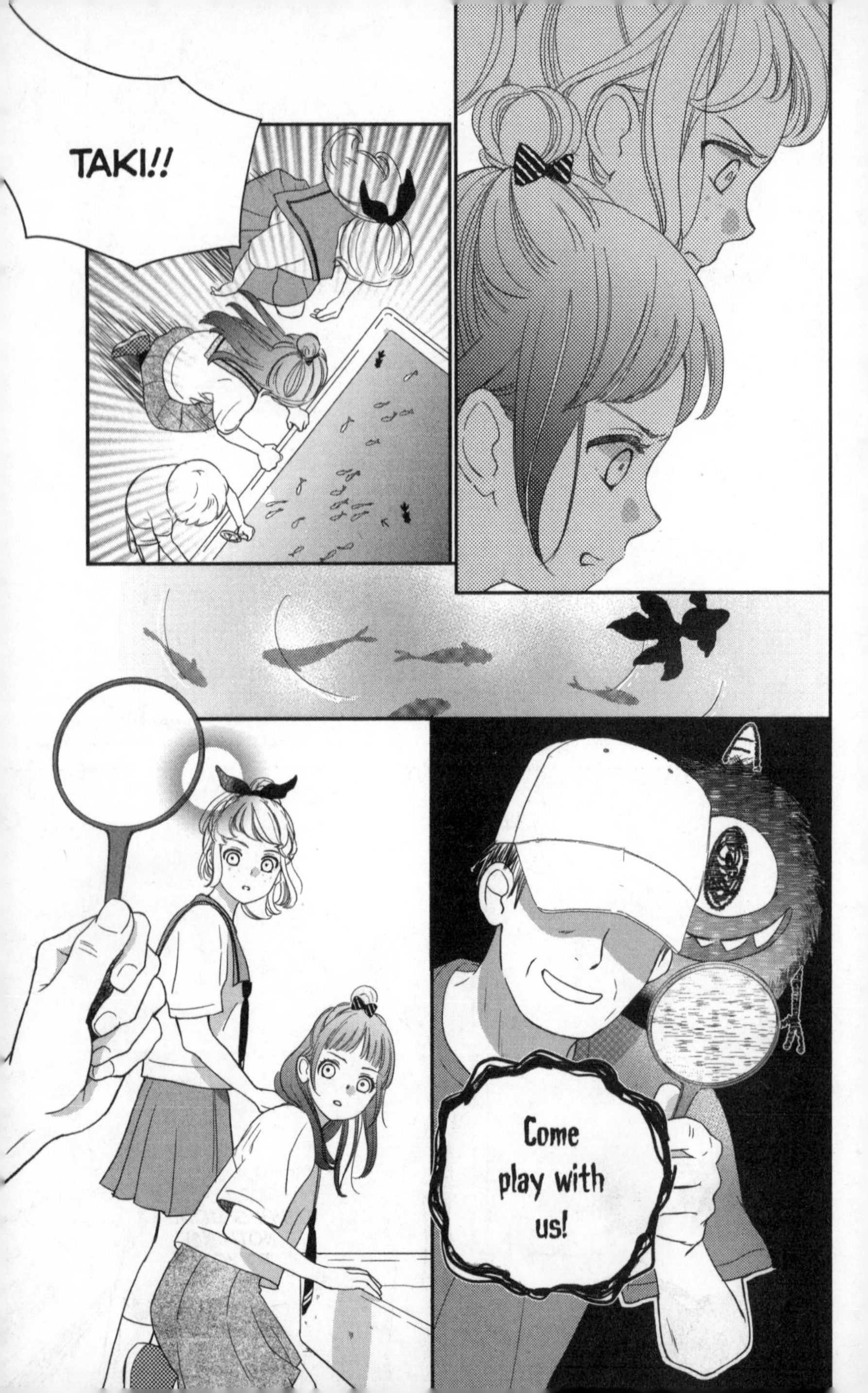
TAKI!!
Come play with us!

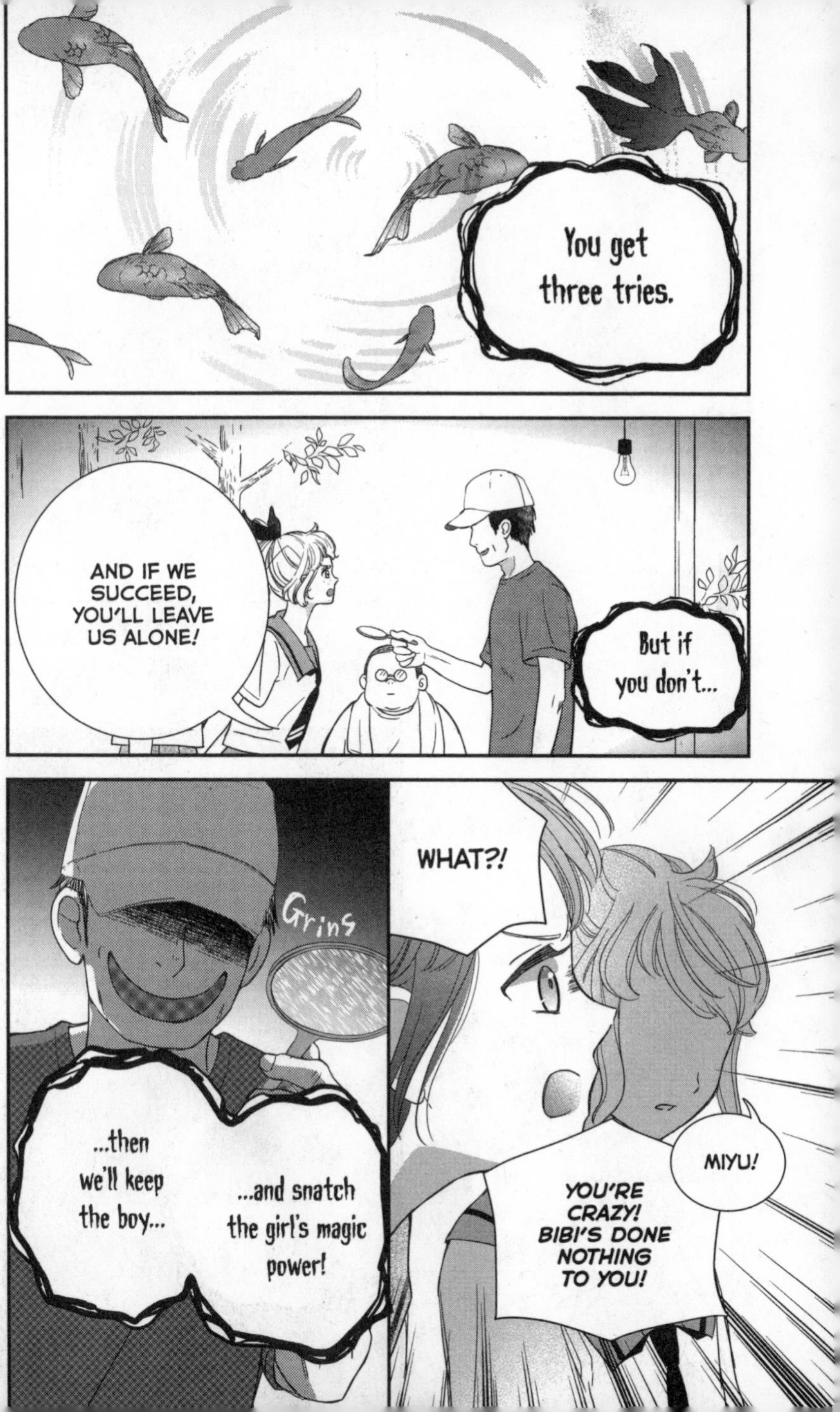
You get three tries.
AND IF WE SUCCEED, YOU'LL LEAVE US ALONE!
But if you don't...
Grins
...then we'll keep the boy...
...and snatch the girl's magic power!
WHAT?!
MIYU!
YOU'RE CRAZY! BIBI'S DONE NOTHING TO YOU!

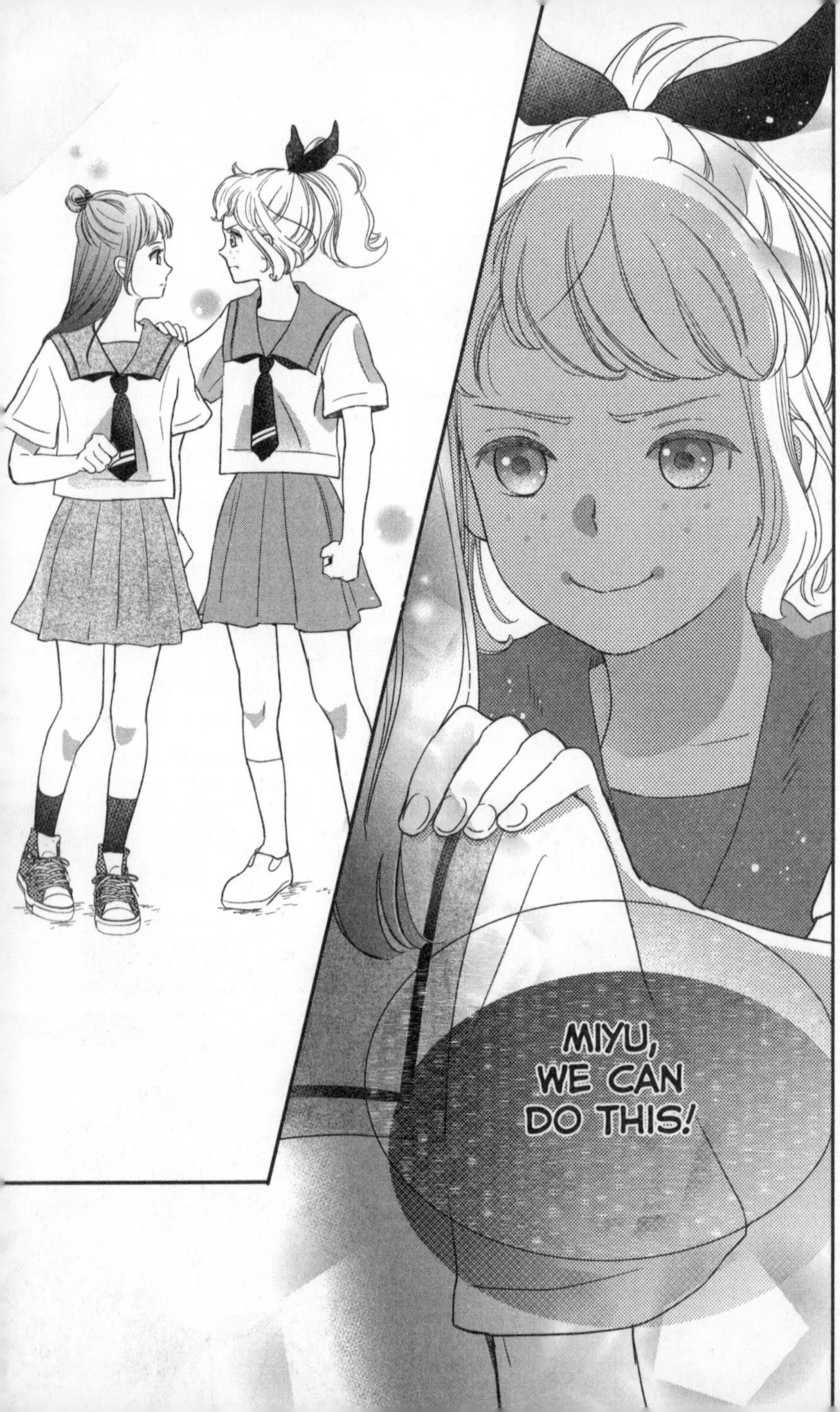
MIYU,
WE CAN
DO THIS!

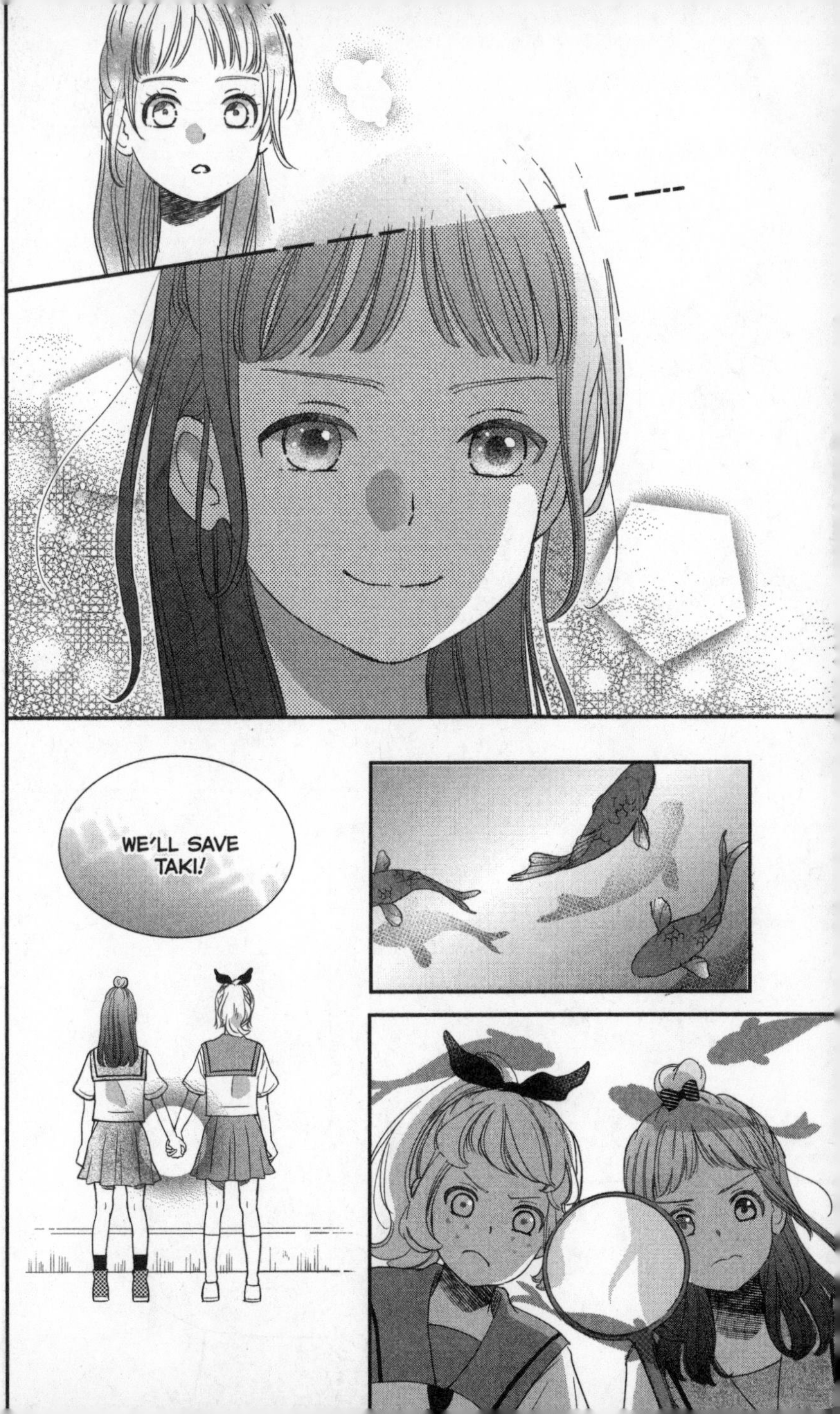
WE'LL SAVE TAKI!

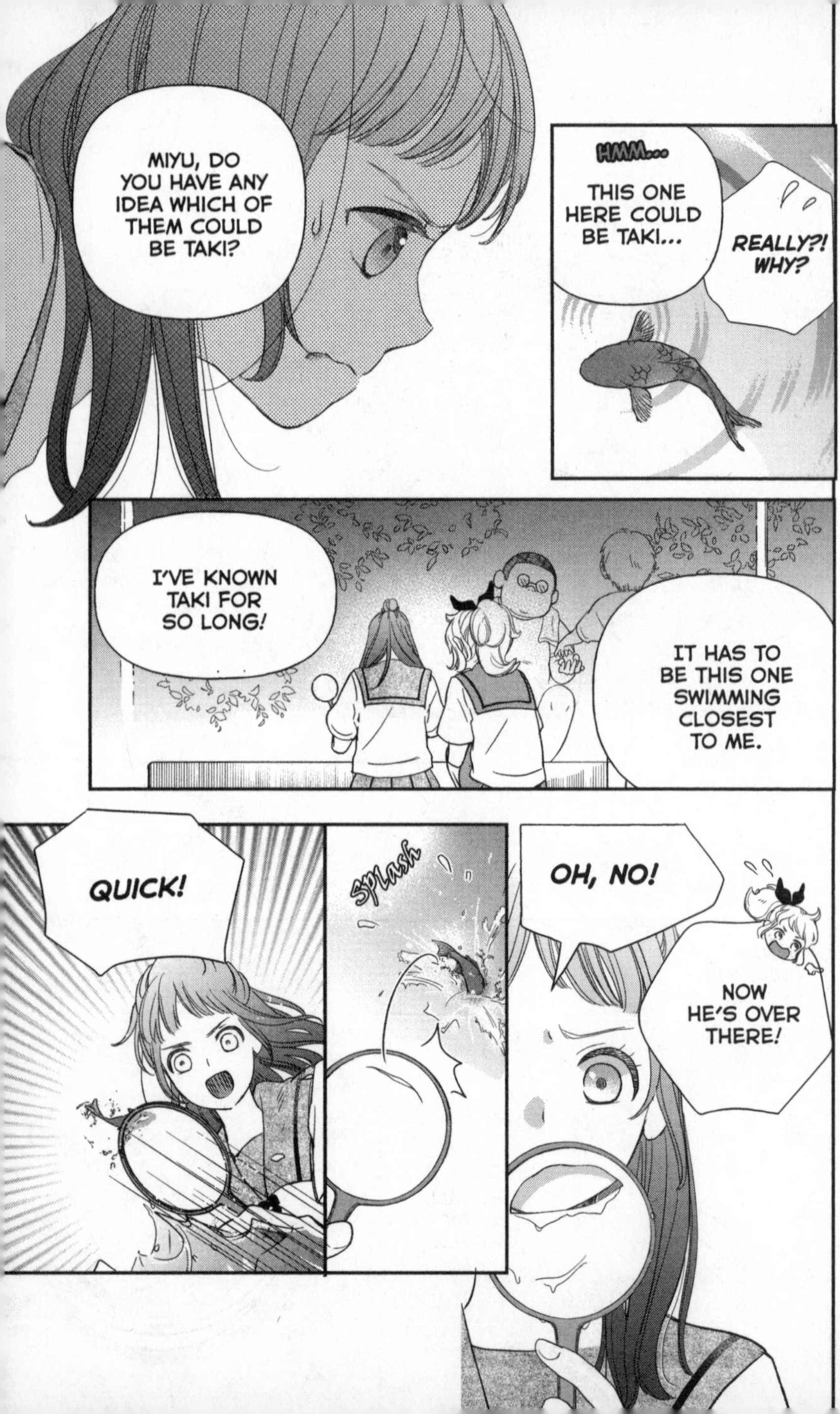
MIYU, DO YOU HAVE ANY IDEA WHICH OF THEM COULD BE TAKI?
HMM...
THIS ONE HERE COULD BE TAKI...
REALLY?! WHY?
I'VE KNOWN TAKI FOR SO LONG!
IT HAS TO BE THIS ONE SWIMMING CLOSEST TO ME.
QUICK!
SPLASH
OH, NO!
NOW HE'S OVER THERE!

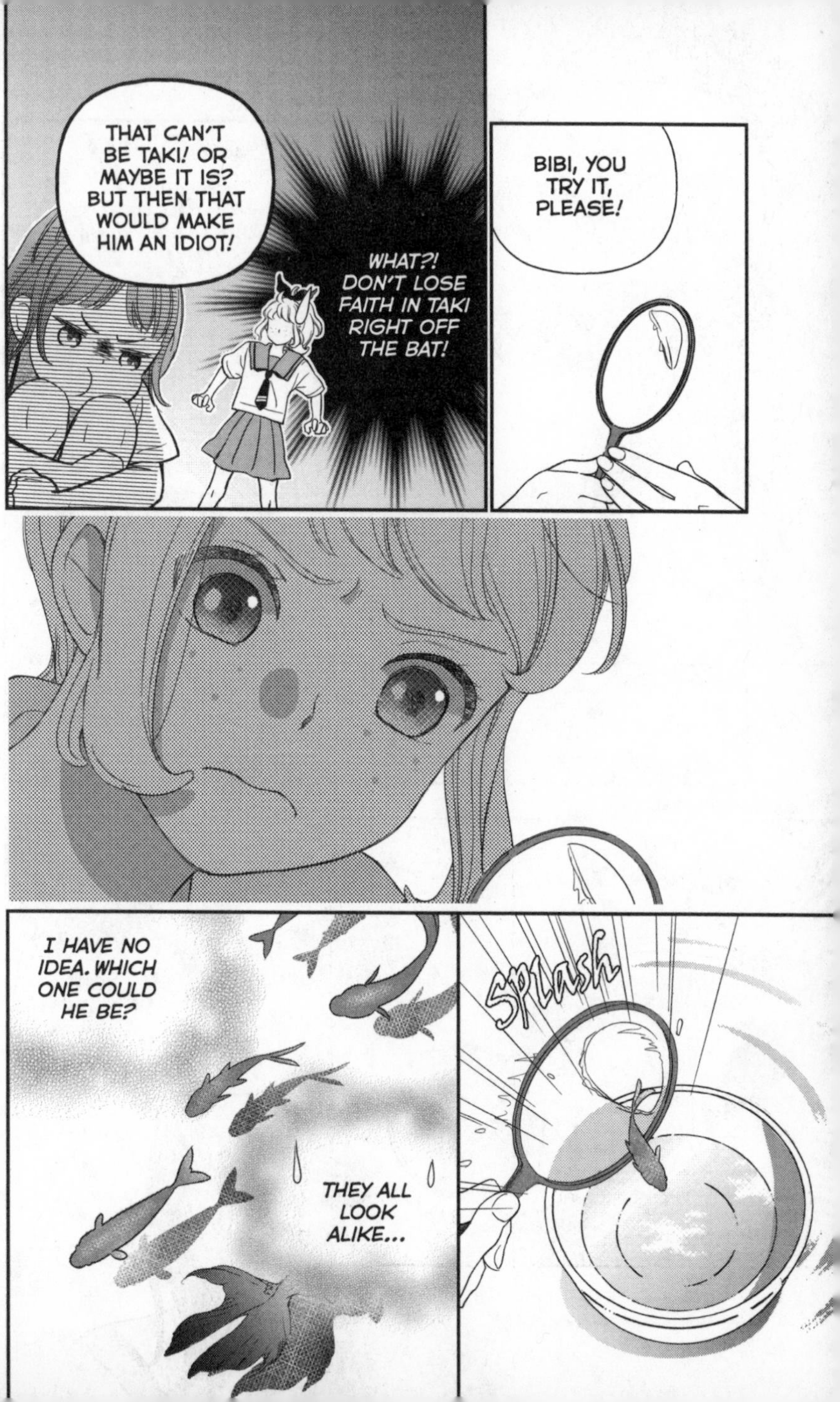
THAT CAN'T BE TAKI! OR MAYBE IT IS? BUT THEN THAT WOULD MAKE HIM AN IDIOT!
WHAT?! DON'T LOSE FAITH IN TAKI RIGHT OFF THE BAT!
BIBI, YOU TRY IT, PLEASE!
I HAVE NO IDEA. WHICH ONE COULD HE BE?
THEY ALL LOOK ALIKE...
SPLASH

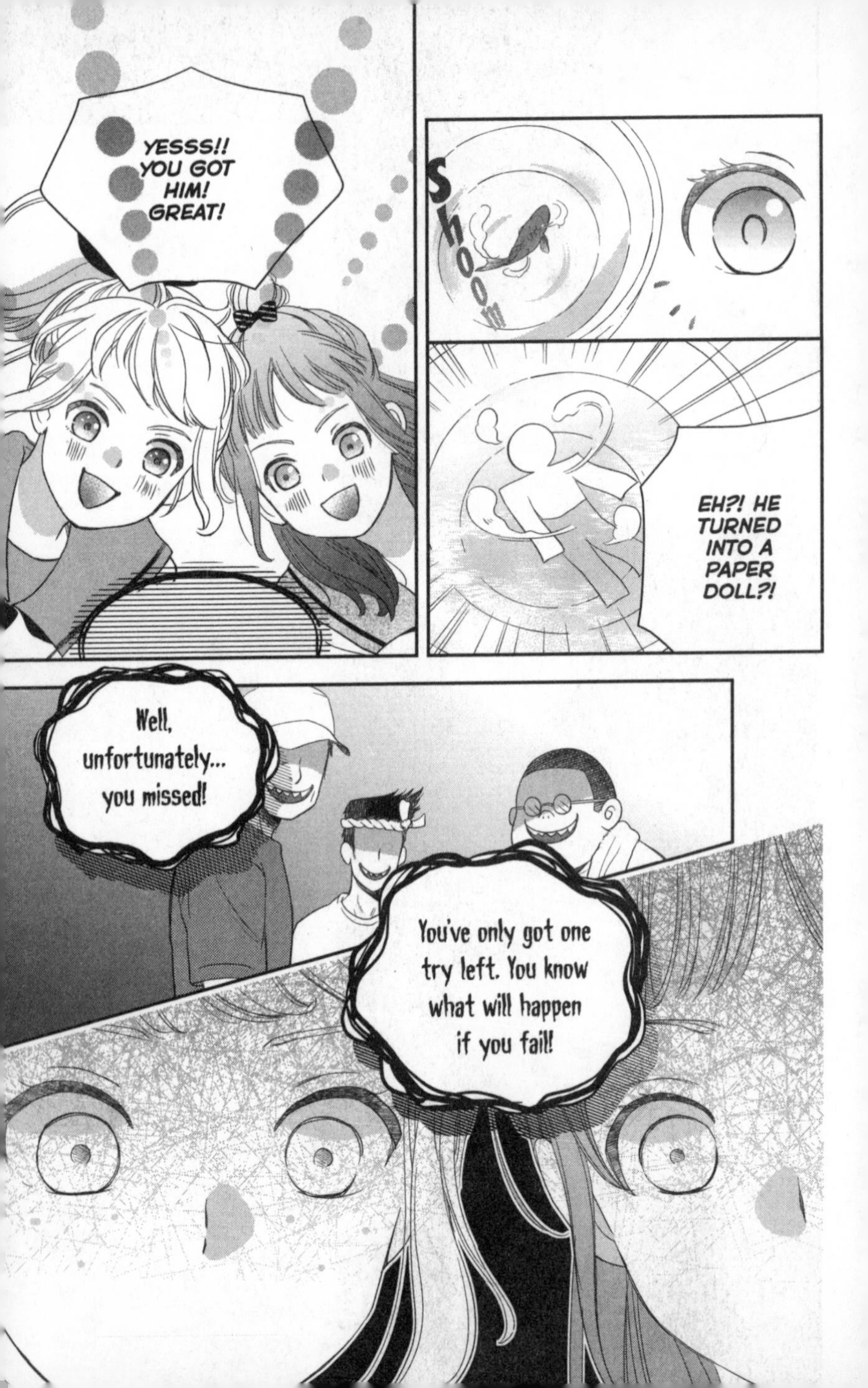
Shoom
EH?! HE TURNED INTO A PAPER DOLL?!
YESSS!! YOU GOT HIM! GREAT!
Well, unfortunately... you missed!
You've only got one try left. You know what will happen if you fail!

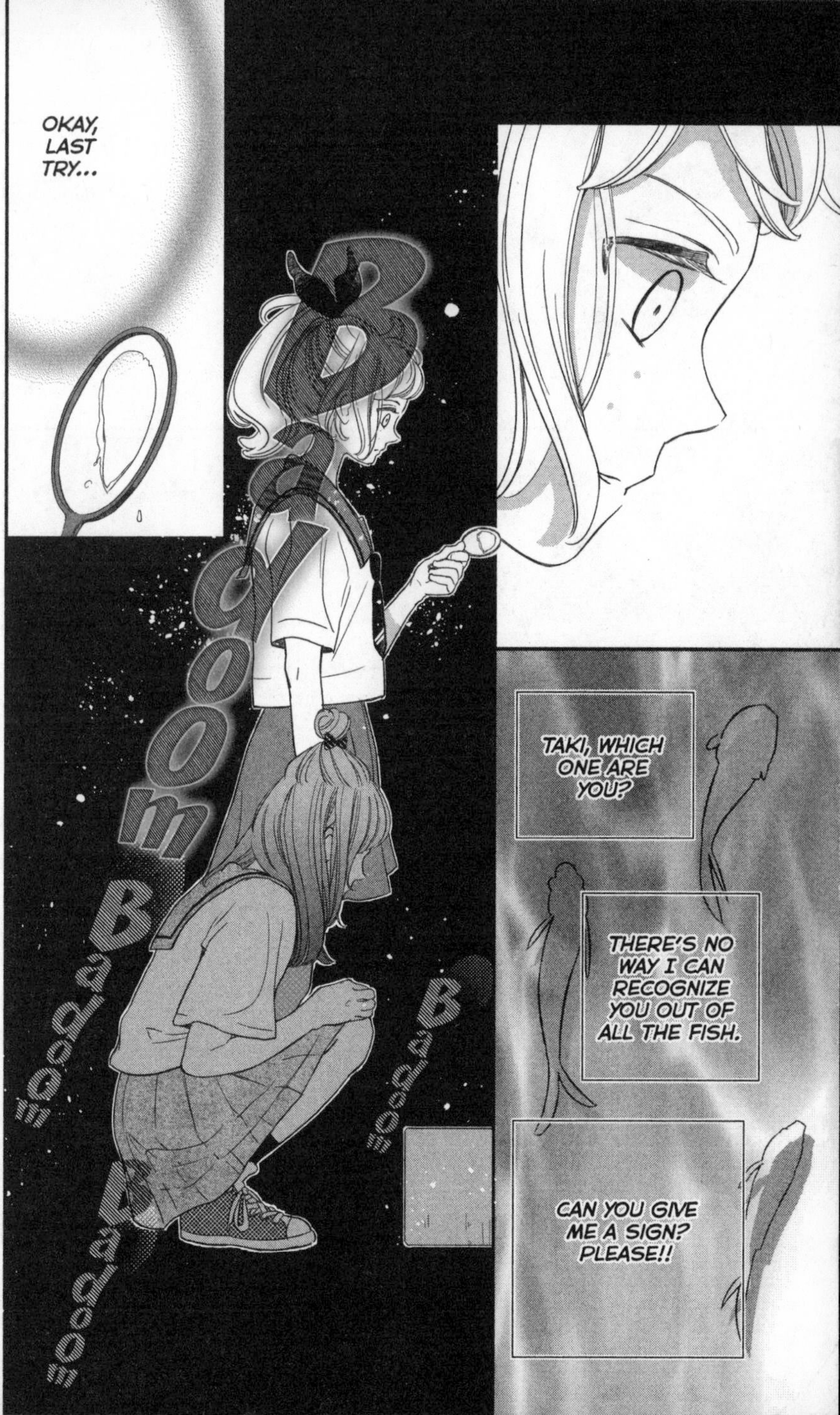
OKAY, LAST TRY...
TAKI, WHICH ONE ARE YOU?
THERE'S NO WAY I CAN RECOGNIZE YOU OUT OF ALL THE FISH.
CAN YOU GIVE ME A SIGN? PLEASE!!
Badoom
Badoom
Badoom
Badoom

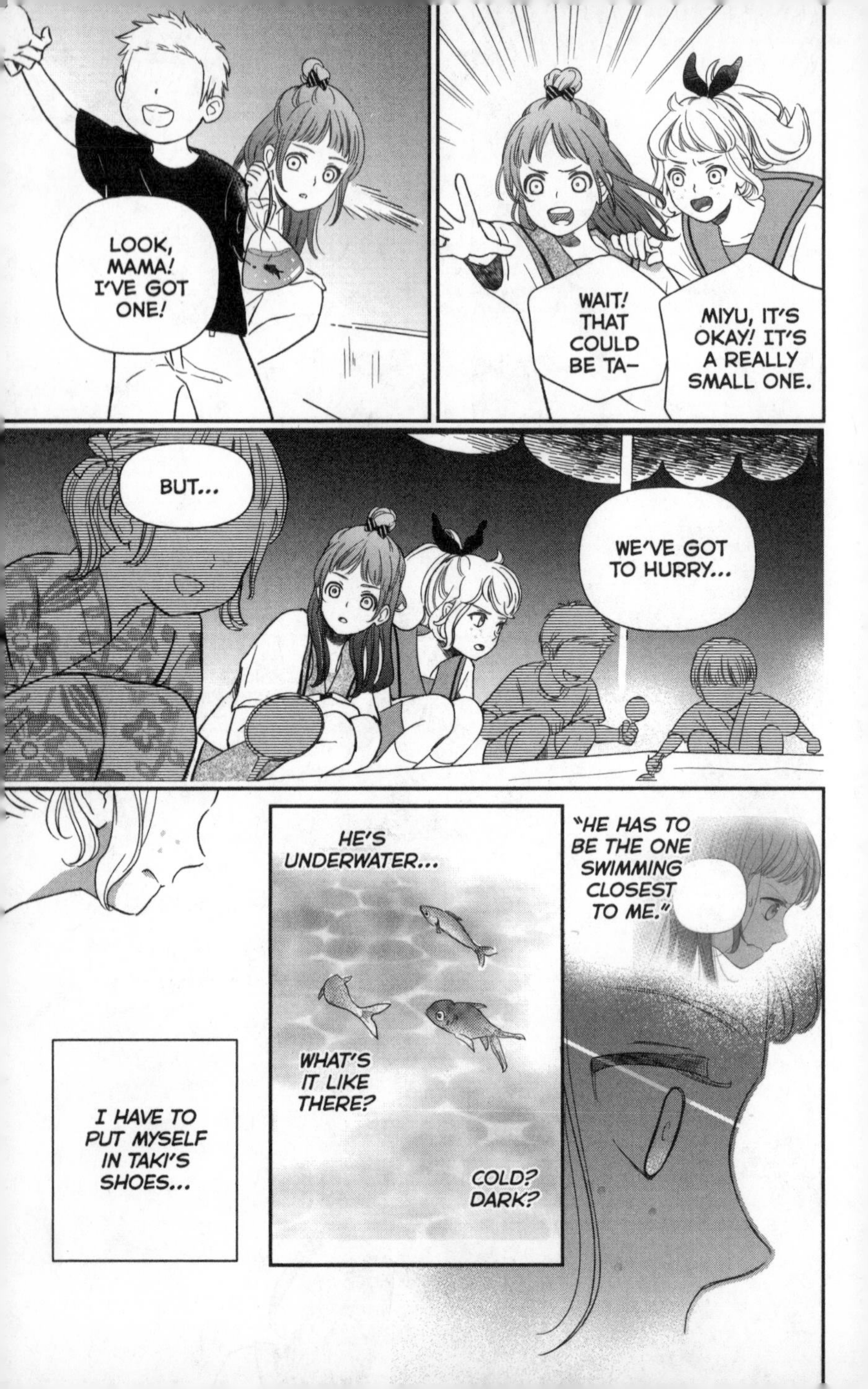
LOOK, MAMA! I'VE GOT ONE!
WAIT! THAT COULD BE TA–
MIYU, IT'S OKAY! IT'S A REALLY SMALL ONE.
BUT...
WE'VE GOT TO HURRY...
I HAVE TO PUT MYSELF IN TAKI'S SHOES...
HE'S UNDERWATER...
WHAT'S IT LIKE THERE?
COLD? DARK?
"HE HAS TO BE THE ONE SWIMMING CLOSEST TO ME."

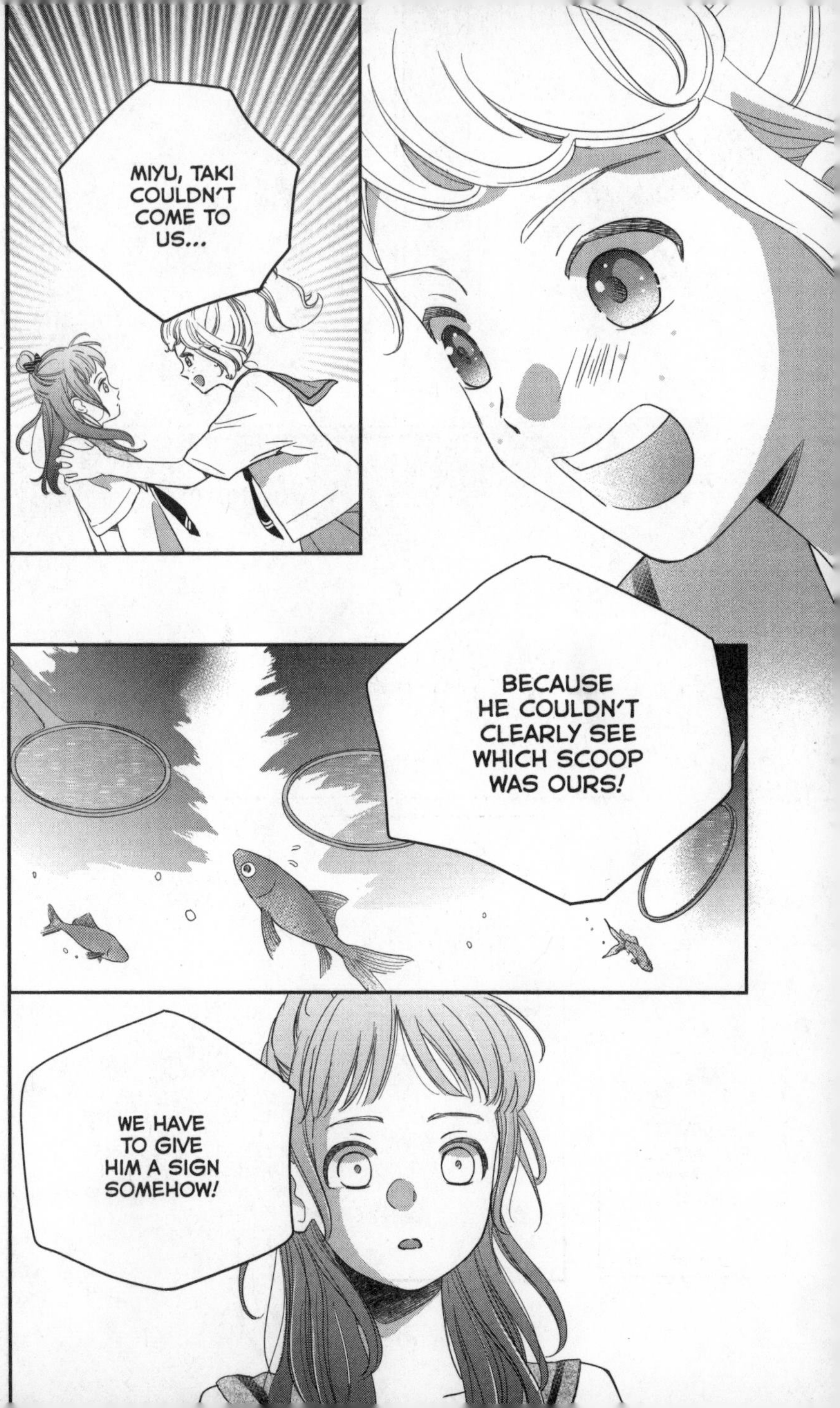
MIYU, TAKI COULDN'T COME TO US...
BECAUSE HE COULDN'T CLEARLY SEE WHICH SCOOP WAS OURS!
WE HAVE TO GIVE HIM A SIGN SOMEHOW!

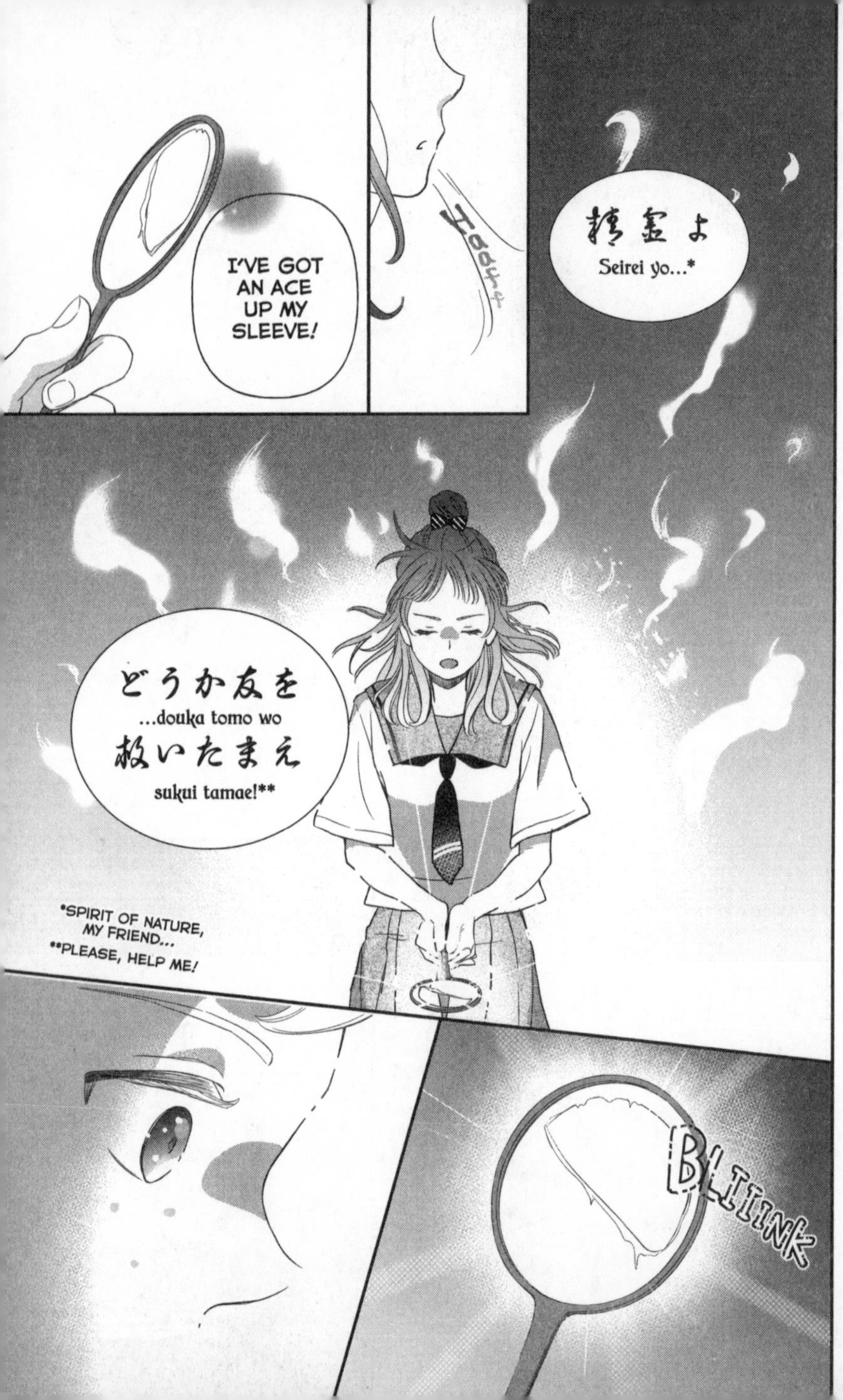
HOOFF
I'VE GOT AN ACE UP MY SLEEVE!
精霊よ
Seirei yo...*
どうか友を
...douka tomo wo
救いたまえ
sukui tamae!**
*SPIRIT OF NATURE, MY FRIEND...
**PLEASE, HELP ME!
BLIIINK

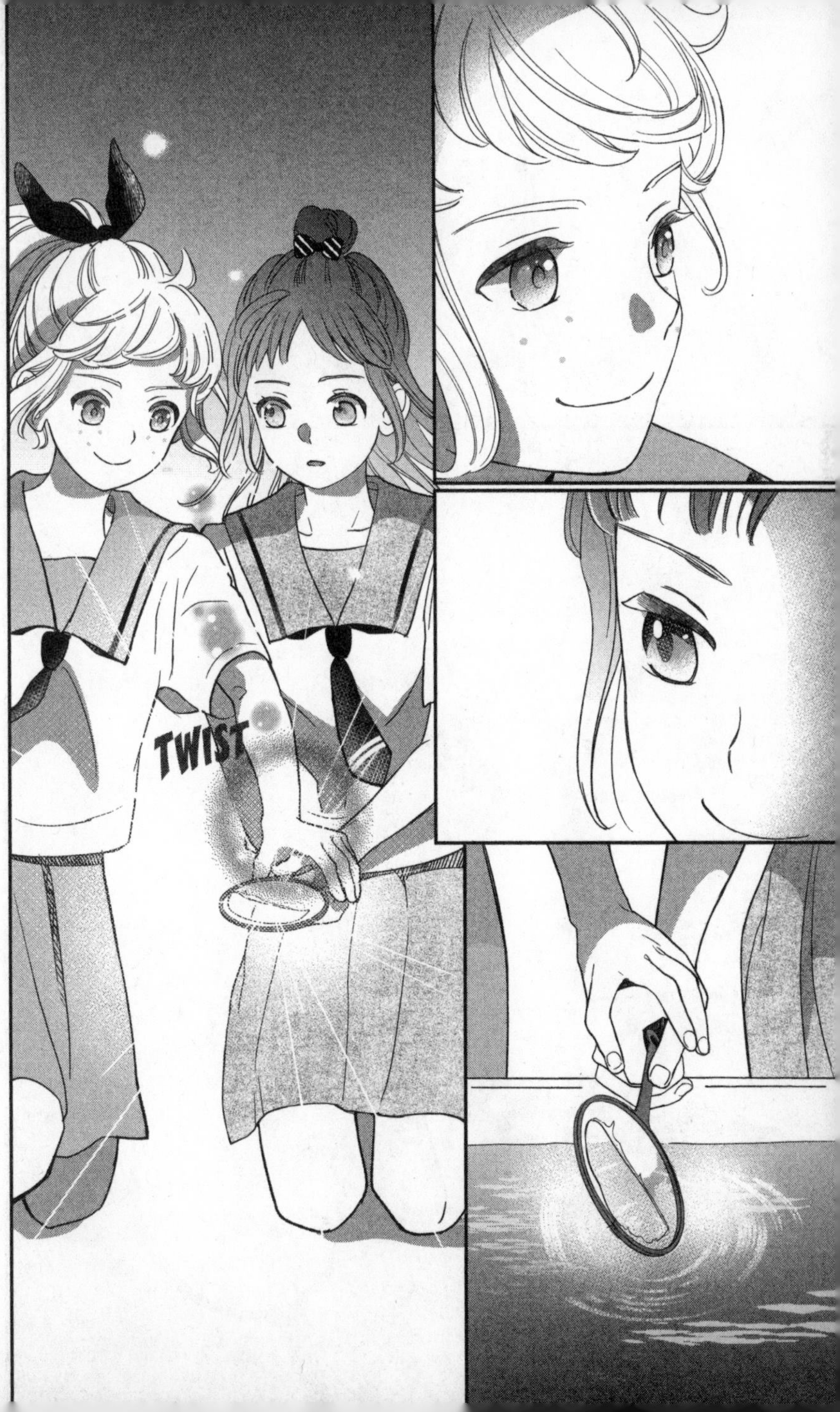
TWIST

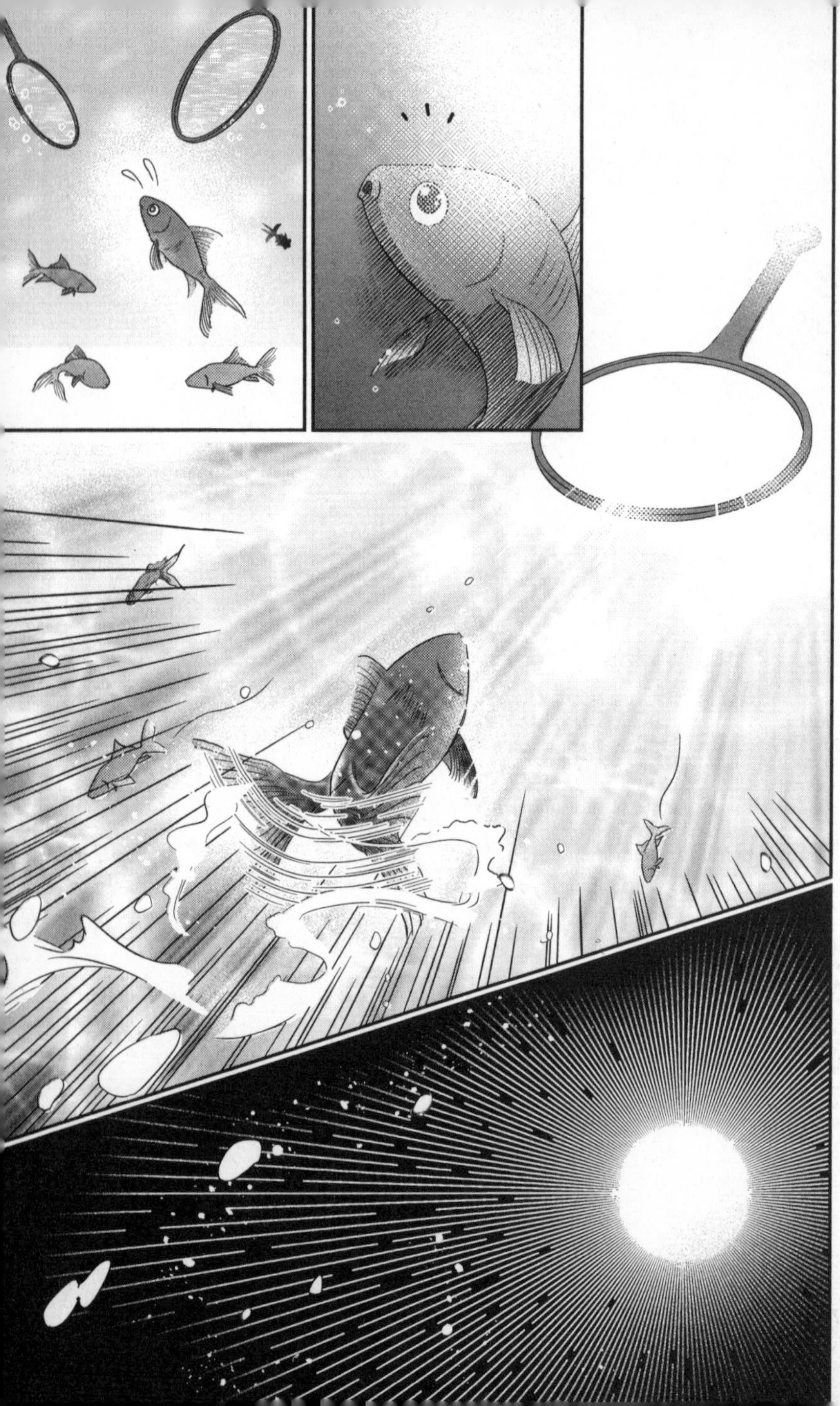

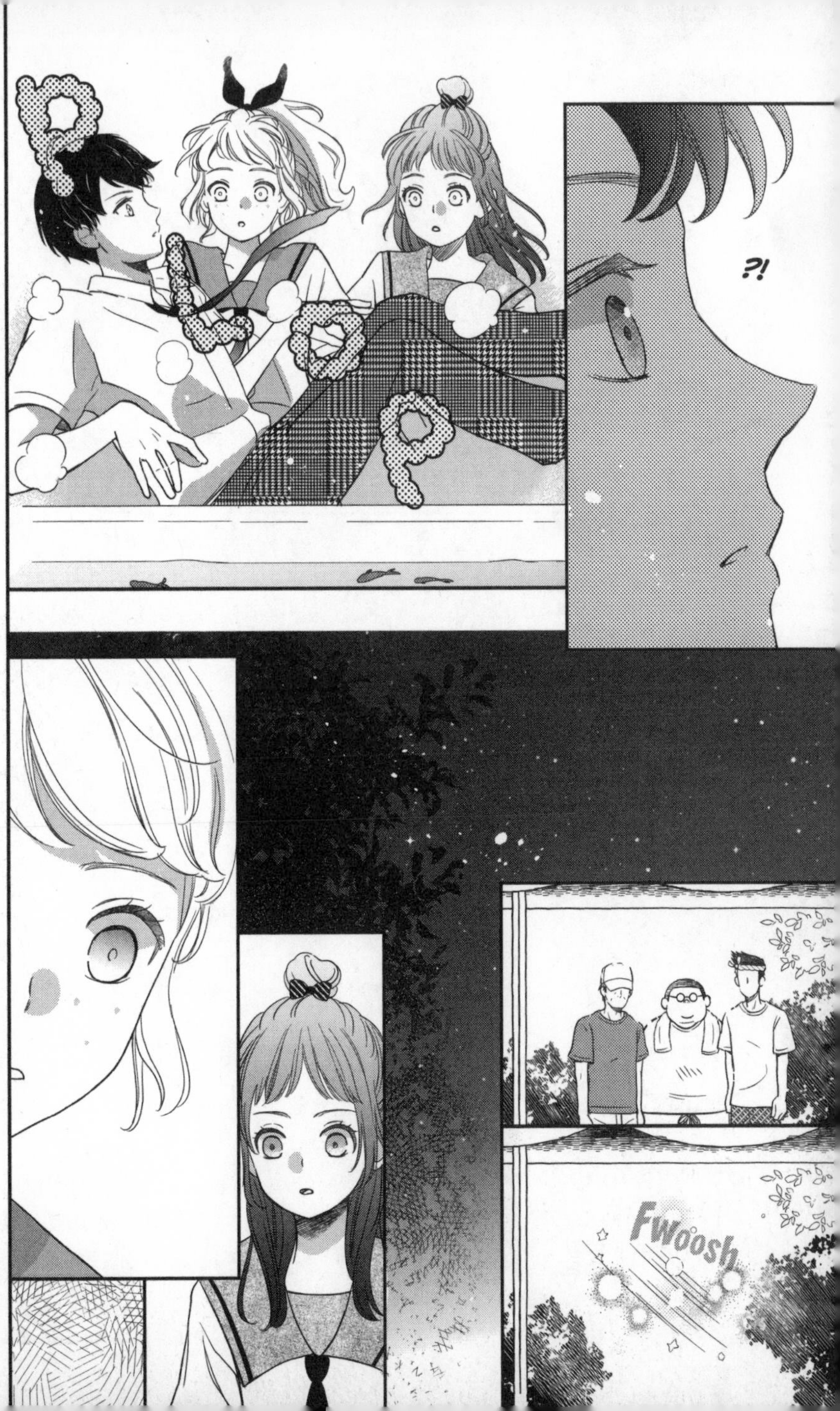
?!
Fwoosh

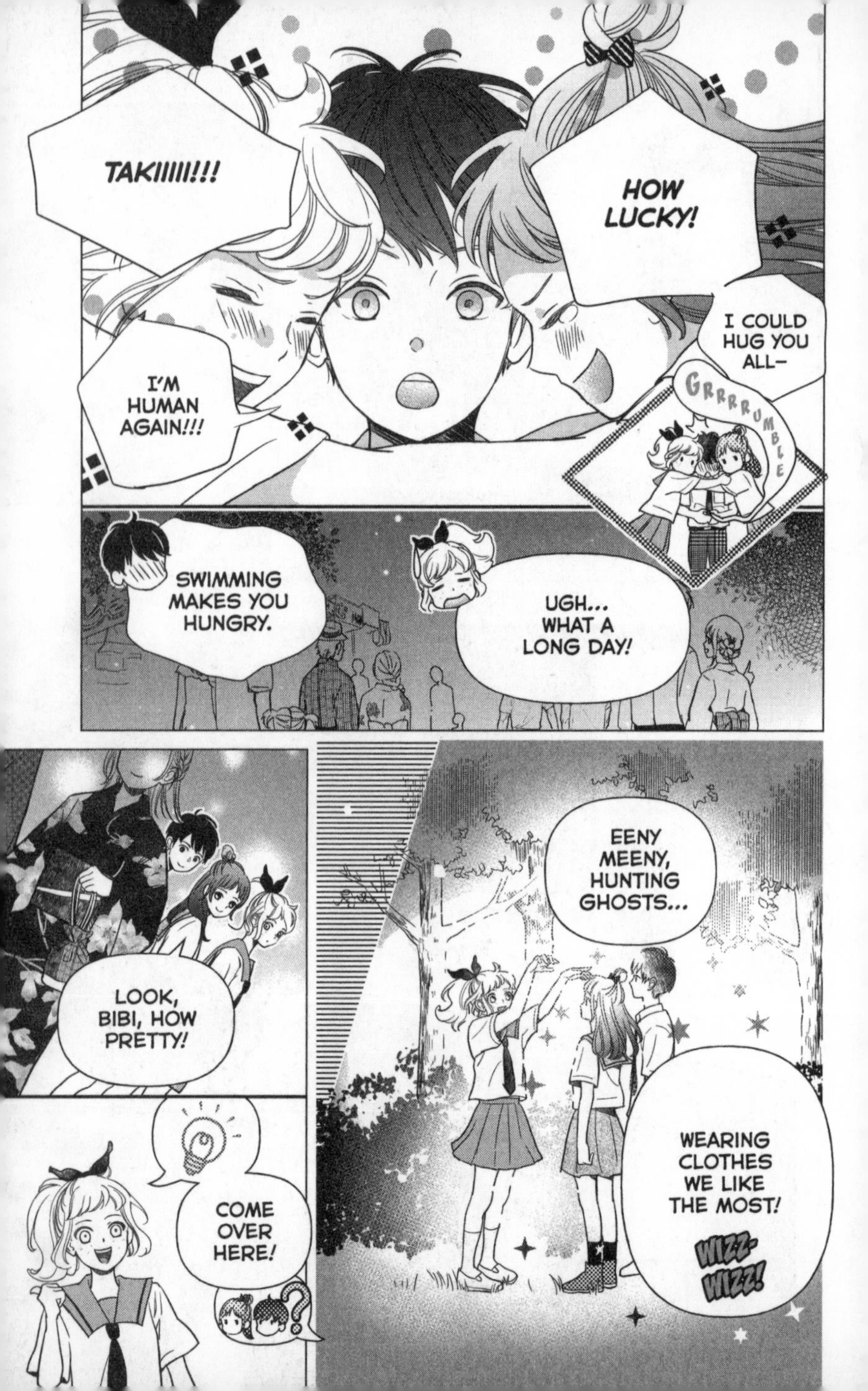
HOW LUCKY!
TAKIIIIII!!!
I COULD HUG YOU ALL–
GRRRRUMBLE
I'M HUMAN AGAIN!!!
UGH... WHAT A LONG DAY!
SWIMMING MAKES YOU HUNGRY.
EENY MEENY, HUNTING GHOSTS...
WEARING CLOTHES WE LIKE THE MOST!
WIZZ-WIZZ!
LOOK, BIBI, HOW PRETTY!
COME OVER HERE!

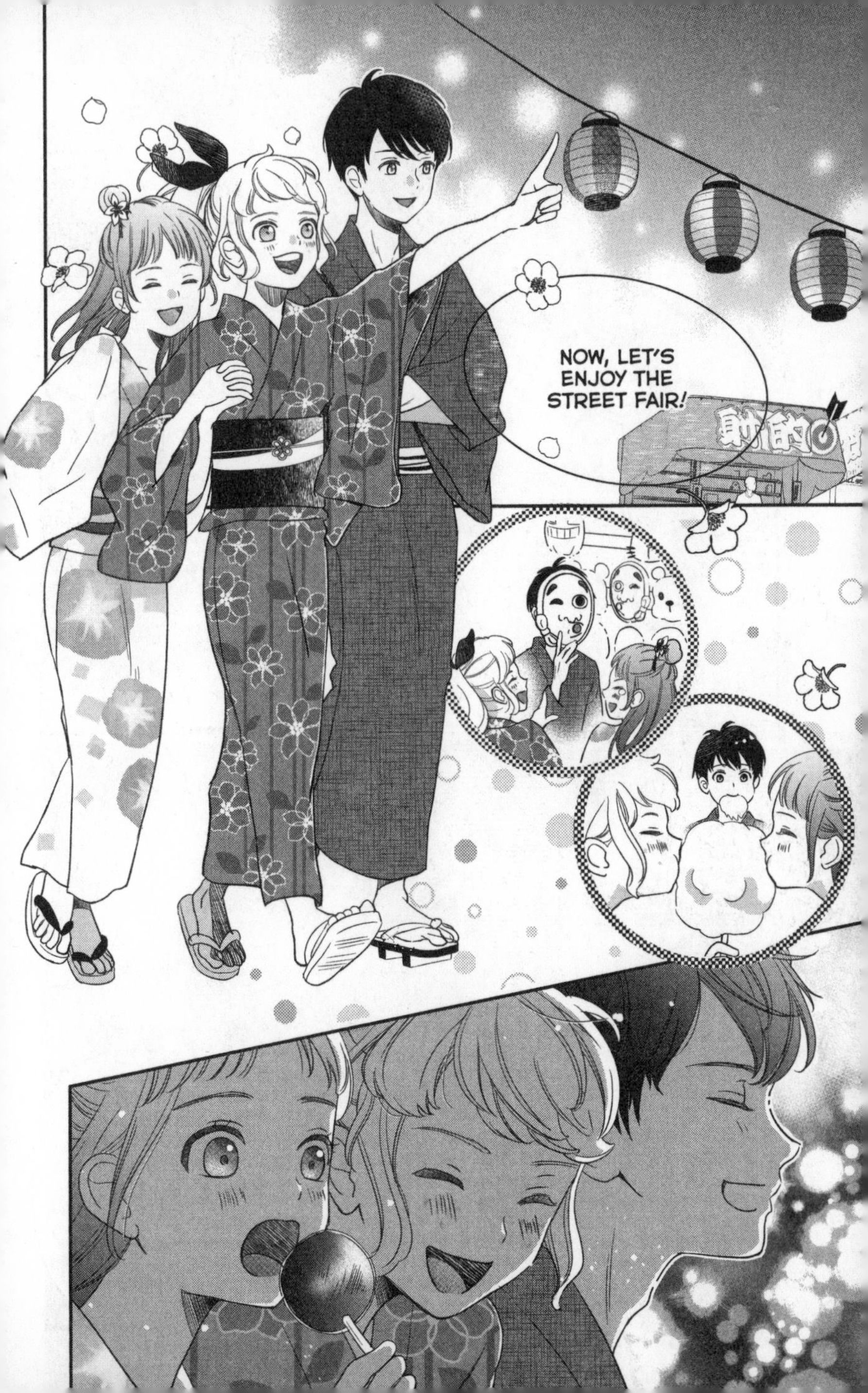
NOW, LET'S ENJOY THE STREET FAIR!

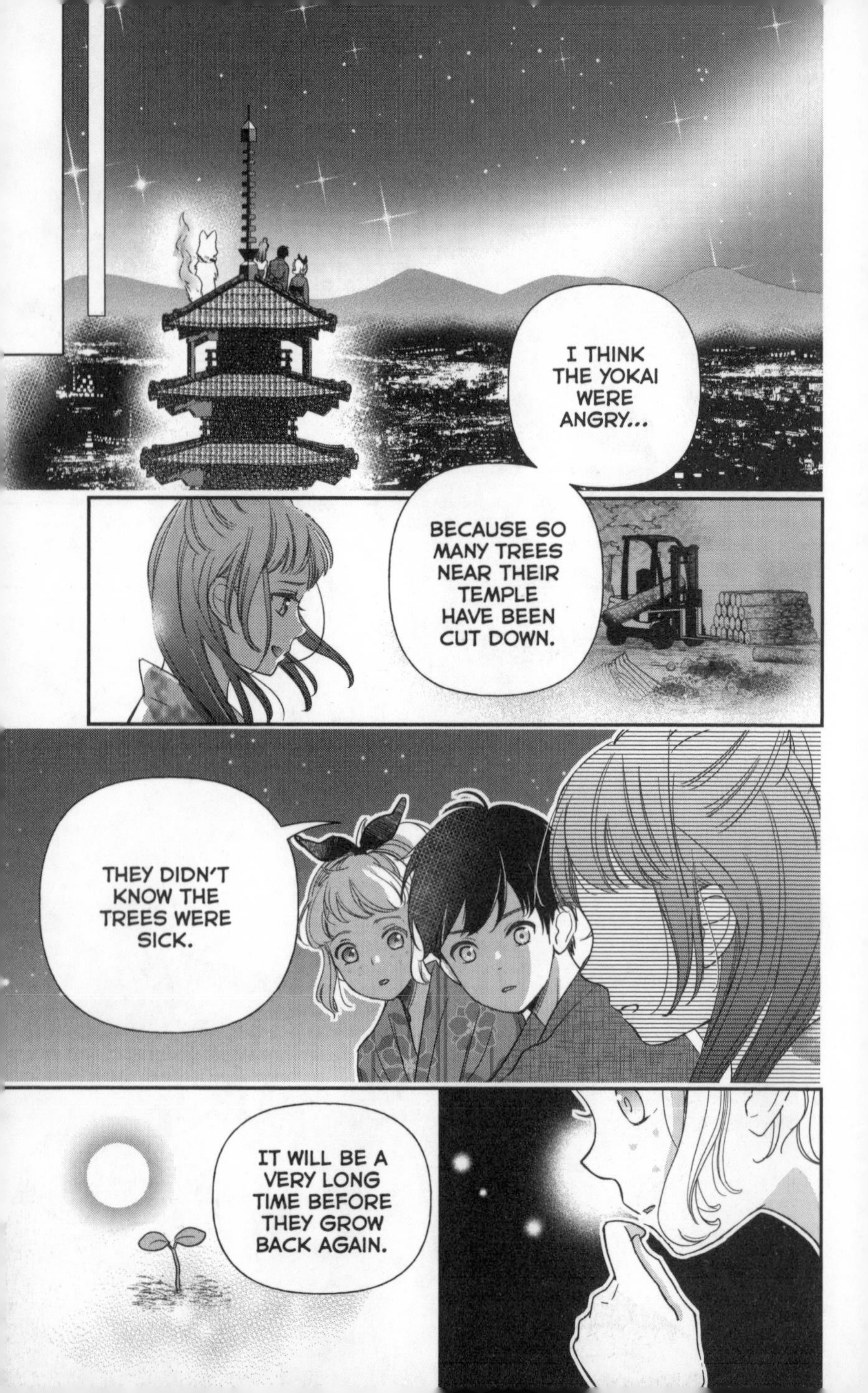
I THINK THE YOKAI WERE ANGRY...
BECAUSE SO MANY TREES NEAR THEIR TEMPLE HAVE BEEN CUT DOWN.
THEY DIDN'T KNOW THE TREES WERE SICK.
IT WILL BE A VERY LONG TIME BEFORE THEY GROW BACK AGAIN.

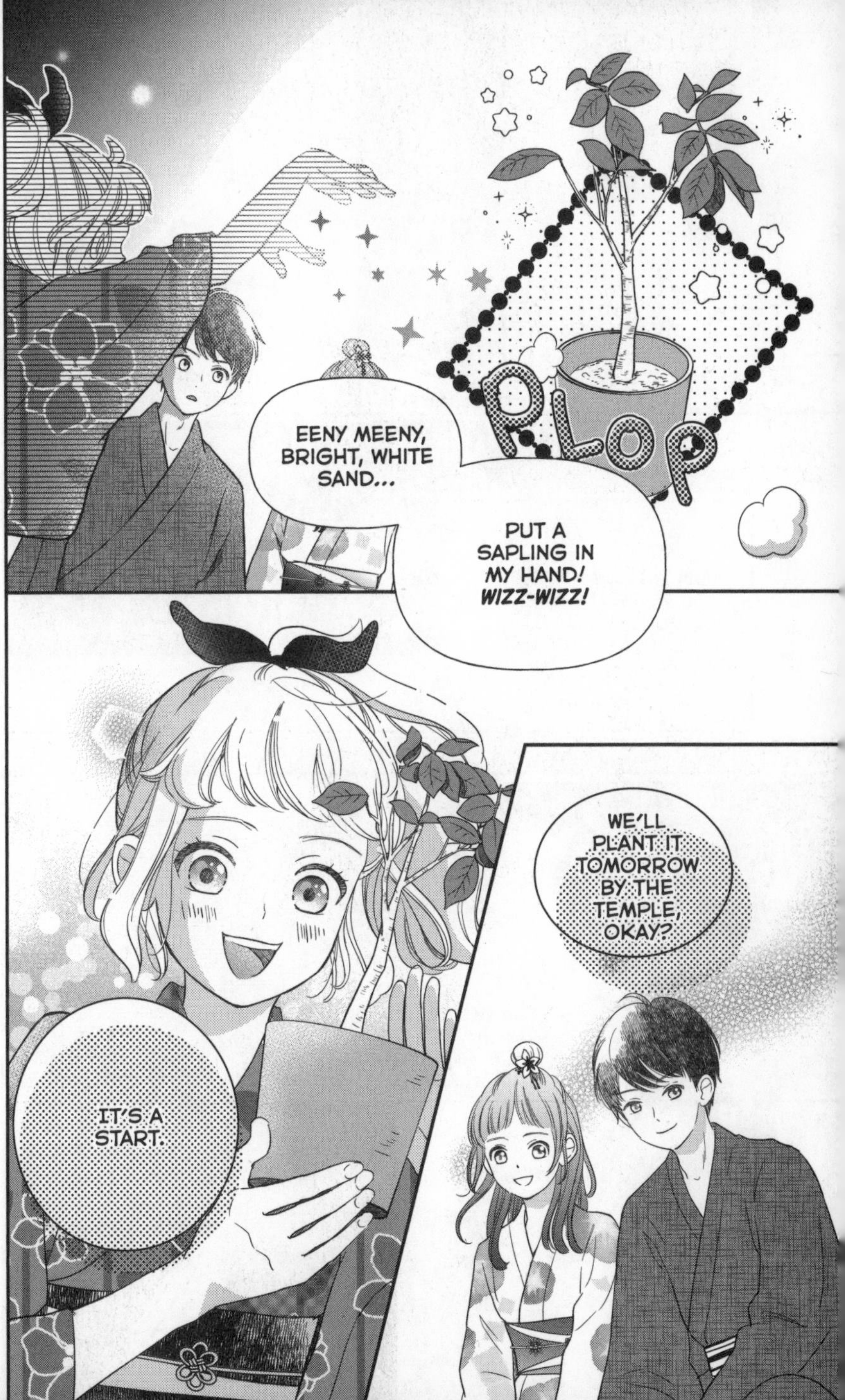
PLOP
EENY MEENY, BRIGHT, WHITE SAND...
PUT A SAPLING IN MY HAND! *WIZZ-WIZZ!*
WE'LL PLANT IT TOMORROW BY THE TEMPLE, OKAY?
IT'S A START.

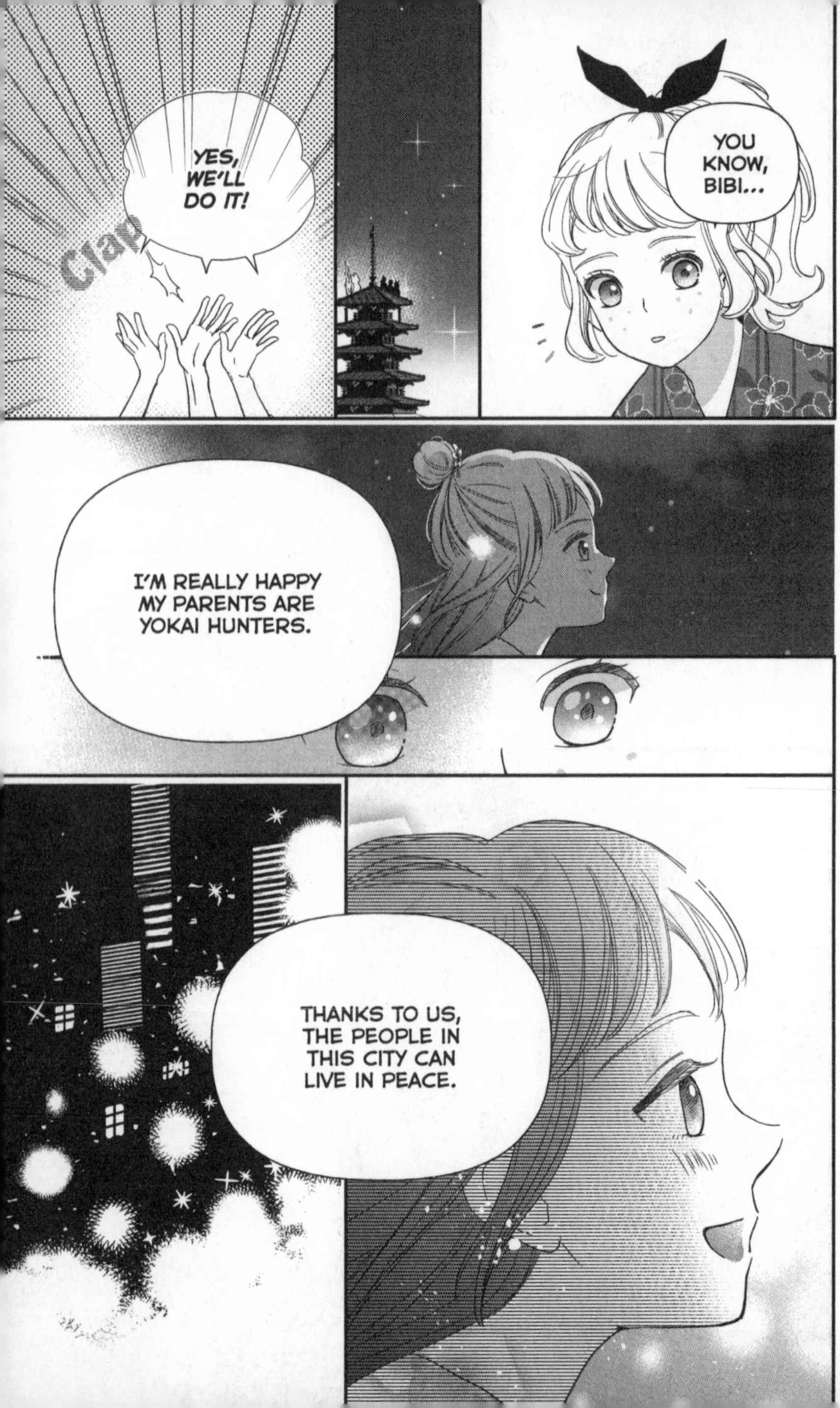
YES, WE'LL DO IT!
Clap
YOU KNOW, BIBI...
I'M REALLY HAPPY MY PARENTS ARE YOKAI HUNTERS.
THANKS TO US, THE PEOPLE IN THIS CITY CAN LIVE IN PEACE.

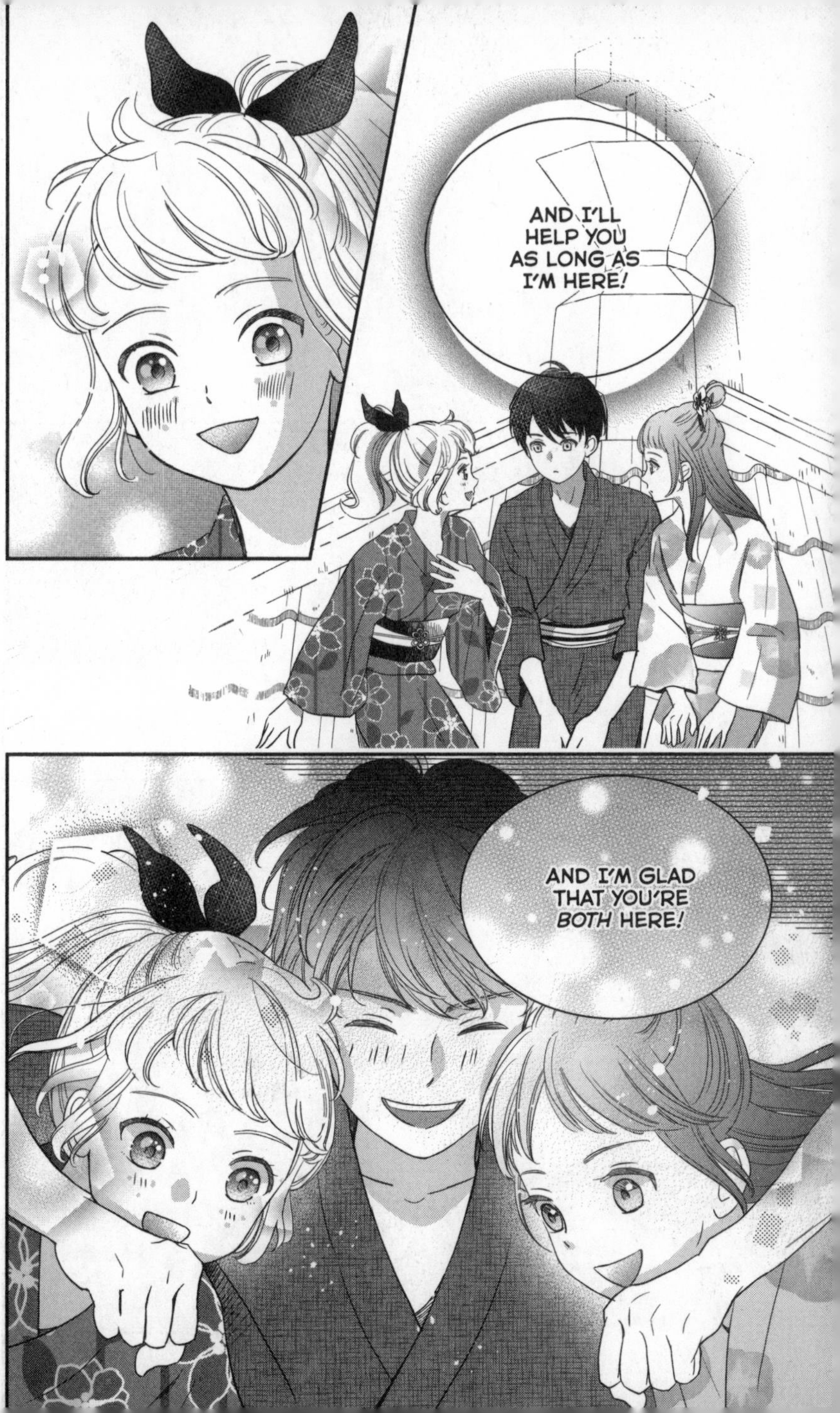
AND I'LL HELP YOU AS LONG AS I'M HERE!
AND I'M GLAD THAT YOU'RE *BOTH* HERE!

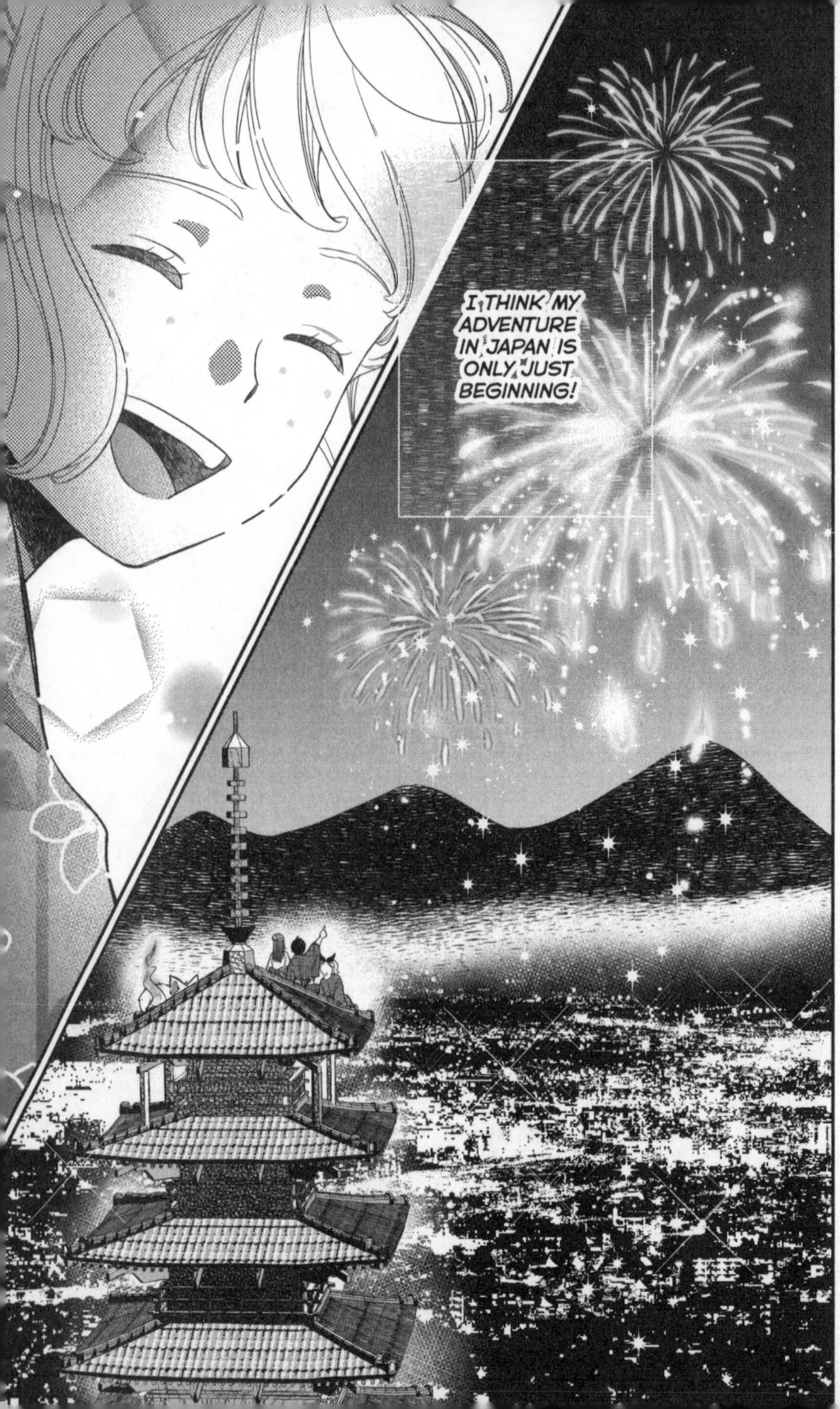
I THINK MY ADVENTURE IN JAPAN IS ONLY JUST BEGINNING!

VOLUME 2

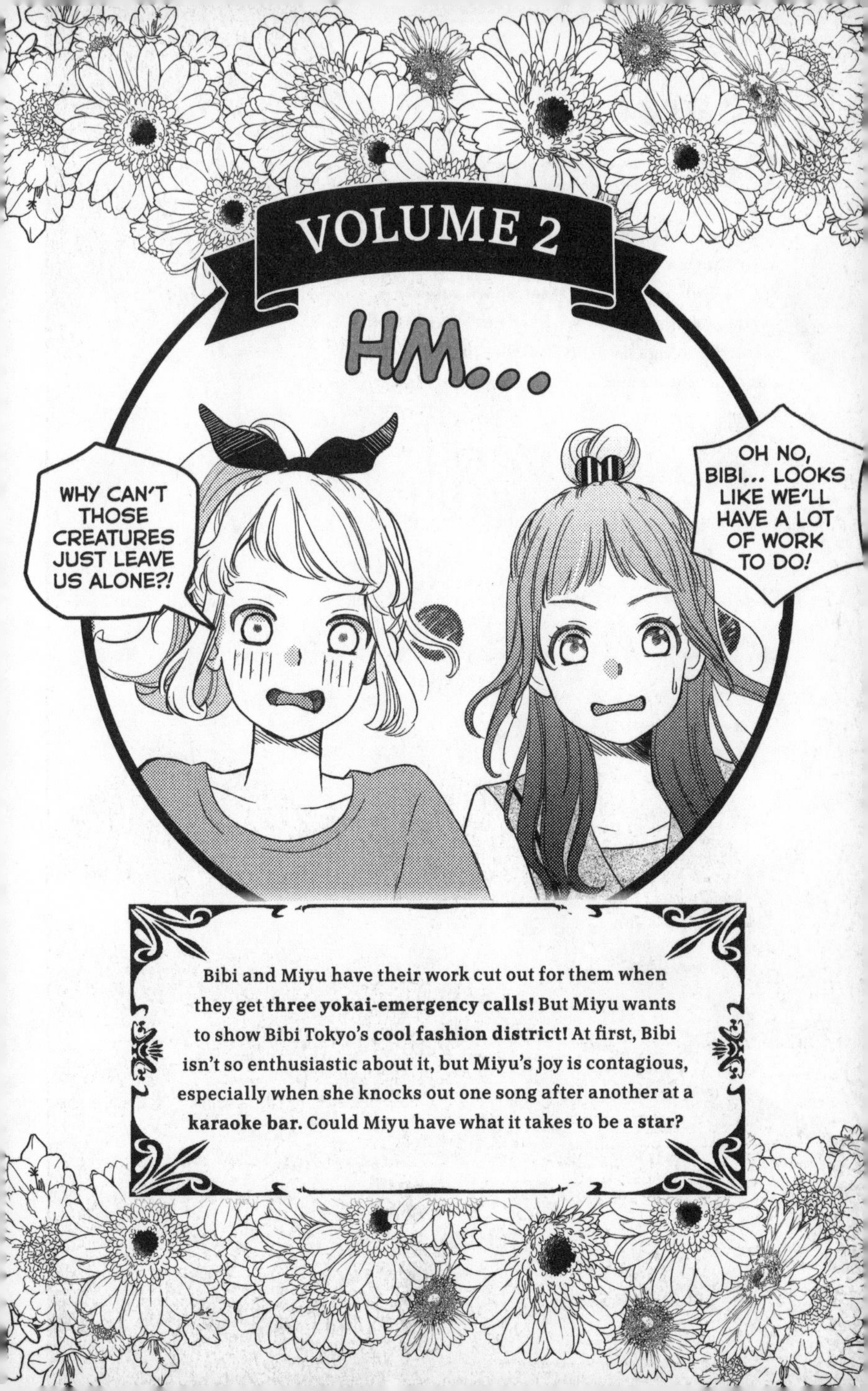
HM...
WHY CAN'T THOSE CREATURES JUST LEAVE US ALONE?!
OH NO, BIBI... LOOKS LIKE WE'LL HAVE A LOT OF WORK TO DO!

Bibi and Miyu have their work cut out for them when they get **three yokai-emergency calls**! But Miyu wants to show Bibi Tokyo's **cool fashion district**! At first, Bibi isn't so enthusiastic about it, but Miyu's joy is contagious, especially when she knocks out one song after another at a **karaoke bar**. Could Miyu have what it takes to be a **star**?

Character Development

Bibi Blocksberg is the leading lady in a children's audio drama originally released in Germany! She's a well-known character, so we spent lots of time designing her. We tried out a variety of different things until we had the final model. Most importantly, we couldn't forget her freckles!

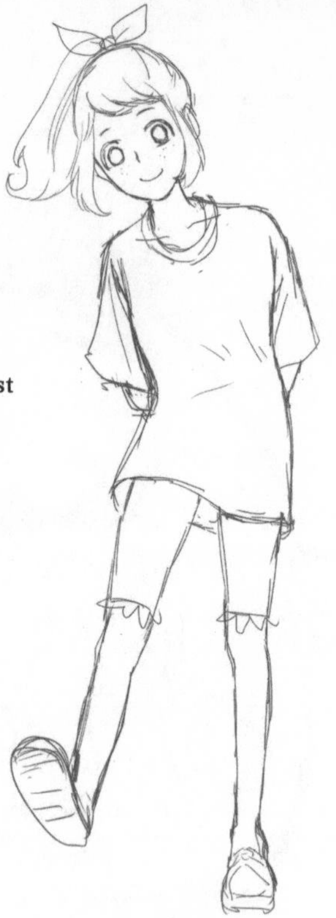

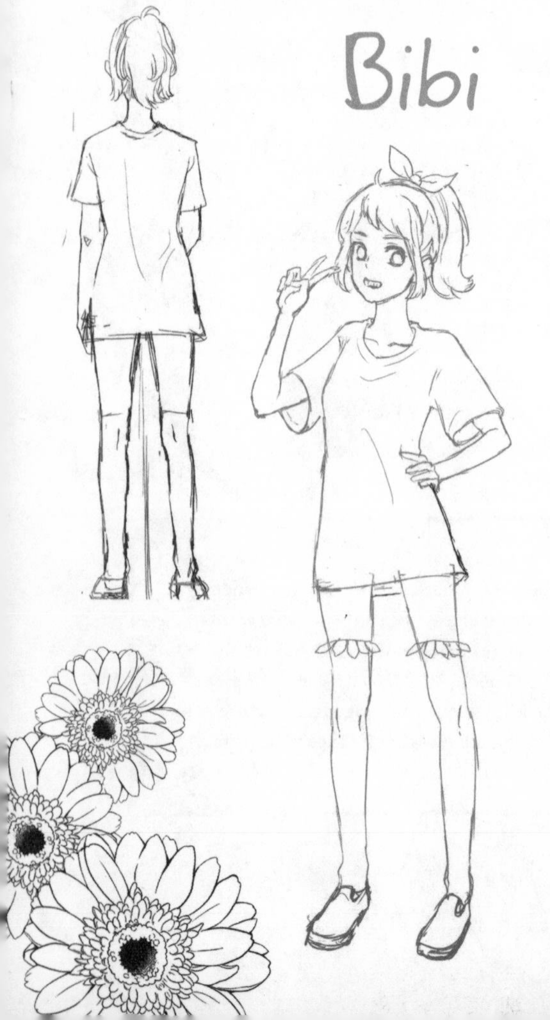
Bibi

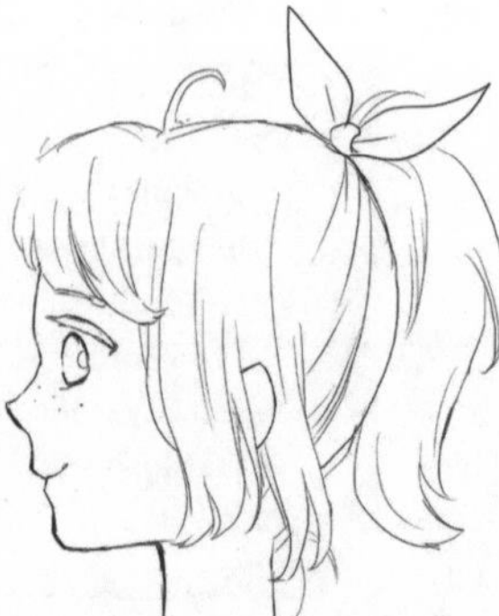

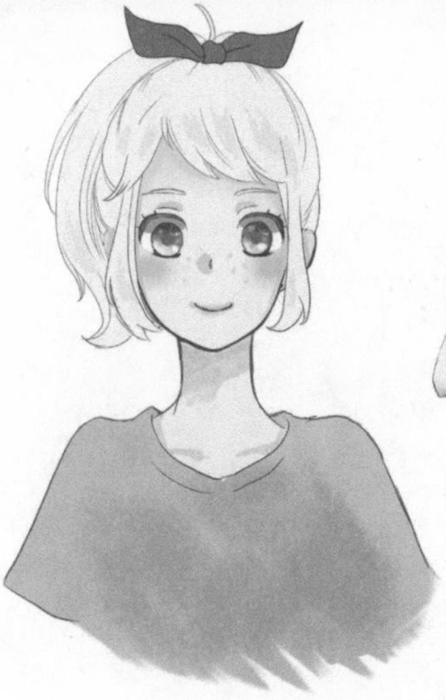

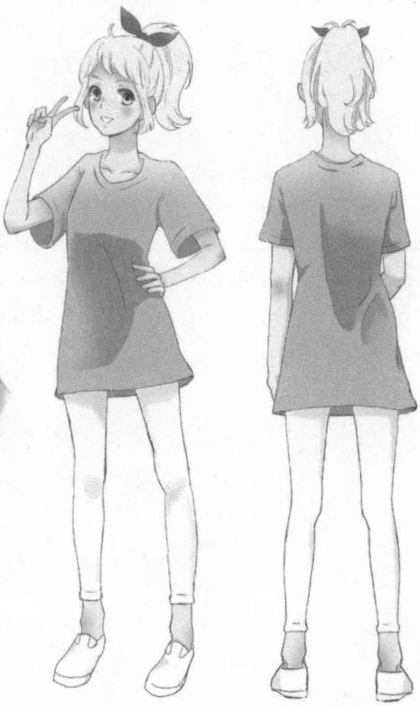

Our final Bibi!

Sometimes, it takes a really long time to get
from the rough sketch to the final illustration.

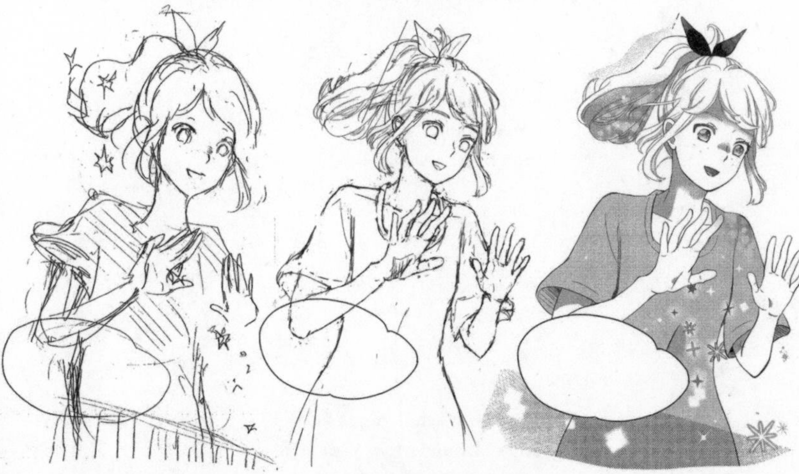

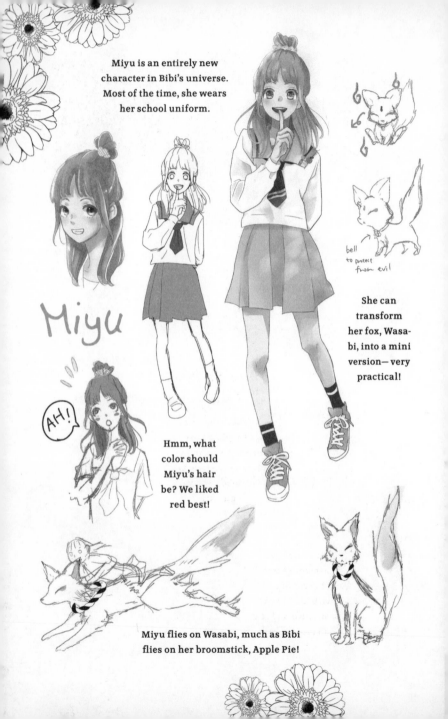

Miyu is an entirely new character in Bibi's universe. Most of the time, she wears her school uniform.

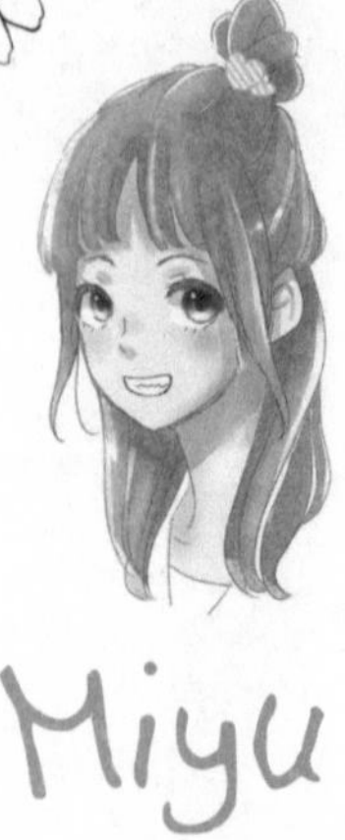
Miyu

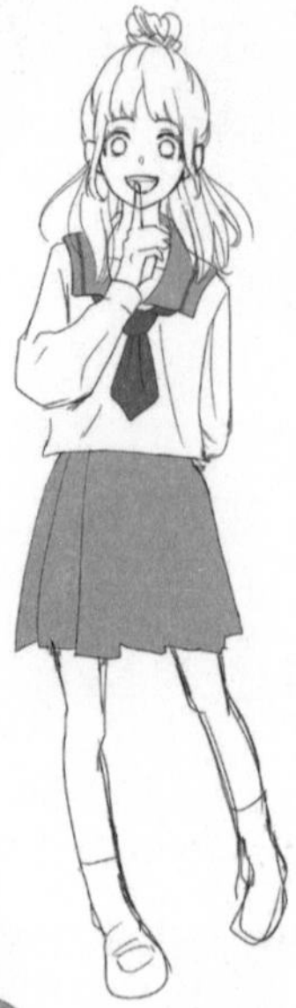

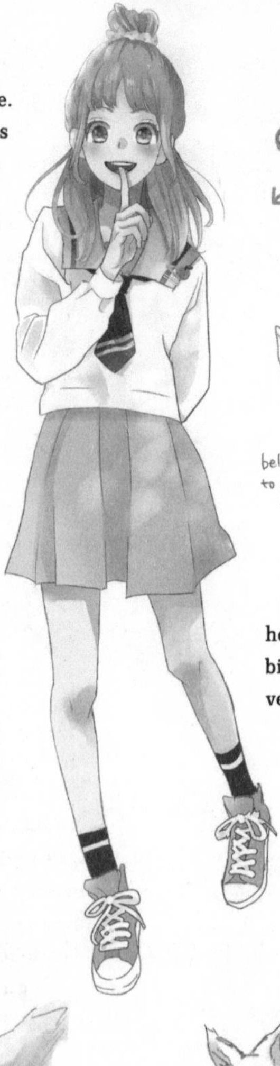

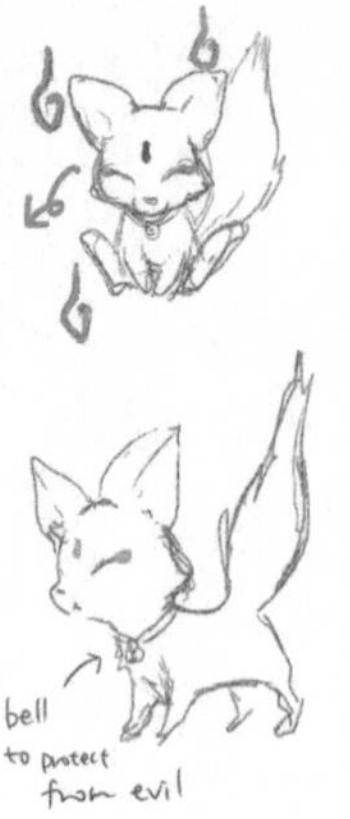
bell
to protect
from evil

She can transform her fox, Wasabi, into a mini version— very practical!

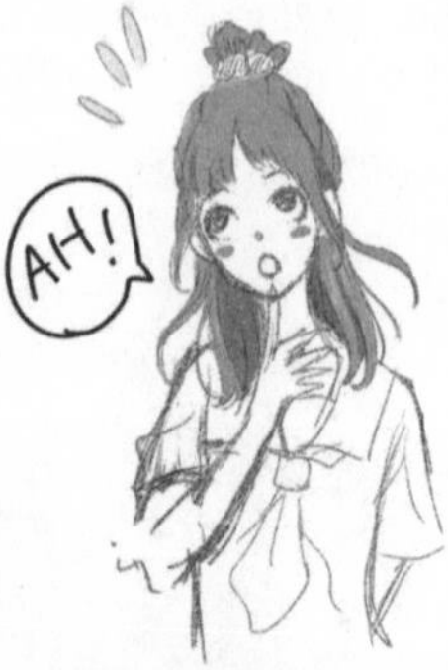
AH!

Hmm, what color should Miyu's hair be? We liked red best!

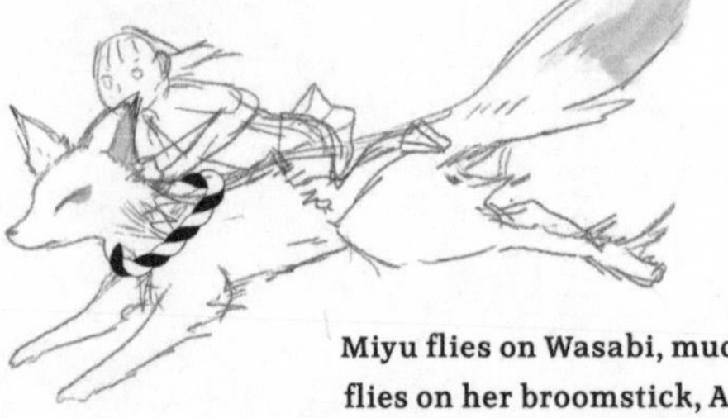

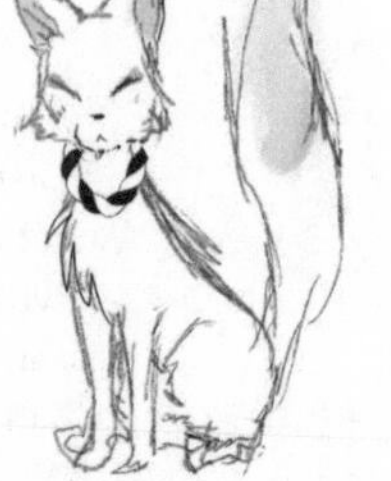

Miyu flies on Wasabi, much as Bibi flies on her broomstick, Apple Pie!

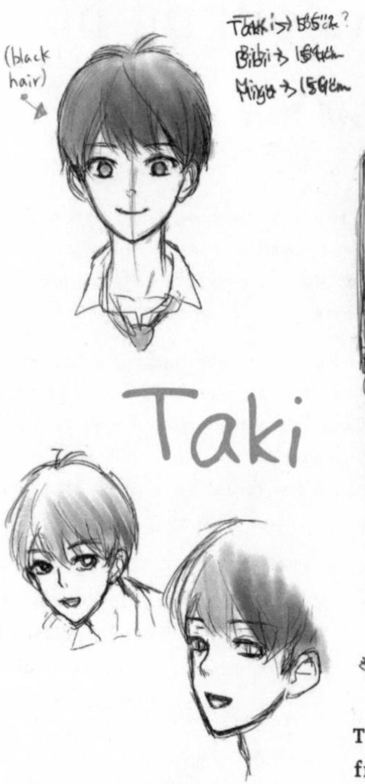
(black hair)
Taki

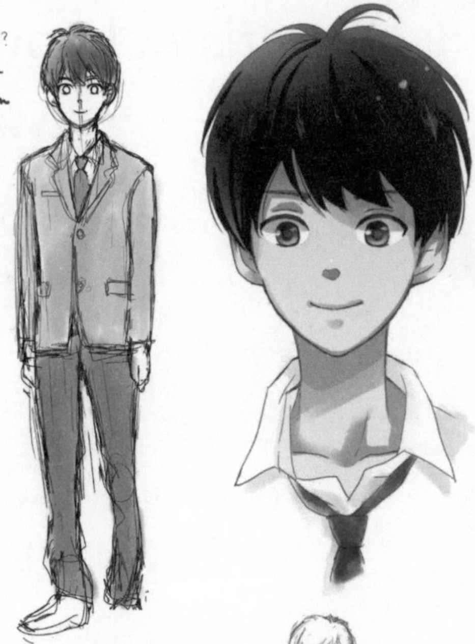

Taki is Miyu's best friend. We wanted him to radiate calm. He's very important because he's the only person who knows Miyu's secret. He also befriends Bibi very quickly!

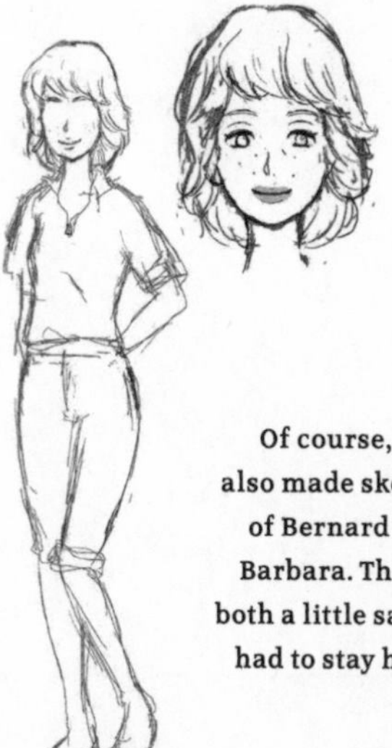

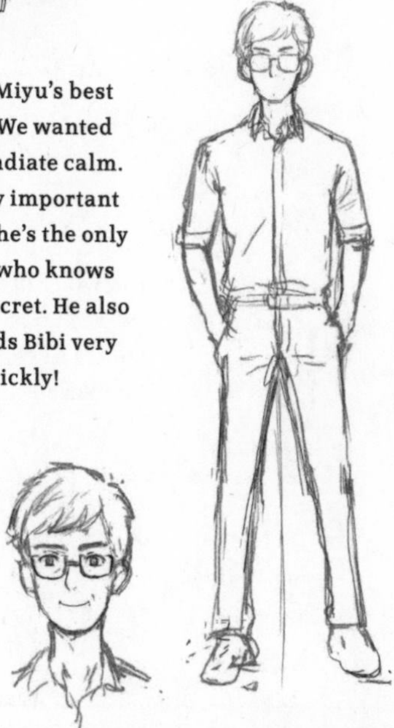

Of course, we also made sketches of Bernard and Barbara. They're both a little sad they had to stay home.

Author's Acknowledgment

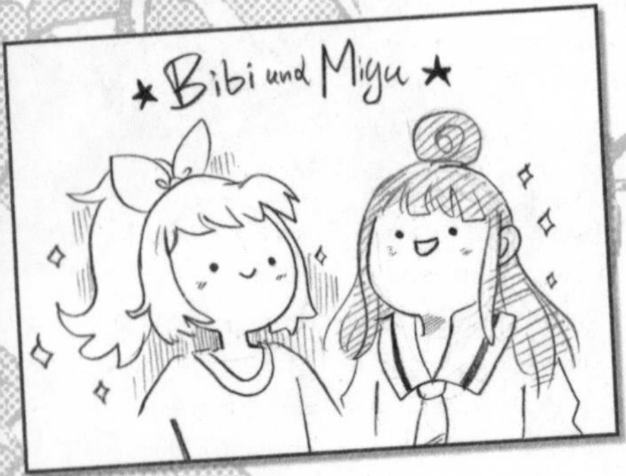
★Bibi und Miyu★

Wow! Here it is!

Bibi & Miyu's first manga!

It's amazing that we really pulled this project together! Hirara did a great job, and Bibi really turned into a manga heroine. What a sweetie!

I've been a fan of audio dramas since my early childhood, and I always thought it was great that the women in the Blocksberg family were the ones who went on adventures. My favorite episode is 'A Surprising Reunion' because it also deals with sad themes.

I hope you've enjoyed our manga just as much! Stay tuned to find out what happens next with Bibi & Miyu! I have lots more ideas for Bibi's time in Japan!

Olivia

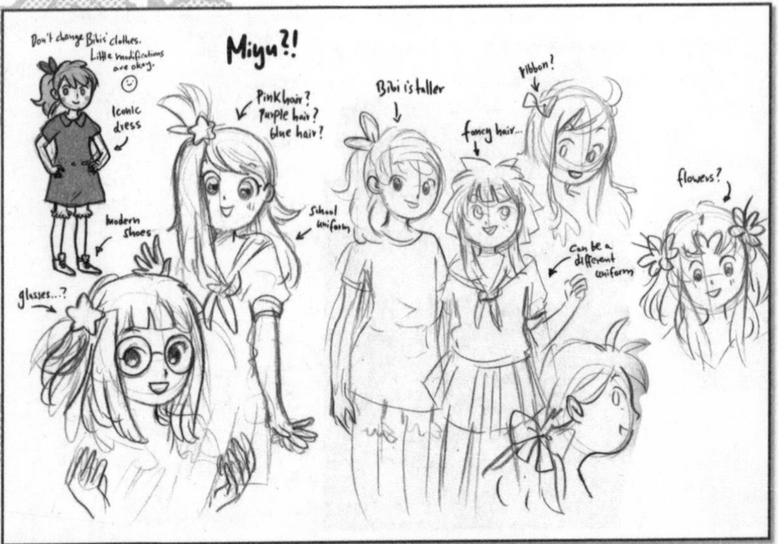
Don't change Bibi's clothes. Little modifications are okay.
Miyu?!
Iconic dress
modern shoes
glasses...?
Pink hair? Purple hair? blue hair?
School uniform
Bibi is taller
ribbon?
fancy hair...
Can be a different uniform
flowers?

Very early sketches by Olivia to get a feel for the characters.

Hi, Olivia! You wrote the story for the Bibi Blocksberg manga, *Bibi & Miyu*. How did that come about?

The idea came from TOKYOPOP; I then came on as the author and project adviser. At the same time, we were lucky enough to encounter Hirara Natsume, who had already worked as an illustrator in Japan and was now living in Germany. I'd already had the idea of making a manga with Bibi for many years, and I'd even written up a couple of sample pages... But they weren't really very good. It's so much better that it's now a reality— and what's more, it looks great, too!

How does collaborating with Hirara work?

I write a rough outline. Then I flesh out the script for each chapter, with the specific dialogue worked out. We get the text translated into Japanese, so that Hirara understands all the details. Although she speaks very good English and German, Japanese is always her first choice. Then, she sketches the rough storyboards, which I look at and give her my feedback about. Then all the documents go to Susanne Stephan at KIDDINX. She decides whether the story fits into Bibi's universe. Then, we continue drawing and rastering pages.

Do you wish you could have drawn the manga yourself?

No, I'm super happy we were able to get Hirara as our artist! When we say we're making a **"Bibi manga,"** it has to look 100% like manga. My drawing style wouldn't work for it at all.

What do enjoy the most in your work?

Developing the first ideas and the beginnings of a story. Seeing where Bibi's journey is going and even what can happen on her trip to Japan is simply amazing. It also thrills me when I can see Hirara's new storyboards, sketches, or the rastered pages. That's always something special!

This is what the translated script looks like. (Translation by Davi Nathaniel.) By the way, this is already volume 2!

2 AM HAFEN (TOKYO BAY)

港で（東京湾）

    MIYU
    Mein schöner freier Abend! Das
    wirst du bereuen!!

    ミユ
  私、今日の夜ゆっくりするはずだったのに
  〜 この〜！！

Bibi und Miyu jagen auf Kartoffelbrei und Wasabi einen Yokai.

カルトッフェルブライとワサビに乗って妖怪を追いかけ回すビビとミユ。

    BIBI
    Mann, ist der schnell!

    ビビ
  もう！コイツ早すぎでしょ！

Illustrator's Acknowledgement

My heart beats for Japan and Germany!

I especially would like to thank Olivia, who made this project possible in the first place. And a big thank you to our translator, Davi, too!

Thank you to my family in Japan and Germany with all my heart for always supporting me.

And thank you very much as well to TOKYOPOP and KIDDINX for the great opportunity to be able to draw this manga! I hope we'll see each other again in Volume 2! ♡♡♡

Hirara

The Making of: Manga Magic!

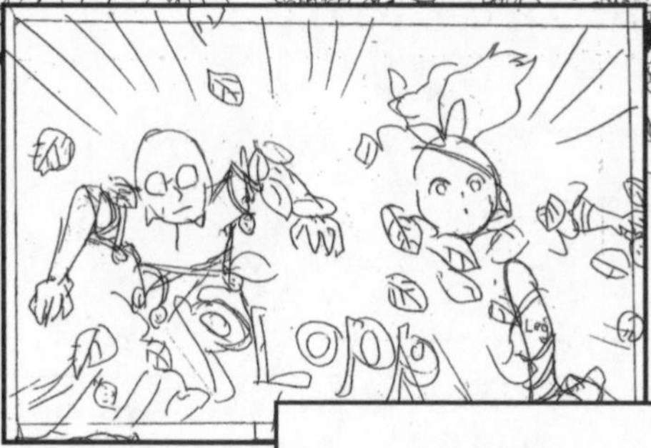
PLopp

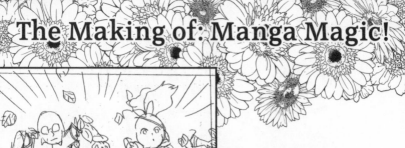

Have you ever wondered how a page of manga comes into being? It takes many steps for a manga to emerge.

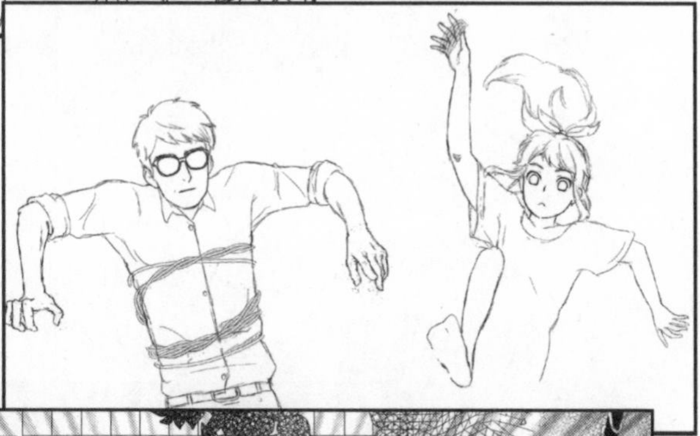

It begins with a sketch of each panel (what the individual pictures in comics/ manga are called). Next comes the rough drawing.

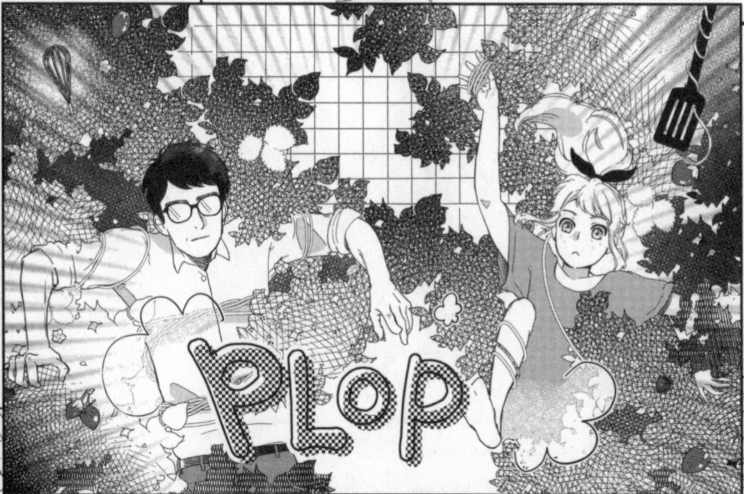
PLOP

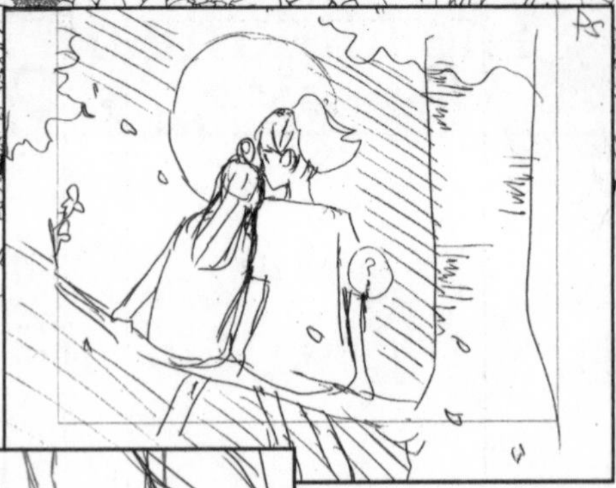
?

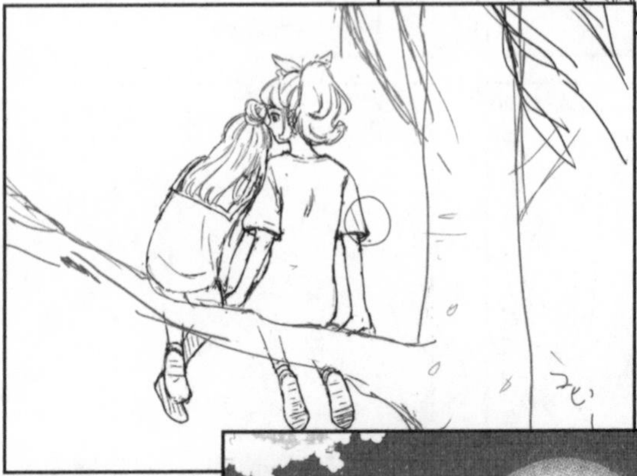

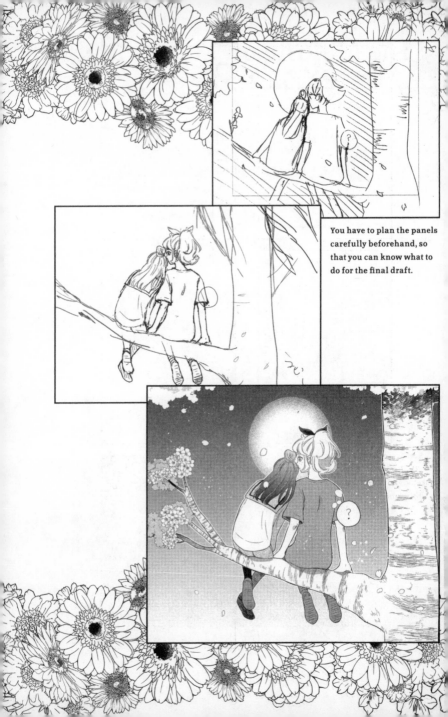

You have to plan the panels carefully beforehand, so that you can know what to do for the final draft.

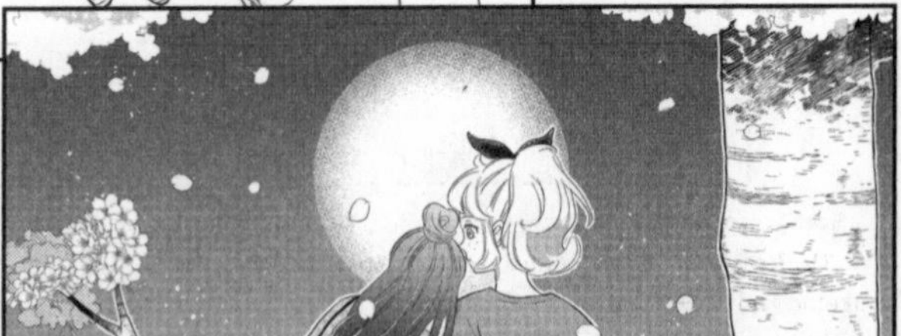
?

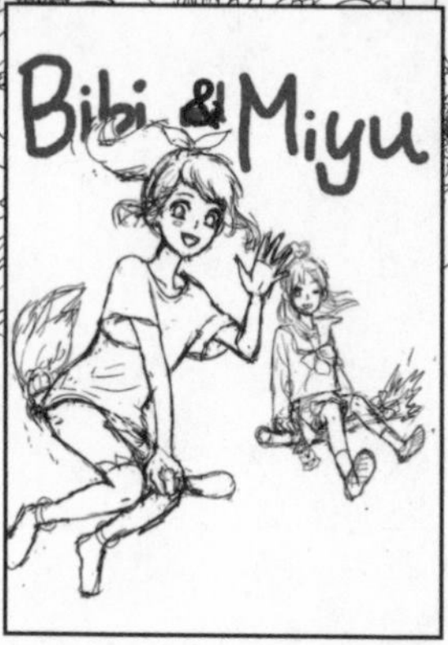
Bibi & Miyu
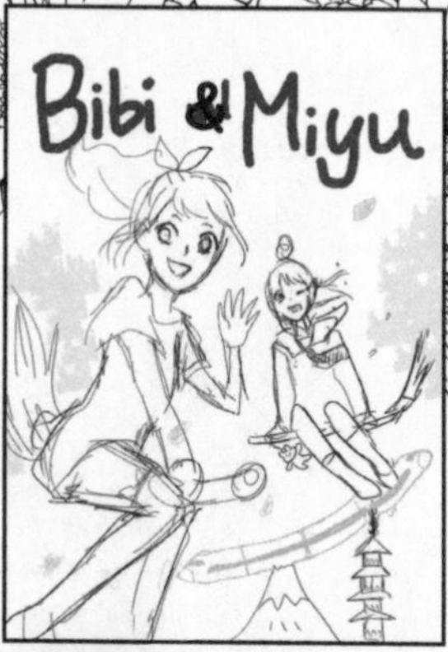
Bibi & Miyu
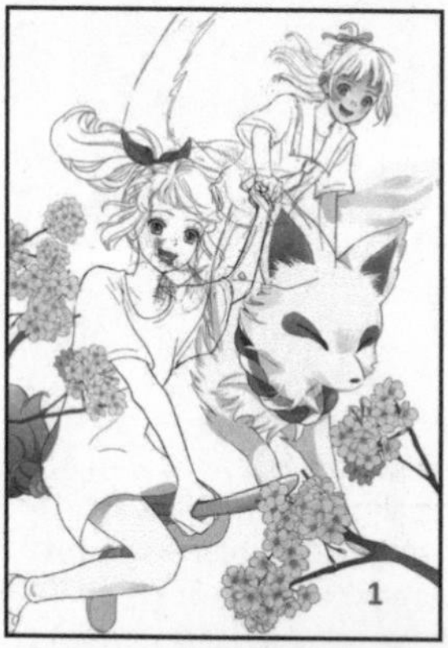
1
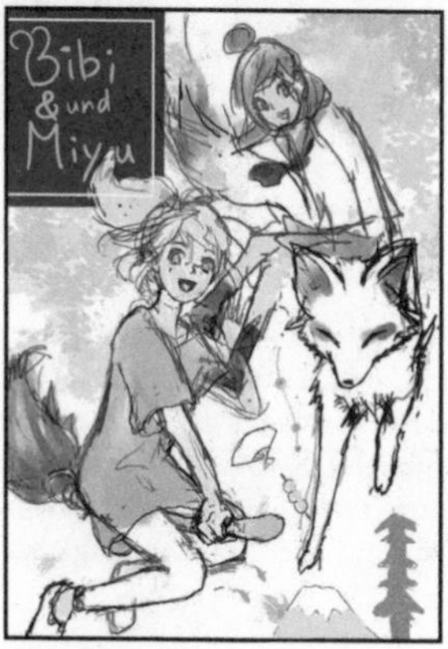
Bibi
& und
Miyu
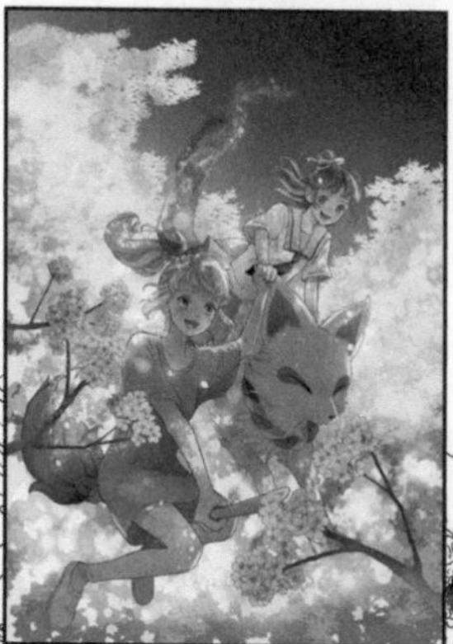

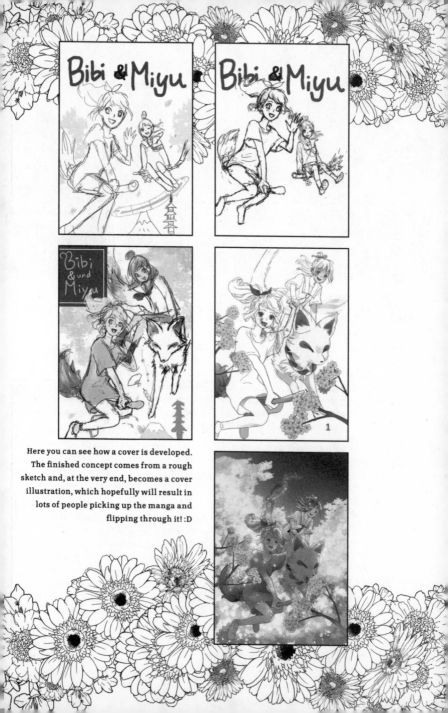

Here you can see how a cover is developed. The finished concept comes from a rough sketch and, at the very end, becomes a cover illustration, which hopefully will result in lots of people picking up the manga and flipping through it! :D

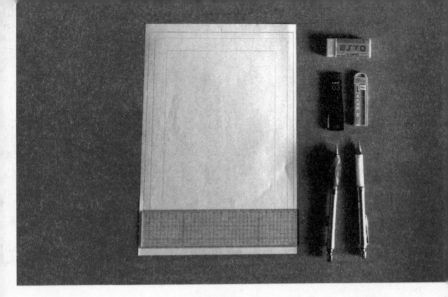

Interview with Hirara Natsume

Hi, Hirara! When did you start drawing?
I was already drawing manga at the age of five. Then, when I was around ten, I started doing it properly, using screen tone, India ink, etc.— things that a real *mangaka* (manga creator) uses.

Did your family encourage you or did they want you to find a "normal" job?
My family always supported me and made sure I could continue drawing. Admittedly, after I finished college, my mother suggested I find a steady-paying job, but my father thought I should do what I wanted. So I listened to my father and never worked at a "real" job, except for some temp work every so often during my studies.

Did you have friends who also drew manga, or did you pursue your hobby all by yourself?

There were many kids in elementary school who drew manga (at their respective levels, of course). But most stopped by the time they were teenagers. Now, of course, I have many friends and acquaintances I met through work who also draw.

Do you have a favorite manga?
I like many of them! But the manga that has influenced my work the most is *Poi* by Yamazaki Takako.

Have you already published manga in Japan? Is it hard to connect with the publishing houses there?
I've already published over a dozen stories in magazines for Shueisha. Four of them were grouped into a collection and released on the market again. It's very hard to establish a connection with a publisher that continues beyond the first meeting.

If a publisher's representative likes your work, then you'll have a better chance of getting an editor to pay attention to you. That still doesn't mean you'll be able to publish your stories any time soon, though. Every month, many magazines hold contests where you can introduce your manga. The readers decide which stories they like best and which artist is good enough to be published regularly in the magazine. The publisher then considers whether to sign you on or not.

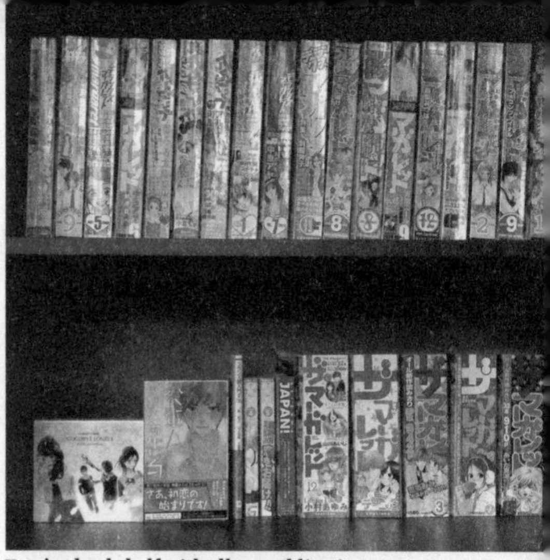

Here's a bookshelf with all my publications.

When did you move to Germany? Do you like it?

I moved to Germany in October, 2015, and I like it very much! There's a lot of nature here (compared to Osaka, the city I'm originally from) and the German "lifestyle" is also amazing. In general, people in Germany have much more time off than in Japan.

Do you go back to Japan often?

I try to visit Japan once a year. When I was a child, I always spent my vacations in the Gifu Prefecture. Every day during the summer, I visited the shrine (this is what Shinto temples are called) in front of my father's house and caught cicadas there!

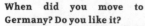

Currently, I have no photos of Osaka (my hometown); that's why I'm showing you something from my grandfather's home.

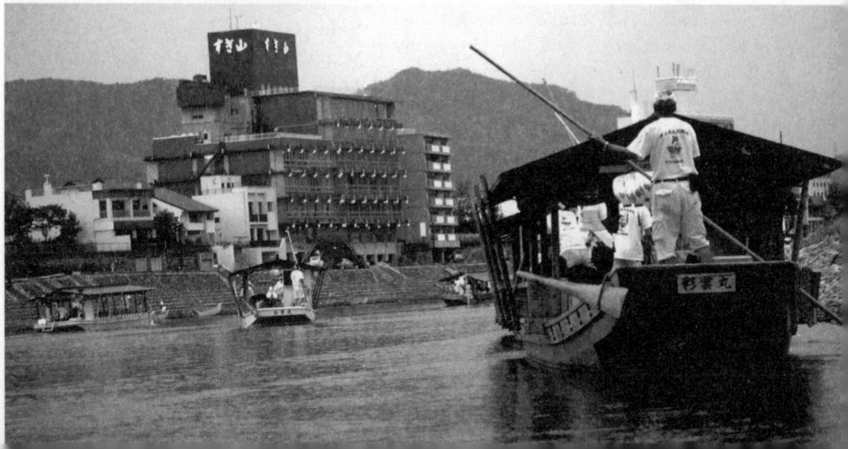

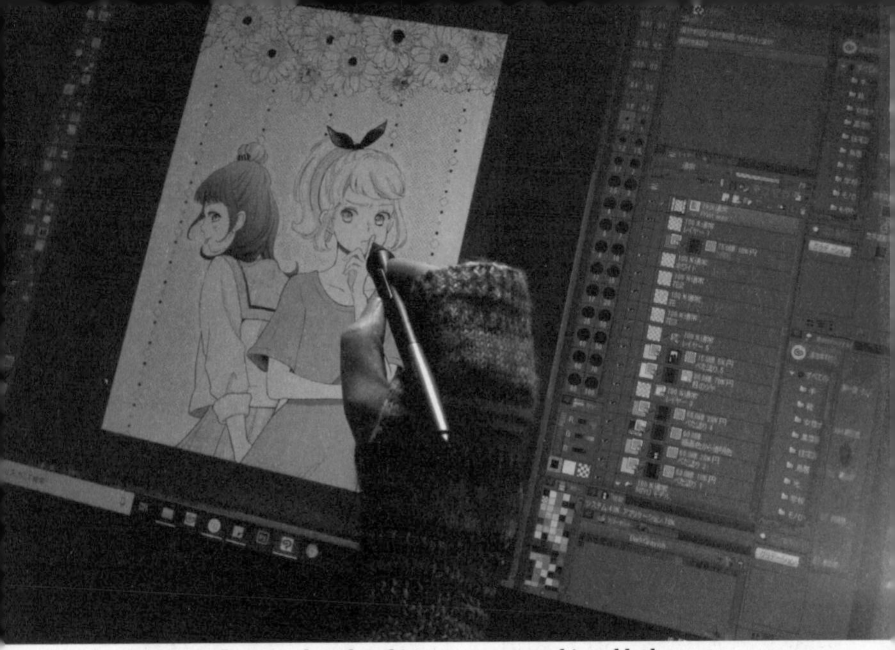

You can see how I work on the Bibi manga on my graphics tablet here.

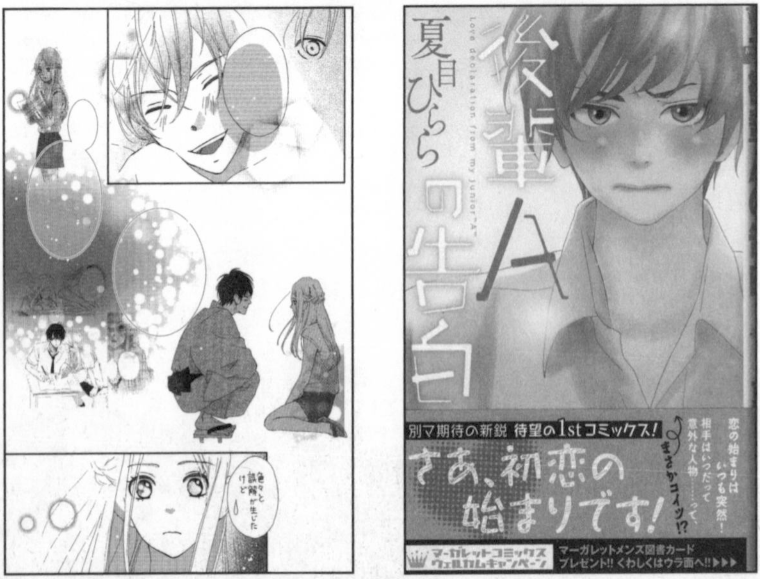
色々と誤解が生じたけど
夏目ひらら
後輩Aの告白
Love declaration from my junior "A"
別マ期待の新鋭 待望の1stコミックス!
さあ、初恋の始まりです!
まさかコイツ!?
恋の始まりはいつも突然! 相手はいつだって意外な人物……って、
マーガレットコミックス ウェルカムキャンペーン
マーガレットメンズ図書カード プレゼント!! くわしくはウラ面へ!!▶▶▶

Here are a few sample pages from my manga in a Japanese magazine.

If someone is visiting Japan, is there any place you'd say is a must-see?

I recommend that everyone visiting Japan should see the Edo-Tokyo Open Air Architectural Museum, the Kyoto Fushimi Inari Shrine, and the island of Okinawa!

What do you like about Bibi?

Bibi's lovable and naive – in the most positive way possible!

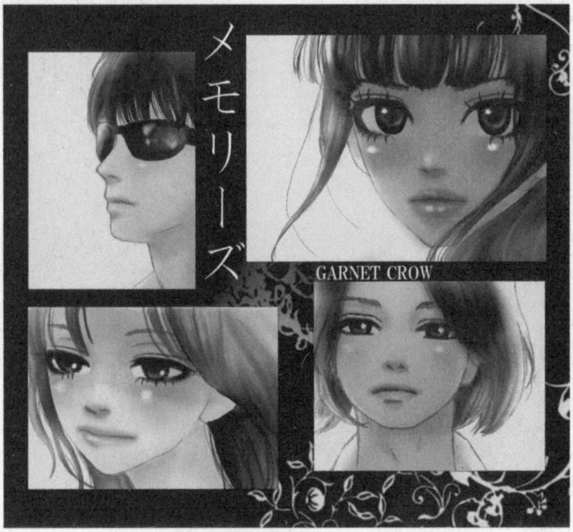
メモリーズ
GARNET CROW

Illustrations for a Japanese book.

What is your favorite part of drawing manga: storyboarding, character design, or something completely different?

That's hard to say! When I draw a storyboard, I'm already looking forward to the rough sketches. When I draw the rough sketches, I'm already looking forward to the detailed version, and as I do the detailed versions, I'm looking forward to the final art, with screentone and shading. Generally, I like when I'm drawing the characters' eyes. They suddenly seem to come to life.

What would you do if you could cast spells like Bibi?

I would cast a spell to transfer my manga directly from my head to the paper.

On the chair, there's a stuffed crocodile, which not only helps me fall asleep but also with back pain caused by sitting for a long time!

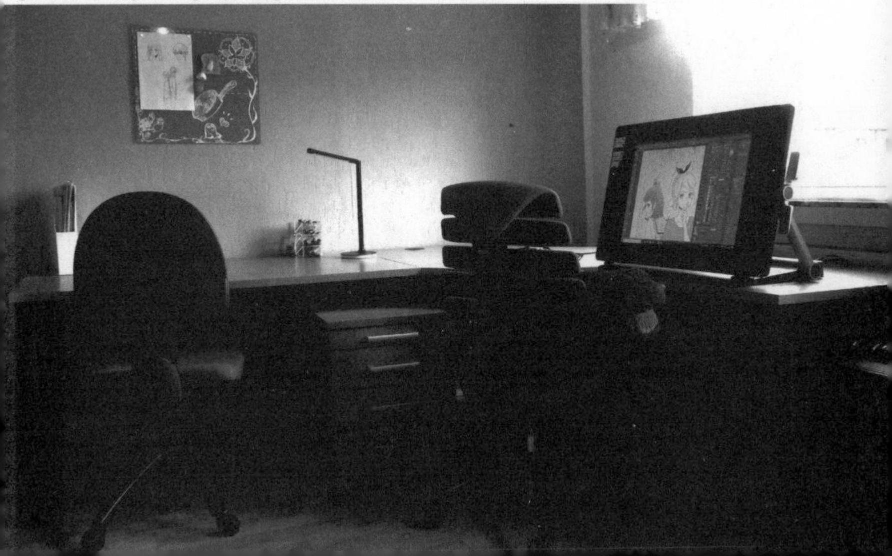

Bibi's Impressions of Japan

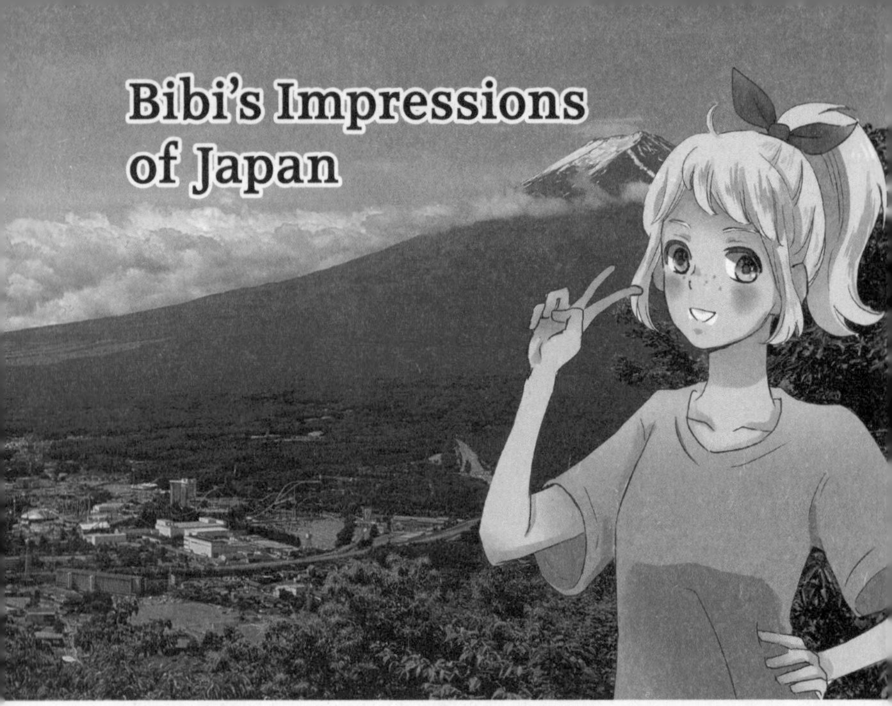

This is my first time in Japan and I have quite a lot to do— both at school and while hunting yokai! **Still, I want to show you the pictures I took on my cell phone!**

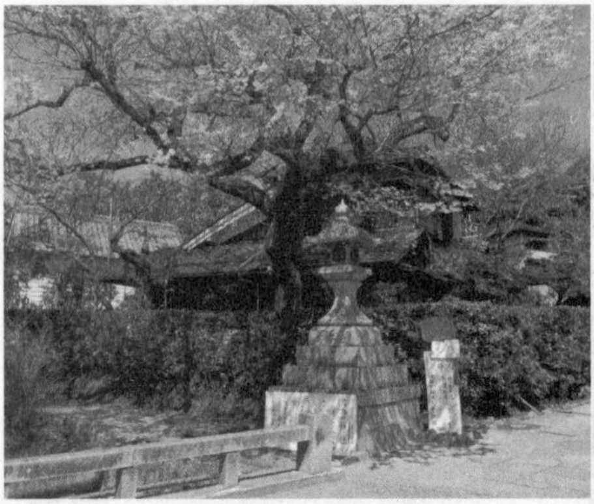

Japanese people adooore blossoming cherry trees! In the spring, everyone is enthralled, waiting for the first blossoms to come out and then **BAMM!** The whole city is suddenly pastel pink. Everyone quickly brings out their cell phones and takes pictures. The parks are filled with people picnicking on blankets. **It's so beautiful!**

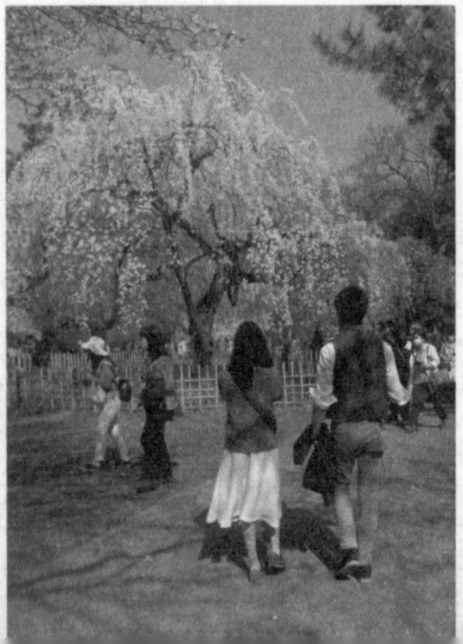

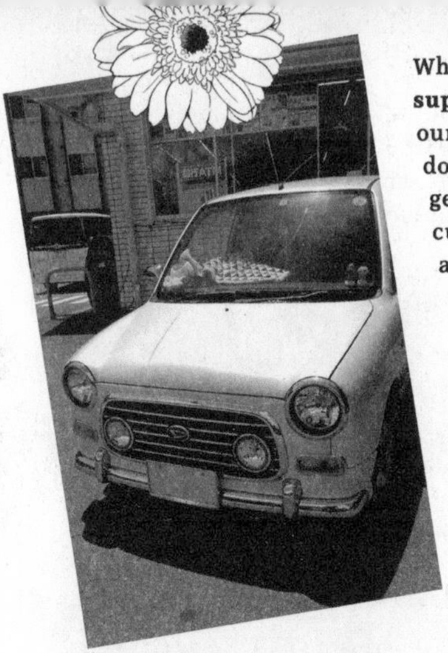

What I find totally cool: in Japan, there are **super-cute cars**— completely different from ours in Newtown! And since big Japanese cities don't have as many places to park, cars aren't generally as large. That's why there are many cute, bug-eyed cars around here that you almost want to hug! ***hehe***

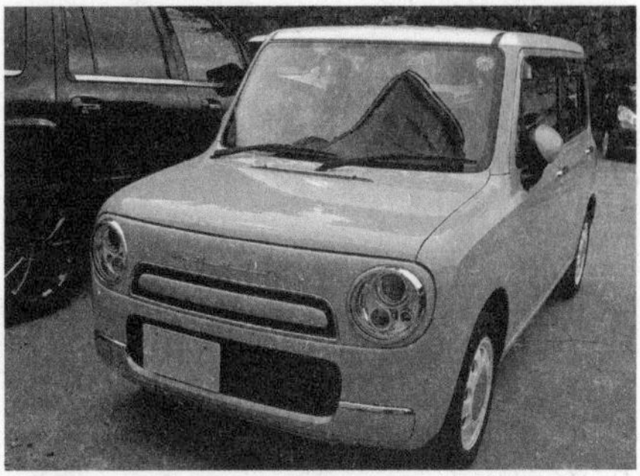

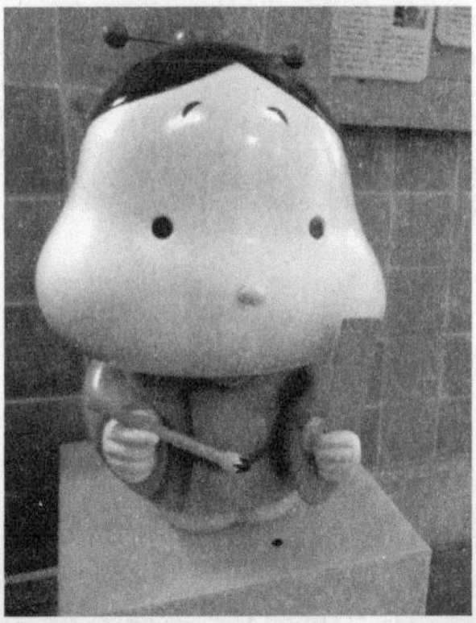

Speaking of cute... **In Japan, there are so many adorable things!** I've seen countless shops with the cutest stuffed animals! And cell phone charms and figures and, and, and—I have to be careful not to go through my allowance too quickly. ***Gulp***

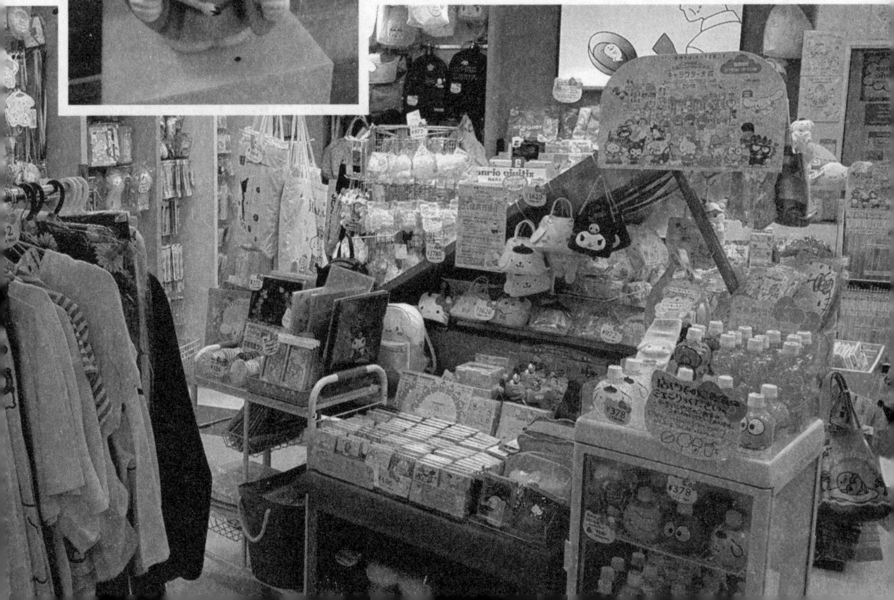

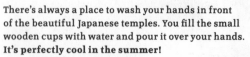

There's always a place to wash your hands in front of the beautiful Japanese temples. You fill the small wooden cups with water and pour it over your hands. **It's perfectly cool in the summer!**

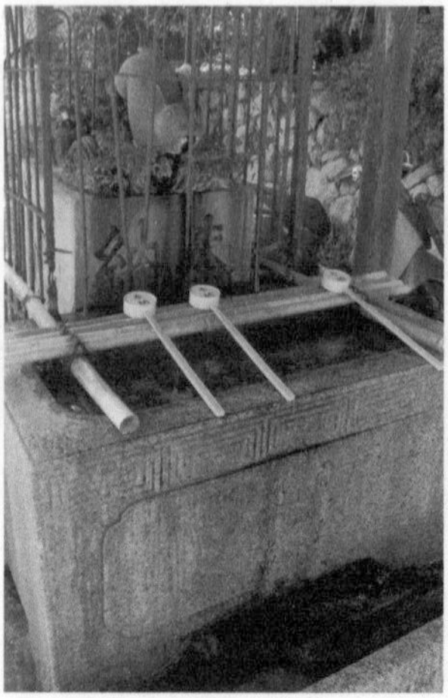

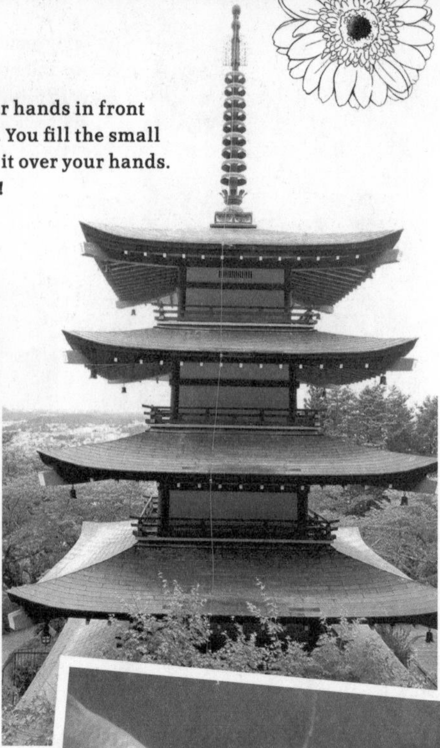

In Japanese gardens, sometimes there are ponds with koi in them! But you should never touch them because it might make them sick! Even though I'd really like to pet them... They look so funny! Wow!

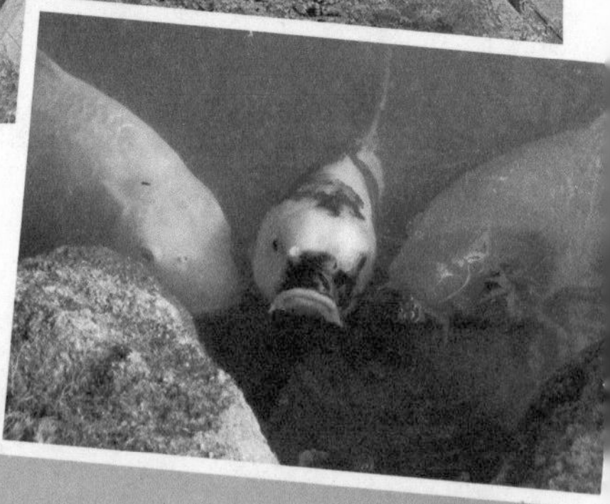

Miyu took this photo of the golden pagoda in Kyoto. I've never been there myself, but Miyu let me show the picture to you. ;)

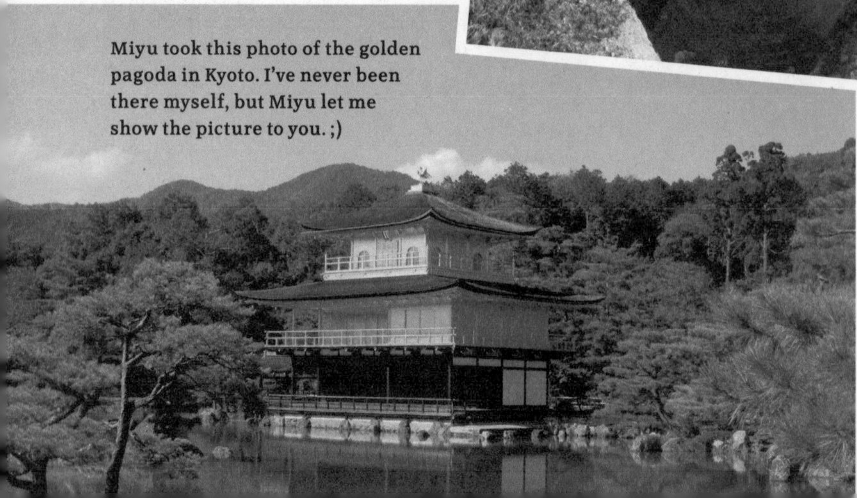

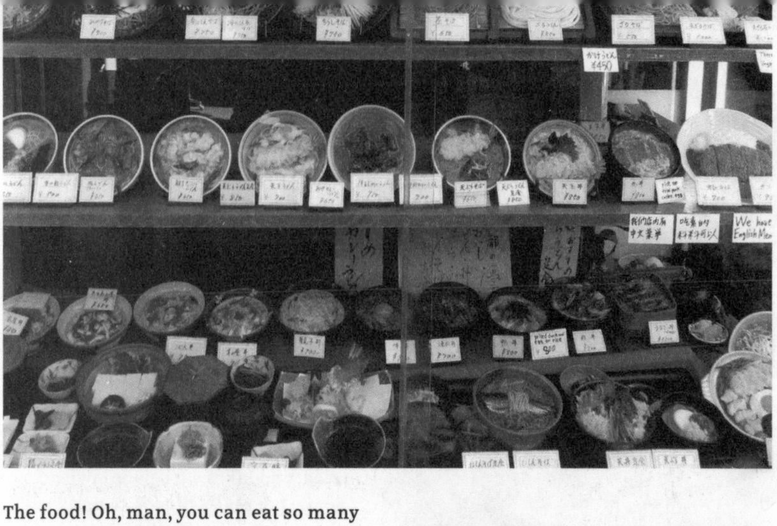

The food! Oh, man, you can eat so many wonderful things here!! Some of it looks weird to me, but most of the time, it's really tasty! Often, things are served on many individual plates— not like at home, where everything comes on one plate. I think this looks really pretty, like a painting.

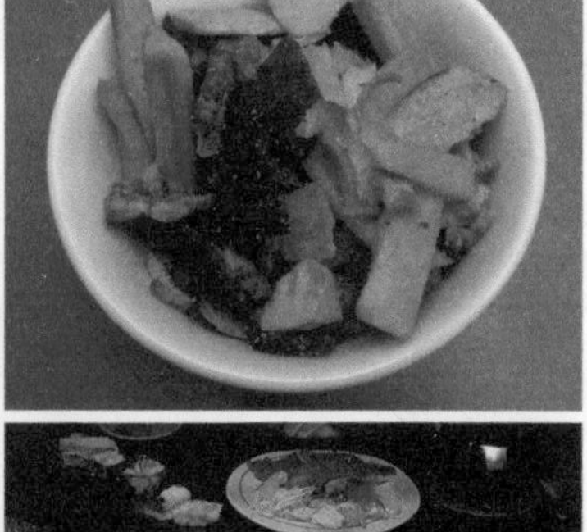

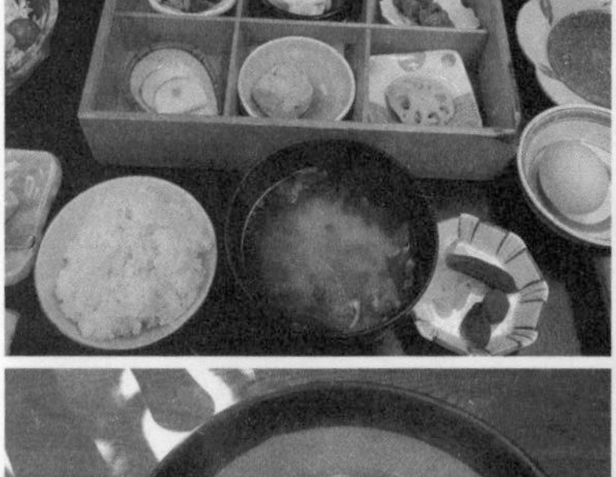

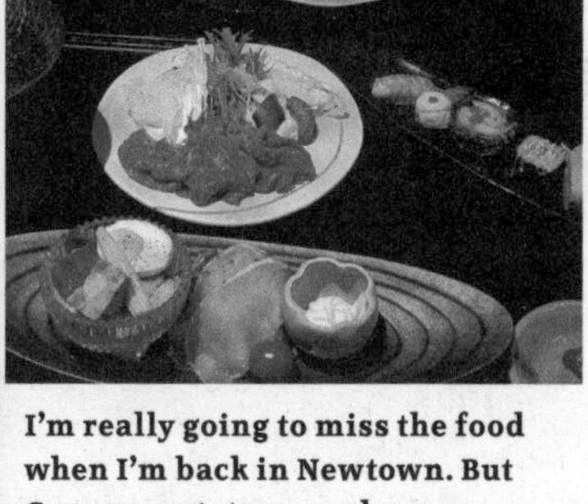

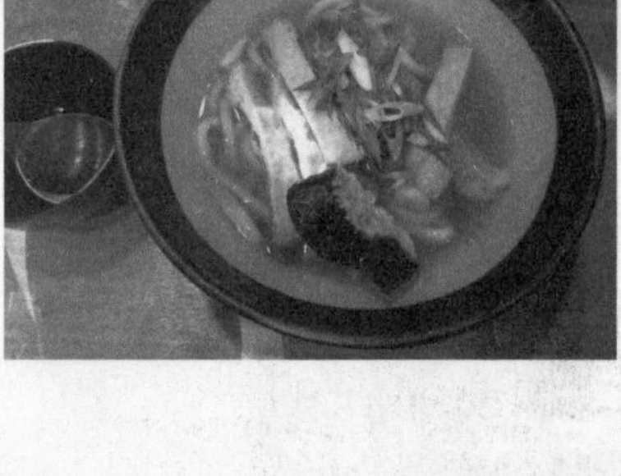

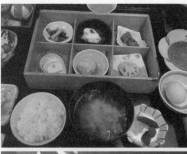

I'm really going to miss the food when I'm back in Newtown. But German potato pancakes are delicious, too! ;)

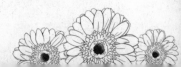

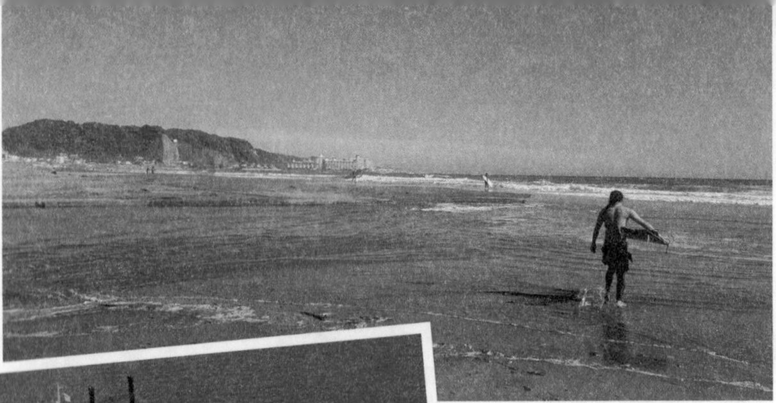

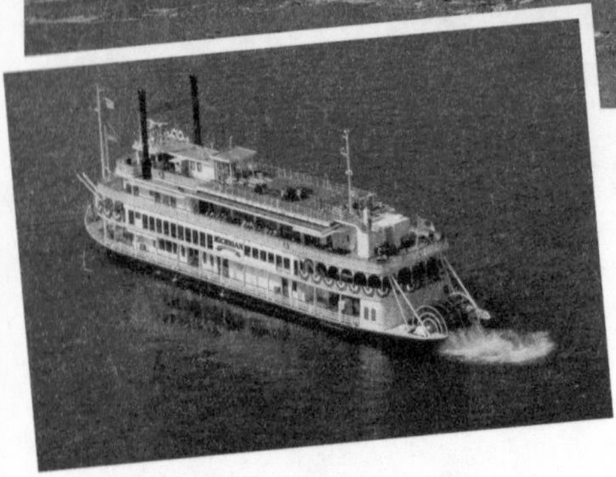

The natural beauty of Japan is so magnificent— the ocean, the mountains, and lakes with paddlewheel boats! I'm really **blown away!**

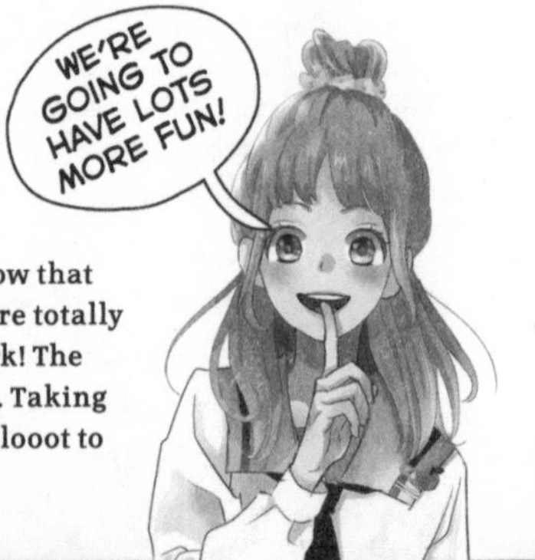
WE'RE GOING TO HAVE LOTS MORE FUN!

The cities are really gigantic here! Of course, I know that Newtown is just a small town and that big cities are totally different, but Tokyo really knocks it out of the park! The city never seems to end. It keeps going on and on... Taking the subway is a real science here: Miyu still has a looot to teach me about it.

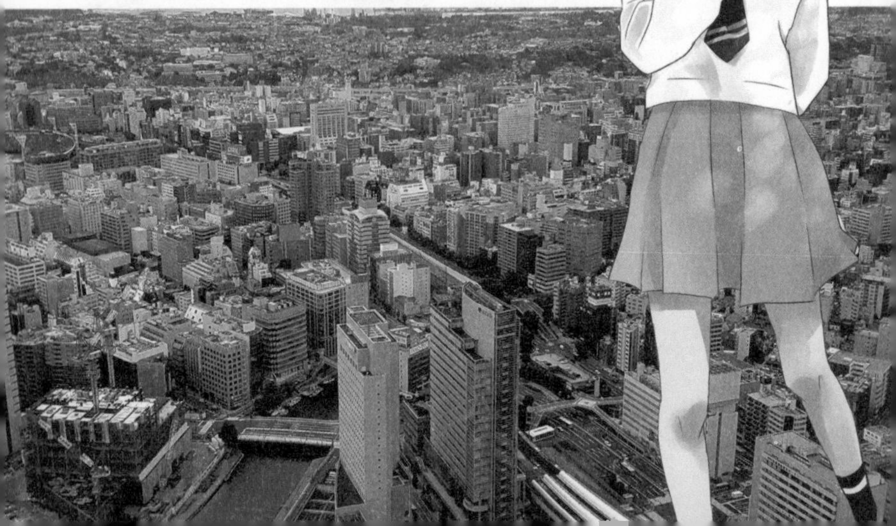

Bibi & Miyu

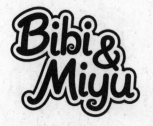

Bibi & Miyu

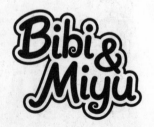

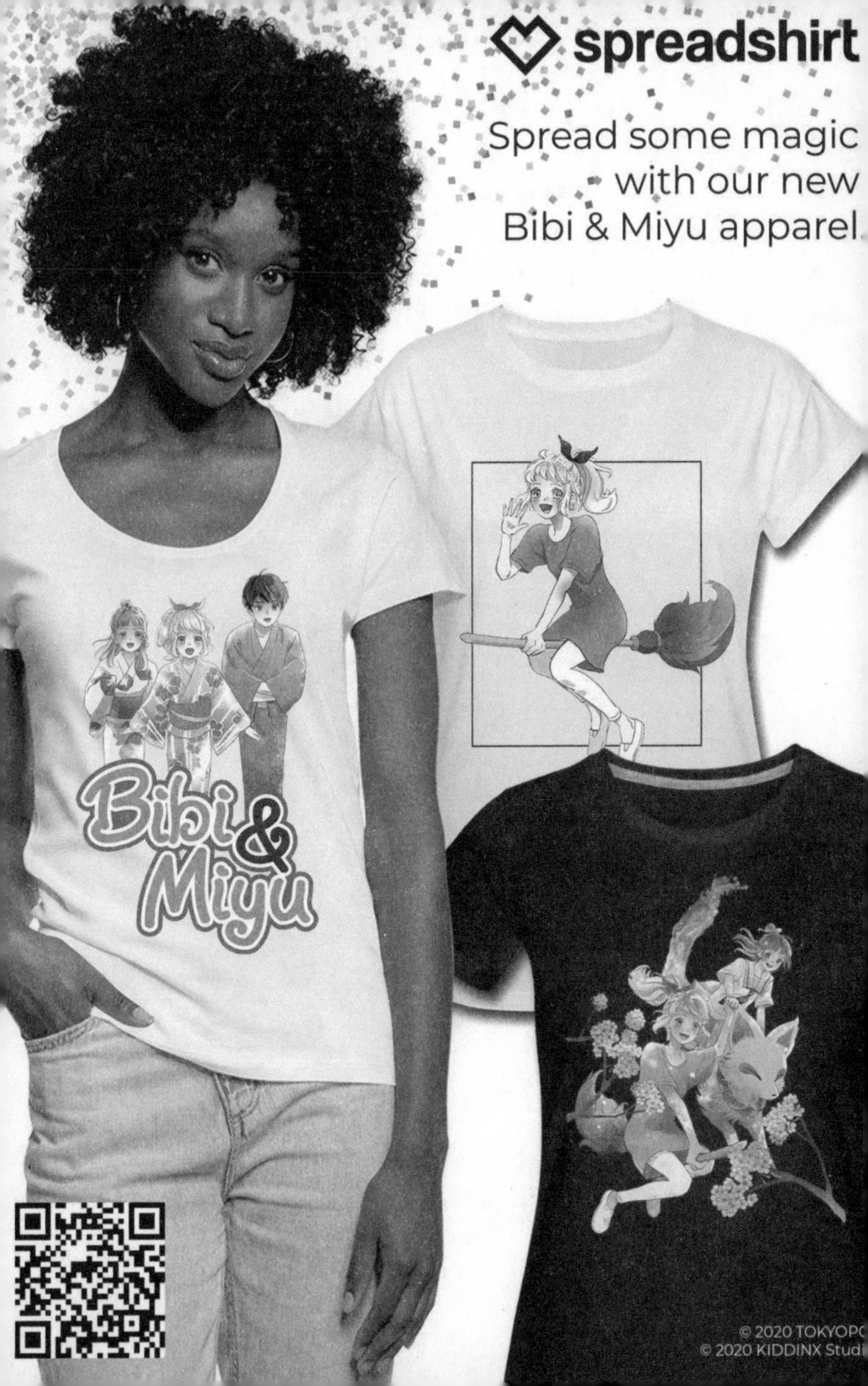
spreadshirt
Spread some magic
with our new
Bibi & Miyu apparel.
Bibi & Miyu
© 2020 TOKYOPOP
© 2020 KIDDINX Studi

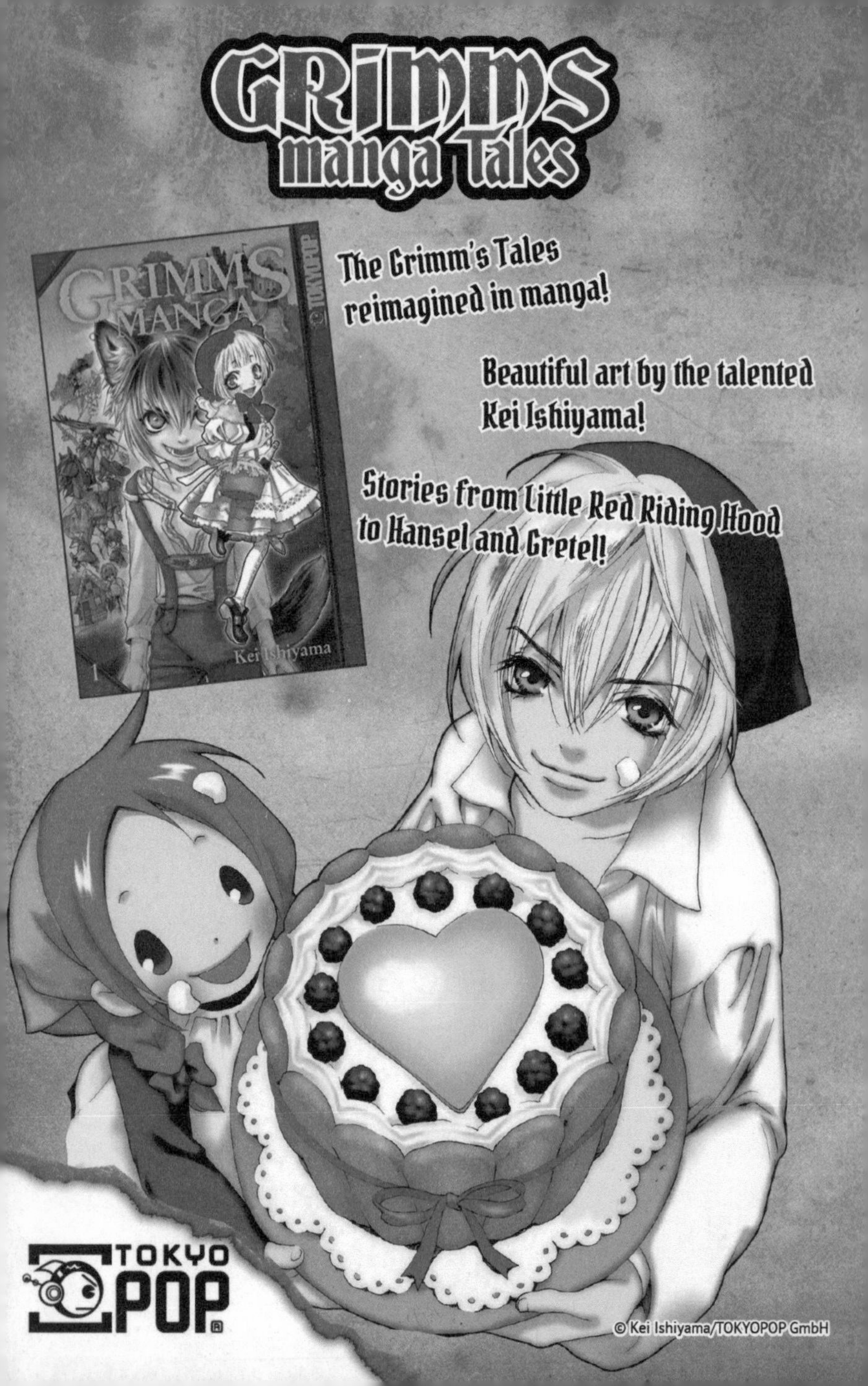
Grimms Manga Tales
GRIMMS MANGA
TOKYOPOP
Kei Ishiyama
1
The Grimm's Tales reimagined in manga!
Beautiful art by the talented Kei Ishiyama!
Stories from Little Red Riding Hood to Hansel and Gretel!
TOKYOPOP
© Kei Ishiyama/TOKYOPOP GmbH

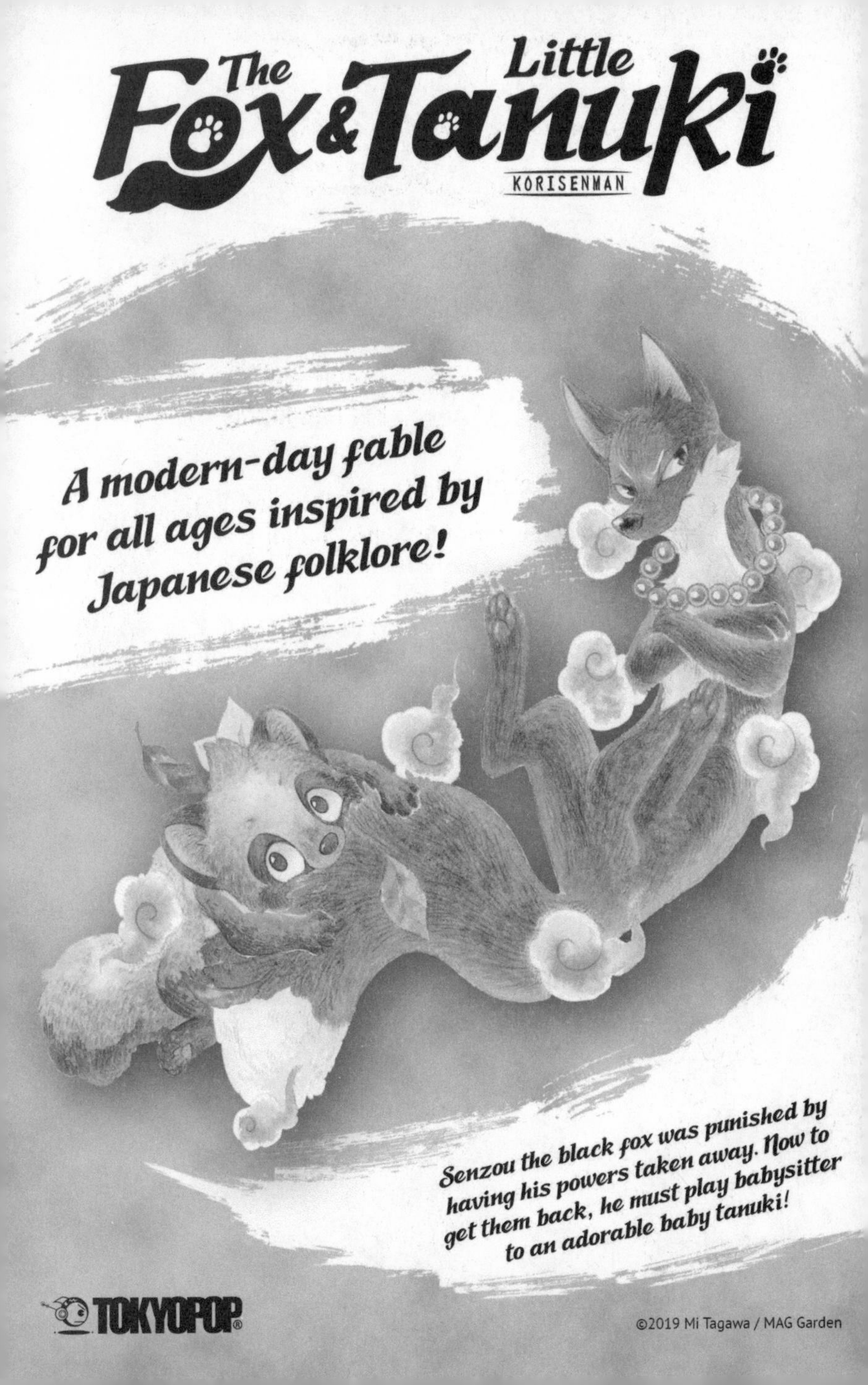

The Little Fox & Tanuki
KORISENMAN
A modern-day fable for all ages inspired by Japanese folklore!
Senzou the black fox was punished by having his powers taken away. Now to get them back, he must play babysitter to an adorable baby tanuki!
TOKYOPOP®
©2019 Mi Tagawa / MAG Garden

Disney *Marie*

★ **Inspired by the characters from Disney's The Aristocats**
★ **Learn facts about Paris and Japan!**
★ **Adorable original shojo story**
★ **Full color manga**

Even though the wealthy young girl Miriya has almost everything she could ever need, what she really wants is the one thing money can't buy: her missing parents. But this year, she gets an extra special birthday gift when Marie, a magical white kitten, appears and whisks her away to Paris! Learning the art of magic is one thing, but getting to eat the tastiest French pastries and wear the most beautiful fashion takes Miriya and Marie's journey to a whole new level!

© Disney

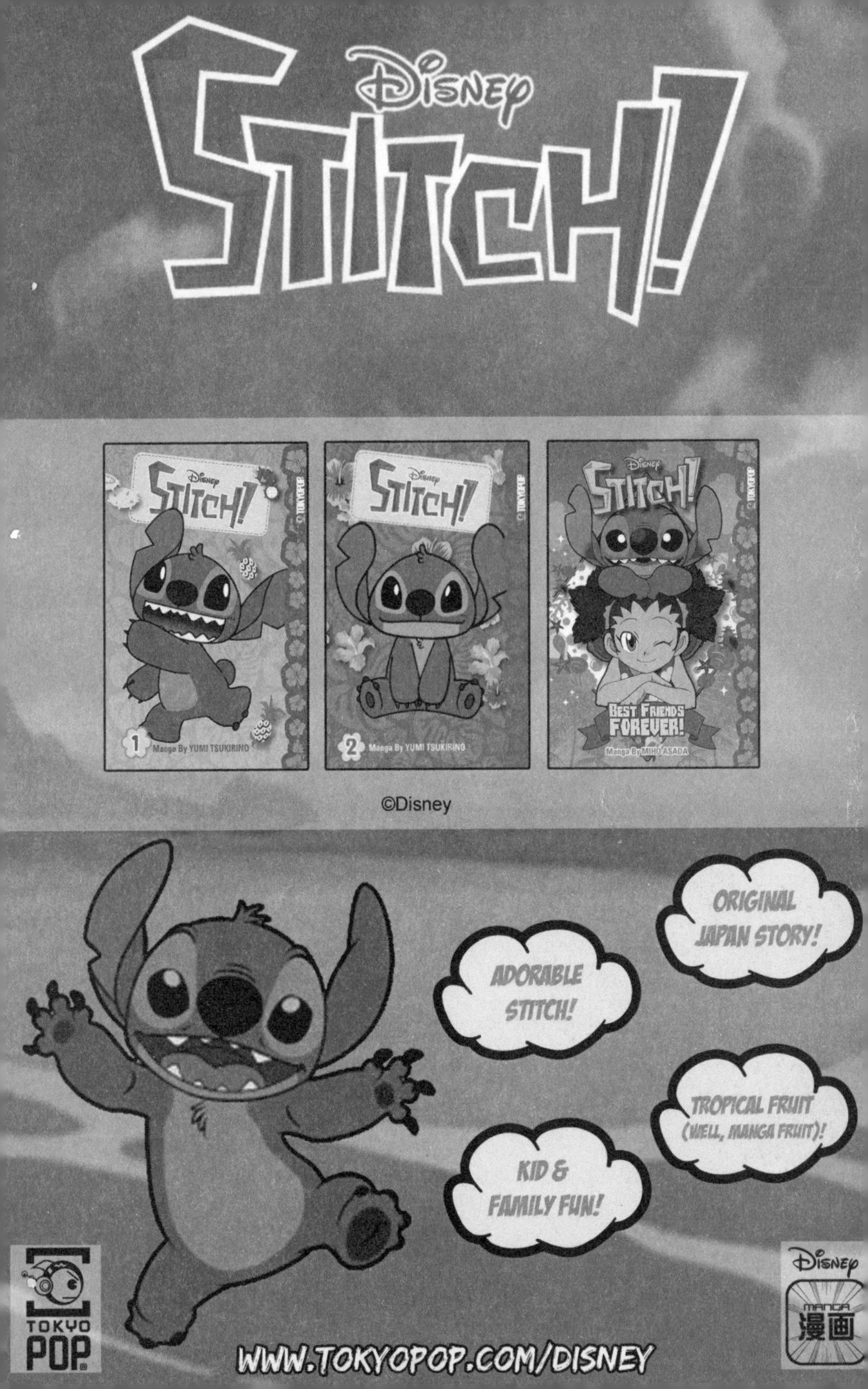
Disney
STITCH!
Disney
STITCH!
1 Manga By YUMI TSUKIRINO
Disney
STITCH!
2 Manga By YUMI TSUKIRINO
Disney
STITCH!
BEST FRIENDS FOREVER!
Manga By MIHO ASADA
©Disney
ORIGINAL JAPAN STORY!
ADORABLE STITCH!
TROPICAL FRUIT (WELL, MANGA FRUIT)!
KID & FAMILY FUN!
TOKYO POP
Disney
MANGA
漫画
WWW.TOKYOPOP.COM/DISNEY

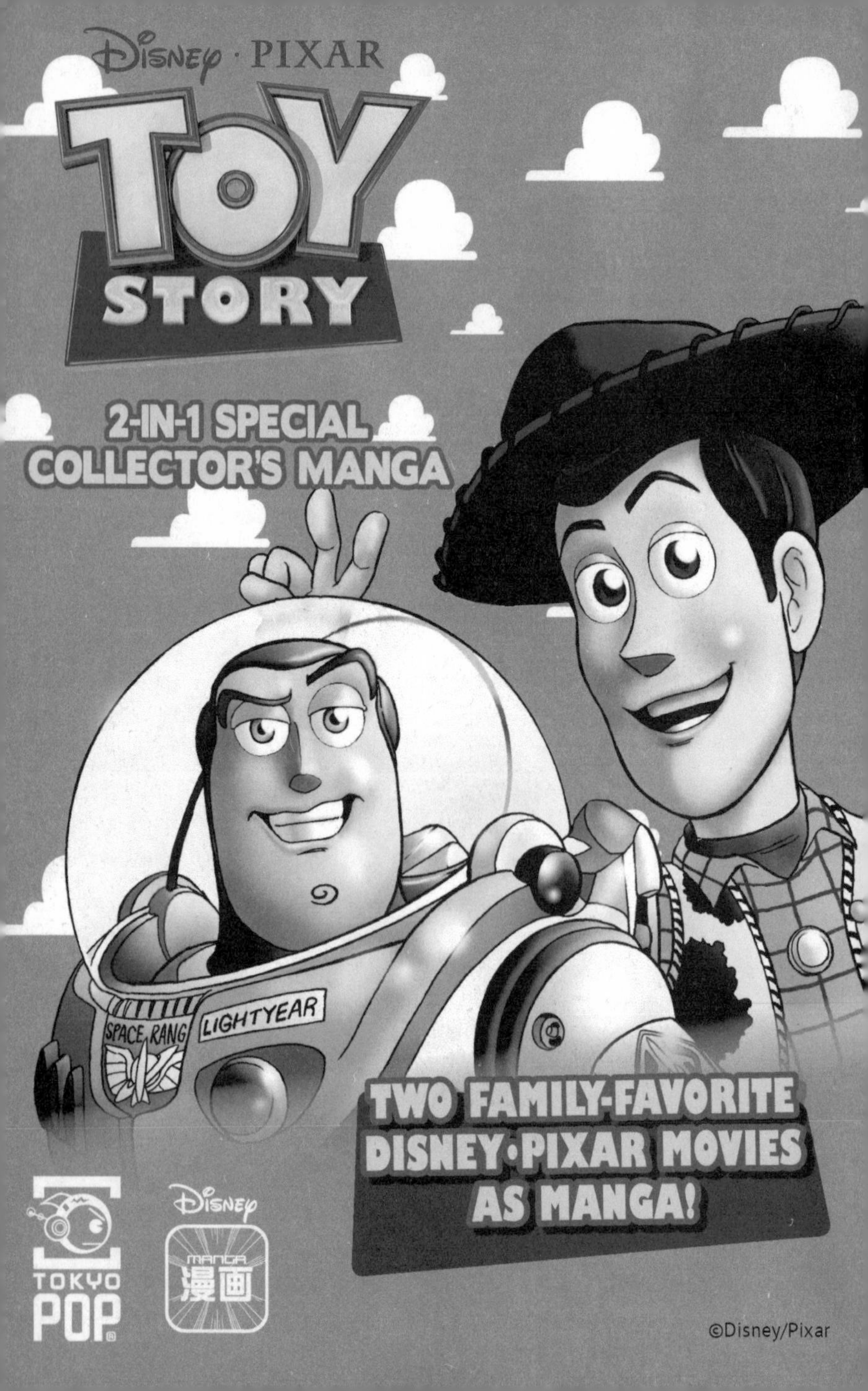
Disney · PIXAR
TOY STORY
2-IN-1 SPECIAL COLLECTOR'S MANGA
SPACE RANG
LIGHTYEAR
TWO FAMILY-FAVORITE DISNEY·PIXAR MOVIES AS MANGA!
TOKYO POP
Disney
MANGA 漫画
©Disney/Pixar

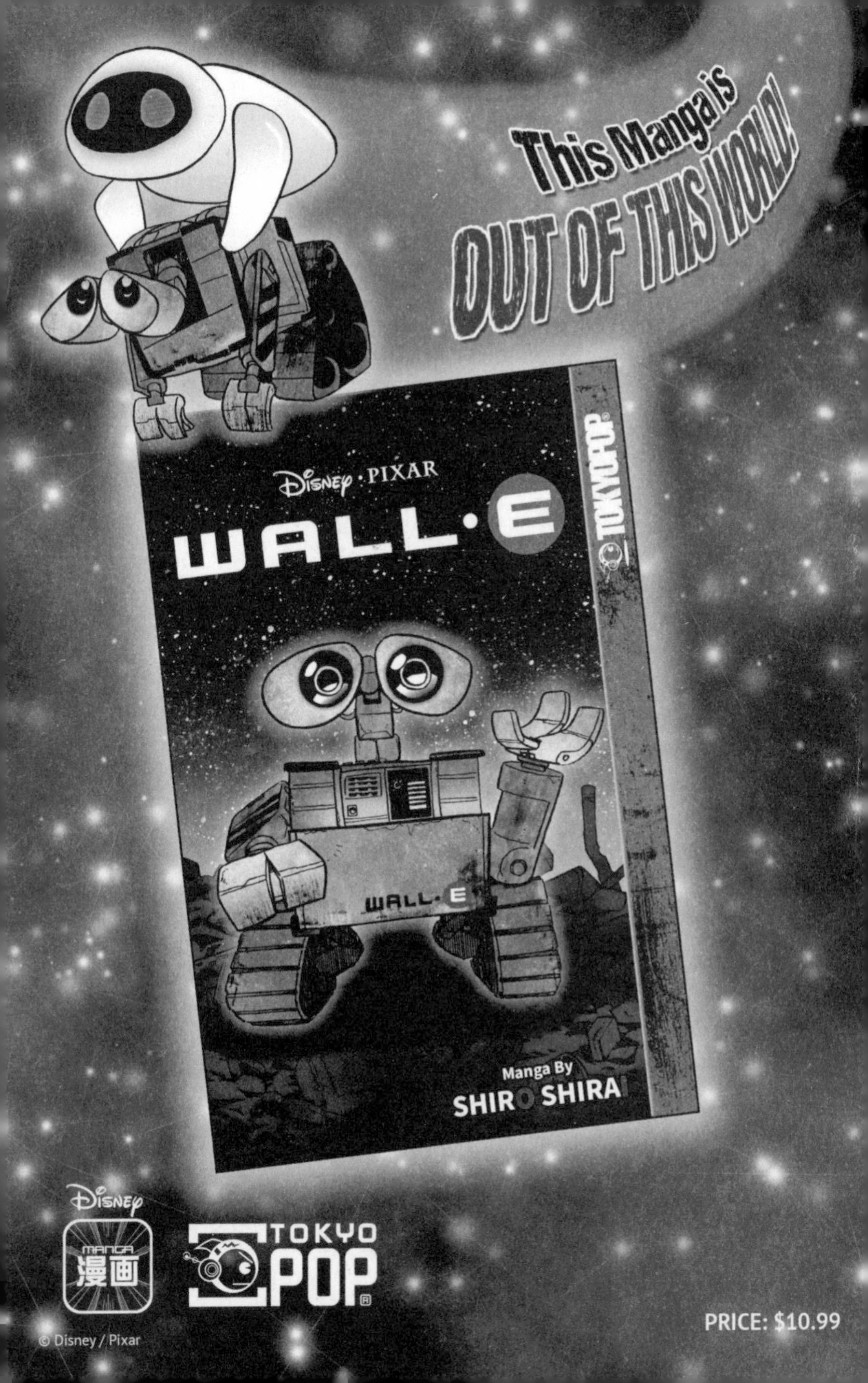
This Manga is
OUT OF THIS WORLD!
DISNEY · PIXAR
WALL·E
TOKYOPOP
WALL·E
Manga By
SHIRO SHIRAI
DISNEY
MANGA
漫画
TOKYO POP
PRICE: $10.99
© Disney / Pixar

DISNEY

MAGICAL DANCE

FEATURING MICKEY, TINKER BELL, STITCH, POOH, AND MORE DISNEY CHARACTERS!

Rin joins a troupe with her fellow students and soon realizes that she has two left feet. She practices day and night but is discouraged by the lack of results and almost gives up on her dreams. Impressed by her passion and dedication, Tinker Bell appears to give her a little encouragement in the form of Disney magic!

FROM THE CREATOR OF DISNEY KILALA PRINCESS!

DISNEY
MANGA
漫画

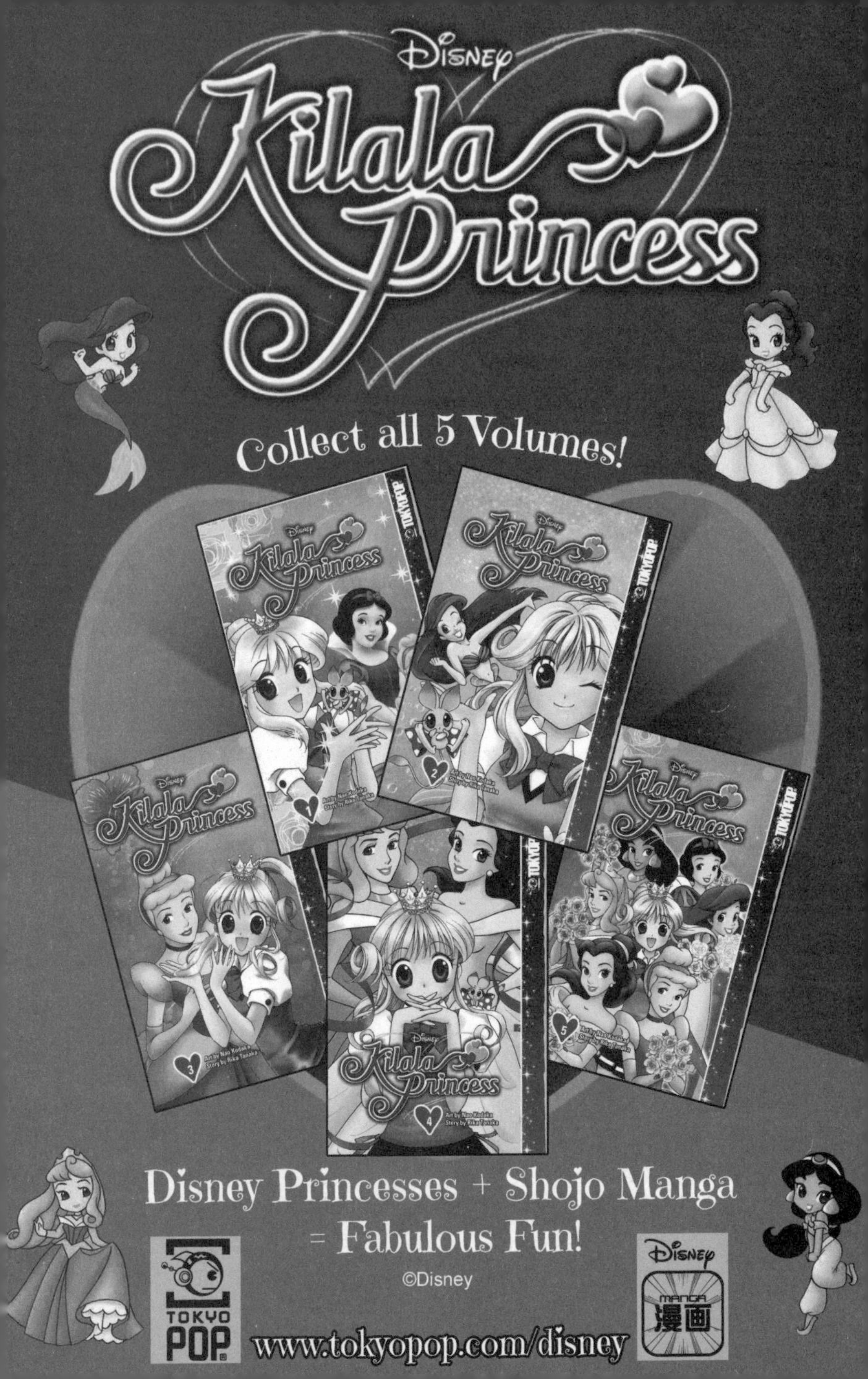
Disney
Kilala Princess
Collect all 5 Volumes!
Disney Princesses + Shojo Manga
= Fabulous Fun!
©Disney
TOKYOPOP
Disney Manga 漫画
www.tokyopop.com/disney

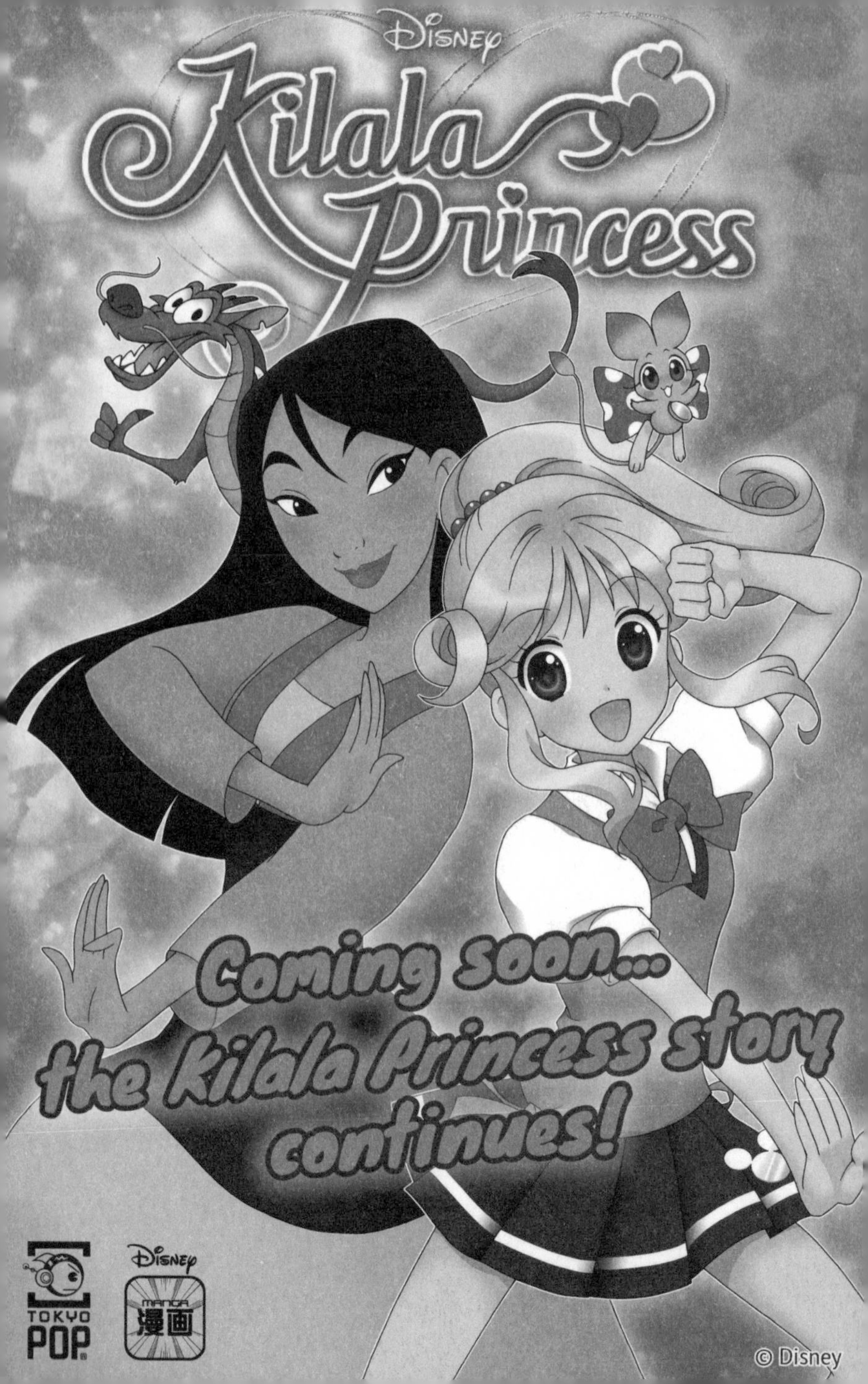

Disney
Kilala Princess
Coming soon...
the Kilala Princess story continues!
TOKYO POP
Disney
MANGA
漫画
© Disney

Full color manga trilogy based on the hit Disney Channel original movie

Experience this spectacular movie in manga form!

© Disney Enterprises, Inc. All rights reserved

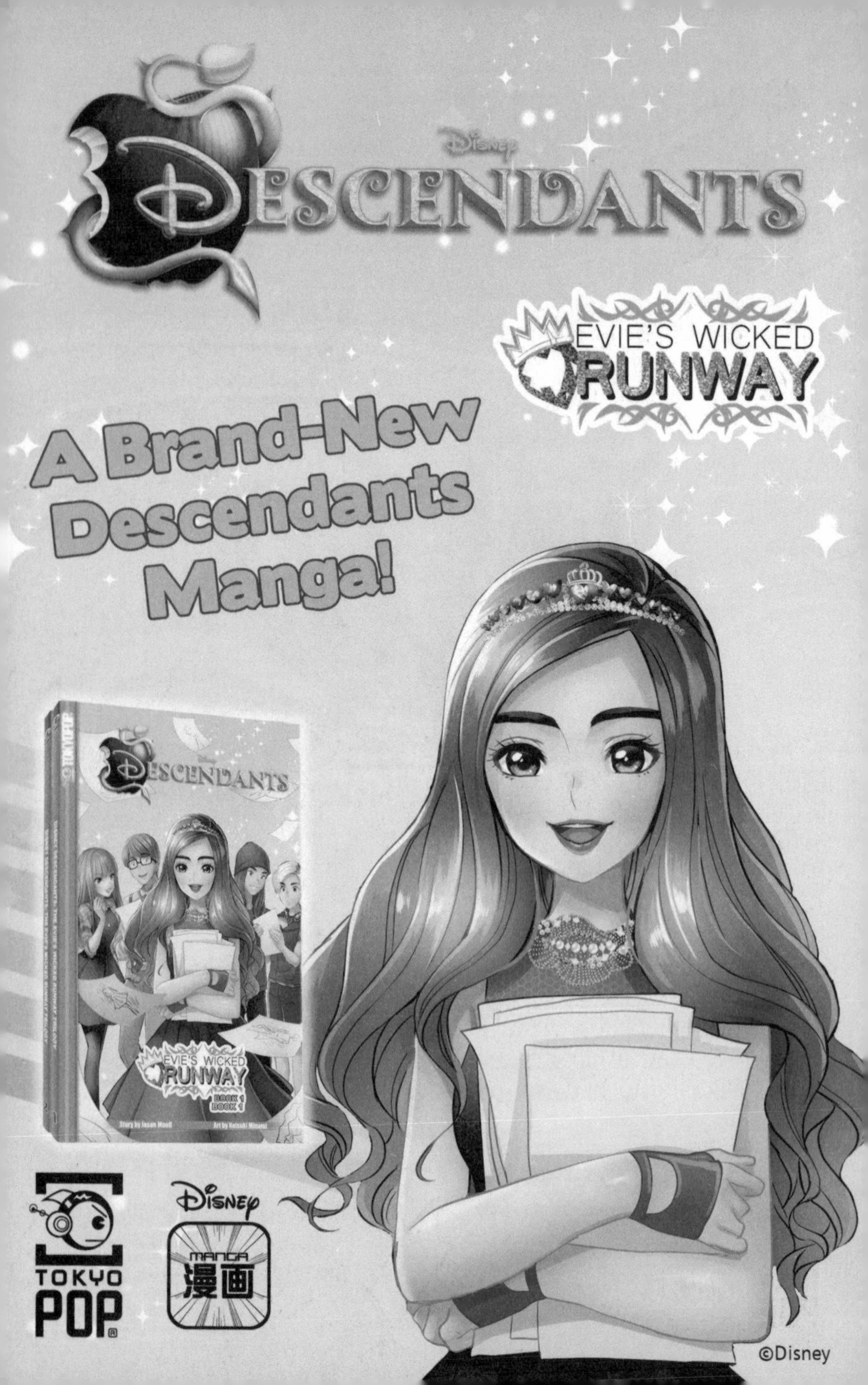

Disney
DESCENDANTS
EVIE'S WICKED RUNWAY
A Brand-New Descendants Manga!
TOKYOPOP
Disney
MANGA
漫画
©Disney

Disney

DESCENDANTS

Dizzy's NEW FORTUNE

THE NEWEST DESCENDANTS MANGA WITH BRAND-NEW VILLAIN KIDS!

The original Villain Kids have worked hard to prove they deserve to stay in Auradon, and now it's time some of their friends from the Isle of the Lost get that chance too! When Dizzy receives a special invitation from King Ben to join the other VKs at Auradon Prep, at first she's thrilled! But doubt soon creeps in, and she begins to question whether she can truly fit in outside the scrappy world of the Isle.

TOKYO POP
© Disney

Disney
MANGA 漫画

Disney
CHANNEL

Check out a few sneak previews of these Disney Manga titles!

SHOJO
- ☐ DISNEY BEAUTY AND THE BEAST
- ☐ DISNEY KILALA PRINCESS SERIES

FANTASY
- ☐ DISNEY DESCENDANTS SERIES
- ☐ DISNEY TANGLED
- ☐ DISNEY PRINCESS AND THE FROG
- ☐ DISNEY FAIRIES SERIES
- ☐ DISNEY MARIE: MIRIYA AND MARIE

KAWAII
- ☐ DISNEY MAGICAL DANCE
- ☐ DISNEY STITCH! SERIES

PIXAR
- ☐ DISNEY • PIXAR TOY STORY
- ☐ DISNEY • PIXAR MONSTERS, INC.
- ☐ DISNEY • PIXAR WALL • E
- ☐ DISNEY • PIXAR FINDING NEMO

ADVENTURE
- ☐ DISNEY TIM BURTON'S THE NIGHTMARE BEFORE CHRISTMAS
- ☐ DISNEY ALICE IN WONDERLAND
- ☐ DISNEY PIRATES OF THE CARIBBEAN SERIES

TOKYO POP

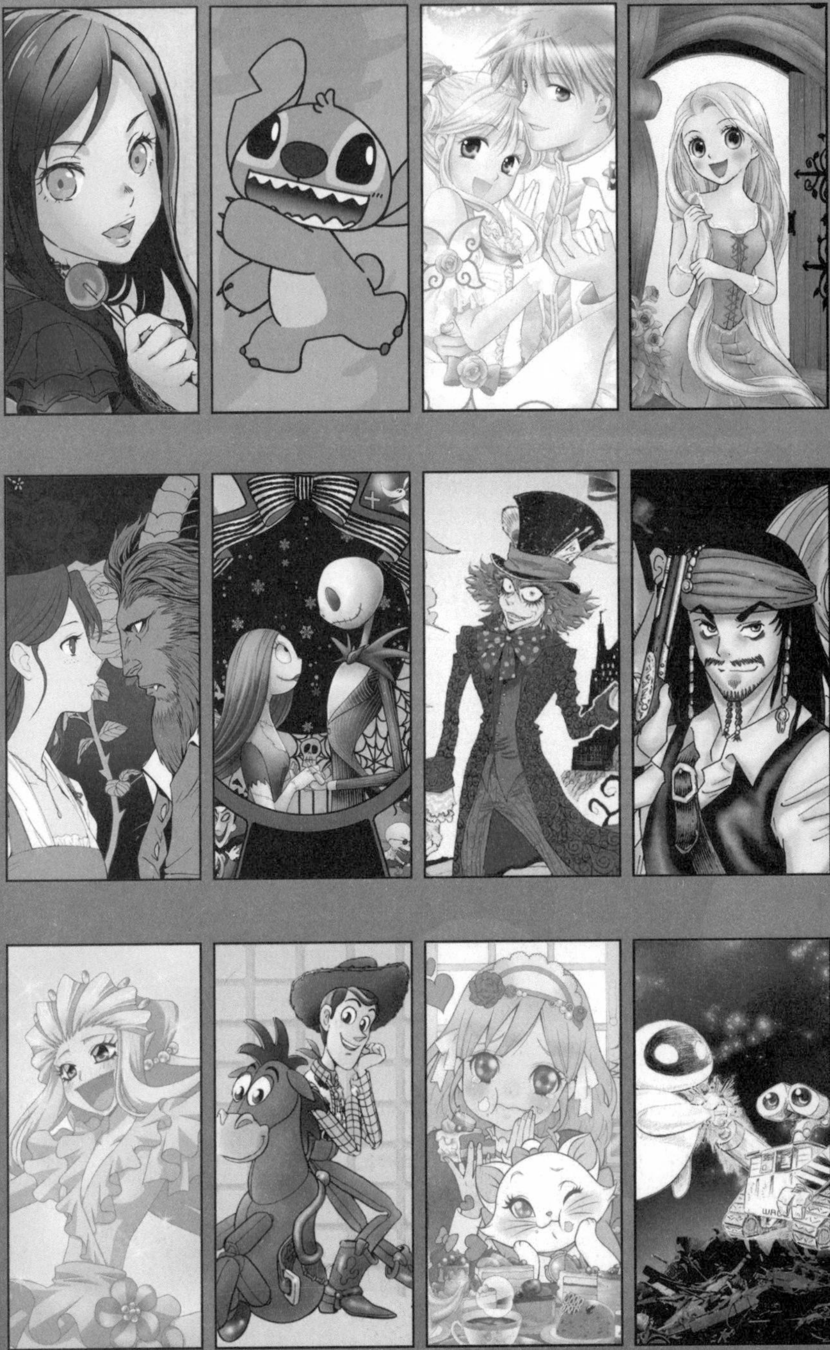

Bibi & Miyu, Volume 1
Art by Hirara Natsume
Written by Olivia Vieweg
Editor: Susanne C. Stephan

Publishing Associate - Janae Young
Marketing Associate - Kae Winters
Digital Marketing and Content Associate - Shraboni Dutta
Licensing Specialist - Arika Yanaka
Translator - Nanette McGuinness
Editor - Janae Young
Copy Editor - Lena Atanassova
Graphic Designer - Phillip Hong
Retouching and Lettering - Vibrraant Publishing Studio
Editor-in-Chief & Publisher - Stu Levy

A  Manga

TOKYOPOP and 🐸 are trademarks or registered trademarks of TOKYOPOP Inc.

TOKYOPOP
5200 W Century Blvd
Suite 705
Los Angeles, CA 90045 USA

E-mail: info@TOKYOPOP.com
Come visit us online at www.TOKYOPOP.com

🅕 www.facebook.com/TOKYOPOP
🐦 www.twitter.com/TOKYOPOP
📌 www.pinterest.com/TOKYOPOP
📷 www.instagram.com/TOKYOPOP

Bibi & Miyu volume 1   First published in Germany in 2019 by
© Hirara Natsume/TOKYOPOP GmbH, Hamburg 2019.
© 2019 KIDDINX Studios GmbH, Berlin
Licensed by KIDDINX Media GmbH, Berlin

©2020 TOKYOPOP   All rights reserved. No portion of this book may be
All Rights Reserved   reproduced or transmitted in any form or by any means
without written permission from the copyright holders.
This manga is a work of fiction. Any resemblance to
actual events or locales or persons, living or dead, is
entirely coincidental.

ISBN: 978-1-4278-6332-4

First TOKYOPOP Printing: June 2020
10 9 8 7 6 5 4 3 2 1
Printed in CANADA